"Impermease is cheap to produce. For over twenty years they've been making it by the megakilo. When I described how it stopped division in rapidly dividing cells I gave the clue to its most dangerous use. It stops cell division in insect pupa. So it's a first class insecticide as well as a contraceptive. The farmer's friend. Accumulated in every woman who's eaten regularly food from crops treated with it. Affluent and starving alike. The starving got it with relief shipments. The poor get it as a discreet additive by governments trying to control runaway birthrates.

"They've reduced the birthrates with a vengeance! That's why the truth hasn't yet been published. Would you like to be a Minister in some country where every peasant would tear you apart if he found you'd sterilized his new bride?

"They've been trying to find a way to reverse the effect, but it's hopeless. The eggs were made infertile twenty years ago. It's as hopeless as trying to bring a twenty-year old corpse back to life!"

"Still through chaos
Works on the ancient plan,
And two things have altered not
Since first the world began—
The beauty of the wild green earth
and the bravery of man."

—T.P. Cameron Wilson

(Magpies in Picardy)

PRELUDE TO CHAOS

EDWARD LLEWELLYN

DAW BOOKS, INC.
Donald A. Wollheim, Publisher
1633 Broadway, New York, N.Y. 10019

Cover art by David B. Mattingly.

FIRST PRINTING, FEBRUARY 1983

1 2 3 4 5 6 7 8 9

PRINTED IN U.S.A.

I

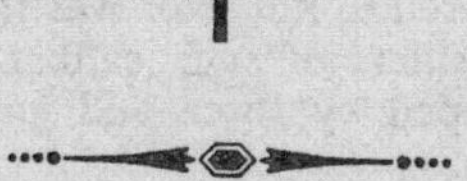

The Atlantic rollers, lashed by the storm winds of the equinox, thundered onto the rocks below the Pen and flung their spray against its walls. Working high on the radio tower, I paused to taste the salt on my lips, watch the gulls wheeling in the updrafts, and look out to sea. For over three years, ever since I had been sentenced, these brief interludes when I climbed to adjust antenna couplings were my only glimpses of the outside world, my only sight of the desolation surrounding the last Federal Penitentiary in the United States.

The last top-security prison on the continent; the final masterpiece of the prison-architect's art. It stood alone, brooding and massive, at the tip of a barren peninsula. To the north, tides were racing into the Bay of Fundy, to the west, a rocky neck of stunted trees and coarse scrub merged into the forests of Maine, to the south, the coast was a curve of white breakers and distant headlands. And out to sea, to the east, night was rising from the Atlantic Ocean. All around me was desolation, a desolation which separated two hundred million peaceable Americans from wild animals like myself.

An octagon of permacrete walls, moats, and watchtowers, of veralloy gates and fences, laced with every sophisticated device the twenty-first century could produce to keep our cage secure. For many kilometers the very soil was contaminated with the residue from physical and chemical weapons, the seas littered with debris and unexploded mines. This bleak peninsula jutting out into the Atlantic had once been a weapon test site and a training ground for amphibious forces. By the time the need for such places had passed, the land, poor by nature, had been made deadly by man. The perfect surround for a secure prison.

The Penitentiary had been built early in the Affluence

when a civilized society recoiled from executing even multiple murderers but had been forced to recognize that such creatures existed. A society which had discovered to its cost that neither punishment nor rehabilitation were protection against those prepared to kill. Nor was the usual prison a sufficient safeguard; killers of such caliber took hostages, murdered guards, escaped by force and guile to leave trails of suffering and death.

An affluent society, too humane to revert to older and more brutal methods of defending itself, had set out to create a completely secure prison where incorrigibles could be held under the most humane conditions possible. The architects had had to meet two specifications: that the prison must be escape-proof, and that the prisoners should be able to lead lives that were close to civilized.

The architects could claim to have succeeded, for nobody had escaped from the Federal Penitentiary on Jona's Point during the twenty years of its existence, and even confirmed malcontents had been hard put to produce genuine complaints about the living conditions within its walls. For the first time in the history of penology a prison was staffed by a carefully selected cadre from which most of the men and women who wanted to become prison guards had been rejected for that very reason. The remainder were well-paid and trained to treat prisoners with kindness, firmness, tact, and continuous vigilance. A dedicated group of strong-minded idealists, none of whom had ever been found guilty of cruelty or the use of unnecessary force. Their paternalism was not regarded as a cause for complaint.

The irony of this humane effort by the Affluence was that the buildings had just been completed and the trained staff installed when psychological restructuring became possible. Within a few years it was made a legal alternative to prolonged imprisonment. More and more incorrigibles had chosen "mind-wipe" instead of the Pen. Some because they did not realize what it entailed, some because they thought they could outwit the system, and some because they welcomed the destruction of their personalities and the loss of their memories.

Others, unable to live without violence in the "free society" of the Pen, committed acts which proved beyond doubt that they were mentally unstable and so incapable of making a responsible decision. They had been certified by the Board of Psychiatric Assessors and mind-wiped willy-nilly. Now, twenty years later, the Pen held only hard-core prisoners; men and women like myself whom no honest psychiatrist could classify as insane but who refused to purchase freedom at the cost of character and memory. And I, Gavin Knox, was among the hardest of the hard-core.

My communicator pinged and I heard a worried voice in my earphone. "How is it up there, Mister Knox?"

"Windy. But the gulls like it!"

Officially I should not have been up there. When I first arrived in the Pen no prisoner would have been allowed to work on the antenna tower, for no prisoner was supposed to see anything of the world outside except via video. But now there was no technician on the staff with the stomach and skill to climb the tower and adjust antenna matchings. In my prepen life I had made more difficult climbs than this, with deadlier bursts than sea-spray whistling past. As the Governor did not like to bring outside techs into the Pen, she had accepted my offer to do the job. I had done it well, and by not making the clamps overtight I had ensured that it had to be redone every few months, giving me these moments in the free air high above my civilized cage.

"Mister Knox, I think you'd better come down now." The voice was even more worried.

"I've still got two Yagis to match."

"You can do them tomorrow. And supper is almost ready. You'll need time to clean up."

"Okay—as soon as I've got the covers back." Satisfied that I had won the promise of another breath of freedom I locked the covers over the matching boxes and began my slow climb down the tower. There would be at least three pairs of anxious eyes watching me on video screens.

I jumped from the base, took a last glance at the stormy world around me, and then looked down through the transparent dome at the secure world below. The Pen had been built as an octagon, with an outer zone for the guards, an inner zone for the prisoners, and a central area of some ten hectares roofed over by lucaplex to let in the sunlight and keep out the rain, snow, and cold. A warm area of lush greenery, of hydroponic gardens and boxed orchards, ringed by byres and pens, sties and bee-hives, with temperature, humidity, and air movements held at optimum for the crops we grew and the animals we bred.

The battery hen, the stalled ox, the tanked lobster, the online cow; prisoners to feed prisoners. Now that there were only some five hundred of us left the Pen was almost self-sufficient in foodstuffs and could be lavish with energy. The test-bed for the first Linus fusion reactor, we generated more electricity than we needed and used the surplus to synthesize the metal hydrides which were starting to replace petroleum in the affluent nations of the world.

There was plenty of work for all, and among us murderers there were men and women skilled in the kinds of work that had to be done. I had given my trade as "electronics technician" on arriving in the Pen, which was partly true. In an establishment packed with complex electronics a good technician had been welcome, especially as the number of competent technicians among the staff had been dwindling.

The voice in my ear gently reminded me not to loiter. I slipped through the hatch and down the ladder; the door leading inwards to the prisoners' zone opened for me and I stepped into the corridor that ringed our quarters. I was back in the sealed center of the prison where the outside world was only a video picture; where we talked only with the images of outsiders. Few prisoners ever met their guards in the flesh and the people we faced on the screens, lacking smell, seemed hardly human.

I turned in my tool kit and checked each item under the eyes of such an image, one of the older women who had been a guard since the days when the Pen had held three thousand murderers. She watched me take off my coveralls but did not order me to strip, and I had already started for the door when she called me back.

"Don't you think you should wash your hands before supper, Mister Knox?"

"Of course! Sorry!" I went to the washbasin, suppressing my resentment of her reproof. It was hard to hate these well-intentioned tyrants. The elderly woman smiling at me from the screen had spent the first few years of her service trying, in the face of insult and provocation, to instil some elements of civilized behavior into urban savages.

It was a long walk to the mess-hall and I ran all the way. The architects had made sure prisoners got exercise by providing plenty of stairs but no elevators. To get from one segment to another one had to go down three flights and then back up another three. I had run up and down fifteen by the time I arrived at the mess hall.

Most of my fellow criminals were already eating, and I went to the serving counter to choose between roast pork, fried chicken, and lobster thermidor. (There were at least two first-class chefs among us.) I took the chicken and looked around for congenial company with whom to eat. A cafeteria designed to feed thousands now catered to only a few hundred and they were scattered in small groups across the hall. I had avoided becoming a regular member of any one clique and sometimes dined alone, though not too often. Any prisoner who showed antisocial tendencies was liable to be psychologically tested and so exposed to the threat of reclassification and compulsory character restructuring. Latterly the Board of Psychiatric Assessors had become more rigid in their definition of "normality" and all "unstable" minds were being wiped. We knew the reason. The Pen was a vastly expensive operation, the electorate was notably less liberal than it had been, and closing down the Pen would now be popular with the voters. The first step in that direction would be to certify as many as possible of us as "mentally unstable"; a diagnosis which justified forced mind-wipe while skirting the legal definitions of insanity.

A woman, sitting alone, glanced toward me. Judith Grenfell, among the most recent of the condemned. Titian hair—that glorious auburn-gold—flashing as she turned her head. When she looked at me a second time I noticed her eyes were green. We had never exchanged more than a few words, but that second glance was an invitation. Living under continuous observation by invisible guards, knowing that everything we said might be monitored and recorded, we had evolved a subtle sign language among us. And as the prison population had fallen in size but risen in education and intelligence that sign language had grown in complexity. I responded to her signal by circling the mess hall, tray in hand, before drifting over to her table, acting like any diffident man seeking to join a pretty woman.

"Mind if I sit down, Judith?" I asked. Manners were a must in the mess hall if one wished to avoid a later scolding from the guards.

"Of course!" She looked up and smiled what the screens would show as a smile of welcome. A smile that told me she had something both private and important to discuss. And a smile that raised her from "good-looking" to beautiful.

There was nothing unusual in sharing a table with a woman in this prison. It had been designed for sexual integration but none of the avant-garde penologists who had founded the Pen could have imagined it would become integrated in fact as well as in theory. Since the eighties of the last century the percentage of violent crimes committed by women had been steadily increasing as sexual equality became one of the better aspects of the Affluence and as more women were trained in the use of firearms. But even by the twenties most murderers were still male.

Yet there were now almost as many women as men among us hard-core incorrigibles. A phenomenon which the experts whose opinions I had read in the library journals had never explained to even their own satisfaction, and all of whom had avoided giving the reason I thought obvious. Women defended their memories and identities more stubbornly than men because women are by nature more stubborn, more pigheaded than most men. And Judith Grenfell, extracting the last of the thermidor from her lobster, looked more stubborn than most women.

Still concentrating on her lobster she murmured, "Are they listening to us?"

I drank my juice and started noisily on my soup. "Not listening. Only taping. But they hardly ever check mess hall tapes these days." I dropped my napkin and, reaching down, I knocked the microphone connection hidden in the leg of the table. "Now the tape will be too noisy to monitor. Daren't do that too often or they'll nab me. So I hope you've got something worth saying."

"You work in electronics, don't you?" She pushed away her lobster and started on apple pie. Prison had not affected her appetite nor spoiled her figure.

I nodded.

"I work in the hospital and morgue."

"Interesting but depressing!" I waited for her to hint at why she should mention her job.

"Joshua Schwartz died last night."

"Poor old Josh. They put him here in the beginning. He held out to the end."

"There are now four bodies in the morgue. They've closed down most of the lockers so there's no cold-storage space left. They'll have to ship those four out soon." She looked at me with an expression suggesting escape.

At one time or another almost every man and woman in the mess hall must have dreamed up some plan of escape and I had listened to most of them. To maintain our morale we still reassured each other that no escape-proof prison had ever existed. Books telling of escapes from prisons, fortresses, camps, chain gangs, and harems were among the most popular reading in the library. The guards must have grown sick of hearing us plan escape for by now they seldom reprimanded us for discussing it openly among ourselves; they probably approved of such talk for its therapeutic value.

To some extent I think the remaining guards admired us remaining prisoners; men and women any of whom could be free with a new name, a new character, and an allowance adequate for reeducation merely by signing a "consent to restructuring" form. Moreover, although all of us had been condemned as killers, few of us later arrivals seemed to be the recidivist murderers for whom the Pen had originally been built. What we were we did not know for we avoided telling each other about our crimes, and only the Governor and her Deputy had the details. I watched Judith sipping coffee, wondering whom she had murdered and why. She didn't look like a murderess, but then few killers look the part. I classified her as a professional woman, with a mouth that suggested passion and a jaw that showed stubborn determination. The kind of woman I had learned to avoid.

She had some ingenious plan she wanted to tell me about and, like all the others, I knew it would be hopeless. The kindest thing to do would be to listen and then gently point out how hopeless it was. To warn her that escape was safe to discuss but deadly to attempt. It was impossible to get out of the Pen, so an attempt to do so was madness and therefore prima facie evidence of that "mental instability" which justified the Assessors ordering mind-wipe. A crunch that for some reason was called "Catch-22."

She finished her coffee and stood up. "Feel like a walk through the woods?"

A "walk through the woods" was usually an invitation to spend an amorous hour among the trees of the orchard. But Judith's green eyes told me that it was not sex she had on her mind. She wanted a secluded place to unfold her plan, and the "woods" provided that. The patches of grass between the potted trees were monitored by microphones and cameras, as was everywhere else within the prisoners' zone, but direct surveillance was relaxed when a couple were in each other's arms. The Governor in her monthly pep talks to us always emphasized that the staff respected our privacy as much as possible; that any voyeurs among them had been screened out long ago.

I picked up my tray. "Suits me fine!" It would suit me very

well to be seen spending the hours before lights-out with a woman. I had been getting hints from the staff that a normal sexual outlet was essential for my mental health and that they would be happier if I sought one more often. I had certainly not been celibate during my three years in the Pen, but my affairs had been brief and intense, fired by physical hunger rather than by a need for female companionship. And that, as judged by our supervisors, partook more of carnality than normality.

We put our trays on the disposal belt and walked together across the mess hall, exchanging pleasantries with the men and women still talking at the tables. It was obvious where we must be heading but there were none of the crude jibes I would have heard had I escorted a woman across other mess halls where I have eaten. That was partly due to staff disapproval of crude jibes and partly because few of our hard-core colleagues were crude by nature.

Outside the mess hall Judith took the first flight of stairs at a run, and I ran after her up and down six more flights before we reached the gardens under the lucaplex dome. She seemed surprised to find me still on her heels, and as we walked between the hydroponics toward the orchard I asked, "Do you check the fitness of every guy you ask to walk through the woods?"

"I haven't invited many!" She glanced at me. "And you're the first to stay with me on that run. You keep in training. Why?"

That was a question I had often asked myself, and to which I had no convincing answer. "I aim to reach the handball finals this year. Did you know handball was a popular game among the debtors in the old Fleet Prison in London? Interesting that it should be so popular here too."

She showed no interest in the popularity of handball but walked quickly past the vegetable tanks toward the comparative seclusion of the orchard. As soon as we were among the first trees, heavy with ripe fruit, she turned toward a strip of grass. I caught her arm. "Let's go farther. To where they're in flower. The cherries have just blossomed."

She glanced at me, as though surprised at some out-of-character remark, then walked with me through the fruiting sector into the division where the trees were foaming with the pinks and whites of cherry, apple, and pear. In the controlled environment of the Pen we could practice continuous rotation of crops so that by walking through the orchard we had gone from winter through fall across summer and into spring. I urged her toward a rustic bench. "Let's sit here and smell the flowers," I said, then added softly, "The local mikes are noisy and the blossoms block the videos."

She seemed relieved to find that I was prompted by practics rather than esthetics, and sat down slowly. "How beautiful! They do what they can to make our lives livable, don't they?"

"This place was designed to pen us up, not drive us mad. If such a thing as a humane prison can exist, this is it." I slipped my arm round her waist and she stiffened. "Found a way to get out?"

She stiffened further and I squeezed her gently. "We need to neck, but keep it light. They'll get nosey if two loners like us turn suddenly passionate!" I kissed her ear. "And speak softly!"

She gave a good imitation of a nervous girl on her first date. "You work in electronics. Can you glitch the cameras?"

"I can dejust some of 'em to foul up their pics at Surveillance Center. Not too often or I'll lose my reputation as their prize captive tech."

"The same with the mikes?"

I nodded.

"What about doors?"

"Cell doors you mean?" We insisted on calling our rooms "cells," to the annoyance of the staff.

"The door of my cell?"

I thought for a moment. "I could fake the interlock. But they'd find it at the next inspection. You'd get blamed. And then—" I tapped my head. "Mind-wash!"

"But not until the next inspection?"

"Not unless you were very unlucky. But what's the point in being able to leave your cell after lock-up? You couldn't go anywhere."

"If you'd faulted the corridor cameras I could reach the sector door."

"And that's as far as you'd get. I can't fake corridor interlocks."

She nodded, then asked, "Do you ever get a clear view of the *John Howard*?"

"I saw her alongside last week. On a camera I was checking. Why?"

"I've heard she carries a minicopter now. The skipper's minicopter. Is that true?"

"She had a minicopter on her poop when I saw her. But if her skipper, or anybody else, tries flying it within five klicks of Jonas Point he'll be cooked by a CPB." The ban on flying in the vicinity of the Pen was absolute, enforced by an integrated Charged Particle Beam-radar system programmed to automatically destroy any aircraft that entered the forbidden zone. Together with our fusion generator and metallic hydrides plant, that system put us among the most technologically advanced establishments on earth.

"I know that! But can you fly a minicopter?" When I nodded she took off on another tack. "Graham Suttler was certified last week."

"Graham was definitely going stir-crazy."

"Naomi Ronston was certified too. I sneaked a scan of her lab reports. All normal by the old criteria."

"Naomi *was* normal! The bastards!" I jerked upright, forgetting my role of lover in my anger. "Are the psych boys turning crooked too?"

"Not crooked. Just more demanding. They've narrowed the normality curve." She shrugged. "Most would classify all of us as crazy without bothering over lab tests. Because we insist on staying locked up in here. Crazy or lazy!"

"The lazy ones quit long ago!" She winced as my fingers dug into her arm. "Sorry!" I eased my grip. "Forced mind-wipe! They'll have to hold me down!"

"And they will."

"They swore they'd never wipe us unless we agreed. Or unless we went lunatic." I made myself talk quietly and calmly. "There've been rumors about closing the Pen since long before they put me here. At one time they talked about shipping the hard-core to Moonbase. That died with the space program."

"Gavin, this time it's serious. Not because of the expense. What government ever gave a damn about the cost of anything they really wanted? But now—I think this Administration wants to use the Pen for something else."

I stared at her. "How can you know anything the rest of us don't? Are they censoring the library?"

"The Governor would quit before she'd allow that."

The Governor was a woman whose image was hard to like but whose integrity I didn't doubt. She had maintained, in the face of growing criticism, the constitution which had governed the Pen from the beginning. And embedded in that constitution was a clause that all information contained in the public media would be available to prisoners. We probably kept ourselves better informed about what was going on outside the Pen than most outsiders. "Then how can you be so sure that the rumors are serious?"

She hesitated. "I'm—I'm a surgeon."

"Not even surgeons know everything! Why should a surgeon know they're going to close the Pen?"

"I work in the hospital and the morgue—as I told you during supper."

"So they're using you as an orderly. Like they're using me as a technician."

"Doctor Shore lets me do more than an orderly's work. He's a good doctor."

"Better than that—he's a good guy!" The Doc was one of the few guardians whom we ever met in the flesh.

She nodded. "A good doctor and a good man. Do you remember that gale three weeks ago? One of the guards working on the wharf was knocked down by a wave. He hit his head and developed an acute subdural hematoma. That's bleeding inside the brain—"

"With rising intracranial pressure which, unless quickly relieved, progresses through coma to death. I watched a man die that way once. We were pinned down and couldn't make the extraction."

"Where—?" She checked a question that would have offended Pen etiquette. "We couldn't evacuate this guard either. Because of the gale the *John Howard* couldn't come alongside to collect him. And because of the CPB's they couldn't lift him out by air. So Doctor Shore had to bring him to the operating room. I helped put in burr holes to relieve the pressure, but that wasn't going to be enough. The Doc knew he had to go inside and—well—he's no neurosurgeon. He asked me to operate."

"And?"

"And I did. Successfully. It wasn't difficult—we've a well-equipped operating room—but it looked impressive to anybody not used to craniotomy. He assisted, and afterward, when we were drinking coffee together, he let slip that forced mind-wipe for all of us is inevitable—and soon! He urged me to accept voluntary mind-wipe while I could. It's much less traumatic than the forced variety. He swore that the Governor, all the staff, would make sure that I requalified. My talents mustn't be wasted! I must practice neurosurgery again. He got quite emotional. 'Accept character restructuring, Judith! Your brain will forget who you were. Your hands will know you're a surgeon!' I said I'd think about it."

"Is that true? I mean about your hands remembering?"

"If they do it won't help much. The hands bit is just the kind of sentimental myth people have about surgeons. My real skill's in my brain. And there it's so tied up with memory that it'll probably go with all my other memories. One reason I've got to get out of here before they strap me to the table."

"You said you'd think about it. What did the Doc say to that?"

"Warned me not to think for too long. The Department of Justice is on the verge of a decision—"

"Justice! Have they got us now?"

"Apparently." She shrugged. "What does it matter who gives the order? The results will be the same."

"If it's Justice, then the Doc's right. The order will come. What that bastard Futrell wants—he gets!" Even mentioning the name "Futrell" sent a surge of adrenalin-anger surging round me. "Okay—what's your plan? Know how to beat the tell-tales?"

Those were our real shackles, the bonds which no prisoner had ever been able to break. On admission I, like every other prisoner, had had a transponder implanted in the muscles of my back, beside my right shoulder-blade. A place which I could only see in a mirror and could not reach without contortion. Wherever I was, whatever I was doing, that transponder was continuously being interrogated by the central surveillance system and was responding with my personal code. If a transponder stopped responding, or if it showed I was somewhere I shouldn't be, then the area was automatically closed and I was isolated. I had seen the system in operation too often to have any hope of evading it. At intervals a transponder failed and some surprised prisoner was whisked away for questioning and returned with a new implant.

But Judith was a surgeon and I was an electronics technician. "Do you know a way?" I repeated.

She stood up. "Perhaps. But I think we've talked enough for one night. Can we come up here again tomorrow?"

"Sure!" I walked back with her through the orchard and gardens as a series of musical chimes rang through the zone, telling us it was time we returned to our cells. She took my arm, perhaps for the benefit of the watching cameras, perhaps because she found the same pleasure in being beside me that I had in being beside her. We strolled along together until the chiding voice of a guard told us to hurry home to bed.

When the lock clicked behind me and I was alone in my cell the small spark of hope Judith had lit started to flicker. The Department of Justice now had responsibility for the Pen, and the Attorney General would make sure that I, as myself, would never get out of this place. And that what I knew would never be made public.

The Pen was an "information black hole." Its constitution insured that all public information would flow into us, but that no information from or about us would ever reach the public. A sentence to the Pen was the civilized substitute for a death sentence, but it was still a kind of death. Legally I had been executed when my sentence was handed down. I would leave the Pen only when I was physically or mentally dead. And nothing I could say, do, or write would ever be allowed to escape to show that I was still living. If I left alive I would leave as naked as a newborn, without a paper to my name. Without even a name. Without a memory. My mind wiped clear of how the Attorney General, Gerald Futrell, had engineered the assassination of his President.

Most prisoners had some self-justifying statement hidden away. Their last desperate attempt to slip something of themselves past mind-wipe. If it had only been a case of surrendering my personality and my memories I would have accepted character restructuring long ago, glad to be rid of both. But I would not willingly get rid of either until I had published what I alone knew.

However hopeless Judith's plan might turn out to be, she was a woman with special opportunities and unique skills. We ourselves would not escape. But the attempt might offer that chance for which I had waited. The chance to pass my story on to somebody outside the Pen.

I took the draft of what I had written from its hiding place and settled down on my bed to check through it once again.

II

My name is Gavin Knox, and in 2016 I transferred from the Special Strike Force to the Secret Service. At that time the Service was still an arm of the Treasury Department, originally charged with catching counterfeiters of the currency and protecting the person of the President. That protection had later been extended to any politician seeking his job.

In 2019 I was Arnold Grainer's only protector when he set out to win the Presidential nomination. I continued as his bodyguard during his campaign, and I was among those guarding him throughout his Presidency. Arnold Grainer was great before he became President, and is among the greatest of U.S. Presidents. That is my opinion, and it will be the opinion of history. In the opinion of most of his contemporaries he was an arrogant, overbearing sonofabitch, elected only because the machine-produced candidates of the other major parties showed themselves too tainted for the electorate to swallow.

Arnold Grainer might be a sonofabitch, but he had shown himself to be an effective, intelligent, and honest sonofabitch, the kind of leader we needed during the crises of the early Affluence, but one whom the pundits decided must be shed when the crises were past. I was assigned to him when he became a serious contender for the Liberal nomination, but before the party mandarins had started to take him seriously. Even the then apolitical Secret Service did not see him as a potential nominee and decided that one agent, myself, was all it could spare for his protection.

As a result he and I traveled together from primary to primary, and for the first few we traveled alone. He acquired disciples as he began to collect delegates and by the time we hit the big states he had a string of media-mongers, mobile politicians and assorted camp-followers trailing astern. During those months I got to know Arnold Grainer very well, while he learned more about me than I like anybody to know.

Some woman once said that to hear the truth about a man you must ask his valet. Today you must ask his bodyguard. Grainer, sitting beside me on innumerable flights between meetings, would ask what I, a nonpolitical Praetorian, thought of his political performance. By then my job had forced me to listen to more peddlers of political bogus than there were counterfeiters of the currency in the prisons of the United States, and I knew what to tell him: that he should curb his natural arrogance, disguise his intelligence, and humble himself before the political verities. He'd laugh, but did stop exposing the ignorance of television interviewers, and his comments on his opponents became too subtle for most of them to realize they had been insulted.

Arnold Grainer had been the General commanding Moonbase during the confrontation with the Eastern bloc and his initiative in contacting the Eastern commander, General Lobachevsky, and the subsequent joint evacuation of both bases probably rescued the world from a panic-inspired holocaust and certainly saved the garrisons of the bases from slow death. As I had been one of the Special Strike Force in Western Moonbase I owed Grainer a personal debt. So did Lobachevsky. For after both Generals had been hailed as heroes Lobachevsky was on his way to the wall. Grainer saved him by letting the Eastern leaders know that if Lobachevsky was disgraced he would make it his personal business to see that every field commander in the Eastern forces got both coded originals and decoded copies of the signals exchanged between Eastern Moonbase and the Kremlin during those hectic days—convincing evidence that many of them, with their staffs and armies, had been slated for sacrifice in the initial nuclear exchange. Knowledge that would make them uneasy about obeying future orders from their Supreme Command.

Grainer only escaped court-martial himself because of his transient popularity. He had used intercepted signals to save an enemy commander when the State Department had planned to use those same signals to blackmail the Kremlin. He was retired as soon as the Administration judged it was safe to retire him. Years later, when Lubachevsky came to power after the convulsions which always accompanied an

Eastern change in leadership, Grainer's action gave him an unique relationship with the Eastern bloc.

The Affluence was an age in which the only heroes the media permitted to survive were those it had created itself. Editors, columnists, and commentators were not comfortable with the genuine article and started to cut Arnold Grainer down to size once he was no longer needed to save their necks. He was a man whom it was easy to dislike, and he infuriated them further by ignoring their criticism and advice. On becoming a civilian he joined Wrenshall in turning veralloy from a laboratory curiosity into the material which threatened the future of every metal-consuming industry. In '09 planned obsolescence was economic dogma and the concept of a cheap, easily worked, wear-resistant alloy was anathema.

Grainer believed that veralloy and other products of high technology could be the basis of a genuine and general affluence. He set out to prove it, and in the process both he and Wrenshall became multimillionaires. Wrenshall continued to mix metals happily. Grainer concentrated on changing the Affluence into the Millennium by converting industrial production into industrial productivity.

Opposed by multinational corporations, international unions, and timid governments of every political hue and economic faith, he saw that logic was useless. Only by political action could he break the strangleholds. To beat the politicians he had to join them. He joined the least rigid of the three parties and put himself forward as a candidate for its presidential nomination. To the astonishment of everybody except his delegates he got it. At that point the Service realized that somebody would probably try to kill him and that many would be delighted if somebody did. A pack of Secret Service men and women surrounded him throughout his campaign. And in 2020 the American people, with that gut instinct which had saved the Republic in the past, elected as their President a man too strong for their tastes and too tough for their stomachs.

By the end of his third year in office Arnold Grainer was so hated by his party's leaders that they were happy to believe the pollsters who were forecasting that he would be the first elected President in over a century to seek renomination and not get it. They prepared to make Vice-President Randolph the people's choice. And during the early months of

2024 most people were saying loudly that they'd never vote for that bastard Grainer again.

When Grainer let his name stand in the primaries but made no effort to campaign, the Party thought he was finished. When he went sailing with Helga and Gloria (both murdered within the year) and with myself on the eve of the New York primary, they were sure of it. They only realized that they were likely to be manipulated and harried by him for another four years when the party members who had cursed him publicly voted for him privately, suggesting that in November the electorate would do the same.

The electorate never had the chance. President Arnold Grainer was assassinated on the twenty-fourth of October 2024, while waiting at Dulles Airport to greet the new President of the Soviet Union.

That was one of his few public appearances when I was not near enough to throw him to the ground. McLean, in charge of overall security, had sent me with a section to investigate a report that there was an intruder on the observation deck of the Airport Terminal. We found nobody but, glancing across the reception area, I saw a curtain move behind the window of a room which should have been cleared.

I called a warning on my communicator and got no answer. The Soviet airliner was turning off the runway and taxiing toward the red carpet where the President was waiting. The rest of my section had already spread out to search the roof. I was alone. I raced along the observation deck, swung down to the ledge by the window where I had seen the curtain move, and was drawing my gun when the man behind the window fired.

His shot shattered the glass. Mine hit him before he could fire a second. I threw myself through the broken window and heard him gasp, "That bitch! She tricked me!" before his voice was drowned by the blood gushing from his mouth. By the time other agents burst into the room he was dead.

I didn't know the President was also dead. A marksman cannot shoot accurately through plate glass and his first round had been designed to smash the window and give him a clear target for his second. For the moment, my attention was fixed on a young man standing on the steps below with a forbidden video camera pointing toward the group around the President. I dropped from the window ledge onto him, fearing that he was the "second gun" in a planned assassination. I had snatched his camera and snapped out the cassette before I even looked toward the apron and saw that the first shot had hit somebody.

The confusion was such that it was minutes before I learned it was the President, and several hours before I found he was dead. He had been whisked away immediately, and I never saw Arnold Grainer again. Later I found he had been killed by an armor-piercing round which had punched through the veralloy vest only the Service knew he was wearing.

Our whole communication system went out of operation; all our careful contingency plans collapsed into chaos. The Service, which had seemed the one efficient organization in the Federal bureaucracy, suddenly showed how far it had deteriorated since becoming the creature of the Attorney General.

When the Secret Service had been transferred from the Department of the Treasury to the Department of Justice its responsibilities had been enlarged and the quality of its recruits had changed. The new agents were men and women who had never known the confusion of combat or the uncertainty of clandestine operations; trained killers rather than experienced fighters. They held political views in a Service sworn to neutrality, and those views would not have been mine had I held any. But until that day I had thought they knew their job; by nightfall I realized they did not.

Eventually I got back to headquarters, but could not reach any senior officer, so I sat down and wrote my report. By then the President's death had been announced and I was turning numb. I was about to leave for my apartment where I planned to get drunk for the first time since I had started to go armed, when I felt the cassette in my pocket. I postponed drinking until after I had screened it.

The camera had been focused on the Presidential party and it showed something I would not have believed possible. It showed the two agents flanking the President flinging themselves sideways at the first shot. Not in front of him as duty demanded, but away from him, exposing him to a second. The agent on his right was Stefan Sline. And the agent on his left was Sherry.

Sherry Cranston and I had once been lovers, a relationship forbidden between agents; a restriction on her freedom which Sherry had resented and which I, infatuated, had ignored. The year I shared with Sherry was the best and the worst of my life. We had nothing in common except our mutual passion and our lethal skills. We opposed each other in almost everything else. She belonged to the new breed of agent who claimed the right to hold political opinions like any other citizen of the United States. And she had never hidden her belief that Grainer as a General and a monopoly capitalist was aiming to become the first American Caesar.

I froze the moment of Grainer's death on the screen and stared at it for a long time. Sline and Sherry had dived instantly and simultaneously; as though they had expected the shot and planned their move. I ran and reran the videotape, looking for some innocuous reason for their joint action. At last I took the cassette and forced my way into the Director's office.

He was surrounded by aides and ringing telephones. I threw out his aides, silenced his phones, ignored his furious protests, and snapped the cassette into his viewer. His protests stopped when he saw the first scene, and when I held the action at the instant that the bullet struck the Director started to shake. He was still shaking when the tape ended.

"It could be that they misjudged the direction, Gavin!"

"It could be," I agreed. I did not have to emphasize the unlikelihood of two trained agents making the same mistake at the same moment.

"Sherry and Stefan—they're two of our best!"

I did not contradict him. "Why was I sent to search the observation deck just before that happened?"

"You were detached?" He stared at me. "I didn't know!" The Director had known nothing and now was finding out too much. "I'm sure there's an explanation. Don't say anything about this to anyone. Not until I've had time to investigate. It must be a tragic coincidence." He stood up, still shaking. "I've got to be at Randolph's swearing-in." He took the cassette from the viewer. "I'll keep this until the matter's cleared up."

"I never want to see it again!" I was not an especial admirer of Humboldt who had been promoted above his ability, but he was of the old school and I trusted his devotion to the Service. If there was an acceptable explanation for what the tape showed, he would find it. I hoped it would be the truth.

I had lost any desire to get drunk, and when I reached my apartment I watched Randolph taking the oath of office. I knew him to be an honest man who had rejected overtures that he betray his Chief and become the party nominee. Now he was looking sad and worried as the Presidency was forced upon him.

Mike Randolph had been a good Governor of Virginia and would be more popular with people and party than Grainer had ever been. He was the first Vice-President in generations who had been allowed to keep a high enough profile to become well-known to voters outside his home state. The refusal to allow another near the throne was a characteristic which most previous American Presidents had shared with the Ottoman Caliphs, the Soviet Secretaries, and the Chinese Chairmen. Grainer had broken with that custom and encouraged Randolph to display his talents. Amiable and intelligent, he got along well with Congress because, unlike his Chief, he believed in the sharing of power and government by consensus.

He was also a true Virginian in that he placed loyalty to his friends above almost every other virtue, and among his friends were the leaders of his party. It would be some time after his almost certain election in November before the electorate realized that characteristics which were virtues in a Governor could be disasters in a President.

Mike Randolph was looking sad and worried. Many of those around him were trying to look sad but were definitely not worried. The cameras panned across the faces of the Cabinet and rested on Gerald Futrell, the Attorney General, a man whom Grainer had admired and mistrusted—the man who controlled the service in which I served. The shock and grief on his face was totally convincing and completely false.

Every assassination generates conspiracy theories. We hate to think that our futures can be drastically changed by some fanatic with a gun. Yet that is what happens with most assassinations, even when the killers are a small group aiming for anarchy. Madman or idiots, killing the wrong man for the wrong reason. We prefer to imagine complicated conspiracies for we would rather be struck by rational evil than buffeted by blind chance. The universe must be deterministic. The good God does not play at dice.

I knew this human tendency, as strong in myself as in anybody else, and I had been suppressing suspicions of conspiracy from the moment I had killed the assassin. The sight of Futrell's face on the television screen made my vague suspicion concrete. And triggered a memory of Helga saying something important—I couldn't remember what. All I could think of was hatred. For there stood a man whose ambitions were great and whose ethics were insignificant.

Professional killers value life highly—their own as well as their victims. That assassin had thought himself safe; he would have been had I not noticed the curtain move. So how had he got into that off-limits room? Why had Sline and Sherry acted in unison to expose the President to a second shot? Why had his armored vest not stopped the first? Why had I been separated from him minutes before it was fired? And had Humboldt been horrified by what he had seen on the tape or by the fact that the tape existed? Those were the questions gnawing at my mind when the telephone rang. And, as I feared, it was Sherry.

Apart from exchanges necessary in shared duties we had not spoken to each other since our last bitter row. So why was she calling me, only hours after the man we had both sworn to protect had been murdered?

"Gavin—I need you! I can't get through the night! I failed so miserably. For God's sake come and talk to me. You were always able to drive out my devils!"

Whatever else was false, that last was true. I had to give the woman whc could still wring my heart the benefit of every hope. "Sherry—I'm on my way."

"You've still got a magcard for my building?"

"I've still got it. I'll let myself in."

"Then please, Gavin—please come at once!"

Every apartment building in the wealthier parts of Washington was now protected by coded interlocks. I found the magcard for Sherry's under a pile of shirts and, as I collected it, I came across my old Walthers .38 PPK, my back-up gun when I had been clandestine. As an afterthought—or forethought—I slipped it into my pocket.

She was waiting for me in a nightdress. "I only collected enough courage to ring you after I'd spent an hour struggling to go to sleep," she explained as she fixed me a bourbon and water, before dropping onto the sofa we had shared so often.

She had evidently tried to go to sleep in the nightdress I had always found the most exciting. I took my drink and sat stiffly in the chair facing her while she arranged herself in a position to match her gown. Madam Recamier in nylon! Even while I hated what I suspected she had done I could not ignore her beauty. Nor refrain from pitying her self-confidence. They had trained her in duplicity so well that she thought she could con a man who had learned the tricks of our despicable trade while she was still in grade school.

"What went wrong this afternoon, Gavin? How could we make such a terrible mistake?"

"Which particular mistake?"

"Missing that gunman behind the curtains. They've identified him, did you know?"

I shook my head.

"He was a hired gun. Who could have hired him?"

I shrugged.

"You killed him, didn't you? I heard you were brilliant. Gavin, you're so damned good at this job! You make the rest of us look like amateurs."

That, essentially, was what they were. Vicious amateurs who didn't play by the rules which govern professionals. "I've been at it a long time, Sherry. I'm one of the old originals. Remember?"

She gave a brittle laugh. "I remember only too well. I wish to God I'd had the sense to value what I had when I had you."

"We had a lot from each other. Some of the best moments of my life."

"Mine too!" She sipped her old-fashioned, then put her glass down. "You were with that gunman when he died. Did he say anything?"

"Yes."

She could keep the tension from her face, but not from her body. The old interrogators stripped their victims for questioning, while hiding their own bodies in cloaks and hoods. "Body-language" is more than a pop phrase. "What did he say?"

"I'll report what he said at the inquiry."

Her guilt was becoming more and more obvious to me who knew her; perhaps it would not be obvious to whoever judged her. It was not for me to make that judgment; that was what commissions and law courts were for. But whatever she had done, was done. It would be merciful to warn her.

She had been trained not to press critical questions against reluctance and switched the conversation to Arnold Grainer. She and I had fought over him so often; argued bitterly in this same room, on that same couch. As far as I believed in anyone outside the Special Strike Force and the old Secret Service, I had believed in Arnold Grainer. I had believed he was the savior of our country. Sherry had insisted he would be its first Dictator. Now she was trying to hide her relief at his death, but her tone when she spoke of him told me that she still held the same opinion.

When she had finished summarizing his virtues I said, "Sherry—you can stop worrying that Grainer was going to wax the Union. He's as dead as Julius Gaius!"

"Gavin—his death has rescued his reputation. He'll be remembered for the good he did. But if he'd won another term he'd have destroyed democracy in America, perhaps in the world." She had leaned toward me, speaking with genuine conviction, showing me her beautiful breasts but for once without ulterior motive. She wanted to convince me. She wanted terribly to convince me.

She wanted to convince me because she wanted to justify to herself whatever she had done. That if she had betrayed her President it was to save her country. She was trying to believe herself a Brutus. And all I now wanted was to help her escape some Philippi.

She saw that I was not convinced, as she had never been able to convince me that the duties of an honorable Praetorian went beyond protecting the body of his Commander. She reverted to the female—as those bastards had trained her to do when she saw her words were failing. She tucked her legs up under her as though innocently showing me herself. A gesture that had always trapped me, and often turned our arguments into fornication.

This time her movement showed me not only herself, it showed me the butt of her gun hidden between the cushions of the couch. I watched her fingers stray toward it. "Gavin, I hear you've seen a video of the shooting. What did it show?"

"It showed the President hit and dropping." So Humboldt had told her! Had he told Sline also? Had he told Gerald Futrell? How many and who were part of this treason?

"Did it show anything else?"

She knew what it showed. And she knew I was the only agent loyal to the dead President who had seen it. She was nerving herself to do what she thought she must do.

"Sherry," I snapped. "Don't! It's suicide for a novice like you to go against a veteran."

"Gavin, I don't understand what you mean." The tragedy was that she didn't. She was even less aware than I had thought. It was my mistake. I had not stopped her soon enough. Her right hand was under the cushion.

"Sherry—"

She made her last and fatal error. She acted precipitously and she signaled her act. "Gavin, I hate to do this! But freedom's more important than either of us. And that video—" She had her gun half out.

It was too late for both of us. I fired from the pocket and I hit her in the heart. Even as I sprang toward her I was thankful I had not smashed the beauty of her face. Even as I bent over her, realizing the enormity of it all, I was glad that her loveliness was marred only by the scarlet patch spreading out across her nightdress from between her breasts.

I had not realized the full enormity. I was still on my knees beside her when Brodnax burst in from the bedroom with Sline at his heels. There was an instant of recognition, of shock at finding her dead instead of me. Then Brodnax fired. I was lucky that he was in first for he was armed with a Jena dart-gun, probably planning to knock out Sherry while they removed my body. Sline had a 9mm magnum which would have flung me across her with my head blown off.

I took a dart in the chest and dropped unconscious.

I woke up in the Service holding cell, charged with first-degree murder. I found that when I joined the Service I had waived my right to an open trial if my offense involved national security. The medieval Bill of Attainder, abolished in England but allowed by the U.S. Constitution, had been revived by Futrell and attainder of the person was used against me. I was flooded with Paxin, the universal solvent of personal problems, and tried in camera. The evidence against me was damning; Sherry and I had been passionate lovers who had become bitter enemies. Paxined as I was, I could deny very little nor gather enough of my mind together to tell the Court the truth, even if my lawyer had put me on the stand and given me a chance to tell it.

He chose to plead that mine had been a crime of passion. That might have helped had I been an ordinary citizen. The Judge rightly said that a trained killer who gave way to passion was too dangerous to be ever again released upon a defenseless public. He sentenced me to imprisonment in the Federal Penitentiary for the term of my natural life. He, and everybody else, assumed that I would choose character restructuring instead. Despite the Paxin my willpower was still strong enough to refuse that offer.

A sentence to life imprisonment was the legal equivalent to execution. For all practical purposes I was now dead. The only message I got from the Service was that both Sherry and I were being recorded as "killed in the line of duty," thus preserving our good names and the Service's honor. And, as the law directed, I was immediately handed over to officers of the Federal Penitentiary to be held incommunicado for ever.

Those officers were still untainted by the venality diffusing through the Federal Government and its Agencies. They let the Paxin leach out of me before they took me before the Board of Psychiatric Assessors, the experts who would decide whether I was sufficiently sane to make an informed decision. If the Assessors decided I was not they could order involuntary character restructuring. The whole operation went too smoothly for me to believe that I was the first obstacle to Futrell's ambitions who had been disposed of by this route.

The Board were still an obstacle of a kind; most of its members were honest psychiatrists. I tried to tell them my true story but they refused to consider anything except my present mental state. The Court had decided on my guilt; the Board's only task was to decide on my sanity. My past actions were not their concern. Psychiatry had outgrown its Freudian diapers. My mental status was judged by my current behavior and by a range of psychological, physiological, and neurochemical parameters. My insistence on dragging up the past might be regarded as showing present mental disorganization. When I saw one member of the Board taking rapid notes while I was disputing this point with the Chairman, I gave up. I had been examined by psychiatrists every six months for years; the Service had always been meticulous about ensuring its agents were sane. I let them run their tests, half-expecting that they would be faked and I would be sent to forced mind-wipe.

I was brought back before a Board that was obviously discomfited at having to admit that any killer was normal in terms of their measurements. The Chairman, a kind, intelligent, and sympathetic physician, did his best to persuade me to accept voluntary character restructuring, but when I still refused he had to certify that I was capable of deciding my own fate.

I was immediately shipped off to the Pen, and here I have been for the past three years. I cannot dispute the ultimate justice of my sentence, only that I have been condemned for the wrong reason. Mine was guiltless but punishable error. I should have stayed beside Grainer. I should have warned Sherry sooner.

I was not an admirer of my own character and would have gladly forgotten my old self. But I must not forget Futrell. Hatred is an emotion which Praetorians cannot afford; one of my few virtues had been my freedom from hatred until I met Futrell. I had hated him—I don't know why—even before he debauched the Service, led Sherry into treason, and arranged the assassination of his President. Now my only ambition was to expose him as a traitor and kill him as a murderer.

I flung down the draft, disgusted with myself. I had set out to write an accurate and succinct account of President Grainer's murder. I had lapsed into verbose, self-justifying sentimentality. Into an hypocrisy as bad as Sherry's.

I had presented myself as a Praetorian outside politics. In my heart I had been Grainer's devoted supporter ever since Western Moonbase. And Sherry had known it. I had killed her before she could kill me. That was a memory I longed to lose, but not at the cost of forgetting to cry "Treason" against Grainer's assassins. To expose them at least; to kill them at best. Those were the only goals I still had.

I settled down to compress onto one page all the evidence against Gerald Futrell. A single sheet that I might hope to slip to some outsider before I was recaptured or killed. When I was satisfied that it was as convincing as I could make it I hid it in the lining of my jumpsuit.

I took my original effusion to the garbage disposer and then hesitated, reluctant to pulp the only literary effort of my life. I looked around my cell, then eased the grill off the air-conditioning vent. I stuffed the bundle of papers up the shaft and round the first elbow where it was unlikely to be found in a cell inspection, even the kind of inspection this cell would get after I had gone.

Perhaps one day in the future, long after the Pen had ceased to be a prison and my words had lost their relevance, some worker cleaning out air shafts would read it, laugh, and toss it away.

Or perhaps it would become a footnote to history.

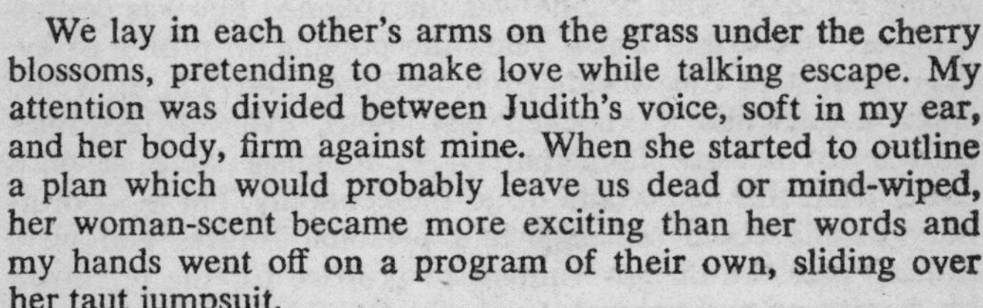

We lay in each other's arms on the grass under the cherry blossoms, pretending to make love while talking escape. My attention was divided between Judith's voice, soft in my ear, and her body, firm against mine. When she started to outline a plan which would probably leave us dead or mind-wiped, her woman-scent became more exciting than her words and my hands went off on a program of their own, sliding over her taut jumpsuit.

She brought them to an abrupt halt as they started to explore further. "Stop it, Gavin!"

"I'm only trying to show our closed-circuit nursemaids that I'm maneuvering for a lay!"

"You're getting me worked up! And this is no time for that." She caught my fingers. "Are you with me so far?"

"I degrade the cameras and mikes in your cell and in the passage. I fake the interlocks in your cell. You haven't told me how you plan to fix the block doors."

"Doctor Shore came to fetch me himself on that night we operated. I saw the codes he used to get from the block to the hospital. So if you can let me out of my cell I can take us as far as the hospital."

"What then?" My hands stopped moving as I became more interested in what she was saying than in how she felt.

"At two in the morning the duty nurse will probably be asleep. There are no serious cases in the ward at present and, like everywhere else, the hospital is short-staffed. We can go through the operating room into the surgeon's lounge. There's a door from the lounge into the guards' zone, and I saw Doctor Shore key that too."

"Did he see you key it?"

She shook her head.

"Maybe the doc was laying a trap. He wants you to volunteer for—"

"Doctor Shore isn't that kind of bastard!" she hissed.

"Okay! Okay!" I hoped he wasn't. "Go on."

"There aren't any circulating patrols now."

"You're sure of that?"

"Certain. Not at night, anyway. The staff knows this place is closing down. They've been leaving to take permanent jobs."

That I knew. The social atmosphere outside the Pen had been changing fast. There was a generalized uneasiness which seemed to have its origin in a sudden decline in births to young mothers. The decline was unexplained but was continuing, so that within a few years the population profile of every country in the world, First, Second, and Third, would show a gap like a knocked out tooth, even if birthrates started to increase immediately. Economists were at odds about what this gap would do to the economy, but most ordinary people could see uncertain personal futures and were putting pressure on government to prepare for the unknown by sacrificing the present—including social luxuries like the Pen. And the staff of the Pen, no longer certain that pensions would be inviolable, looked around for jobs that would continue into old age.

"Once we're into the guard zone we can reach the elevator to the morgue."

"The morgue? Why the morgue?"

"I told you! Cold-storage is full. There are four bodies waiting to be shipped out on Saturday morning. It's high tide at six, just before sunrise." The sailings of the *John Howard* were governed more by the tides than by the clock.

"You mean we switch with the corpses? That won't work. If we take their places—"

"We don't go out in place of the bodies. We go out *under* the bodies. The coffins come in one size—large. They're deep enough to take a corpse with a hundred and fifty centimeter waistline. Poor old Josh was down to skin and bone by the time he died, and Greta was a small woman. They pack the coffin with foamed styro to make a nest for the body. We can burrow our own nests under that."

"My God!" I stared at her, appalled.

She stared back. "Don't soldiers sometimes hide under dead bodies?"

"Fresh dead bodies! And I've never had to—" I swallowed.

"Okay, so we're nested down underneath Josh and Greta. What then?"

"The coffins are already in the shipping container. On Friday I'll be helping them move Josh and Greta from the cold-storage lockers to lay out in the coffins. The lids will be off and the container left open so that they can be checked in the morgue and at the inspection station. That's where they'll put on the lids and close the container. Then it'll go through the tunnel, out onto the wharf, and be loaded on the deck-rails of the *John Howard*."

"And crews in the morgue and the inspection station will examine the coffins and every square centimeter of the containers. They'll be scanned by thermistor beams, gas analyzers, and God knows what else. They showed me what they do to anything that goes out of here. When I first arrived. So I'd see how useless it was to try. Didn't they show you their gadgetry?"

"They did. But two years later. By then most of it wasn't operating to spec—I saw that. As you said, they're short of techs. I'll bet the ones they have aren't wasting time fixing things they consider useless gadgets. Two inspections by guards should be enough to pick up any nut trying to go out with the garbage."

"They should. And probably will."

"How closely would you inspect a coffin and a body at dawn on a March morning? Would you move poor old Josh around to probe underneath him?"

"Maybe. Maybe not. Okay—we can hope they won't. So they snap down the lids. Close up the container. And slide it aboard. The *John Howard* puts to sea. It's a six-hour trip to Clarport. At about eight Surveillance Center finds we're missing. They'll radio her to come about and alert the guards to shoot us on sight. Or are you hoping Surveillance will let us lovers sleep late on a Saturday morning? That we'll be buried and digging our way out before they come to dig us up?"

"There'll be no digging by anyone. All prisoners from the Pen are buried at sea."

"Balls! When I arrived they made me sign a form saying where I wanted to be buried when the time came. And if cremated what was to be done with my ashes. I said I didn't give a damn what they did with my body, just so long as they made sure it was dead first. But they insisted I made a choice and signed the form. It didn't offer sea burial as an option!"

"That form's a fake. A justifiable fake, perhaps. It makes

some people happier while they're alive if they think they've chosen the place where they'll be planted when dead. In fact, no corpse leaving the Pen ever reaches the mainland. The container they use to haul away the coffins is like a garbage container. It's loaded onto the same deck rails. When the *John Howard* reaches deep water, and that should be well before eight o'clock, the Skipper stops the engines, reads a non-denominational burial service, and pulls the 'dump garbage' lever. The container tips, the side swings open, and the coffins slide overboard like garbage bales. Those coffins have a concrete block built in at the foot. I've checked on that! So they're shot out into six hundred meters of water and go straight to the bottom."

"And we swim back to the surface after the *John Howard*'s sailed on?"

"Gavin, if you haven't managed to get out of your coffin by then, you deserve to go down with it! We leave the container when it starts to tilt and the side swings open, grab the minicopter, and take off. By then we should be outside the CPB zone."

"How the hell do you know so much about this sea-burial business?"

Judith hesitated, then murmured, "Greta was a Believer."

"A what?"

"A Believer. A disciple of the Teacher." She paused, then added, "So am I."

I was not as surprised as she expected. I had become used to the paradox that as the educational level of prisoners rose so did the prevalence of superstition. Among us were a Baptist minister, an Episcopal priest (both female), a Rabbi, a Jesuit, and a Suffi Mullah (all male). How this collection of ecclesiarchs came to finish up in the Pen I couldn't imagine, though I knew why they chose to stay. They were fanatics who refused to surrender their sacred memories and would not desert the little flocks each had gathered around her or him. They practiced a kind of applied ecumenism in that they did not raid each other's congregations for converts and presented a solid religious front to the prison administration. I suspected they were all hankering after the crown of martyrdom.

In addition to these representatives of established religion there were numerous other clusters of people who gathered for prayer and meditation. The "Believers" were one such group and I knew that their "Teacher" was a revivalist having some success on the outside, although I did not know which particular superstition he was reviving. Anyway, he led the kind of "back to land" movement which appeals to people who have never had to live off the land, and had established rural Settlements to which his followers could flee "from the wrath to come." Much the same program as was being sold by many of the other gurus who were flourishing in the lush economy of the Affluence. Although to have converted a surgeon like Judith and a first-class intellect like Greta he must be offering something more nourishing than the pabulum his rivals were dishing out.

So when Judith admitted she was one of his followers I only nodded. "How did that help you learn about this sea-burial stuff?"

"We Believers have—well—certain restrictions on how we should be buried. A funeral pyre is best. An earth burial is worst. A sea burial is acceptable."

"You have a kind of theological ecology?"

She ignored my remark. "When Greta was dying she grew frantic. She'd been a Presbyterian, and when she was sent here she'd asked to be buried in her family vault. Now she was horrified at the prospect of being parked among the decaying bones of her ancestors. Doctor Shore promised her that she'd be buried at sea. His promise let Greta go to the Bridge happy."

"The Bridge?"

"The Chinvat Bridge. The bridge the soul crosses on its way to the judgment. The Teacher uses certain Zoroastrian revelations in his exegesis of Good and Evil, Light and Darkness."

In other words he'd lifted picturesque metaphors from established superstitions to construct his own brand of revelation. "So the Doc was trying to reassure Greta that she wouldn't be food for earthworms. And I'm sure the Doc would lie to make a dying patient happy."

"I was at Greta's bedside with him. And he didn't want me to think him a liar. Later he told me that some prisoners, after they had died, were buried at sea. Greta's going to be one of them."

After thinking about it for a while I saw the rationale. "Not just Greta," I said slowly. "All of us. We were all declared officially dead when they sent us here. They wouldn't want to have our bodies turning up outside, years later. So the answer's obvious—dump us with the garbage!"

"Not with the garbage. Like the garbage. Do you believe me now?"

I nodded.

"And what about my plan?"

"Judith, it's the best I've heard. But it still founders on those damned transponders."

"I'm a surgeon. I can take yours out."

"And we'll be isolated and hauled off for mind-wipe within minutes. Those things stop transmitting the moment you get them free. They're powered by the myopotentials of the muscles they're in."

"I know how the transponders work!" she said, with a trace of impatience. "They have a pair of fine wires running among the muscle fibers. The wires act as both power pick-ups and antennae. If you hold them firmly between your fingers they'll go on transmitting well enough to satisfy the central surveillance computer."

"How do you know?"

"I've helped at autopsies. Taken transponders out and tested them. I managed to implant Greta's into a rabbit. The computer tried to insist that Greta was alive and in the animal colony!"

"If you fool around with those things—"

"I wasn't fooling around. I was finding a way of keeping ours going after we've gone." Her whisper became intense. "I can take out yours, plant it in a rabbit—"

"A rabbit? What rabbit?" Prisoners weren't allowed to keep pets.

"Rabbits from the test colony. We use them for bioassays. When there are a couple under test over a weekend they let me keep them in my cell for observation. It saves having to come and escort me down to the colony on a Saturday and Sunday just to take a rabbit's temperature. I've set it up so that I'll have a pair under test starting Friday night. The surveillance center will go on reporting we're in my cell, and maybe they won't interrupt us for half the morning."

"Us? You've only switched mine. How are you going to switch yours?"

"I won't. You will!"

"Me? Impossible! I've seen the mess amateur surgeons have made of each other's backs trying to dig those damned things out."

"I'll show you how. I've already got a surgical kit, local anesthetics, everything needed, stashed away in my cell. We can rig mirrors so you can watch me take out yours. Then I'll guide you while you take out mine."

"You'd really let me cut into your back?"

"I'd let you do it without anesthetic if that was the only way to avoid mind-wipe. Gavin, are you game?"

"It's the only game there is."

"I want one promise from you before we start to play."

"What's that?"

"You're not desperate to get out of the Pen just to get out of the Pen. You've been programmed to kill somebody!"

"Programmed? Me? What the hell do you mean?"

"You're no murderer. In fact I'd call you cautious, sympathetic, and sensitive." That was the first time for many years that anybody had called me sympathetic or sensitive. Before I could deny the charge she had gone on, "But when you talk of escape you go glazed. You're not a hater, but you hate someone. You've had a defined hatred planted in you."

"That's a lot of bull!"

"I don't think so." She shrugged. "I'm betting everything on this escape because there's something I've got to do. It's not particularly dangerous, but I'll need help. So before we agree to go together I want your word that you'll help me with my task before you start on yours. After that, I'll help you."

"I won't need anybody's help." I brought myself under control. The face of Futrell had risen in my mind and set me shaking. "But I promise to help you first—if we get out."

"Good." She sat up and patted her Titian hair. "Then we'd better ask for permission to cohabit Friday."

"Why not tonight? So we can plan some more?"

She eyed me. "Gavin—you're not planning on planning tonight! But sure—we can ask. The old hen on duty won't let us. She'll tell me to think it over and come back when I'm sure I want to commit myself."

Judith was right. When we went to the interview booth and asked the Controller on duty if I could spend the night in Judith's cell, the elderly woman on the screen smiled benignly, gave us a brief lecture on human relationships, and advised Judith to consider a little longer before she gave herself to me. "Ask again tomorrow, after you've had time to think."

"Thank you, ma'am," said Judith. I grunted.

We walked together toward our cells while I seethed and Judith chattered. When we came to her corridor she said,

"Wait here, darling. There's a book in my room I'd like you to read. I'll fetch it for you." And she had shot off before I could say that I didn't want to read any damned book that night.

She returned with a paperback, *The Lighted Road*, some kind of religious tract. As she kissed me she whispered, "My story's hidden in there. I've got another copy, so file that one in the library tomorrow. On some back shelf." She kissed me again. "See you at breakfast."

I walked slowly to my cell as the curfew chimed; more frustrated than excited.

IV

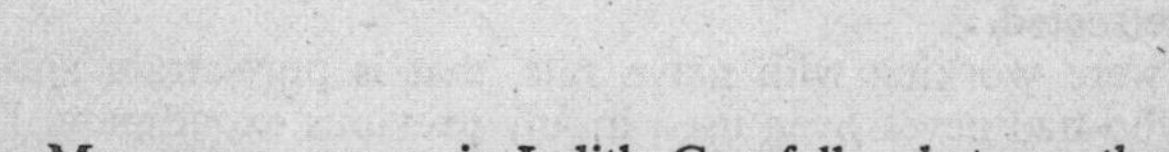

My—your—name is Judith Grenfell, whatever they may call you now, and I am—was—a neurosurgeon (MD Hopkins '20, Chief Neurosurgical Resident Bethesda '24, Staff of Mercy Hospital and Research Associate NIH '24—'26). For more about our past life read my obituary in the Journal of the National Institutes of Health.

Officially I am dead. I was found guilty of premeditated murder and sentenced to life imprisonment in the Federal Penitentiary. I have now served one year and don't expect to serve much longer, for they are planning to close the Pen and restructure the remaining prisoners. That will wipe me out and bring you into being. If you exist I do not. But I am hoping that our body retains some remnants of my beliefs and that, if you ever read this, you will see where your—our—duty lies.

In '24 I went to NIH Bethesda as a Research Associate and joined a team investigating neurotransmitters. It was headed by Doctor Eugene Drummond, and the others were James Cranston and Audrey Sullivan. They were both neuroscientists and both are now dead. I was convicted of murdering them.

I did not and I don't know who did, but that is not important. What is important is a discovery we made and which has still not been published. Whoever you are, I beg you to make sure that it is.

Our project was the investigation of Aleptin, a synthetic neurotransmitter, and we used Paxin as the control drug in a double-blind cross-over study. We chose Paxin because it had been (we thought) well-researched, and was reputed to be so safe that it had recently been deregulated and could be bought "over the counter" without prescription. There had been some objections to its deregulation, and the American Medical Association had bitterly opposed the sale of an effective drug obtainable without first seeing a doctor. But when the Directors of Medicare showed that seeing a doctor was costing the taxpayer some ten billion dollars a year (five hundred million office visits at twenty dollars a visit to get prescriptions for a drug purported to be much safer than Aspirin), the opposition died and the American Medical Association retreated.

We were working with naive rats, that is pure-strain animals who had never been used in any previous experiment. I was doing the surgical implants and, as the junior member of the team and for another reason I explain below I was also supervising most of the pre- and post-drug tests. One of the tests was a standard maze-run to measure exploratory behavior (the orientation phase of the learning process). In group after group that exploratory behavior was reduced by Paxin, the effect to be expected from a minor tranquillizer.

One evening when I was alone in the lab watching the rats run the maze, I noticed that some showed a definite asymmetry; they consistently took right forks. This was sufficiently unusual for me to record which of the rats were right-turning. The next day a technician came from the animal colony to apologize for having inadvertently issued me a group which had been used in an operant conditioning experiment months before, and when I checked the protocol of that experiment I found that the operant response had been to turn right.

None of the rats had shown any right-turning tendency in their no-drug run but some had shown it strongly in their post-drug. I broke the double-blind code for that group, expecting to find those were the animals treated with Aleptin. They were not. All the right-turners had had Paxin.

That was an exciting observation, but it was also disquieting. I hope you can see why. Paxin was being used by half the populations in all the affluent nations of the world. And my observation suggested Paxin was a chemical reinforcer of conditioned behavior, at least in rats.

It might not have that effect in humans, but if it did the implications were so enormous that I repeated the experiment a number of times during the next few weeks. The statistical significance rose to probability levels which approached certainty.

Jim and Audrey knew that I was staying behind in the lab most evenings, and assumed that it was to sulk as well as to run rats. Team morale was bad because soon after my arrival at NIH I had become infatuated with Jim and we had shared a brief but hectic love affair. This had not endeared me to Audrey, his previous partner, and she had used her not inconsiderable charm to win him back from me. In fact I had not met either of my two colleagues outside the lab since I had been dumped by Jim.

My discovery of the "Paxin effect" however was of such potential importance that it transcended personal feelings. I showed both of them my data and asked them to try and replicate my results while I carried out another survey of the human literature. Doctor Drummond was in Europe attending the World Conference on Impermease or I would have shown my data to him also.

When we met again two weeks later Jim and Audrey not only confirmed my results, their own findings suggested that Paxin in rats was an even more powerful reinforcer than I had suspected. And my search of the human literature had turned up a number of observations which, viewed in the light of our new knowledge, hinted that Paxin had the same reinforcing effect in man.

We were too excited by our discovery to let mutual hostility affect our decisions. We agreed that we must keep our results confidential until we had shown them to Doctor Drummond who was, after all, the leader of our team. His name would appear first on anything we published and the papers we planned would probably be referenced as "Drummond et al." Jim and Audrey were already starting to resent that prospect. I myself would be proud to be among the "et al" in the authorship of a paper I was sure would be seminal, but I could not resist writing up what we had done. I included in my draft both our own findings and a catalog of those quotations from human experimentation which supported our hypothesis.

When Doctor Drummond returned from Europe we showed him our data. He was initially skeptical, then interested, and finally absorbed. We ran some groups to convince him and, once convinced, he went straight to the Federal Therapeutics Administration. He left us an enthusiastic scientist; he returned a troubled civil servant.

FTA had gone into spasm on seeing our results. Here was a drug they had decontrolled under Administration pressure, and we were showing that it had an unexpected and socially significant side-effect. The Director of FTA pulled down a security screen over our study, and ordered Doctor Drummond to surrender all our data. He invoked the recently passed Social Stability Act and warned us we would be prosecuted if we mentioned our work to any unauthorized person. He certainly succeeded in frightening Doctor Drummond, who tried to calm our anger at the FTA's gag by emphasizing the public uproar if people learned they had been gulping down a drug which encouraged them to act like conditioned rats!
stood why the Administration had pressured FTA into mak-

Jim, in particular, was furious and said that he now understood why the Administration had pressured FTA into making Paxin easily available. Others must have already discovered the "Paxin Effect"; the Administration must have known about it for some time and were using it for their own ends. Everybody is conditioned to some extent by social pressures. We all stop automatically at a red light, and tend to move back when a policeman tells us to. Paxin would make us jump back and would reinforce the average citizen's tendency to obey authority. The drug was a social stabilizer. With public agitation developing over the sudden decline in the birth rate, the Administration was in need of all the social stability it could get, and the last thing it would welcome was news of an unexpected drawback to a widely touted drug.

That was the first time any of us realized how the Social Stability Act allowed the Administration to tighten its hold over all information dissemination. As soon as I suspected that the gag would be applied to us I stored my draft in the NIH "data-dump," the mammoth computerized filing system where the mountains of data produced by NIH research are stored for possible future reference. I filed mine under "Meprobamate," an obsolete drug which nobody had worked with for many years and so an address which nobody was likely to access for many more.

Jim continued to protest the gag and finally by-passed Doctor Drummond, who had been acting as an unhappy intermediary between us and the FTA. He told the bureaucrats bluntly that he would only respect their security order long enough for them to prepare a soothing public statement on Paxin and amend their regulations so that it was returned to the list of Schedule II Restricted drugs. In the heated discussions he had with FTA he must have let slip the information that I still had my draft report, for several days later Doctor Drummond urged me to turn it in. I told him that I had put it where there was no chance of it surfacing accidentally and that I did not intend to retrieve it while the gag was in force.

Two days after I had refused to surrender my report I got a note from Jim asking me to drop round to his apartment at seven that evening to discuss our future plans with Audrey and himself. The message was marked "Very Important," and was the first invitation I had had from him since we split. I couldn't get an answer when I phoned, so at seven I dutifully went to his apartment.

The door was unlocked and I let myself in. The lounge was empty. I went to look in the bedroom and found Jim and Audrey in a collapsed missionary position. Both were naked and both appeared to be dead.

I was confirming that they were when two detectives burst into the apartment. I was standing by the bed with blood on my hands and the murder weapon on the floor. A gun I had never seen but which the records later showed I had purchased. And which bore my fingerprints.

I was arrested and charged with a double murder. Because of the FTA's ukase neither my arrest nor my trial were made public and my court-appointed lawyer wouldn't believe me when I tried to tell him the truth. What the judge believed was the plethora of genuine evidence that I had quarreled bitterly with Audrey and the purely synthetic evidence that I had threatened to kill both her and Jim.

Even Doctor Drummond, one of the few people allowed to visit me in jail, seemed convinced that I had killed my colleagues. He tried to suggest that our frustration over not being allowed to publish our research added to my own frustration at having lost Jim to Audrey, had led the three of us into one of those escalating quarrels which result in killings. If I would tell him where I had hidden my draft he would produce it as evidence which might persuade the authorities to reduce the charge against me.

By the time Doctor Drummond had finished outlining the reasons for me to surrender the draft I knew what would happen if I did. I'd be silenced, as they had silenced Jim and Audrey, and Drummond would be next for the axe. I told him that by refusing his offer I was prolonging his life as well as my own. He was trying to argue me out of such an absurd idea when his visiting time was cut short, and he left lamenting my fate and worrying about his own.

I was found guilty and sentenced to life imprisonment, and an addendum to my sentence confirmed my confidence that I was not paranoid, but was indeed the target of an Administration growing desperate. For I was sent to the Pen without the routine examination by the Board of Psychiatric Assessors, and without the option of voluntary restructuring until I had served at least one year. The Judge tried to pretend this was "a partial punishment for my revolting crime." (The concept of punishment is returning to the judicial process with a vengeance, as the Administration becomes more frightened and the public more bitter.)

It was not my punishment the Administration wanted, it was my draft. They didn't want my memory wiped until I'd told them where my report was hidden. The accidental reappearance of my data in the hands of any reputable scientist would blow the whole Paxin play.

They had not allowed for the integrity of the Federal Penal Service. Immediately after I had been sentenced the FPS took me into custody and, as the law directed, held me incommunicado. Inadvertently they saved me from the intensive interrogation that is also starting to become customary with an Administration determined to maintain law and order. Or perhaps the FPS did know what would happen to me if I was given to the police and purposely protected me. Whatever the cause, I was vastly relieved to arrive here because it was the only place where nobody could get their hands on me.

Now my fears are being renewed. Not fears for myself; I am already doomed. Doomed to either clandestine execution or regulation mind-wipe. If the Pen is closed down and all the remaining prisoners restructured I may be detached and surrendered to the police for interrogation. In which event you—my new persona—will never exist.

Or the Administration may have given up on me, and is too involved in other mounting problems to trouble itself with interrogating and executing me. If I am restructured and you are born from me, I pray to the light that this letter will reach you and that, somehow or other, you will gain access to the "Meprobamate" file at NIH and retrieve my—our—report. It *must* be published. The implications of Paxin when used as a social stabilizer are too immense for the decisions about it to be made by some faceless group.

V

The similarity to my own entrapment was not coincidental. I lay awake half the night fitting the various pieces of the jigsaw together and the nearer the picture approached completion, the uglier it looked.

When I sat down opposite Judith at breakfast the next morning she played with her roll and avoided my eye. "Well—what do you think?"

"You write like a true scientist."

She took my remark as a compliment. "Thanks. But I mean about—"

"At times the woman breaks through. Unexpectedly. The sudden changes in style are disconcerting."

To glare at me she had to look at me. "About what I say! Not about how I say it!" She bit her lip. "I suppose everybody here claims they're innocent!"

"Not me. I admit I killed a woman." I saw the shock in her face. "But you—you never killed anybody in your life." I sipped my coffee. "Tell me—those detectives who caught you red-handed. Did either of them have laid-back teeth? Look rather like a shark with acne?"

"One looked like a rat with acne."

"Near enough. I wonder how many of us hard-core holdouts were framed?"

Her eyes widened. "Were you framed too? Are there others like me?" She looked round the mess-hall, as though seeing her fellow-prisoners through fresh eyes.

"None of 'em are like you, Judy. But I'm damned sure most of the later arrivals aren't premeditated murderers. That woman priest, for instance. Look at her holding forth over there! Can you imagine her killing anybody on purpose? Equally, can you imagine her keeping quiet about any evil she's unearthed? I'll bet she stumbled on something the Administration didn't want publicized and started to shout it from the rooftops. So she was grabbed and gagged under the Social Stability Act. There must be dozens who were either maneuvered into fixing themselves or were framed."

"Then why don't they talk about what happened to them. The old ones talk about nothing else."

"Why didn't you tell everybody what happened to you?"

She looked down at her plate. "Because I thought nobody'd believe me."

"Judy, that's only part of the truth. The other part is because you're ashamed of what you did. Fall in love with a man you'd snatched from a colleague. Hate her for snatching him back. Then him for dumping you."

"Damn you, Gavin—"

"That woman priest probably had an affair with a choir girl. So she feels guilty, though not about whatever they hung on her. My guess is that it's much the same with most of the others. I know I'm ashamed of what I did. Although that isn't why they canned me. They canned me to keep me quiet. Like they did you."

Judith sat silent, considering my hypothesis while I finished my breakfast. I pushed away my plate and asked, "All set for tonight?"

"You still want to try?"

"I hate the prospect. But the choice is between taking an outside chance and never getting outside." I stood up. "Got your gear and rabbits?"

She nodded.

"Then I'll fix the mikes and cameras. After supper we'll go and plead for permission to make love."

"I've asked already. The Controller gave me a long talking-to. Warned me you were a bad bet. When I wept and swore I loved you, she gave way." A flush flooded Judith's cheeks. "May the Light forgive me for lying in my teeth!"

"All in a good cause." I bent and kissed her for the benefit of our watching colleagues and the ever-scanning cameras. "See you at supper!"

Once more we stood hand-in-hand facing the image of the Controller while she lectured me on my lax morals, and hoped that this time I would form a meaningful relationship with a fine young woman. In return I repented of my licentious past and asked only that I be allowed to share with Judy our remaining years in the Pen.

That took the fire from the old girl; she must have known that within a few months Judith was scheduled to be wiped from my mind along with all my other memories. Her eyes glistened and she sent us off with her blessing to enjoy our night of love. "You laid it on pretty thick!" snapped my partner as we reached her cell.

"I was aiming to make her feel guilty so she'll leave us together as long as she can tomorrow morning." I slipped an opaque cover over the lens of the monitoring camera and masked the mike. Then I bent to fake the interlock on the cell door. "Now they'll only see us as blurs and hear us as noise. We can move out when we're ready." I straightened and turned. Judith was still standing by her bed, as though starting to doubt the wisdom of what we were doing. "Come on, girl! This is no time to ruminate! We're committed."

That stung her into action. She pointed to a chair. "Take off your shirt and sit astride that. Hunch forward. Shift around so you can see your own back in the mirror." She took a large rabbit from its cage and sat it on the table facing me. It looked me over, then continued eating lettuce. "Watch carefully. So you'll know how to dig out my transponder."

Now that the moment of truth had come I had my own moment of doubt. "You're sure—?"

"I'm sure of nothing except this is the only chance we've got." She draped me with a sheet of transparent plastic, then flattened it out so it stuck evenly across my back. "Swing your shoulders forward. I have to go under the medial aspect of your right scapula. The edge of this bone here!" She began to probe my skin. "Make the first injection here." She prodded a spot about three centimeters from my backbone and then took a syringe from a tray she hooked out from beneath the bed with her foot. I winced at the sight of the long needle. The rabbit on the table stopped chomping lettuce to watch.

"Just a prick!" I jerked. The rabbit blinked. "Now I'm infiltrating. Keep injecting as you push the needle in so that you anesthetize the tissue ahead. It shouldn't hurt. Tell me if it does. You've got to go right into the body of the trapezius." She sank the needle in up to its hilt, then drew it smoothly out. "Same thing here—and here—and here. Along the line I've marked."

The rabbit lost interest and returned to chewing lettuce. I clenched my teeth, not from pain because after the first prick there hadn't been any, but at the thought that I would soon have to do the same thing to her.

"Good! That's fixed you. Now for George." She left me with a numb strip to bend over the rabbit, turning back his fur to expose a shaven patch along his shoulder. She gave him the same series of injections she had given me. George didn't even alter his chew rate.

"You'll both be ready for surgery by the time I finish scrubbing. Five minute scrub by the clock in this antiseptic. Can't use gloves as I have to grab those two transponder wires with bare skin as I lug them out." She continued scrubbing. I sat worrying. George went on eating.

He stopped as her scalpel opened up a three-centimeter incision in his back. He resumed as she spread it open with a retractor and peered down the hole. "Well into muscle," she remarked with satisfaction, and packed wet gauze into the gaping wound. "Now for you."

"Can I have some lettuce to munch on?"

"Pay attention and don't attempt humor!" She rinsed her hands, picked up a fresh scalpel, and poised it over my back.

The edge to her voice awakened the memory of my first weapons instructor. The tone used by all determined teachers to keep lighthearted trainees in line. The tone Judith must have used on brash medical students. I watched her in the mirror as she drew the blade along the line of puncture points left by the needle. A scarlet slash appeared as plastic and skin opened together.

"No need to hurry, but cut boldly. Don't chop and scrape or you'll leave a scar and the patient will curse you for life." She made another smooth stroke and I recognized her skill. It is always a pleasure to watch an expert on the job, whether it's a whore or a surgeon.

"Keep a bloodless field. When you cut a small artery put on a snap." She reached into me with a pair of scissorlike forceps and snapped them onto something deep in the incision. Then she mopped up blood and said, "See it? That black thing down there?"

I saw it. The encapsulated body of the transponder, its two veralloy leads disappearing into a red mass which I presumed was my trapezius muscle. The thing telling the surveillance computer that I was alive and at present in Judith's cell.

She was separating leads from muscle mass with a fine probe. "Don't bother with this when you find mine. Just grab it, rip it out with one jerk, and hand it to me stat!" She reached into the incision with her fingers, gave a quick twist, and thrust the transponder at me. "Clamp onto those wires! Clamp hard!"

I clamped so hard the leads cut into my fingers. Unless the transponder continued to tell the computer that all was well with Gavin Knox the alarms would start ringing.

"Give!" Judith had to jerk the thing from me. She pushed it down into George, then carefully maneuvered the leads among the muscles. "You don't have to worry about this part. I'll be doing it."

I sat and worried, conscious of the slit gaping in my back and the electromagnetic radiations I hoped were still going out from the transponder. George froze momentarily, then returned to his lettuce.

Judith spread a white compound along the margins of his incision, then held it closed. "Polyurethane surgical adhesive," she explained, glancing at me while still clamping George. "Give it two minutes to set. And keep it off your fingers or you'll have to cut them apart. There! That's done it!" She left George and returned to me. "Very nice!" she congratulated herself, peering into the slit in my back. "No bleeders." She removed the retractor, spread adhesive, and then held my incision closed as she had held George's. Finally she stepped back and ripped off the plastic sheet.

I jumped and cursed. "Sorry," she said in the automatic voice used by doctors and dentists after they have inflicted an instant of agony. "You're done. Now go to work on me."

This was the moment I dreaded. It is one thing to dress the wounds of a comrade ripped by a mortar shell. It's another to cut in cold blood. I stood shaking while Judith placed another rabbit beside George and gave him a helping of lettuce. "Here's Rupert." She took George toward the cage.

"No!" I said, snapping back from the prospect to the present.

"What do you mean? No?" She looked at me as if I were some junior contradicting the Chief of Surgery.

"That cage is metal. Put him in it and you may screen the transponder. Or weaken the signal enough for the computer to send a guard to find out what's going on."

"Lucky you think electronically, Gavin." She placed George gently on the bed. "Stay there, rabbit. Or I'll knock your head off!" She rubbed the base of his ears, so that he stopped eating to enjoy the new sensation. When she spoke to me it was in quite a different tone. "Don't sit there gaping.

Go and start scrubbing. Ask questions while you're washing your hands."

I scrubbed away, trying to select the most imperative from the many important questions I wanted to ask. Judith pulled a fresh set of instruments from under the bed and prepared Rupert's back. Rupert stamped his foot once and was mollified by a slice of carrot.

"Keep scrubbing! Five minutes by the clock!" She unzipped her jumpsuit, turned it down to the waist, and took off her bra. "You're a surgeon now, Gavin. It's considered unethical to stare at a patient's breasts except for clinical reasons. And you're going to operate on my back—not my front!" She took her seat astride the chair, shifting her position to get a good view of the area I was about to cut into. I continued to scrub.

"Five minutes is enough. Leave some skin on your hands! Dry them on that towel. No! The sterile towel. Spread out the plastic. Stretch it tight. Use the flat of your hands. Gavin, for God's sake, get a grip on yourself! I'm the one who ought to be shaking."

I stepped back to calm myself and study the operative field, determined to make my incision along the skin stress-line as she had told me, trying to remember whether that was the same as the direction of the muscle fibers I must part without cutting once I was through the skin. I reached for the scalpel and was stopped by my patient.

"So you're one of those bastards who don't bother with anesthesia for minor surgery, are you, Doctor?"

"Sorry! Of course!" I picked up the syringe and approached her back with the needle.

"If you wish to give the maximum amount of pain when making an injection," she remarked coldly, "Use a blunt needle and push it slowly through the skin, thus exerting the most pressure for the longest possible time on the cutaneous pain receptors. Gavin! For Christ's sake go in like I showed you! One swift, firm thrust. Similar to rape!"

"Damn you, Judy—I'm doing my best!" I rammed the needle through the skin and into the muscle.

"That's better—Ouch—the idea is to inject the anesthetic ahead of the needle. Not to push the needle ahead of the anesthetic!"

I did not apologize, and by the time I had made the fifth injection I was getting the hang of it. Judith snapped, "Now scrub again while the stuff you've shot into me takes effect.

From the amount you've used I'm expecting to lose all feeling in my fingers at any moment!"

I scrubbed away in silence. I was no longer nervous. Only angry. And I stayed angry even after I realized that had been her objective.

I picked up the scalpel. Cut boldly, she had said. One smooth sweep of the blade through the skin. Another with the back of the scalpel to separate the muscle fibers. They parted as they should. Then a bright red fountain sprayed from the incision.

"Snap! Get a snap on the bleeder! That's right. You've got it. Well done. Leave it for the moment. You may have to tie it off later. Mop out the blood. I told you to keep a dry field! You've got to be able to see what you're cutting, and blood's opaque. Slow and easy. Good! That retractor's got a ratchet. It's not there for ornament. Use it! Give yourself a full exposure. You're not a damned cosmetic surgeon prettying up some fat softig. And keep your fingers out of the incision until you're sure what you're grabbing. Okay, that's enough! Move back and mop your brow. I don't want you dripping your filthy sweat into my rhomboideus major! And for God's sake use a sterile towel. That's the one I spread over George!"

I stepped back, dried my face, and admired my handiwork. The black body of the transponder was clear in the base of the incision.

"Okay—you've had your time out! Get a good grip on it. Now—don't worry about me. Rip it out and hand it over. That's the boy!" She grabbed the bloody thing from my hand, jumped over to Rupert, and rammed it into him, ignoring the retractor sticking out of her shoulder and the blood running down her back. I pressed a sterile dressing against her incision while she held Rupert's closed.

"It's working, thanks be to the Light!" She let go of Rupert and returned to slump forward astride the chair, leaving me to extract the snap, stanch the bleeding, and close the incision as best I could.

I spent some time tidying up before I was satisfied with the results. "There!" I said. "You're repaired."

"At last!" She came back to life and spirit, studying my workmanship in the mirror. "We'll make a surgeon out of you yet, fumblefingers!"

"They must have forgotten to feed you a child this morning!" I began picking up bloody swabs from the floor.

She said nothing but stood up to inspect first the rabbits and then me. Finally she went to lie face-down on the bed. After a few minutes she reached out a hand to grip my fingers. "We've done it!" The triumph in her voice, the squeeze of her hand, soothed the bruises on my psyche.

I cleaned the floor, flushed the handbasin, and put the instruments back under the bed. Then I sat down beside her. "What now?"

"We can't start moving before two. So we get some rest."

"Rest and recreation?" I suggested, patting her bottom.

"It's unethical for a surgeon to fondle a patient's backside," she mumbled, her face still cradled in her arms.

"That's for professionals. I'm only an amateur."

"You were better than some interns I've had inflicted on me!" She pushed my hand away.

I caught her wrist. "Judy, we may never get another chance after tonight. Let's take what we can get while we can get it!"

She lifted her head and studied my face. At last she said, "Okay—if you really want a last bang as much as all that—I'll oblige."

I didn't want a "bang" and I didn't want to be "obliged." I wanted something from Judith which I hadn't yet earned and she wasn't prepared to give. "Forget it! I shouldn't waste my strength screwing around."

"And I need sleep. We'll have lots of excitement later." With that ambiguous remark she dropped her head back onto her arms and was asleep within two minutes. The way I had been able to fall asleep at her age, even when I had thought I would only awaken to die.

I sat watching her and wondering what kind of person she really was. Then I switched off the light, took the opaque cover from the camera lens, and unmasked the microphone before going to stretch out beside her. If Surveillance looked at us now they would see only the outlines of a couple sleeping contentedly together, weary from making love.

I shivered in the chill of the morgue, nerving myself for the next step in our macabre escape. When we had slipped from Judith's cell and sidled past the corridor cameras, when she had demonstrated that her memory of the door-codes was not perfect, when we had scurried through the hospital to the security of the Surgeon's Lounge, I had been too conscious of our immediate peril to worry about our destination. When we sprinted along the passages in the guard zone and took the morgue elevator I was better prepared to fight any guards we met than to face the cold silence we found.

There was a deathly chill about the place. In the middle of the room, on the rails leading to the doors across the exit tunnel, was a container the size of a cell. One side was open and inside were four coffins. Their lids were hinged back and in each the body of someone I had known lay face upward in that sickly imitation of life shown by wax flowers on untended graves.

I followed Judith slowly into the container. "You take Josh. I'll go out under Greta." She had a physician's concern for the dying and indifference to the dead. "Come on, Gavin! You must have handled more corpses than me."

That was probably true, but the ones I had buried or dug up had either been freshly killed or dead for some time. Judith picked up Greta's stiff body, laid her gently on the floor of the container, covered her with the black cloth on which she had been lying, and tossed me a plastic garbage bag. "Stow the styro you dig out in that. If we leave bits lying around the guards may start to look for rats." She burrowed into the foamed styro. "Plenty of room down here!" She looked across at me. "Go on, Gavin! Move old Josh out of the way. You know he'd want to help us. And he'll be as mad as hell if we foul things up now."

He would be. I put him on the floor; the wasted husk of the man who had come here twenty years earlier. I covered him with his grave-cloth as Judith had hidden Greta, and began to make a nest for myself in the foam of his coffin.

Judith had finished hers and disappeared into it. "Not too cramped!" came her muffled voice. "Greta's no weight. And she's not leaking!"

I had forgotten that bodies sometimes leak and inspected Josh. He was dry, thank God. The refrigerator had desiccated him. I climbed into his coffin and found there was just enough room for me to lie flat on my back, though I hoped I would not have to lie there too long. When I clambered out I found Judith inspecting the catches which would hold the lids closed. "We'll have to take a strip of metal along to slide these off after they've clamped us down."

"Are you sure they don't use nails? Or screws?"

"Fairly sure. But we'd better include crowbars in our kits in case they do. There's a workbench in that corner. See what you can find."

I found two heavy wrenches. They'd make useful clubs at any rate. I stowed one in each coffin. "Have they got metal detectors?"

"Metal detectors, ultrasound imagers, fluroscopes, heat sensors, sniffers! There's every damn thing in that inspection station. But I don't think any of them are working."

I hoped they weren't, and went to hide the garbage bags filled with the foam we had removed to make our nests. When I came back to the container Judith pointed to my coffin. "You get in first. You're a tighter fit than me, and I'll arrange Josh and his cerements."

"Who'll arrange Greta on top of you?" I asked as I lowered myself into the foam.

"I can fix myself." The light disappeared as she spread the black grave-cloth over my embedded body. I was alone in the dark silence, the constricted space, used in one type of interrogation equipment. I tried not to think about that technique.

Josh's cold weight rested on my chest and stomach, but I could breath, move my head a little, and reach the metal strip and the wrench. I felt my flash. Sounds from outside were muffled but presently I heard Judith's shout, "I'm in position. How about you?"

"I'm as good as I'll ever be."

"Breathe slowly if you have anxiety build-up!"

"Okay and out!" I shouted back.

I lay sweating and then, the last thing I had expected to do, I fell asleep. I was awakened by the sound of footsteps, and a man's voice above me shouting, "Joshua Schwartz. Check!"

"Poor old Josh!" A woman's voice, and a flash of light as the corner of the grave-cloth was lifted. A metal rod came probing down past my right arm. "Just Josh!" the woman's voice called and the cloth dropped back.

I'd hardly had time to sweat for myself, but I had plenty of time to sweat for Judith as the inspection team probed the two other coffins before they came to hers. But, as she had forecast, people were not at their most zealous at dawn on a Saturday morning and assumed that one quick thrust into the foam was enough to ensure that nothing else was there. "Search complete and negative!" the man was reporting, as he must have reported many times on past mornings when the dead had left the Pen.

"Take it away!" The container went bumping and lurching forward, tilting slightly as it slid down the rails toward the tunnel entrance. We were going through the walls and into the inspection station where the meticulous searches were supposed to take place. I got my hand round the handle of the wrench. These guards might be innocent men and women, only doing their job. But if they found me I planned to take as many with me as I could hit.

No sound had come from Judith. I had a terrible vision of her dead beneath Greta, a stab wound through her heart. Then of her lying in agonized silence, blood and bile pouring from a punctured gut. The vision was so vivid that I was about to throw Josh off me when the container slowed and stopped. We had reached the inspection station and if she was injured I would soon know.

As an inspection it was a farce. Whoever checked the container was both incompetent and careless. Even in my coffin I could hear a counter clicking at a rate which would have alerted me. A loudspeaker shouted that the heat radiation from the container was above limits; the inspector yelled back that the heat detectors always read high. I felt I was radiating enough heat to trigger every sensor in the Pen. Judith had been right. The instrument search was now a formality. The sensors were either inoperative or far off calibration. After less than a minute in the station the loudspeaker called, "Okay! All clear. Close up, ready to ship."

The coffin lid came down and the clamp snapped home. No nails in my coffin, thank God! The container side crashed closed and we began to bump forward. My relief that we had escaped detection was tempered by chagrin. In a way all of us prisoners had been proud of the complex systems which held us incarcerated. Now the staff had grown so slack that those systems had deteriorated until they were little better than masses of bogus gadgetry to overawe rather than use. *"La Legion c'est ma patrie,"* another gang of scoundrels had once claimed proudly as they cursed the regiment that was marching them through hell. Men grow loyal to the most absurd organizations if given enough time. If I'd been running the Pen I'd have been putting on simulated escape attempts at irregular intervals to keep the staff on their toes.

The container jerked to another halt. We must be on the wharf waiting to be loaded. I heard the low throaty wail of Old Groaner, the foghorn that had roared its warning from Jona's Point since long before the days of radio beacons and radar. It had continued to roar after the Pen had been built, warning mariners of danger even after the seas around the

Point had become verboten to every ship except the *John Howard*. An anachronism that lived on because no bureaucrat had dared to take the responsibility for pronouncing it useless. An anachronism which we prisoners had listened to with affection because it had told us something about the world outside—that there was fog around the Pen.

The container shuddered as the loading rails locked between ship and wharf, then lurched as it was thrust by the hydraulic rams up onto the ship's deck. The afterdeck, I prayed. A final slam as it was gripped by the ship's clamps. We were aboard. At last I could escape from my coffin.

That was harder than I had expected, and the *John Howard* was already rolling and pitching as she left the lee of the Point before I was able to slip the catch and climb from under old Josh. The container was ringing like the inside of a drum with the noises that fill any closed compartment in a rolling ship. I snapped on my flash and lurched across to Judith's coffin. She had not yet been able to get it open.

The pallor of her face, the desperation in her eyes, showed that she had begun to believe that she never would. When I eased Greta aside and litfed Judith out she clung to me in a way that cured the wounds my male pride had suffered during the past twelve hours. I sat down slowly, my back against the side of the container, and held her in my arms, cradled her head in my lap.

Presently her breathing slowed and she scrambled to her feet. "Thanks! From now on you can take me any time you want, any way you want!" She shuddered. "All I could think about was that block of concrete under my feet!"

I had forgotten about the weight that would drag coffin and contents down to the bottom ooze. I shuddered in sympathy. "Now to find a way out of this damned box!"

The wrenches, which I had collected primarily as weapons, now proved their worth as wrenches. We had planned to wait until the container started to tip and the side swung open, as that would give us a moment to get out before we were shot with the coffins into the sea. Now, searching with my flash, we found a manhole in the side facing aft, and with the wrenches we were able to slacken the bolts sufficiently to let in a blast of sea air and a gleam of light.

I squinted through the crack. "We're on the afterdeck, thank Christ! Right up against the poop."

"And the minicopter's on the poop?"

"Should be." I looked up at her, my flash throwing her

face into stark relief. "We've got to get out of here now and chance being seen. Once they start to dump we'll never have time to reach the minicopter, warm the motor, and take off before we're spotted."

"Then get cracking on those bolts!" Judith had regained her old form.

VI

We crouched together in the gap between the after end of the container and the poop bulkhead. The *John Howard* was rolling heavily as she swung southwest toward Clarport, the seas breaking over her and the spray driving over us. Off the port beam the Pen was shrouded by mist and rain. Overhead was a turmoil of low clouds. A bad day for a crossing, but the weather would hide us if we could get into the air without falling into the ocean.

I eased up the poop ladder, hidden from the bridge by the container, and my heart sank. I slid back down and hissed in Judith's ear, "They've got double lashings on the chopper. We'll have to get the lines free before we can release the holdfasts round the skids."

"Translate!"

"The minicopter's locked to the deck by quick-release clamps round the skids. The poop's a landing pad. But the Skipper's got his toy tied down with extra ropes. We've got to free those before we can grab it. And when we do—God knows how we're going to lift off while she's rolling like this." I glanced at the sky. "It's not going to be any better out in the bay."

"Can we cut the ropes?" Judith asked.

"We could if we had a knife."

She reached inside her suit and produced two scalpels. "I brought these along. Just in case."

To use on the guards or on herself? "They're too light. Those lines are lurax."

"These scalpels are veralloy. They'll cut any rope. Let me try."

I hesitated, but she could use a veralloy scalpel better than I could. "Okay! But stay flat on the deck so the container'll hide you from the bridge." She started up the ladder. I gripped her ankle. "And hang on! One hand for yourself at all times. There's nothing to stop you if you start to slide. And she's pitching like hell!"

She nodded and pulled herself over the edge of the pad. I eased up the ladder to watch her work, cursing our luck. Even if she cut the lashings, how could I lift the minicopter off? If the ship hadn't been rolling around like a drunken senator I might have been able to hold the chopper steady long enough for Judith to throw the clamps and climb aboard. I'd learned the basics of minicopter flying during my Strike Force training, but not even our top pilots would have tried to take off in this sea; in fact the hydrofoils from which we'd flown wouldn't even have put to sea in this weather.

Judith knew too little to know we were attempting the impossible. Flat on her stomach, sawing away at the lashings with one hand while holding onto the struts of the minicopter with the other, she was determined to push on to the end. I watched the last lashing whip out in the wind, and caught her hands as she dragged herself to the top of the ladder. The ship pitched and we fell together to the bottom.

When she had recovered her breath she gasped, "Anybody spot me?"

"No sign anybody did." I hesitated. "Judy, I don't see how I'll be able to get that thing airborne." And I explained why.

She pushed her wet hair back from her face. "We can do it if we try. Don't you understand yet, Gavin? The Light hasn't allowed us to come as far as this only to be captured or drowned. We're being tested. We can make it. If we don't it's because we've failed. And if we fail, then we're not fit to succeed."

Tested to destruction! Judith's religion seemed to treat this world as a kind of boot camp in which humans were screened and trained before going on to take part in the serious business of the Universe. A crazy concept which might help her but did nothing for me. "Then perhaps your Light will—"

"It has. Already. When the container starts to tilt that'll hide the minicopter. You climb aboard and start the engine. I'll throw the clamps when you signal. Then you take off."

"Without you? Like hell!"

"I'll come on the skids."

"On the skids? You're mad! You'll be blown or knocked off the moment I try to lift. In this wind and sea—"

"I'll rope myself to the struts."

"Judy—"

"Move it! They're heaving to! Skipper's about to dump."

Jona's Point had disappeared astern. We must be at least ten kilometers from the Pen, and the *John Howard* was preparing to get rid of her load. We heard the clang as the bolts holding the container's hinged side crashed back. The Skipper was shouting on the bullhorn, "Forasmuch as these, our brothers and sisters—"

Judith began to shove me up the ladder as the inboard edge of the container started to rise. "Go, Gavin, go!" she screamed. "It's the only way. Get that motor turning!"

At least we'd go fighting. I clawed across the pad to the chopper and pulled myself into the cockpit. The container had tilted high and we were still hidden. But the moment the turbine fired and the blades began to turn, the guards would start aft. And the instant the container dropped back onto its rails, we'd be exposed to their view and their guns.

I checked the controls and instruments. All standardized. UN regulations. Every aircraft, every auto, no matter where it was made or who made it, must follow the same control-display pattern. And the minicopter itself was a popular US model. Fully fueled with hydrides—the Skipper probably got them free from the Pen's surplus. I put my hand on the starter and looked down at the skids. We were committed. I must do my best. If my best wasn't good enough for the Light, then we were for the Dark.

Judith had wound a cut lashing round herself, binding her body to the skids. Would her knots hold? Most women can't tie a knot that doesn't slip. But Judith was a surgeon. Hers should be good. She had one hand on the clamp-release, was signaling "Ready" with the other.

The container had reached maximum tilt. Its seaward side swung open. The Skipper's voice came on the wind, "We therefore commit these bodies to the deep—" I pressed the starter.

The rotors turned. The turbine gasped and fired, hesitated and died. I held the starter down. The turbine tried again, gasped again, and kept turning.

The four coffins shot overside into the welter of sea foam. The Skipper broke off his nondenominational burial prayer to shout, "What the hell?" The container dropped back onto the deck with a crash that shook the ship. The turbine roared and spluttered. Three guards were tumbling down the bridge ladder. A fourth, on the bridge, was aiming a rifle.

It was the next stern-lift or never. I speeded the turbine and signaled Judith. She struggled with the clamp-release. It wouldn't free. The moment passed. The *John Howard*'s stern dropped into the next trough. The Light was pitching us every curve ball in its repertoire.

The ship corkscrewed in a cross sea at the moment that the rifle stuttered. The burst went wide. The first of the guards down the bridge ladder slipped on the wet deck and the two behind fell with him. The rifleman was snapping on another magazine. Judith had both hands on the clamp-release. The stern started to rise.

I signaled. Judith tugged. The turbine roared. At the critical moment when the crest lifted the clamp came free. The minicopter was tossed into the air. A burst ricocheted off the deck.

The rotors got a grip, lost it, and we dropped alongside the ship into the trough between waves. The turbine roared again and we were starting to rise when the next crest caught us, foaming around struts and over skids. Judith was submerged.

I hauled out the overdrive control, an action likely to stall a cold engine. It started to fade, then decided to try. Power poured into the rotors. They tore us, airframe shuddering, out of the grip of the sea. I glimpsed Judith limp across the skids, and then I was into the overcast, fighting to retain control of a minicopter whose turbine was alternating between full power and failure.

I cut the overdrive and the turbine settled into a steady purr. Below me Judith was still limp. If not already drowned she'd be dead of exposure within minutes. I rammed open the throttle and dipped through the clouds. About five kilometers ahead the seas were pounding onto a rocky coast. I dived toward the only stretch of shingle in sight.

I touched down as gently as I could, and dropped from the cockpit to frantically attack the lashings. She had tied them well and they freed easily. I rolled her onto her stomach, pumped water from her lungs, then turned her on her back and started mouth-to-mouth resuscitation. She gasped and opened her eyes. "Gavin! I promised any time, anyway! But not right now!" She sat up. "Where are we? In hell?"

"In Maine! And we've got to move. The hounds will be after us."

She began to shiver. Her jumpsuit was soaked. I helped her

up into the cockpit, and dragged a rug from behind the seat. "Get that suit off and this around you, before you freeze." I turned up the cabin heater, which didn't help much while the motor was still cool. Then I took off. The overcast was our best hope.

She fumbled at her zippers. "Gavin—I've got no hands!" I glanced sideways. They were white claws.

I switched the copter to auto and set it to fly southwest through the clouds. I pushed her hands into the heater blast and began to unzip her. After a struggle I managed to peel off her soaked jumpsuit. I had undressed women in a minicopter before, but never when it was flying and the woman was freezing.

I wrapped her in the rug, then found a windbreaker to pull over her shoulders. She began to sob with pain as feeling came back into her fingers and toes. That was a good sign. I concentrated on flying the copter, glancing down through gaps in the clouds. All I could see below were patches of wet woods.

"The proximity indicator," she whispered. "Aircraft at seventy-two!"

Three, a little above us, flying southwest. Had they vectored in on us already? I started to turn and came out of the clouds. "Minicopters, by God!"

Three civilian minicopters, flying in a group but not in formation. And another four farther inland, heading the same way. They must all be going somewhere, but they weren't after us. I eased over to fall in astern of the nearest group. A flock like this might confuse the radar search. "Where the hell are they going?" I muttered.

"Up ahead!" Judith raised a mottled hand. "They're landing."

Beneath us was only forest. It would be hopeless to try to hide in that, even if I could see a place to put down. I know about people-hunting in jungle; airborne sniffers would smell us out in no time, once they knew roughly where we were hiding.

We passed over a road, cars moving along it in a steady stream, heading toward a group of buildings surrounded by hectares of permacrete. "A rural shopping mall!" said Judith.

After being out of circulation for three years, it took a moment for me to appreciate what she was saying. Minicopters were forbidden to fly near cities or to land in populated areas. But out here, in the boondocks, they were the transportation of choice for farmers, miners, and foresters. Shopping centers to serve such people had sprung up and the one ahead of us was large and obviously popular. Cars were streaming in from the highway; minicopters dropping down from the sky. I followed the copter ahead into the landing pattern and put down in the next parking slot. It was starting to rain, and people were running from cars and copters toward the dome covering the mall. Every rustic within range seemed to have come shopping at the same time.

I cut the motor. "What's going on? Why the rush?"

"Nine o'clock on a Saturday morning." Judith glanced around. "Will they have tracked us here?"

"Maybe not yet. We've hours at the best—minutes at the worst. We've got to lose ourselves in that mob. Come on!" I began to open the door.

"Like this?" She was wearing only a windbreaker and a blanket. "Help me back into my suit."

Judith's fingers were not yet fully functional and cramming her back into a wet jumpsuit was an exercise in applied gymnastics. The shoppers who glanced at us as they hurried through the rain looked quickly away. We were obviously some kinky couple who chose to copulate in a minicopter at nine on a Saturday morning in a parking lot. I was more afraid of the police arriving with Judith half-naked than of shocking the rustics. When she was more or less dressed I jumped out. "Let's make a dash for it!"

The rain had turned into downpour. We ran toward the mall among other scurrying shoppers and stood dripping amid potted plants and ornamental fountains. Judith looked only a little wetter than the rest of the crowd, but she was shivering as well as dripping. I guided her to a store where flocks of women were rummaging through racks of clothing. "Join that mob. Pick out something warm and try it on."

Her teeth were chattering. "I've no cards and no cash."

"Tell anybody who asks that your old man told you to buy yourself a dry dress. He'll pay when he comes to pick you up. But get rid of that jumpsuit. It's a dead giveaway if the cops come looking."

"You'll be back?"

"Of course!" I took the windbreaker and gave her a push toward the store. "If I can't liberate enough cash you'll have to fade into the crowd. The shoplifter magstrip is usually hidden in the hem. Go on! And pick something sensible and inconspicuous, for God's sake!"

I left her wandering between the racks and set out to gather the cash we needed before we could go anywhere. I went to the nearest bank because, as some bank-robber once remarked, that's where the money was. The tellers had not yet opened their windows but the bank was already filled with damp customers, queuing up or completing slips at tall desks round the edge of the room.

I joined the crowd, watching for suitable marks. These bucolics still preferred cash to cards and were preparing to pay it in or draw it out. Presently a large red-faced man laid down his checkbook and a pile of checks on one of the desks and began to complete a paying-in slip.

I went to stand beside him and started to make out a similar slip. By opening my windbreaker at a critical moment I sent a puff of air along the desk which blew his checks among the feet of customers crowding into the bank. He didn't recognize the source of the sudden draft but dived into the crowd to recover the checks from among their muddy boots. By the time he returned, cursing and counting, I had acquired his slip and one of his blank checks. When he couldn't find his slip he cursed again and began to make out another while I moved to a desk on the far side of the room.

The Secret Service had been founded to catch counterfeiters and forgers. My basic training had taught me the methods of both and turned me into a fair penman. By the time the tellers opened their windows and my mark was making his deposit I had produced a reasonable facsimile of his signature on a check withdrawing a tenth of what he had just deposited. Two thousand dollars—a sum large enough for our immediate needs but too small to arouse teller interest.

I gave the computer time to enter the appropriate credits, then joined the queue at another window. It inched forward while I listened to those around me complaining of the weather, the price of hogs, and the Government, in that order. When I presented the check the computer approved it and the teller hardly looked up as she gave me the cash. I left the bank slowly, counting my money in the manner of a careful countryman.

Outside in the mall I bought myself a long plastic raincoat, a wide-brimmed rain hat, and a woman's purse. I slipped twenty fifties into the purse and went to see how Judith was doing.

I found her inspecting herself in a knit dress of drab design, her face showing her dislike of the effect. Only a few hours out of the Pen, in imminent danger of recapture and mind-wipe, she was still a woman buying a new dress. "Perfect!" I muttered, laying the purse down beside her. "There's a grand in that. Get yourself a raincoat with hood. Then wait for me in the coffee shop by the Eastern entrance."

She nodded without looking at me and I went out into the rain to walk among the rows of cars in the agitated manner of a driver who cannot remember where he is parked. As the sumptuary laws had restricted the scope of auto stylists they had switched their talents to the design of advertisements and left the designing of autos to the engineers who built them. The result had been a notable improvement in taste and a trend toward standardization. With color choice limited, most cars looked remarkably alike. I went searching for any auto in which some hurried shopper had left the keys, but these rustics were a careful bunch and I had covered a large part of the lot without success when I saw a GM "Auditor" swing in to park.

Its owner got out, locked up, put the keys in the right-hand pocket of his raincoat, and ran toward the mall entrance. I walked after him into the automat where he flung his coat across a chair and went to purchase breakfast from the dispensers.

I collected an empty coffee mug, put my own raincoat across the same chair, and sat down at the same table. I then began to search my pockets, transferred the search to my raincoat, and then to his. The keys of the Auditor were on the same ring as his other keys so I was able to detach them and have the rest stowed back in his coat while he was still waiting for his fried eggs to emerge from the slot at the dispenser. By the time he got back to the table I was leaving the automat and heading for the coffee shop where Judith should be waiting.

She was both waiting and eating. The sight of her consuming doughnuts made me realize how hungry I was but we had already had more than our share of good luck, Judith's Light had beamed upon us, and I dared not demand more. She joined me in the Mall, still munching a doughnut, at the moment when we heard the wail of a distant police siren and froze in mid-chew.

"Relax! We're not the only crooks they're after!" That did not convince me but it started her chewing again. "I've got an auto. A dark-blue Auditor. Wait for me in the passenger pick-up shelter outside the Eastern entrance. I'll be round to collect you in ten minutes. Make sure it's me. There are hundreds of dark-blue Auditors in that lot."

"What can I do to help?"

"Pray to Saint Ditmas."

"Saint who?"

"Ditmas. The patron saint of thieves. If I don't arrive within fifteen minutes turn on your charm and pick up a lonely farmer. Guys are usually helpful to a girl who's been stood up. Especially a pretty girl like you!" On the impulse I kissed her, then faded into the crowds thronging the mall.

I walked out of the Western entrance into the rain to find three State Troopers charging toward me. I continued walking toward them, and was knocked aside. "Outta the way, buster!" The shoppers clustering in the entrance, wiser in the new ways of the police than I was, parted to let them through. I continued toward the Auditor, forcing myself to act with a calmness that was almost a parody.

Judith was waiting and whispered, "Saint Ditmas did his stuff!" as she slipped into the seat beside me.

"Go on bribing him!" I muttered as I headed the Auditor toward the exit. "Here comes the cavalry." Two State Trooper helicopters were angling in to land. A squad was jumping from them as I turned onto the highway.

After a few kilometers Judith reached in her purse and gave me a chocolate bar. "That was the only eatable in the machine. But your kiss deserved some reward."

"Better than rubies!" I tore off the wrapping. "Best meal of my life."

"Where are we going?"

"Hucksters Haven. North of Boston."

She did not ask me why but sat watching the road astern and the sky above. The girl had the instincts of a good tail-gunner. I sweated out an hour of uneventful driving and only began to relax when we reached the first packaged liquor store, an indicator of the commercial jungle ahead. Next a block of low buildings that screamed "Warehouse Sale Fabulous Furniture" and then we were among every form of scabrous growth an uncontrolled highway can develop.

There were dozens of second-hand auto dealers scattered among the other hucksters. I picked one which displayed a selection of Cadillacs as well as hordes of Auditors and Accountants, parked behind a Howardsons, and opened the trunk.

Judith followed me round to the back of the car. "What are you planning to liberate now?"

"A socket wrench. And here's the right size." I patted the rear fender. "Thank your owner for looking after your tool kit." I crouched to loosen the bolts holding the rear plate. When I had them finger-tight I stood up and faced her. "You stroll over among those Cadillacs, radiating wealth. Charm that salesman who looks as though he hasn't sold a car or had a girl in months. Turn him on! Make him think he's a bigger attraction than the Caddies. Fascinate him, so he'll ignore a slob in a long raincoat who's kicking tires on used Auditors."

"Keep his attention on me while you steal a plate?"

"Exactly! You'll make the big time yet! And carry on conning him after I've walked off in disgust. Keep the charm going. Promise to return after you've asked Daddy to buy you a Caddy. Then go to that Austrian abortion—"

"That what?"

"That cream-colored coupe."

"I think it looks rather nice."

"Then suspend thinking and do as I say. Pretend to get into it, wave to him if he's watching—as he's likely to be. Then change your mind and go into Howardsons. As though you've decided to visit the john. Exit this side. By then I should have the new plates on."

"And the old ones where?"

"On one of the several hundred Auditors in that lot. It'll be some time before the cops start checking all dark-blue Auditors in all the used-car lots in Massachusetts."

"But won't the dealer notice when he sells the car?"

"Probably not till he gets to sell it. And the turnover in that lot doesn't seem rapid."

"Okay—I charm and you switch. Though God knows how I can charm anything dressed like this. And with a face that's spent the morning in a coffin and under the sea."

I studied her; she did look part worn. "You'll do," I said, to raise her morale.

"Gavin—you're a bad liar. For this job I'll have to refurbish my face. But don't change anything about yourself. You look a slob to the life!" She laughed and disappeared into Howardsons.

I stood fretting until she emerged, looking as though she really might be in the market for a Cadillac. The very rich wear the weirdest garments, but they wear them in a way that shows what they are, with an assurance we lesser beings never seem to learn. Her face was now a study in elegant beauty. And she added to her act by going to the Austrian Abortion, seemed about to get in, glanced at the Caddys, and started to stroll toward the lot with an air that brought the salesman hurrying toward her even before he had seen her face.

I was ignored as I went around kicking tires and jumping on rear bumpers. I found an Auditor of the same year and much the same condition as the one we had borrowed and went down on my knees to inspect the rear shocks. I got up with our plate on and its plate under my droopy raincoat. After that I kicked a few more tires and then wandered off in patent disgust.

Judith tended to overact and she gave me a few nervous minutes while she dallied with the salesman and used the washroom. We exchanged only a few brief remarks until we reached the thruway and I headed southwest.

"Where are we going now, Gavin?"

"Buxton—just outside Greater Washington."

"Washington suits me. But what's at Buxton?"

"My grandfather's grave."

She swiveled around to stare. "I'm religious-minded myself. But that's extreme. Can't your grandfather wait until we've had some sleep?"

"I'll sleep easier after I've checked Gramps."

"Then you won't mind if I grab some now?"

"Sleep all you like. I'd rather drive than be driven."

She tilted back her seat, stretched out, closed her eyes, and within two minutes was snoring softly. Asleep, with her face repaired and the lines of strain relaxed, she was a damned good-looking woman. I was tempted to kiss her again, and only refrained for fear of waking her. Life was quieter with Judith asleep.

She came partly awake when I stopped for fuel and food but only woke fully when I finally reached the dirt road behind the Buxton Cemetery. By then it was dusk and though the rain had stopped the cemetery was shrouded in mist and the trees were dripping water. I had parked on the grass shoulder beneath an overhanging oak so the first thing Judith saw when she sat up was a row of iron railings.

"Where the hell are we? Back behind bars?"

"Behind Buxton Cemetery. My grandfather's last resting place. That's Washington—over there!" I pointed to the carpet of lights, starting a few kilometers away from the rise on which the cemetery stood, and spreading to the horizon.

"And what's up here?" She got out of the car to look quickly around her. The way a cat looks around for hidden threats when suddenly put out of doors.

"This is the balanced, self-contained community of Buxton. An elegant habitat of luxury homes for the upwardly mobile. Sited to integrate unobtrusively with an authentic historical setting."

"Gavin—I've just woken up. Talk like a condemned murderer, not like an advertising copy-writer!"

"Sorry! Post-Pen euphoria!" I joined her by the railings. "Those are the luxury homes. Their yards end at this dirt road. Half of them are empty. With no kids, who needs a house that size? The only thing in Buxton with any history is this graveyard. Note the old oaks, the worn headstones, and the high spiked railings. They were put up to protect the dead from body snatchers. They've been kept because the cemetery's been declared an historical site. Also to prevent people from taking the stones for their back-yard patios."

"And where's this grandfather of yours we've come to visit?"

"Follow me." I moved along the fence checking landmarks until I came to an upright which gave slightly when I pushed at it. They had repainted but not repaired. I pushed hard and it swung back, leaving a gap just sufficient for someone of my build to squeeze through. I gestured to Judith. "Ladies first!"

She hesitated, and I did not blame her. A deserted cemetery at dusk is not the place where a woman would want to be alone with a convicted killer. But the reason for her hesitation was less rational. "I'll dirty my dress getting through that. Why don't we go in by the gate?"

"The gates are locked at eighteen hundred hours. This cemetery is under the care of the Bureau of Parks."

She looked at me, shrugged, and squeezed through the gap into the shadows beyond.

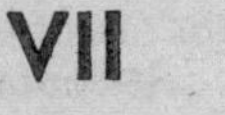

VII

We stood together, looking down at my grandfather's grave. "Good!" I said.

"Good? What's good about this place? We start the day in a morgue. We hide in coffins. Now you dragged me into a cemetery! What kind—?"

"Judy—stop bitching! We nearly got shot. We almost got drowned. You've got a new dress. And we've done the impossible—escaped from the Pen. Luck's been with us so far, but—"

"Not luck—light! The Light's guided us, tested us, and we've passed the test. For some purpose, Gavin. Remember that! And I doubt it was to pay our respects to your grandfather!" She bent to read the inscription. "Robert MacDonald, 1919-2011, 'In the Arms of the Lord.' What does that mean?"

"Remembering Gramps, it means that God is probably female."

"A graveyard's no place for blasphemy!" She glanced away into the shadows.

"God help us all if He hasn't got a sense of humor." I ran my hand over the headstone. "My father was a Minister—Presbyterian, of course. His father was a soldier—of the free-lance variety. My father had me educated. But it was Gramps who taught me how to survive. 'War's like clap. It's mostly the amateurs who catch it!' Good advice for a healthy youngster with a yen for excitement."

"You've brought me in here to listen to that kind of nonsense?"

"I've come to get help from Gramps."

"What? More bad advice from his ghost?"

"Better than advice." The main gates were about fifty meters away and securely locked. The dusk was deepening and there was nobody in sight. I knelt on the grass.

"I'll throw up if you start to pray!"

I tested the blocks around the grave, felt one loosen, and eased it out. "I endowed this plot in perpetuity to keep Gramp's memory green. And to give myself an emergency cache." I reached into the space behind the block and pulled out a 7mm Luger, wrapped in preserving plastic.

"A gun!" Judith jumped back as though I had produced a devil's hoof.

"Two guns!" I extracted a Jeta. "One with slugs; one with darts." I felt around in the cavity. "Spare magazines for both. Also money, ID's et cetera, and a badge." I laid my collection on the edge of the grave, then slid the stone carefully back into place.

She picked up the badge. "Secret Service!" she breathed, then looked at me. "So you're one of those!"

"I used to be. Until I got killed on duty three years ago. You can read my eulogy in the *New York Times*. That was before the Service had acquired its present reputation."

She followed me in silence back across the cemetery and through the gap in the railings. "Gramps still has some things I may want," I explained as I fitted the loose rail into place.

"What are you going to do with those guns?"

"Kill a man. Perhaps several men."

"You swore you'd help me before you went off to enjoy yourself!"

"And I will. After I know what you plan to do. But before you go into that I need sleep. You slept from Boston to Baltimore. There's a Holiday Inn back there by the thruway."

"Gavin, you can try it. But things have changed in the last three years. They'll want to see ID's if we register. And I haven't got one." She slipped mine from the plastic pouch in which my papers were stored. "And this is outdated. You'll be arrested if you use it."

I started the motor. "Then I'll show my badge. That's usually enough."

"It'll be more than enough. It'll send the desk clerk into shock and bring the manager fawning. The US Secret Service now has much the same reputation as that other SS—the Schutzstaffein—once had."

I cursed, and cursed again when I pulled up outside the office of the Holiday Inn. Not only was the desk clerk checking

ID's, he was comparing photographs with faces. I drove off down a side road, then stopped to think.

"We'd better sleep in the car."

"Car be damned!" I snarled. "I need a bath as well as a bed. We'll try one place which used to prefer not to know its guests' identities. If it's still operating."

The "Sybarite" was not only operating, it was booming and renting each room several times a night. I left Judith in the car, and when the desk clerk asked for my ID I showed him the picture of President Truman on a hundred dollar bill. I signed the register as William Miller, a past Secretary of the Treasury, and after paying for the room in advance, left the hundred on the desk. As the clerk palmed it he murmured, "Channel Three's the popular choice tonight."

Our room had that smell peculiar to rooms often used but seldom cleaned. Judith sniffed, then stood staring at the ceiling-mirror above the king-size bed. "Interesting!"

"This is supposed to be more interesting." I switched to Channel Three and went to the john. When I came back she was watching with fascinated disgust a life-size full-color image of two naked women doing things to each other which were novel to me. "You're a doctor, so that must be old stuff."

"I'd never even imagined—" She switched channels and ran through a gamut of pornography.

"SM seems to have recovered its popularity while I was away," I remarked, feeling along a wall panel for a pressure point I remembered. I found it, released the catch, and the panel slid open on a closet the size of a small room. I hung my raincoat on a hanger and began to unzip my jumpsuit. Judith switched her attention from the video to me.

"That's a hell of a big closet!"

"It's more than a closet." I stepped into it and closed the panel.

"Gavin!" I heard her muffled cry, and then her hands on the wall, searching for the catch. She failed to find it after several minutes of searching and complaining. At last she shouted, "Gavin! Please! Don't leave me!"

I slid the panel open to face first her relief, then her fury. "What the hell did you think you were doing?"

"Testing!" I said, stepping back into the room. "Making sure nobody could get that open while I was inside." I peeled off my jumpsuit and put it on a shelf. Then I placed my guns, badge, money and papers on another shelf. "This is the modern equivalent of the seventeenth-century priest's hole. The place English Catholics hid their priest when the Protestant posse came riding around. If a police posse raids this place the man dives in there to hide with his clothes."

"And what's the woman supposed to do? Offer herself to the cops to save the man's skin?"

"The lady stays watching the pictures. There's no law against watching dirty movies in the privacy of your motel room." I crouched down in the closet, feeling around for another catch. "For special clients there's also a special exit." A hatch opened and a ladder led down into darkness. "A passage between the walls. Serves double duty. For politicos who wouldn't like to meet a constituent on their way out. And for clients who like to watch others at work in the flesh." I smelt the dank air rising from the hatch and snapped it closed. "This place can't have been raided in years. Or it doesn't still cater to politicians and voyeurs. But there's our line of retreat if they corner us. Put your clothes with mine so we can both leave dressed if we have to leave fast. I'm going to take a shower." And I went into the bathroom, leaving Judith fumbling with her zippers and staring at the video screen.

She was probably regretting her rash promise to let me have her any way I wanted. I suppose neurosurgeons are not experts in sexology and she had not realized there were so many ways I might want. When I came back from my shower both her clothes and mine were neatly folded together in the closet and she was in bed with the sheets up to her chin. I got in beside her, switched out the light, and fell asleep while still counting the ways.

She was shaking me and I was fumbling under the pillow for my Luger. "Your guns are with your clothes," she said. "Drink your coffee and come to your senses before you start to play with them."

I sipped the liquid in the styrofoam cup, choked, and complained, "We'll never again get coffee as good as the Pen's!" Then I looked around. The sight of myself in the ceiling mirror was revolting. The sun was struggling in through a gap in the drapes. "Christ! It's after ten. We should be out of here!"

"Relax! The cleaning woman is advancing slowly and without enthusiasm. She won't get to this room before noon." She produced fresh rolls from a plastic bag. I started on one, then grabbed a copy of the "Post" she had put on the bed, scanning it fast, then checking it column by column.

"I've searched it already. Also the news—radio and video. Nothing about us. Not even a hint."

"They're not going to admit that their escape-proof prison's not escape proof." I felt like a writer searching the papers for reviews of his novel and finding his masterpiece ignored by the critics.

"They won't give anybody else a chance to confirm it. It'll be forced mind-wipe for all of them. Did you think about that, when we planned our escape?"

I hadn't, perhaps because I had never thought we would succeed. And I didn't want to think of it now. I went to the window and peered past the curtain at the parking lot below. Ours was the only car left. The Sybarite's overnight guests usually checked out early. "We'd better get moving." I grabbed for my underpants.

"Here!" She tossed me a pair of plastic-wrapped briefs and undervest. "Those are clean. Your others stink. And shave before you dress. I put a razor and cream in the bathroom. I did some shopping while you were dreaming."

She shouldn't have taken off alone, but the immense pleasure of being able to shower without a camera lens aimed at me, of putting on non-regulation underwear and a garish but obviously civilian jumpsuit, cancelled my annoyance. "Thanks," I said as I slipped on a pair of red sneakers.

"Here's some camouflage." She pulled a pair of brown coveralls with "Epsteins Electronics" in large letters across the back. "Poor Epstein went bankrupt last month. I got these cheap." She began to pack our Pen clothes into the overnight bag. "I'll dump this in the first garbage compactor we pass." She checked the room. "All clear, so let's move."

"Where to? I haven't had time to decide—"

"I've been up since seven and I've decided already. We both need ID's, credit cards, driver's licenses, money, a place to hole up. And I think I know where I can get some of them."

"Where's that?"

"For once, let me surprise you."

When we had left the Sybarite astern she directed me to the beltway and then to the Alexandria cutoff. "We're heading for Mercy Hospital," she explained in answer to my repeated demands. "That pile over there. Drive into the parking lot. Not that lot—it's strictly Staff. Interlopers towed on sight. Use the patients' lot. It's not really full. Give the guy ten bucks and he'll show you a place."

"How do you know?" I asked as I parked the car.

"I was a visiting consultant. Nobody'll recognize me. I didn't come here often and they think I'm dead." She led me inside, through a crowded lobby, down an empty corridor, and finished in a room filled with benches on which were sitting men and women in various stages of dissolution.

"Geriatrics and Psychoneurotics," she announced. "You're one of the latter. Take a seat and say you're waiting to see Doctor Randolph if anybody asks. Which is unlikely. Patients often sit here ignored for hours. I'll be back in twenty minutes." And she disappeared through a pair of swing doors into the bowels of the building.

I slumped down on a bench and hid behind a discarded newspaper, watching a stream of decrepit or neurotic humanity shuffling in and out, changing seats, or trying to attract the attention of receptionists who seemed expert at ignoring everybody except the occasional visiting intern. If the statistics which pointed to a vanishing birth rate were valid, then within a few years many other places were going to look like this hospital waiting room. I was considering that gloomy prospect when Judith reappeared, but a very different Judith from the one I had known.

She was wearing a white coat with a name tag, "Doctor Margaret Randolph," pinned to her chest and a stethoscope around her neck. Her return to familiar territory had aged her six years and raised her to the local aristocracy. She radiated confident competence. The sick moved aside for her with the anxious courtesy of poor patients toward a physician. Instinctively I jumped to my feet when she addressed me.

"Are you Mister Jones? Then come with me, please!" She turned and went striding away without looking back, as though it had never occurred to her that any patient might fail to follow when told to do so.

I did follow, trying to mimic an anxious patient to match her performance as an arrogant physician. I followed her through a maze of corridors until we came to a row of doctors' offices. She pointed to an alcove. "Sit there please!" and disappeared through a door marked "Doctors Only—Strictly Private."

Presently she emerged from another door, a scarf around her head, a shopping bag in her hand, and a worried look on her face. "Ah—there you are, Sam. The doctor said everything would be fine if I took the pills and got plenty of rest."

She clutched my arm. "Come along now. We've still got to get the shopping done."

"You're enjoying this playacting!" I muttered as we reached the Auditor.

"You enjoy shooting people!" She pulled the scarf from her hair and shook it so it fell free. "Drive to the Summit Auto Rentals on the corner of Sixth and Pine."

I turned the car down Pine. "You're not a boss physician now! You're a murderess on the run."

"I'm Doctor Murial Zworken." She waved a driving license and an ID at me. "A brown-haired, bird-brained dermatologist, at present vacationing in Mexico. She looks enough like me to pass. And she keeps a spare ID and license in her hospital locker because she's always leaving them at home. Also—" Judith looked out of the window, "She's a good egg and would give them to me gladly if she knew the mess I'm in."

"You're going to rent a car?"

"This one may get hot. Murial's secretary says she's not due back for a week. That should give me time for what I have to do before you go off to do your thing. There's the rental place. A block down. Drop me here and wait. Follow me when I drive out."

Her habit of authority still lingered and I watched her smiling at the rental agent as she got into a black "Superb." Her smile did more for her than her card. A typical glitterati! After ten blocks she turned toward the Sheraton-Ritz, waved me over to wait, and drove up to the main entrance. The doorman sprang to open her car door, then hurried to activate the hotel doors ahead of her. She disappeared with the nod of thanks that went with the style of car. The procedure was reversed when she emerged, keys in hand.

The doorman indicated how to reach whatever accommodation she had chosen and accepted her tip with the reverence which showed she had given him exactly the right amount. As she circled she stopped abeam of me to hiss, "Chalet seventy-three. Round the back. Surveillance knows you're arriving in half an hour. The chalet has a private garage. The doors will be open. Drive straight in and they'll close behind you. As far as the hotel's concerned you will then cease to exist."

Something like entering the Pen! I drove round for half an hour, wondering if I should leave Judith to get on with her program. She seemed better equipped to survive in her own world than I was. But I had promised, and she might need me. I rejected the thought that I might need her and turned toward the security gate at the entrance to the Sheraton-Ritz parking lot exactly on time. It lifted for me as promised and I found Chalet seventy-three among other chalets, all surrounded by trees and arranged so that none could observe the arrivals, departures, or doings of neighbors. The garage doors were open, I parked alongside the Superb, and they closed behind me at the same moment that another door opened onto the chalet lounge.

Judith looked up from her study of the Washington phone read-out. "Fix yourself a drink. Even you SS would have a job busting in here."

"I'm not SS," I protested, tasting my first bourbon in more than three years. "I was Secret Service in the days when we protected Presidents." I dropped into an armchair served to match my contours and looked at the luxury around me. "Murial Zworkin's credit must be good."

"She's a dermatologist," said Judith without looking up and as though that explained everything.

"Better than the accommodation I provided last night."

"The video programs are more sophisticated. And more evil." She spat out the "evil" as if she were about to confront it.

"I promised to help you before I went off on my own. So how can I help?"

She wrote down a number from the read-out—a sign of her essential innocence—and studied me. "I'm not sure that I still want your help, Gavin. I'm not planning anything that involves guns."

So smart! So self-confident! And so godamned ignorant! I couldn't leave her to walk into some interrogation room with the same confidence that she had walked into Mercy Hospital. "Judy—when you're running for your life, anything may involve guns. And we're running for our lives. You and me. The Justice Department may not want to publicize that we're out of the Pen with our minds intact. But they'll have every agent they can spare and every Police Chief they can trust trying to grab you and kill me. For Futrell I'm a fused bomb rolling around loose!"

"Gavin!" She looked down at her hands. "It's not that I don't want you with me. I just thought you were only staying because you'd promised—" She chewed her lower lip.

"I've got to stay with you. For now at any rate. First, because I want to be with you. Second, because if I leave you they'll catch you, sure as hell. And when they catch you they'll have you squealing within the hour. Telling them where I was and what I was doing when last seen."

"I'd never—" She stopped and paled. "If that's what you think—then stay!"

"It's what you think, too. It's why you were glad you were put in the Pen before the police got you. Isn't that right?"

She nodded, then looked up and smiled. "Anyway, my mother used to be fond of telling me how nice it would be to have a man around."

"Okay—so I'm staying around. What are you planning to do?"

"First, I'm going to call Doctor Drummond and arrange a meeting." She reached for the phone.

I jumped over and caught her hand. "Drummond? The guy who sold you down river?"

"Doctor Drummond didn't betray me. He may be a bit dumb outside the lab, but he's decent and honest. He never understood what was going on. I've got to tell him. He's still at NIH—the only person I know with access to the memory banks." She tried to lift the phone.

I held it down. "Your Doctor Drummond may be everything you think. But they'll have bugged his phones by now. They'll have bugged the phones of everybody you might call. They'll have a stake-out on his home and his lab. If you try and contact him through either they'll grab you."

"But I must speak to him."

"Where else could you reach him? Is there any place he goes regularly, but not so often that they'd cover it?"

She thought for a moment. "He often went to the Archers Club. Or so Jim said. I never heard Doctor Drummond mention it."

"The Archers Club? No, I'll bet he didn't! If you want to call him there, you'd better let me do the calling."

"Why?"

"If they hear a woman, they'll hang up. It's that kind of a club."

"Nonsense! Doctor Drummond isn't that kind of man!" She keyed the directory, read the number on the screen, and picked up the phone. I picked up the extension and sat back.

"Archers here!" said a voice.

"I'd like to speak—"

Click. Judith sat as silent as a girl in a beer commercial.

"Some of the best men I know are that kind," I said. "Want me to try and arrange a meeting for you?"

She nodded.

I keyed the Archers again. When the receptionist answered I said, "I long to contact Eugene!"

"Lucky you! Eugene's steaming now. I'll page him. Who shall I say's calling."

"Hermes, the messenger of the gods and the lover of men."

"That's cute!" A giggle. "I'll tell Eugene to fly to the phone."

I covered the mouthpiece and said to Judith, who was holding the extension as if it were a fused grenade, "Listen, but don't speak! Nod if you recognize his voice."

"Eugene here!" A somewhat breathless voice. He had hurried to the phone. I glanced at Judith and she nodded.

"This is Hermes, with a message not from a god but from a goddess. A straight chick with glow-hair and green eyes who gave me a fifty to pass the signal that she's mad to meet you. A chick who had to blow last year and now she's on the lam. Has a mole on her bottom and she burned her left pinky. Was mixed up with you in some hot trank. Remember the chick?"

"I don't think—"

"They called her Juicy Fruit! The rats!"

"Juicy what? Rats? Good God! You mean—"

"I mean she wants to talk paper. She said you were sure to remember Juicy. Said that if you were in Sam's on 24th and K at exactly sixteen hundred she'd call there and ask for Slammer Sims. So take a table with a phone and tell the waiter you're Slammer. Mister—that's all I know! I'm just a messenger boy. Hermes, that's my name. And I'm running too. She paid me to pass this signal. She's a real nice chick and needs to talk. So be at Sam's, Slammer. At eight bells and don't tell nobody. Over and out!" I hung up.

Judith was staring at me. "Why that mixture of jargon?"

"The boys at the desk listen in. Maybe tape. I synthesized a slang. The desk boys won't get it. Even the cops may not, if they ever listen. But Eugene got it."

"Juicy Fruit!"

"Nearest I dared come to Judy. And I fed him enough clues."

"I haven't got a mole on my bottom!"

"I presumed Doctor Drummond had never seen your bottom. So he may think you have. The cops know you don't—they'll have your description, including all marks and scars. But they probably didn't bother to record the one on your left little finger. Maybe Doctor Drummond noticed it."

"He was there when I burned it. There's no mark left." She held it up. "Or hardly any mark. But what was all that about Sam's and Slammer?"

"I stopped him bellowing your name. If he wants the contact he'll be in Sam's on time. I know that bar and it's still going strong. I'll be there at four p.m. If he doesn't turn up—take off and don't try to contact him again."

"I think you're being absurdly cautious!"

"I've just spent three years in jail because I wasn't! So for my sake play it my way. Here's Sam's number. Don't call directory. Appropriate a coin phone well before four. Have that Superb parked round a corner, ready for a quick takeoff. And leave fast when you've made the contact."

"But I have to meet Doctor Drummond. There are things—"

"Don't waste time gabbing on the phone. Once you're sure it's him, tell him to drive to Buxton and park in the lot by the cemetery gates. Tell him to arrive at nineteen hundred exactly and be alone. To flash his lights, get out of his car, and walk over when he hears you call his name. Got it?"

"Why—?"

"I'll give you the why's after he's agreed to be there. Goddamn it Judy! You know surgery. I know duplicity. Drummond may be dead straight, but he may have a crooked shadow. I don't want your meeting converted into a stakeout. So once he agrees to the time and place hang up and head for Buxton. In the rush hour traffic it'll take most of two hours. No time for him or anybody else to set up something complicated. Park your car in the driveway of that empty house one block over from where we parked last night. And wait for me."

"What will you be doing?"

"Drinking beer in Sam's and watching Drummond for tails. When we leave here we'll get a pair of CB radios. Listen out on yours. If I tell you to blow—get out of the Washington area fastest. And don't come back. Because they'll be combing the city for you."

"Then how will I meet you again?"

I shrugged. "You'll be too hot to approach for months. And so will I."

She seemed to accept the fact that if Eugene Drummond

betrayed her, or if he was being followed, then she'd have to escape as best she could. And that I would have kept my promise. "If I do have to run, here's where I'll be heading." She scribbled "Sutton Cove, Maine" on a hotel pad.

I took the pad, tore off her note with the five top sheets, and flushed them down the john. She was an innocent-at-large. "So you'll double back to Maine? Maybe that's smart, because they won't expect it. But what's at Sutton Cove?"

"The Settlement where my mother lived. She died five years ago but I went there often as a girl and after I graduated I used to visit every two weeks. They don't have a doctor so I ran a clinic. They like to see a doctor who's a Believer, as I am. They think I'm dead. But I know they'll take me back, and thank the Light for returning me alive."

"And the cops will thank their stars when you walk into their hands. If you're a Believer they'll be watching every Settlement in America."

She shook her head. "Even before I went to med school I knew that Believers didn't get far in the medical profession. And I've never had to tell anybody I was. It's not each Believer's light that's supposed to shine, but only the True Light. Believers who don't join a Settlement are expected to live good lives, but not to hold themselves up as something special. And not to try for martyrdom unless there's a good reason. As all the great religions have some access to the Light we can use the one most natural for us. The Teacher says—"

"Damn the Teacher! You mean that when the Service sifted your background they didn't find out you were a Believer? That your mother lived at Sutton Cove?"

"Even my father couldn't find out where my mother was. And he employed the most expensive outfit in your business—Gratton and Gerrard. Heard of them?"

"They're not in my business! But I've heard of them all right. Pay them enough, give them the data, and they'll find you if you're hiding in hell!"

"My father paid them a lot. He wanted to get mother back. Not because he loved her—or me. He wanted to make her break the deed of gift under which I got a lot of money when I became eighteen. My father was good at making things and breaking people. He was never able to have a second go at mother. Or at me after I was eighteen." She paused. "That's why I've no brothers or sisters. No family. And he's dead."

"And those visits to your mother? Those clinics you ran in Maine? Didn't anybody know where you were going?"

She shook her head. "My father's lawyers went on looking for mother for years after he died. To try to collect from her. In the end I paid them off myself. My friends knew that I had a lover somewhere in Vermont. A passionate lover with a jealous-hearted wife!" She laughed. "And so I did. But he only had my company at irregular intervals."

"So!" I studied her laughing face, irrationally angry with her for being skilled in certain types of deception. "Your Teacher doesn't seem to bother much about the usual morals!"

Her laughter died on the instant. "Oh yes he does!" She looked at the carpet, then at me. "Not for making love, but for hurting that wife. And I learned how much it hurt when Jim dumped me." She stood up. "So if things go wrong I've a refuge. At least—I had one. Now I've told you, so it may not be safe anymore. Not after what you said about interrogation. If they catch you—"

"I'll be too dead to talk. I've already covered that possibility. There was a silencer capsule in Gramps' grave. And it's in place!" I pointed to my mouth. "So if we're both hunted I may come to Sutton, but I won't be bringing anyone with me."

"Gavin!" She bent down and kissed me. "That's in return for the kiss in the mall."

VIII

Sam's was a bar where blue and white collars mingled and nobody questioned anybody. The small man sitting on the edge of his seat in the next booth was the kind of midager who could disappear in a crowd of ten. I studied him as I enjoyed a bourbon and he toyed with a Martini. His changing expression was worth watching; the eyes may be the mirror of the soul but you need the movements of the mouth to glimpse the character. Doctor Drummond was chewing his knuckles and licking his lips.

An intellectual, a scientist, a weak man determined to be strong, carrying his courage in both hands. He had told the barman that his name was Slammer and he was expecting a phone call. Now he was watching the waiter as if it were the waiter's decision whether he got one.

The phone in his booth rang, and he grabbed it. He was too excited to speak softly, but I was the only drinker close enough to hear what he was saying. "Yes, this is Doctor Drummond. . . . Gene Drummond. Judy, is that you? . . . Thank God! Where are you? . . . But I've so much to explain! . . . Meet you where? . . . The parking lot? . . . I will! I will! . . . Yes, I know where it is. . . . Yes, I'll make sure nobody's following me. Judy, you were wise to phone me here! . . . Judy?"

She had evidently hung up. He looked at the phone, then stared at infinity. The instrument's squeal brought him back to Sam's and he went into a flurry of action: tossing back his Martini, calling for the waiter, paying his bill, rushing from the bar. Nobody took any notice, nobody followed him. After a few moments I followed him myself. Nobody followed me.

He trotted across the street, then seemed to remember that Judith had warned him about tails. He stopped, looked vaguely around, saw nothing that matched his image of a tail, and got into his car. I watched him drive away and waited until I was sure he was clean. Then I went to the Auditor, now equipped with Virginia plates.

"Juicy Fruit!" I called on the C.B. "Come in!"

"This is Juicy." She was terse. "Go ahead."

"No customers here. No signs of interest. I'm heading south."

"See you. Over and out."

It was still daylight when I reached the realtor disaster road—Lee Avenue in Buxton. The Superb was parked in the driveway of an empty house that did not look empty because it had curtains and lights, the desperate attempts of the developers to make the street appear populated. I circled the block and turned down the dirt road to park under the same oak tree as the night before. I had picked my back-up cache with some care. In fact during Gramps' funeral I had spent most of the service deciding his grave was the place to bury the essentials for a fast move if I ever had to make one without official approval. I was then little more than a rookie in the Special Strike Force, but already experienced enough to know that to extract special equipment from any service always took too long. Over the years, as my career had changed direction, so had the nature of the essentials but the site itself was still prime.

I had known that if I ever had to use it things would have got hot or turned sour. That either I'd be after someone or someone would be after me. A clear takeoff would be important and the road behind the cemetery gave that. A kilometer farther on it joined a hardtop which dipped down a hill to an underpass and merged with a cloverleaf providing six separate exits.

Judith emerged from the back yard of the empty house as I got out of my car. "Gavin, Doctor Drummond's honest. I could tell by his voice he was glad to hear me."

"Excited, at any rate!"

"And he didn't argue about meeting me here." She looked around her and shivered. "Though I wish you'd chosen somewhere else."

"Judy, you know why I did. It gives us the edge if we're jumped. And we could be. Drummond seems honest. I think he is. But I'm still the careful type." I eased the broken rail aside and motioned her through. "My car to hide our entrances and our exits. Trees for air cover. No lights. No visitors left. It's about lock-up time." I caught her arm as she started forward. "There!" A clang came from across the cemetery as the gates were closed. "Nobody can wander in and we can leave fast." I listened to the cemetery attendant's car fading away. "Now we can move. But keep off the gravel."

"And walk on the graves?"

"They don't crunch."

She followed me, lagging a little, across the cemetery to the main gates. "They're shut! Will I have to talk to Doctor Drummond through bars?"

"Perhaps. But not here." I went to work on the lock and left the gates ajar. "When Drummond arrives make sure it's him and that he's alone. Then call him over. Tell him to join you under the trees and to slam the gates behind him. They'll lock. So nobody'll be able to slip in after him. And he won't be able to bolt."

"He won't want to bolt. He wants to talk to me."

"Then take him back among the trees so you can talk without being targets."

She considered my suggestion. "And where will you be?"

"Prone—behind Gramps' grave. Covering Drummond and ready to shoot anybody who interrupts your conversation."

"Gavin—I tell you—there's no need for guns! Doctor Drummond's not a violent man."

"He's a timid little man. But he's got the guts to meet a convicted murderess at dusk in a deserted graveyard. I was watching his face when he heard your voice. He was either genuinely glad to hear you, or he's a character actor of talent. He's not trying to trap you. I don't think he even knows that you've escaped from the Pen. He wants to believe they've let you go. And I'll bet he hasn't the sense to arrive armed."

"Doctor Drummond has the sense not to own a gun!"

"Good for the Doctor. But the goat on a tether doesn't know it's bait for tigers—or jackals. If they arrive—then there'll be shooting."

"Gavin—I don't want any shooting!"

"Nor do I. But my neck's on the block beside yours. If the Feds arrive—bolt for that loose railing, push it closed behind you, and take off. When you reach that mess of cloverleaf traffic—get lost!"

"What about you?"

"I'll have cover and a clear field of fire. The fence will

delay 'em. I'll only wait long enough to confuse, and then I'll be away before they surround the cemetery. It'll probably be hours before they realize we're not in it. They won't expect to be shot at. And nobody likes going in among trees at night after a marksman!"

"Promise you'll head for Sutton Cove?"

"Maybe. But not tonight. Probably not for months. I've got my own job to do. And I don't want to bring grief with me."

She touched my hand. "Gavin, aren't you being theatrical?"

"Worst case theater. What do you want me to do with Drummond if the worst happens? Kill him? Slug him? Or leave him hiding among the graves?"

"You're not to hurt him! He trusts me. I can't leave him. If I have to run I'll take him with me. I'll drop him off when I'm safe." She made a gesture. "But I don't think there'll be any need—"

"Dragging Drummond along will cut down your chances of getting clear."

"Gavin, if things go wrong—if we lose the Light—then look after yourself. It's because of me you're here."

"Judy, I'm here because I want to be."

"If I've led Eugene Drummond into a trap, then I've got to get him out of it."

I started to protest, then shrugged. She was probably right. I was being frightened by memory-shadows. "Okay! Eugene's your baby. Make sure he snaps the gate locked behind him. Take him back out of sight. And, for God's sake, stay out of sight. However safe it seems." I kissed her.

She touched my cheek, then moved into the darkness under the trees. I went to lie behind Gramps' grave, fitting the shoulder stock, the thirty centimeter barrel, and the night sights to my 9mm Luger. I was now armed with something close to a sniper's carbine, and I started to estimate a range-table while waiting for Drummond.

He arrived exactly at seven and there was enough light for me to recognize his silhouette when he stepped from his car. He flashed the headlights four times, then stood waiting. I could almost smell his fear.

"Doctor Drummond! Over here!" Judith was calling to him from the cemetery gate. I cursed the silly girl.

"Judy!" He ran toward her across the parking lot, pushed the gate open, and took her in his arms. Judith remembered to slam it, but they remained beside it, looking into each others' faces, overcome by God knows what emotions. I didn't want to show myself to this Drummond and whoever else might be watching so I could only lie on the damp ground and damn them both.

"Judy! Thank God they let you out. And still you! I thought I'd never have a chance to explain."

"They didn't let me out, Eugene. I escaped."

"You escaped from the Federal Penitentiary? How could you? Nobody escapes from that place!"

"I have. Mind unwiped. And you're the first person I had to see. To tell you the truth."

"I already know the truth. Or most of it. I realized the truth soon after they'd taken you away. I went to the Director. I went to everybody I could think of. All I could get from anybody was that, guilty or not, it was already too late. You were now a new person, living a new life. I was told not to try to find you. To leave you alone to be happy. And Paxin's still covered by the Social Stability Act. Judy, they're clamping down on everything to do with pharmaceuticals. This Impermease business—"

"Impermease is something else. It's the facts about Paxin I broke out to publish. If I tell you where my data are hidden, what will you do with them?"

"What I've decided to do anyway. Go to Europe. Visit every research center where there are colleagues I can trust. Tell them the truth about Paxin. It's Impermease they're really worried about now, but that Paxin business is still damnable. And the way they murdered Audrey and Jim—the way they treated you—" He shuddered. "Horrible!"

"Who killed them?" Judith's voice was fierce and too loud.

"I don't know. At the time I assumed it was you. May God forgive me! Then—after you'd said my life was in danger—that made me think." Drummond stood back from her and spoke in clear clipped tones. "I don't know who did the actual killing. But I'm certain about who ordered it. Gerald Futrell—the Attorney General! He's the man who's running America now, Judy. Only those of us who see the inside workings of the Administration seem to realize it. He's got the President—all the cabinet—following his orders. He's using the Impermease disaster to justify every kind of subtle tyranny—"

"Eugene, are you still in danger?"

"Me?" He gave a little laugh. "No more than anybody else. They left me alone after they'd frightened me into keeping my mouth shut. And they seem to have forgotten about Paxin. Even if the public knew what Paxin does, I doubt that they'd stop taking it." Through the dusk I could see him pass his hand across his forehead. "With things going the way they are—I've used it myself. It helps at times."

"I've used it too. But not all the time." She caught Drummond's arm and turned him to face her, his back to the gate. "If I tell you where the report's hidden, will you swear to publish?"

I began to relax, although I still wished she would move him away from the gate.

"I swear I'll do my best to have it published. It'll have to be in Europe. No American journal will touch anything that's ever been covered by Social Stability."

"If you can't publish in Europe, will you swear to have it duplicated and copies mailed to everybody who'll understand what my report means?" She was gripping him by both arms, almost shaking him.

A searchlight struck from across the parking lot. A bullhorn bellowed, "Hold it! Hands high! You're both under arrest!"

The tableau held for an instant, then vanished as I shot out the searchlight. Somebody beside it shrieked. A hail of bullets came humming through the trees, ricochets screaming high into the night above the cemetery.

Judith had reacted the instant I fired, pulling Drummond down with her. Both were flat on the ground. She seemed unhurt. He was moaning, "Judy, I didn't know. I had no idea!"

I scrambled to them. He was bleeding. "Back to your car, Judy!" I hissed. "Take off before they cut you off! I'll follow in mine. Get moving while I cover." I rolled to the nearest grave as another spotlight flashed on, probing erratically. I shot it out before it picked us up.

More wild bursts hissed overhead. Judith, her arm around Drummond, crawled away into the darkness. I glimpsed a shadow racing for the cemetery gate, waited for a head to show against the night sky, then hit it with one shot. The shadow dropped into darkness.

Our attackers were reacting rather than thinking. They had probably slapped a radio transponder onto Drummond's car as a routine precaution, then sent a team after him to discover what he was doing at dusk in suburban Buxton. When they had seen he was meeting the woman they were hunting they must have assumed they had an easy snatch and gone into their usual brutal drill. They'd met rifle fire and fallen apart, shooting wildly at every shadow they thought had moved. By now they would be radioing frantically for reinforcements, reporting that they had a gang of armed revolutionaries holed up in Buxton cemetery.

I was moving from grave to grave in the darkness under the trees, firing only when I saw a target. My night sights were proving their value. I picked up a cluster of shadows working their way round the margin of the parking lot and put a burst among them. A woman screamed and the shadows scattered. I turned and ran across graves and gravel paths.

I had almost reached the far railings when a blow on my left shoulder spun me round and sent me sprawling. I struggled up with my left arm useless. I grabbed my Luger with my right, found the gap in the railings, squeezed through, kicked it closed, and staggered to the Auditor.

Drummond was hanging onto the door while Judith was trying to drag him away across the dirt road. Lights were coming on in the inhabited houses. When Drummond saw me he made a weak gesture of defiance and Judith shouted, "No—that's Gavin! He's my friend. Gavin, help me get Eugene to my car!"

A chopper roared out of the mists overhead, its searchbeam probing among the trees of the cemetery. "Faces down!" I gasped as we crouched by the Auditor, hoping the leaves of the oak tree were thick enough to hide us. Apparently they were for the chopper continued to follow a standard search pattern, methodically angling across the cemetery.

Drummond hung onto the door. "You've got another car? Then go to it, for God's sake! Leave me. I'm finished. Lungs!" The whistle of air through a puncture wound, the blood he was coughing from his mouth, confirmed his diagnosis.

"No!" Judith continued to tug at him.

I hit her with my good arm, knocked her sprawling across the road, dragged her semi-conscious into the overgrown backyard beyond.

"Help me in!" Drummond had got the door of the Auditor open and was trying to climb behind the wheel. "I'll decoy!" He spat blood. "Least I can do." The questing chopper came overhead a second time and its beam flashed off the car. "That thing will follow me. I'll lead it as far as I can."

He wouldn't get far. I can recognize the face of death on the features of a wounded man. He moaned, "Save Judy! Please!"

I took him at his word. With only one arm I had little choice. I shouldered him behind the wheel of the Auditor and he gripped it with both hands. "Start the motor!" he gasped.

I started the motor. "Straight ahead, down the hill, through the underpass, into the cloverleaf." I was careless of how many innocent motorists he might kill so long as he led the hunters away from Judith.

"Headlights!" he moaned.

I switched on the headlights, grabbed my Luger, and stumbled across the road to where Judith was starting to get up. I pulled her down.

Drummond roared the motor; the tires spun and gripped. The Auditor skidded and swerved away along the dirt road, the picture of a panicked driver. I held Judith down among the weeds as the chopper sighted its target and darted off. Moments later a car came around the corner of the cemetery and roared past, chasing the tail-lights of the Auditor.

I managed to get to my feet and urged Judith across the yard to the Superb. She was starting to get in when from down the hill came a dull thud. An instant later there was the screech of brakes and a second thud. Judith stood with the door open to stare past the houses at the glow rising from beyond the hill.

"Oh God! He's crashed!"

"He's hit the underpass!" There was a sullen rumble from the valley. "So have the Feds!" The glow was changing from dull red to brilliant white. Hydride packs don't explode like gasoline tanks nor catch fire as easily. But if they do burn they burn in a feedback combustion, reaching temperatures which turn everything around them into a fine ash. Including bones.

"Eugene!" She had her hand at her mouth. "He never hurt anyone in his life!"

"He's finished it by killing himself and a carload of Feds. With luck they'll assume we're among the ashes. It'll be days before they'll be able to sift for dental fillings. Maybe they melt. Or maybe they won't bother." I was losing orientation in time and space. "For Christ's sake, get under way while they're watching us burn!"

She shuddered, started the car, then noticed my arm hanging loose, the blood running down my sleeve. "Gavin, you're hurt!"

"Flesh wound. Move us out of here before I get one in the head."

"Let me look at it."

"Look all you like when we're on the other side of Frederick. Now—move!"

She glanced at me as I slumped down in the seat beside her, then turned the Superb up the lighted street. But once we were out of Buxton she parked on a dark lane and I was too weak to protest when she pulled the coveralls and jumpsuit back from my shoulder.

She studied my wound. "You won't last to Sutton Cove."

I lost consciousness.

I regained it outside a packaged liquor store on some deserted highway. She was forcing me to drink brandy against my objections that alcohol was not the treatment for gunshot wounds. Then she started to use her panties as a first field dressing, snarling, "They're clean, dammit!"

I remember her pouring brandy over the panty-pad. As a disinfectant I supposed. Then pouring the rest over me. Of my gasping, "What the hell are you doing?"

"Disguising you as a drunk!"

I sank into a fog of alcohol, surfacing later to ask, "Where are you going?"

"The nearest Settlement. At Sherando. They should take us in." She didn't sound certain they would. "I'll never get you to Sutton alive."

I remember waking and watching her face, intent over the wheel, greenish in the dim light from the instrument panel. Of trying to tell her to slow down; she was driving like a mad Mormon. Of waking under the glare of a flashlight; the face of a policeman looming through the open window.

And Judith saying, "I'm Doctor Zworkin. Here's my license and ID. This specimen's my husband—more drunk than damaged. He hit somebody his own size for once! I'm taking him home to repair."

"Take him away, lady!" The flash went out and the head disappeared. "Call us if you want help."

"Thank you, officer. I will. But I think the most he'll be able to do is throw up."

A dirt road winding between wet woods. A crowd around the car. Being carried. Lying half-naked on a high table, strange faces around me, Judith bending over me. "Gavin! We're here! At the Settlement. We're safe!"

"You? Are you okay?"

"I'm fine." Her face came closer, gray with fatigue and concern. "I've got plasma running into you. You're out of shock. But your left brachial plexus is damaged. If I don't operate your arm will be paralyzed. I can't promise a perfect repair."

I remember muttering, "Rewire it right or cut it off." Then the stab of another needle and she faded away.

The golds and greens of the Shenandoah Valley glistened in the morning sunlight, and away in the distance the Appalachians faded into range after misty range. I sat on a fallen tree to rest from my long walk and enjoy one of the loveliest views in North America. Since my discharge from the Settlement hospital I had made it my custom to go walking in the early morning, exploring a little farther every day as my strength returned. On this May morning I had managed to reach the foothills of the Blue Ridge Mountains before having to halt and recover my breath.

The Sherando Settlement was about five kilometers away, a cluster of stone buildings crowning a low hill, surrounded by fields of corn and wheat, green pastures and grazing cattle, tree-filled gullies and winding streams. A picture of peace and calm prosperity. The only twenty-first-century intrusion was a bulldozer lumbering down the road from the Settlement to continue digging a reservoir at the base of the hill.

Judith and I had found refuge here, but now that I had almost recovered from my wound it could not be my refuge for much longer. Sherando was a community of Believers, and while I admired their discipline, their organization, and the ordered life they lived, I was not of their simplistic faith. They had welcomed Judith as a fellow-Believer and accepted me only because I was with her. And for only as long as I was not fit to leave. Suspicious of me at first, as they were suspicious of all outsiders, after two months they were beginning to treat me as one of themselves. Which I was not. And neither, I suspected, was Judith.

They were followers of the Teacher, living a communal life within two hundred kilometers of Greater Washington. During the thirty years since they had founded their Settlement in this Virginian valley they had converted a cluster of temporary buildings into the strong stone houses which covered the crest of the hill. Starting as a band of back-to-the-soil zealots they had developed into the kind of wealthy religious commune many other fundamentalist sects had attempted but few had achieved. Like their Puritan predecessors they were pragmatic and sensible. And like my own ancestors who had settled the northeastern seaboard five hundred years before they were united in the belief that they were the chosen of God. If their God—their Light—existed and had chosen anybody, I knew He had not chosen me.

Sherando was like a small self-contained city, inhabited by some five thousand self-satisfied citizens. Its founders must have included some wealthy converts or have had generous benefactors, for they had been able to purchase a prime site for their Settlement, and over the years they had continued to expand by buying up neighboring farms. Sherando was now the center of an agricultural complex; an affluent rural community in an affluent urban age.

It was affluent for the same reason that most Mennonite communities were prosperous. Both consisted of hard-working farmers who eschewed luxuries and labored for God as well as for themselves. But while the Mennonites avoided such modern conveniences as electricity and horseless carriages, the Believers in Sherando employed any modern device they judged useful. They were digging a reservoir with bulldozers, they ran a high-powered radio station which kept them in contact with Settlements in other parts of the world, and they had a stock of modern weapons stored in their warehouses. They did not use any chemicals developed after 1990, those for some reason had been forbidden en bloc by their Teacher, but their farms were producing crops as rich as any in the valley. Moreover they sold at a premium to the hosts of ignorant city dwellers for whom "organically produced" meant "manure only." In fact, they used quadravalent carbon compounds as freely as had the farmers of the twentieth century. Only those developed after 1990 were verboten.

Sherando was a contented and fruitful community. Almost every woman over sixteen seemed to be either pregnant or suckling; its young females were still as fertile as girls everywhere had once been, a fact which outsiders were beginning to notice. Sherando was not my kind of society, but it was one of which I could approve. Judith did not.

She had operated superbly on my shoulder, but that was

the last surgery she had been allowed to do. There were already eight physicians in the Settlement and Judith, unable to give her name and qualifications, had not been accepted by them. In any case a female surgeon would not have been welcomed. The protectiveness of Sherando toward its women limited their scope and, Judith claimed, was reducing them to their old inferiority under the guise of preserving Sherando as an oasis of human fertility. Moreover, although she was as devoted a Believer as anyone there, she was by no means a Puritan. She muttered about "Islamic heresies," and resented having to live in the hospital while I had been allotted a room in the Bachelor Cloister. There was no spinster equivalent because there were, in effect, no unmarried post-adolescent women in the Settlement.

There was certainly a strong Puritan strain in the place; something that Judith insisted was no part of what the Teacher had taught. Personally I found it refreshing to live for a while in a community with a firm moral code, at least while I was too weak to find its sexual restraints uncomfortable. And my stay was only temporary, while it looked as if Judith's would have to become permanent. Unless she chose to leave with me.

I did not want to leave until I was fit enough to go after Gerald Futrell, and though Judith had done a first-class job of nerve-splicing I had not yet recovered the full use of my left arm. I was going to need both my arms and all my skills to get within killing distance of him. As Drummond had told Judith the Attorney General was now the power behind the Administration, and was probably better protected than the President.

So my immediate aim was to stay in Sherando until I had acquired the strength and the means to complete what was my main mission in life. And sitting on the hillside in the spring sunshine I studied Sherando and wondered about ways to avoid being thrown out.

I could, of course, become a convert. That would have let me stay but would also have subjected me immediately to the rigid rule of life which the Believers either followed or were made to follow. I would have to surrender my guns and my money to the Settlement Council, and I would have to do whatever tasks the Council directed me to do. Nor would it be sufficient to say that I had been converted to the Light; I would have to demonstrate that I had been to the satisfaction of the Elders, the group of older men who ran the place. I doubted whether I could satisfy them; I have no great talent for hypocrisy. Becoming a convert was a stratagem of last resort; my problem that morning was thinking up a way to postpone having to make the committal.

Looking down at the trail leading from the Settlement I saw a horseman riding toward me. As he came closer I recognized the rider as Deacon Anslinger; one of the leaders of the Puritan party and a powerful member of the Council. A tall, black-haired, vigorous man of about thirty, he was wearing a broad-brimmed hat, a frock coat, riding breeches, and polished black boots. He looked rather like those pictures of Southern planters in advertisements for bourbon, and the whole effect would have been absurd except that Anslinger was the type of man whose clothes, while they might be unusual, were never incongruous. He also wore a gun-belt and a revolver under his frock coat; the only man in the Settlement who went armed.

He trotted his horse up the trail toward me, and I stood up. He must have seen me leave the Settlement, judged that if I was fit enough to walk this far then I was fit enough to keep on walking, and had come to tell me so. The best I could hope for were a few days to collect what things I had and perhaps try to persuade Judith to come with me.

Anslinger rode well and the coat of his black stallion gleamed in the sunlight. I am no judge of horseflesh; in fact I consider horses to be untrustworthy and foolish animals. An opinion I had kept to myself for they were used for much of the farm work, and Sherando had developed a breed which was proving popular with recreational riders in the surrounding Affluence. The horse which Deacon Anslinger was riding was an unusually fine specimen, even to my untutored eye. I said as much when he dismounted and came to join me.

That evidently pleased him. "A fine animal to look at, a valuable animal to use, Mister Smith." (Judith had wisely given both of us names which were obvious aliases when we had arrived covered in blood and reeking of alcohol.)

"You're starting to use horsepower here."

"We are preparing to face the Wrath to Come. The Wrath against which our Teacher warned us. Preparing for the day when the oil wells will no longer pour forth their plenty, when the fusion reactors are silent, when the oceans no longer provide hydrides to power the machines. For the day when we return to healthy ways, to natural ways, to the ways of our forefathers."

I glanced at him. "Do you really think things will become as bad as all that?"

"That is the future which the Light has illuminated for those of us who walk in the way of the Light. The future which is darkness for those who hide in Darkness."

"You'll be better prepared than most." I nodded toward the rich fields surrounding the Settlement.

"Fertility, Mister Smith! Fertility! An island of human fertility set in a once-fertile valley. Did you know that the Shenandoah was called the 'breadbasket of the Confederacy'? We are going to restore it to its old richness."

"The whole valley?"

Anslinger waved his riding crop north and south. "We are saving many farms from Washington dilettantes and developers by purchasing them from farmers growing too old to farm and without grandchildren to inherit. We are paying very generous prices for the land surrounding the Settlement. Surely you can see why, Mister Smith? You are an educated and intelligent man. You can read the future better than most outsiders."

I agreed that the future was starting to look grim.

"Grim to those who have the insight to look and the courage to see." He laid his hand on my shoulder. "Have you considered facing that future here with us?"

"Deacon, I'm not a Believer."

"Anyone with a skill we need is welcome here. We hope that the stranger within our gates who remains as our guest will learn our way of life and be illuminated by the Light which shines upon us all."

"Skill? What skill?"

"You are a fighting man. I do not know who you are nor whence you came. But you arrived with two guns and a bullet in your shoulder. Judith brought you here. She is an arrogant and willful woman, but I think she is a good judge of men. And men will be needed to defend Sherando."

"Defend Sherando? Defend it against what?"

"Against the rabble who will try to take from us that which is ours."

I assumed he meant that the locals might try to snatch some of the girls reputed to be fertile. "You think there'll be more than the Sheriff can handle?" Sheriff Jenkins was an elderly and amiable man whose job was a sinecure. The Believers in Sherando were law-abiding by nature and religion. Those who proved otherwise were thrown out.

"Sheriff Jenkins needs competent deputies. Many more if we are ever attacked by a mob."

"You've got over a couple of thousand able-bodied men down there." I gestured toward the Settlement. "That should be enough to drive off any mob."

"Two thousand males! Only a handful of men. The Settlements were founded by pacifists. They have the weapons but lack the will. And it is the Will which triumphs! We must prepare Sherando to face the dangers which lie ahead. The Council has made me responsible for those preparations. I have already started to do what I can. You see those bulldozers?" He pointed with his riding crop. "They are digging a lake. A reservoir for water storage through a dry summer. The soil they throw up will serve us as ramparts through a violent season."

I began to see what he was getting at. "Ramparts can give an illusion of security, Deacon Anslinger."

"That I know. What was it the Swedes used to say? Something to the effect that other nations defended their men with walls. The Swedes defended their walls with men. We must prepare to defend those ramparts with men. I have earth to form into ramparts. I have males who must be formed into men. But I need trained fighters, like yourself, to aid me in building up a defense force." He slapped his crop against his boot. "You may be the kind of man I need. While your wound is healing would you consider aiding me in that? The Council and I would both be grateful if you do."

I chose my words with care. "I may not be the kind of expert you want."

"That we can only discover if you agree to demonstrate what you can do." He walked toward his horse. "If you're interested in staying on for a while as our guest, come to my office in the Council Chamber later today, after you have considered my suggestion. Then we will discuss it further." He swung up into the saddle. "It would be wise of you to come!" He raised his riding crop in salute and went cantering back toward Sherando.

I walked slowly after him. Both invitation and threat were clear. I would be allowed to stay if I was willing to become his hit man, and if he liked the sound of what I had to say about defending the Settlement.

I really didn't have much choice. I was certain that I was still being hunted by the Feds and I was in no shape to survive that kind of hunt. I had no refuge outside Sherando; I felt secure within it. And in any case what Anslinger was asking me to do seemed something worth doing. These people would have to get together some kind of self-defense force to prepare for a worst-case outcome. I studied the layout of the Settlement as I walked toward it and began to appreciate that whoever had chosen this site had had something more than communal agriculture in mind. The hill on which Sherando had been built was a natural strongpoint in nineteenth century terms. And the kind of fighting likely to occur if Anslinger's scenario proved correct would be nineteenth-century fighting.

I went to discuss Anslinger's proposal with Judith. I found her in the hospital cleaning instruments and, as was often the case these days, she was in a foul temper.

"So Anslinger's offered you a job as one of his resident thugs, has he?" She threw down the instrument she was cleaning. "This is no place for you! There is Light here, but there is also Darkness. There is Good but also Evil. And you don't know enough to tell one from the other. If you stay in Sherando you'll be drawn into a struggle you don't understand and destroyed not knowing why."

A couple of nurses on the far side of the room were beginning to look at Judith, and their looks were not friendly. I signaled her to meet me outside on the plaza, and when she arrived I asked, "Can't we go somewhere private?" I attempted humor. "What about a walk through the woods?"

"Do you want to get me classified as a wanton woman? Whatever you have to say, say it here. That gaggle of so-called nurses can't eavesdrop. But they can see I'm not seducing you!"

I glanced around. There was less privacy inside Sherando than there had been inside the Pen. The plaza was the main square and, paved with permac, it reminded me of a parade ground. To the south was the main entrance to the Settlement, to the north the Council Chamber, to the east the Hospital, and to the west the Bachelor Cloister. We were probably being watched from all sides but nobody was within earshot. "Judy, I'm thinking of accepting Anslinger's offer."

"I thought you escaped from the Pen to kill somebody! Given up that idea now you've got a place to hide?"

"Damnation—I'm not fit yet. I got wounded saving your ass. Remember?"

"And you remember I shafted myself when I brought you

here. I saved your life. I could have headed for Sutton Cove. We're quits in ass-saving!"

"Okay! Okay! But I have to stay somewhere until I'm fit to go. And I happen to like this place, even if your Believers aren't all you cracked them up to be." I looked into her face. "What's got into you, Judy? What's so wrong with Sherando? Why that sermon you gave me inside?"

She went from insulting to sullen. "I don't like being hassled by Anslinger and his gang."

"Hassled? Anslinger's going to have to hassle a lot of people around here if Sherando's going to survive. The Deacon's not my ideal type, but he's prepared to fight for what he believes in. Which is more than I can say for most of the draft dodgers hiding out in this place!"

We parted on that note and later that day, when I found Anslinger in his office, I told him I'd like to try to earn my keep and what did he want me to do?

He studied me across his large desk. "Was I right this morning? When I identified you as a professional soldier?"

"I was. Ten years ago."

He stood up. "Come with me, and we'll find out if you can help."

We went through a maze of offices down into the basements beneath the building. "This was built as a refuge in the days when we feared nuclear war," he explained, as we went along a permacrete tunnel and through three veralloy blast doors into what looked like an operations room. On one wall was a relief map of the Settlement and the surrounding terrain. He pointed to it. "Give me your ideas on how Sherando can be defended."

"Against what?"

"At first—against an armed mob."

"With what?"

"Say fifty riflemen. Plus a few rocket launchers and machine guns."

I studied the map, intrigued in much the same way that one becomes intrigued by a casually encountered chess problem. Presently I said, "If you've got launchers, guns, and fifty riflemen you can drive off any mob." I picked up a pointer and tapped the map. "A couple of launchers and two guns to cover the bridge at the bottom of the hill and that road out of the woods. Guns in the top windows of those corner buildings to sweep the approaches across the fields. They're granite and as good as blockhouses." I paused, trying to picture how a mob would probably attack the Settlement. "No local gang's going to walk far. They'll come in trucks and automobiles and park 'em in the fields over by the highway. So set up your launchers and guns in the Settlement, ranged on those fields. Split your fifty men up into two squads. One squad you keep here as your reserve. The other squad, the best men you've got, are the strike force. Their job will be to move around the flank and brew up those parked cars. Most of the mob will go howling back when they see their precious wheels burning. Then you hit 'em with the ranged rockets and machine guns. The reserve squad makes a sortie and chases the stragglers. The squad who's fired the autos cleans out the woods." I stopped, suddenly realizing that I had not been solving a problem in chess but outlining how to kill the most people as economically and quickly as possible.

Anslinger laughed. "Very neat! Very neat indeed! Where did you learn that kind of thinking?"

"Special Strike Force," I admitted. The reputation of the SSF had deteriorated since my day.

But Anslinger seemed to approve. "SSF eh? As an officer?"

"Yes." An officer of the noncommissioned variety for most of my service, but made Temporary Lieutenant after all our real officers had been killed during one particularly bloody foul-up. I had held that commission long enough to be eligible for transfer to the Secret Service, so I could honestly claim officer status. And rank was evidently important to Anslinger.

He rubbed his hands. "Beside myself, you're the only man in this Settlement who's had any military experience. I was a GSOIII at the Pentagon."

"Intelligence!" I sounded impressed, as he meant me to be. In fact a Staff job in Washington, while offering access to people in power, was hardly a source of combat experience.

"That was before I heard the Teacher. Before I saw the Light."

I *was* impressed. A preacher who could convert an armchair warrior and a female neurosurgeon. individuals from opposite ends of the human scale, must have the fire of a John Knox and the persuasiveness of a John Wesley. One day I must make it my business to hear this Teacher perform.

Anslinger had returned to studying the map. "Now tell me how you would plan to drive off an attack by the National Guard."

"The National Guard? You're expecting the Governor to send in the National Guard?"

He shrugged. "He might—if the pressure on him built up. I hope not, of course. But how do you suggest we prepare for it in case he does?"

"The National Guard will come with tanks and gunships. Our modern citizen-soldiers know a lot about machines; not so much about fighting. And they dislike walking. They'll be green fliers and novice tankmen. But they'll still have gunships and tanks. And you won't be able to stop those with machine guns and rockets. Even the National Guard have sintered veralloy armor now."

Anslinger nodded. "Imagine we've got Strelas."

"Strelas? You've got American Strelas?" They were the US equivalent of the one-man guided missiles the Soviets had used with such deadly effect.

"A few," he admitted. "But nobody here knows how to use them. And if you use them wrong—"

"If you use the Mark Five wrong you'll kill yourself and your buddies. Use it right—and no tankman or flyboy will stay around!"

"Do you know how?"

I nodded. This was escalating into something much more complicated than planning to drive off some undisciplined mob. "Any mortars?" I asked hopefully.

"A few old 81mm."

"They're still as good as the best—if the gunner knows his job."

"At present there aren't any gunners. Maybe you can change that." He eyed me. "And what if a unit of the Strike Force attacks us?"

"If even a squad of the SSF arrives, then you run up the white flag pronto. You won't have a chance. Twenty Troopers could handle fifty farmers—five hundred farmers—even if you were armed with nukes. Believe me—I know"

"I believe you. But I'm sure things will never get as bad as that."

"If you start shooting down National Guard gunships you're liable to have an SSF Section descend on you soon afterwards!"

"Maybe! Maybe!" Anslinger clapped me on the shoulder. "Now let's go up to my office and arrange the terms under which we can profit from your military expertise." As he led me back through the tunnel he added, "Please treat our discussion as highly confidential. And don't repeat what I told you about our possible weapons. There are a lot of defeatists out there, naive old men still hanging on to power. I've persuaded the Council that some measures of defense are necessary, but they don't yet appreciate how draconian those measures will have to be." When Anslinger moved into his role of Sherando Combat Commander he changed both his style and his language. "Gavin, I'll fix it for you to get a job you'll enjoy!"

"A temporary job."

"Temporary at first. Of course."

"I'm not a Believer—so I'll want more than food and accommodation. Like you—I can see trouble ahead. And guys with my background will be in demand again." I wasn't really interested in anything more than having a safe place to recuperate, but if I was to be eased into the role of mercenary, then I must act avaricious.

He sat down behind his desk and studied me. "We will offer you a salary. Paid in gold. But there will be other perquisites available to those skilled outsiders who serve the Light by aiding the Settlement."

"Other perquisites? Such as?"

He did not answer me directly, but toyed with a calculator on his desk as though the instrument might help him decide what manner of man I was. "I trust that the Light will fall upon you, and that you will decide to become one of us. But, whether you become a Believer or not, I hope that you will stay and marry Judith."

"Marry Judith?" I stared at him, then laughed. "Judy will have something to say about that!"

He reverted from Combat Commander to Deacon. "Judith is an unusually willful woman. But she is fertile and intelligent. We do not want to lose her genes. Her husband will have to be a man with sufficient strength of will to reeducate her in the true role of womanhood. She must make up her mind to marry very soon. You may be the man to persuade her. And we are about to revive some of the old tried and true methods of bringing erring Believers back into the Lighted Way. Methods both physical and psychological. I hope that you will be able to persuade Judith to marry before such methods are needed in her case." There was no humor in his voice or his eyes. "In this sterile age a fertile woman who remains unmarried is an abomination!"

I gave Judith a week to cool down from our last encounter, then I ran her to earth in the yard behind the hospital. She was washing bedpans.

"Some job for a surgeon!" I joked.

That was the wrong joke. She looked up at me and snarled, "I've been demoted to orderly. They'll have me scrubbing floors soon!" She straightened and pushed back a lock of her Titian hair. "Those macho incompetents! They don't know their ass from their elbow!" Her language had deteriorated with her status. "I tried to tell 'em some of the ways surgery's advanced since Lister. So they tossed me out as OR nurse. And now I'm cleaning toilets to earn my keep." She studied me and her green eyes were hard. "How's the Deacon's pet military adviser making out?"

I shrugged. "Somebody's got to do it. And nobody else can. But I didn't come here to swap insults. I came here to help you."

"Help me? How?"

I shifted uncomfortably. How the hell was I going to introduce the subject of matrimony? A subject I had always avoided. "Judy, you're the only unmarried woman in the place."

"So?"

"Well—I'm not the marrying kind. But I'm willing to make an exception in your case." I again attempted humor. "Let me take you away from all this!" I pointed at the bedpans.

She threw down the one she was cleaning and advanced to face me. "Put it plainer, Gavin Smith!"

"I've decided to stay in Sherando for a while." I took the plunge. "I'm willing to marry you."

She stared at me. "You think you're doing me a favor by offering me your unpleasant self? Rescuing me from spinsterhood?" She took a deep breath and blasted on. "Why didn't you mention marriage before? When you were trying to back me up onto your bed?"

"Judy—I'm not trying to do you a favor. I mean, if you're going to stay here—well—it'll make it easier for you if you're tied up with some man. Like all the other women are. We could split later if you didn't like—" My voice trailed away under her glare.

"Is this an original idea of yours? Or am I part of the package Anslinger's selling you?"

"Of course you're not a part of any deal! There isn't any deal! I'm only suggesting you marry me for your own good."

I wasn't saying what I meant to say, and what I was saying was the wrong thing.

She stood with her hands on her hips; the classical picture of the outraged female. "And who suggested marrying you would be good for me?"

"Nobody. But Anslinger did mention—"

"Tell your pal Anslinger to go and jump into that lake he's having dug! I didn't break out of the Pen to hole up in this heretic Settlement with an escaped con as a husband!" She snatched up her washrag. "I'd rather go on cleaning shit out of bedpans for the rest of my life than share a bed with you, Gavin Knox—or whatever your name is!" And with that verbal overkill she swung on her heel and marched back into the hospital, her face flushed and her hair gleaming.

X

The constructions of surface fortifications is an art which declined with the development of high explosives in the nineteenth century, and was made archaic with the arrival of nuclear warheads in the twentieth. Military engineers were ordered to build fortresses long after they had become obsolete death-traps—Maginot, Corregidor, Siegfried, Dienbienphu, Moonbase—gaunt memorials to engineering success and military error. From the time when Jubal Early fought his way north up this very valley every infantryman has known that the best fortress is a hole in the ground and his best defensive weapon an entrenching tool.

However if Sherando was ever attacked, something I still though unlikely, it would be by mobs or bandits with neither nukes nor artillery. In designing its defenses, therefore, I had looked to military history rather than current practice (the Settlement had an excellent library, with restricted access). Standing on the earthworks the bulldozers had flung up on each side of the main entrance I felt rather like an artist viewing his first attempt to paint in tempera because oils were no longer available: the reviver of an antiquated art. The last great builder of effective fortresses had been Vauban, Marshal of France and Chief Engineer to Louis XIV; I was his lonely successor, building this small fortress in the Shenandoah Valley after the pattern of the great fortresses he had built to defend France. And I had enjoyed learning what he had taught. The placing of inner and outer ramparts, of running outworks, of angling defensive faces flanked by other faces; a polygon of major and minor bastions with intersecting fields of fire. All utterly useless against airborne attack, heavy artillery, or properly handled armor. But impregnable, if properly defended, to unorganized mobs or untrained troops.

I had worked hard through the first half of the summer creating something of doubtful value in real war but impressive to those who knew nothing of war. The mere fact that masses of earth were being bulldozed around, ramparts raised, ditches dug, angles measured, fire fields laid out, had done much to convince the Council that all this activity proved its own necessity. That defenses were needed. And that I was needed.

One of Sheriff Jenkins's new deputies came scrambling up the rampart. "The Deacon has a visitor in the Council Chamber, Mister Smith. He would like you to meet him there." The Deputy spoke with respect. The population of Sherando had become increasingly respectful of Anslinger as his influence had increased and, by extension, had shown increased respect for me. The fate of certain Settlements in countries where government was collapsing had added weight to Anslinger's insistence that if we didn't want that to happen to us we had better start doing something about it now while we still had powerful friends in Washington and Richmond. He had also quoted the Teacher to prove that failure to defend the Centers of Light (the Settlements) against the Forces of Darkness (all outsiders except collaborators like me) was a sin against the Light. Deacon Anslinger had a genius for combining common sense, political insight, and religious dogma into an argument for reaching Puritan goals by draconian methods.

A request from him was tantamount to a command. I slid down the rampart and walked across the plaza, wondering which of the friendly outsiders now regularly visiting Sherando I was to meet. Of one thing I was sure; until the defenses of the Settlement were finished Anslinger was not going to betray me to anybody.

I was not quite so sure when I arrived in the Council Chamber to find Anslinger and three of his tame Elders in conference with a small brusque man whose clothes were civilian but whose manner was Army. "This is Gavin Smith, Colonel Forsyth," said Anslinger when I entered. "He has had some military experience."

"Military experience?" barked the Colonel, turning to give me a parade-ground inspection. "What kind of military experience?"

"Special Strike Force. Ten years ago." I returned his inspection with the stare with which we of the elite had surveyed lesser breeds within the armed forces of the United States.

"SSF?" He looked at me sharply. "What rank?"

"Lieutenant, sir."

He liked the "Sir." "What unit?"

"The Third."

"Third, eh?" He warmed slightly. "Then you were in Bolivia."

"Not Bolivia, sir. It was the Second that got cut up in Bolivia. I was in Libya, Socotra, Brunei—and others!" I decided not to mention Moonbase.

"And your Commanding Officer?" He was still not sure of me.

"In Libya and Socotra—Colonel Fowler. Until he got zapped. Then Colonel Jewett."

"Jewett eh? So you served with Jewett" He nodded his head approvingly. "Know anything about stores and supplies?"

"Only that they usually didn't arrive. Or went to the wrong mob. In the Third we learned to live on what we took in. And off the country!" I was becoming irritated at this peremptory interrogation by some little Quartermaster Corps Colonel.

"By God—that's right!" Instead of being insulted, he laughed and slapped his right leg. It was a prosthesis. "That's why I got this. And why I'm in the Corps. When I had both legs I was in the Second."

So that was the source of his disdain! It was not the fussy self-importance of a Quartermaster Corps Colonel, but the attitude natural to anyone who had ever served in the Special Strike Force.

Anslinger, dismayed by the abruptness of the interchange between the Colonel and myself, broke in, "Mister Smith didn't give me the details of his military service."

"He was Third Strike—so I'm not surprised! Does he know what we want him to do?"

"I haven't mentioned it to him, Colonel. I thought you had better meet him first."

"Now I have!" He swung on me. "Lieutenant—your past is your business. Did you realize that a general dispensation was issued over Socotra? Probably not—it was only circulated to those under threat of civil action. You weren't one, eh? I'm just as glad. Bad business that!" He shook his head. "Well, these days I'm only concerned with the proper care and maintenance of stores and supplies controlled by the Department of Defense. Did you know that the Sherando Settlement is likely to be designated an official Defense Depot?"

"No sir."

"Good! You weren't supposed to know. But you know now! You will not mention the fact to anybody else."

"Colonel—one of the things I learned with the Third was to keep my mouth shut about anything the Army did—however crazy."

Anslinger again looked dismayed, showing how far away he had been from the real Army. The Colonel laughed. "Sometimes crazy like a fool! Sometimes crazy like a fox!"

"They were both the same to me then. They still are now."

"Spoken like a Trooper! Well, since you're here, I'm prepared to approve the establishment of a Defense Depot at Sherando. Deacon Anslinger will explain the details." The Colonel turned to Anslinger whose concern had changed to relief. "Tell your Council that the Depot is in being as from today. Shipments will start arriving shortly. They will come in civilian trucks with armed escorts wearing civilian clothing. The escorts will be responsible for the unloading and proper storage in those stone warehouses you've built. Let Lieutenant Smith keep an eye on them—he should know about weaponry. Who were you with, Deacon? Intelligence Corps—of course!" He managed to inject just the correct amount of contempt into that last phrase. Anslinger looked pleased; he did not realize he had been insulted. Colonel Forsyth was the genuine article!

"And you'll be visiting us upon occasion, Colonel?"

"Depends on the occasion, Deacon. But I'll certainly be back. Good day, gentlemen." He turned toward the door. "Smith, I'd like a word with you outside."

I glanced at Anslinger, who nodded approval, so I followed the Colonel out onto the plaza. He went limping across it and only stopped for me to catch up when he was well out of earshot of the buildings. "Persuade these yokels to keep their hands off the hot stuff or they'll blow their bodies to Hell and their brains to Hades! Understand?"

"There'll be CBW agents among the supplies you're going to store here?"

"There will. Some real beauts! Horrible stuff, most of it!" He shook his head. "But there'll be plenty of small arms ammo. And other standard items they can use to bang away with—if they have to!" He looked at the earthworks. "You planned this layout?"

"No sir. It's modified Vauban."

"Vauban?" He looked puzzled, then laughed. "Back to the seventeenth century, eh? Well, you're probably right. And you're doing a good job. Glad to see it." He paused, then added softly, "I'm going to retire here—when the time comes." He held out his hand. "Nice to know I'll have somebody to talk to."

I watched his car drive out through the gateway and walked back to the Council Chamber. Anslinger and his allies were in animated discussion, and the Deacon broke it off to greet me. "Nicely done, Gavin. You had me worried for a moment. But we've passed the test. The Colonel was hesitant about approving a Depot here until he was sure there would be somebody familiar with the material he's going to store." He rubbed his hands together. "Once the Army fills the Depot—then I guess we'll have everything we need. In case of need! Eh, Gavin?"

"Only after we've got men who know how to use it." Use it on whom, I wondered.

I had hardly spoken to Judith for a month; I had seen her shaking out rugs or dumping garbage, and on those occasions she had made quite a performance of not seeing me. She had continued to retain her spinsterhood, and I decided that Anslinger's warning was a distant threat; that his old tried and true methods of maintaining discipline would have to wait until the situation outside the Settlement made it obvious to the whole population that their existence was at stake. Law and order were still being maintained in most parts of the United States, and Anslinger had no immediate excuse for persuading Council to revive the methods of Dracon.

Judith was changing. In the Pen she had been a competent and self-contained person. During our escape she had shown herself to be brave and essentially sensible. Her rejection of me as a husband was not sensible from the practical point of view. From our brief exchanges, from her looks and words, I felt that she was on the verge of doing something desperate.

I thought I could understand why; she had lost her cause, the reason for which she had risked her life and her memory. It was now obvious that Paxin was a dead issue. Most outsiders knew it was a chemical reenforcer of learned behavior and didn't seem to care. They used it as an escape from concern about their personal futures. And in Sherando it was not needed—Believers were quite sure of their physical and spiritual futures. In any case it was a post-1990 chemical and therefore evil by definition and banned by rule. Even if she recovered her report from the data banks of NIH its publication now would cause hardly a ripple. And all this meant not only had Judith lost her reason for suffering and escaping, it meant that Eugene Drummond had died in a pointless undertaking.

The rigid social structure of the Settlement made it difficult for any single man and woman to be alone together. I, as an outsider, was free from many of the restrictions which constrained Believers; Judith, as an insider was not only constrained but watched to make sure that her behavior did not offend the Light. The first chance I had of talking to her privately was on the night that President Michael Randolph spoke on the State of the Union.

The importance of his address to the nation was emphasized by the fact that it was carried live in prime time by all US and Canadian networks, and relayed by Settlement cable. Outside TV was banned in Sherando, and as most of the cable programs were educational or inspirational I had given up watching television. That night I went to the General Assembly, one of the few opportunities for men and women to mix, and managed to get a seat next to Judith.

She greeted me without warmth but with relief. My presence as an ostensible suitor was of some value to her as protection against the disapproval of those around us. And when the President started to speak we became too engrossed to worry about what they thought.

Michael Randolph was a good speaker, a better speaker in fact than Grainer, for whom he had often spoken. That evening he spoke without notes, an honest American speaking to other honest Americans. Simple, straightforward, and utterly convincing. He must have convinced most viewers across the nation. The words were his, the voice was his, the phrases were his. Only afterward did I realize that the concepts were those of the Teacher and the plans were those of Grainer.

He started with the traditional Presidential invocation, "My fellow Americans," but thereafter said little that was traditional. He told the youth of the nation that they must prepare to carry a double burden. "The burden you carry now and the burden which the generation after you would usually carry. Because statistics make it certain that generation will be smaller than even the pessimists have suggested. In middle age you will have to support us as we grow old and the new generation of children who will be born when the birth rate again starts to rise, as rise it surely will!"

"The poor dumb bastard believes that!" whispered Judith.

"We Americans can meet the challenge, as we have met other challenges in the past. You of the rising generation will not be left to meet it unaided. Today I am placing the nation on a war footing. But not the kind of war in which the youngest and best of us have to suffer and die. A new kind of war; a war against future poverty and suffering. Now, while America is in the bloom of her full strength, all of us must direct our every nerve and sinew to serve the nation after we are gone."

"Now he's misquoting Kipling!" muttered Judith.

"Quiet, damn you!" I hissed.

"At present American industrial production is increasing at a rate unprecedented in our history. A rate of increase not achieved even in past wars. The programs initiated by my great predecessor, President Grainer, are now bearing fruit."

"Grainer?" whispered Judith. "The President who thought himself king!" I almost slapped her.

"I am shifting America into a war economy. But not to produce the weapons of war. I am not diverting the energies and skills of the American people toward the creation of engineering and scientific miracles whose only purpose is to destroy, whose only end is to be destroyed. Our efforts will be to build every variety of useful product, from the most complex electronic equipment to the simplest of hand tools. To build things to serve both the present and the future.

"We live in a prosperous age, the most affluent age in human history. That prosperity, that affluence, will continue. But it must be an affluence without excessive luxury. The kind of prosperity which demands sacrifices, the full-employment which in the past has only occurred during periods of rearmament and war, the times when every citizen was needed to produce the weapons our fighting men and women needed to defend our country. From now on the skills and labor of every American will be needed to create products of permanent value. Not to be shot in the air, or sunk in the sea, or exploded in the earth. We must start to produce for preservation. We must produce to serve our posterity."

I began to see the object of all this political rhetoric.

"In this tremendous national effort we must all make sacrifices, as we have willingly made sacrifices in the past when our nation was in peril. We must practice accelerated cost-containment intervention, turn away from the tawdry and the superfluous. We must not squander energy, materials, and human effort on making things to fill a created demand, on novelties to titillate our taste for novelty, on responses to the caprice of changing fashions. We must concentrate on the creation of things which have durability and use. And, as a personal opinion, educated as I am in the views of that great creative American, Thomas Jefferson, I believe that in creating such things we will also be creating beauty. The real beauty shown by the useful and the good."

"There will be work for all, good wages for all, rewards for all. And all of us must join together in this great and humane effort. We cannot allow the private interests of selfish groups, whether they be those of capital, or labor, or self-elected elites, to interfere with our common effort."

I didn't like the sound of "self-elected elites" nor, judging by her frown, did Judith.

Randolph continued to exhort us to unite in productivity, to create surpluses for which the Administration would provide a market. Vast storage depots were already being erected. Supply bases on which we ourselves could draw later when the productivity of an aging population started to fall. Supplies which future generations of Americans would surely need.

He finished with a word from those Americans, about eighty-five percent of the population, who were either pure consumers or whose jobs had no possible relevance to future needs. He urged them to shift to vital industries, to learn new skills, even at the cost of some personal privation. "My Administration will supply without charge the equipment and materials so that every American can preserve those possessions for which he or she has no pressing present use, but which will be of great use in the low-production phase ahead. Each one of you can make your own personal gift to the future, secure in the knowledge that some future American will accept your gift with gratitude."

It began to dawn on me what Randolph was attempting; he was trying to give meaning to lives that would seem increasingly pointless as people aged and their civilization decayed. To inspire every individual to commence some task which would occupy him or her during the bleak days ahead. It was not the speech of a posturing politician but the attempt of a President to give leadership to his people.

Randolph was doing his best, and was doubtless getting his message across to millions. But Grainer would have done it better; not perhaps in his words but by his acts. And certain of Randolph's statements stirred the strings of my memory; remarks I had heard Arnold Grainer make some six years before.

Suddenly the situation came into focus. Grainer had known! He had known then what was about to happen now. Back in 2020 he had known. That was why he had plunged into politics, had fought to win a presidency he had never enjoyed.

Had he been a secret disciple of the Teacher? Or had he had access to the same knowledge that had set the Teacher off to preach withdrawal from the Affluence to his privileged followers? Whatever the truth, Arnold Grainer had fought to gain the power that would let him work for the well-being of the many rather than the survival of a believing elite. He was not here to complete it because he had been murdered to serve Gerald Futrell's ambition!

I began to shake with fury at the immensity of Futrell's treason, so that Judith laid her hand on mine to calm me. By the time I had regained control of my emotions the President had finished and the commentators had started.

They were switched off abruptly and Deacon Anslinger appeared on the screens, explaining what the President had really meant, and how it was going to affect the situation in Sherando. From now on Anslinger would be dominant on the Council, and soon his rigorous recommendations would become the Settlement's way of life. I got to my feet and pushed my way to the door; I had to get out into the fresh night air and decide what I myself must do.

Judith had come out after me and for a few minutes we were alone on the plaza. I wiped my forehead. "They're switching to a war economy. Self-elected elites and other minorities are going to get stomped. Especially if they've got something the majority wants—like kids and fertile girls. The storm's coming. And now it has Presidential approval to blow!"

She glanced at me. "The Teacher warned us. That's why we've been gathering in these Settlements."

"Judy—you'd better get out of this one!"

She bit her lip and whispered, "Gavin, I must talk to you alone. But where?"

I must talk to her too! I thought for a moment. "Tomorrow morning I'll be checking stores in the Depot. Go to the side door at ten and tap three times. The Depot's verboten to everybody except myself and Anslinger, so don't let anybody see you. The door's down that alley which leads to the warehouse where they store old agricultural machinery. Know it? Then if I'm alone I'll let you in. If I don't it means Anslinger's with me, so beat it fast."

"Thanks! I'll be there." She pressed my hand and slipped away into the crowd pouring down the steps from the General Assembly.

Why did I feel protective? She was an eminently self-sufficient person and under most circumstances probably better able to look after herself than I was. But the circumstances in Sherando, in North America, in the whole damned world, were abnormal. And while sitting beside her during the President's speech I had been aware of her isolation among these Believers and of the tension building up within her. Judith's superficial calm hid a wildness which, I sensed, made her capable of doing almost anything. She was on the verge of doing something wild.

The Depot was a stone building, half sunk into the ground, and looked almost as if it had been designed as an ammunition store. Without windows and with only a few scattered light bulbs it was a gloomy place. As I waited for Judith the next morning I heard a motorcycle turn down the alley and go on past into the warehouse at the end. Apparently the rider had not spotted her, for a few minutes later there were three quick taps on the side door. I went to open it.

Judith slipped in from the sunlight and stood looking around into the gloom. "What is all this stuff?" she asked.

"Sufficient weaponry to arm a brigade."

"What's it doing here?"

"Ostensibly, the Army's stockpiling it for our descendents. So they can start blowing each other apart again. I think it's really for use by Sherando if it's attacked. Somebody up there in Washington likes us!"

She pointed to a stack of blue-white ammunition carriers. "What's in those things?"

"CBW agents."

"What agents?"

"Chemical Biological Warfare agents. Those containers are mixed HCN and nerve gas."

"Nerve gas!" Her hand went to her mouth.

"Pre-1990 chemicals, so they don't break your Teacher's prohibition. But over there," I pointed to a stack of containers checkered red and yellow, "is something new. I don't know what it does, but I'll bet it's something horrible!"

"How could they allow such chemicals into a Settlement?"

"Judy!" I caught her shoulder and turned her to face me. "When things go sour, weapon-prohibitions aren't worth a damn. Anyway, you didn't come here to talk about how Sherando's sliding into heresy!"

"No." She studied my face. "I came to tell you that yesterday Anslinger warned me to get married—or take the consequences."

I looked at her, then said gently, "You're the only single woman in Sherando over sixteen. You've got to marry someone if you're going to stay here. I admit I came at you like a patronizing fool. Now I'm asking you like a humble suitor. Please marry me."

"Gavin—I can't!" She looked away from me. "Not now, at any rate."

I sighed. "Then they won't let you stay."

"They won't let me go!" She gave a short laugh. "I'm a valuable item on the Sherando inventory."

"I know you're a good surgeon, but—"

"I'm not valuable because I'm a surgeon. I'm valuable because I'm a woman. A fertile woman. Anslinger's demanding that I marry and start breeding. The bastard's after my genes!"

"How do you know you're fertile?" I saw her expression. "Scrub that question! Tell Anslinger to stuff it. I'll speak to him. If he insists—he can't stop you leaving. This is still a free country."

"Free for some people perhaps. But not for us!" She turned to look at me. "Anslinger has found out who we are. He wants to keep us in Sherando. Me to breed. You to fight. If we bolt he'll sic the Feds onto us. He's hand-in-glove with the local cops. He'll probably make a deal with them to bring us back to Sherando after they've caught us. He as good as told me so yesterday."

"Judith—we can leave any time. Who's to stop us?"

"Leave? On what? With what? To go where?"

I hesitated. I had not thought about leaving after Anslinger had asked me to stay, and so I had never considered how I might. Now that Judith had made me think about it I saw the problems of trying to escape without transportation, ID's, or credit cards.

"Ever hear of a place called Jonestown?" Judith asked suddenly.

"Vaguely. Wasn't that some settlement where they all killed themselves on orders from a religious maniac called Jones? Back in the seventies?"

"They started out as religious idealists; poor people trying to build a better life for themselves. Some of them turned into devils. All of them acted like sheep. They killed each other, and then killed themselves. Jones became a sadistical brute. Anslinger's starting down the same evil pathway. Oh, he's not a madman like Jones. He's very sane. As sane as the Puritans who hung witches in Salem."

I stared at her. "Judith that's balls! This isn't a collection of huts on the edge of the jungle." I remembered the terrible pictures I had seen in the encyclopedia as a boy, and gestured toward the stone building around us. It might not be beautiful but it was solid. "We're not trying to scratch a living from a rain forest. This place has lasted thirty years. It's well established. It's prosperous and strong. It'll be even stronger when I've finished the fortifications. The people here may be zealots, but they're not superstitious fools. The Elders aren't religious maniacs."

"The Elders are a bunch of elderly fumblers who follow Anslinger because they can't see where to go and they won't see where they're going! They've been under his thumb ever since the first mob attack on a Settlement scared hell out of them." She paused, breathing quickly. "Sherando was founded by genuine Believers. They built it up. They made it what it is today. They're still Believers, but they're confused and frightened. When Anslinger talks about austerity, about the need for discipline, all that fascist crap, they think he's talking good sense. He's roused the Puritan in them. And that's not what the Teacher taught."

"I've never been able to work out what the Teacher actually taught—or teaches." I was trying to cool her down by shifting the subject. "Is he still alive?"

"He's alive." The glow that came into Judith's face when she spoke of the founder of her religion was almost as disconcerting as the flush of anger when she spoke of how Anslinger was distorting his teaching. "He's withdrawn to meditate." She gripped my hand. "Gavin, if you'd heard him, then you'd believe as I do."

"Maybe." What kind of man was this Teacher? A man whose name alone could change Judith from a sensible scientifically trained neurosurgeon into a gullible innocent? I had given up trying to show her the fallacies in the religious mish-mash she called her faith. "I can't fault Anslinger for putting some backbone into the Council. I know they're moving toward a closed society. But that's what they've got to become within the next few years. This is going to be a Settlement under siege. The sooner he can persuade people to think in terms of survival the better the chance they have of surviving."

"You think that's how a society survives? By absolute obedience to whatever fanatic has grabbed control? Hard work and harsh discipline for anybody who dares to oppose the laws the leaders lay down?" She clenched her fists. "That's what it turned into at Jonestown. Jones used to have anybody who didn't obey his whims thrashed in public. That's the spectacle Anslinger's going to start here. And this morning he warned me I'll be the first in line for a public flogging unless I marry fast. And marry him or you. He thinks him and you are my genetic match."

"Marry him? He's married!"

"Polygamy is about to be introduced. We're diverting into the Mormon pattern. Along with a lot of other less pleasant things. Including capital punishment."

"Whip you? He wouldn't dare! I'll stomp the bastard if he tries—"

"Quit coming the heavy, Gavin!" Judith sighed. "Anslinger will have the mass of these decent people here behind him. All the women and most of the men would agree that I have to be brought into line. A fertile woman without children is an anathema. I'm going to have kids, all right. But at a time I choose and by a man of my own choosing." She saw my face and touched my arm. "Don't look so upset! I won't be calling on you to make some grand gesture. I'm not planning to stay around to become Anslinger's second wife—or his first victim."

"What are you going to do?"

"Take off. I've been getting ready to go ever since I realized that Anslinger was taking over."

"Go where?"

She shrugged. "I haven't mentioned Sutton Harbor to anyone. And I asked you not to. Have you?"

"Of course not!" I felt sick at the thought of Judith on the run, alone. She'd never reach Maine. "I'll come with you."

"Like hell you will! I haven't planned for a partner. Not on this escape!" She saw my hurt and gripped my hand. "Whatever I may have said in the past, you're better off here. You've shown that you're too cynical to be caught by Anslinger's cant. And there will be fighting. However rotten the leadership—there are five thousand basically decent people here. They'll need men like you when the fighting starts. If you help the Settlement survive you'll be serving the Light in your own way."

"Damn the Light! It's you I want. Okay—take off for Sutton Cove. But don't be surprised if I turn up there later." I caught her arm. "Judy, you'll never make it alone!"

She reacted like a goosed girl. I had said the wrong thing and she had interpreted it the wrong way. "I'll be waiting for you—but I won't hold my breath!" She walked toward the side door. "Now let me out of this store of evil!"

I followed her, protesting, careless of whoever might be watching us. Judy was about to do something desperate. I had either to stop her or go with her.

She strode down the alley, her skirts swinging, her head held high. She was a stubborn, willful, crazy, arrogant bitch! She was exactly what Anslinger had described so well. Here I was, with an assured position in one of the few strongholds that were likely to survive the next few years. There she was, being followed by a man who loved her and could protect her. Once she had married me, nobody would dare to insult or threaten her.

Instead, she was choosing to embark on a desperate journey across an unsettled countryside, swarming with thugs and rapists. And I was going to have to go with her, whether she wanted me or not. It was I, not her, who was still being hunted by the Feds. They didn't give a damn about her by this time. I wished I felt the same way.

We reached the end of the alley, to where it opened onto the plaza. She had the sense to stop in the shadow of a building when a black limousine came through the main gates and turned toward the Council Chamber. "What Washington bigshot's come to make a deal with Anslinger today?" she snarled.

I was too worried about Judith to be interested in nervous

politicos. "Judy!" I said, grabbing her arm. "For God's sake show some sense! You can't just walk off through the woods!"

She shook off my hand. "I'm not an idiot, Gavin Knox. When I said I've been preparing to get out of this hell-hole I mean I've been preparing as carefully as I did when I got us out of the Pen. Worry about your soul! Not about my body."

"Damn my soul! How are you going to make a break?"

"You'll know after I've made it. I trust you, Gavin. But—" She stopped, her hand to her mouth, staring across the plaza. "Oh God!"

"What?" I turned to look.

And I saw. Standing on the steps of the Council Chamber to greet the new arrival was Deacon Anslinger and a group of Elders. Getting from the limousine, glancing suddenly toward us, was Gerald Futrell.

XI

I can't remember what I did when I saw Futrell. I can only remember a surge of hatred, a surge which swamped everything except the face of the man I meant to kill. Judith tells me that I reacted like an automaton; reaching for a gun that wasn't there, standing rigid with one hand fumbling like a machine on automatic which has encountered some unprogrammed obstacle.

She says that after a moment of confusion I knocked her aside as I swung around and went striding back down the alley. I remember an instant of savage frustration at finding myself unarmed facing my enemy, then the insistent need to get my gun and blow him apart. Judith says she followed me between the houses, through the hallway of the Bachelor Cloister, and up the stairs to my room. I have a vague image of her anguished face as I loaded the Luger and the Jeta. Of her hanging onto my arm. Of my saying, "That's Futrell. I've got to kill him."

I remember her voice. "You can't! Not here!"

"He was brought here for me to kill." None of this makes much sense to me now, but at the time my logic seemed as clear and sharp as the blade of a fighting knife.

She slapped my face and I remember the shock. Like hitting a faulty video camera, her blow brought things back into focus. She was standing in the doorway, challenging me to push her aside. "They'll kill you!"

I answered slowly, reaching for my lost conviction. "That doesn't matter. Just so long as I kill Futrell first."

"They'll kill me! Doesn't that matter either?"

The shock of her words added to the shock of her blow. I found myself suddenly uncertain. She pushed me back into the room, closing the door behind her. "Gavin—you've been conditioned. I suspected it before. Now I'm certain. Fight it—for God's sake! For my sake!"

"For your sake?" I shook my head. "What the hell's going on?" Then I realized what was going on. I had been about to act as a human missile. A missile targeted on Gerald Futrell. I still hated the man. I would still kill him if I could. But not at the cost of my own life—or Judith's. I looked around, snatched up my body-belt and buckled it on. In it were my badge and my money. "We've got to get out of here. Together. But we'll have to wait till it's dark."

"We can't wait! Futrell recognized you. They're coming after you now."

There were heavy steps on the stairs and the door was flung open. In the doorway stood two of Anslinger's cronies, both Elders and both armed. Men who had previously shown me respect. Their attitude held no respect for me now.

But they were still uncertain. One stepped forward to glare at Judith. "What are you doing in the Bachelor Cloister, woman?"

"Let her go, Jason!" said the other. "Mister Knox, Deacon Anslinger wants to see you at once. Come with us!" He looked at Judith. "You'd better get out of this building quickly. A woman can get into bad trouble for being found in bachelor quarters."

She glanced at me and I caught her quick nod. We were back in unison. I shrugged and started down the stairs, the two Elders behind me. Judith came last, sobbing for the benefit of Jason.

At the foot of the stairs I swung around, grabbed Jason's shirt, and pitched him forward, adding a neck-chop as he fell. Judith had thrown her arms round the second Elder, preventing him from drawing his gun. I hit him twice and flung him on top of Jason. Then I glanced out of the front door. The agents who had been in the limousine with Futrell were standing around it, waiting for us.

"Out back!" I called to Judith. We went through the ground-floor lounge, out of the window, and away into the maze of narrow streets among the boxlike married quarters.

There I stopped, recovering my full sanity. There was now no hope of my getting close enough to Futrell to shoot him. He must have recognized me. Anslinger had sent his thugs after me. What was going on between Sherando and the Attorney General? And how was I going to get Judith out of the mess I'd landed her in? The Elders hadn't come for her. But if she was caught with me she'd suffer with me.

She tugged my arm. "Gav—wait here! Trust me." And she darted away up the alley.

There was nothing else I could do. The whole Settlement would soon be isolated and searched. There was nowhere we could hide. And what the hell was Judy up to?

The lane was strewn with bags of garbage waiting collection. A biker appeared round the corner and came weaving among them like a skier running the gates in a grand slalom. I jumped back into the shelter of a yard as it skidded to a halt. The visor went up. It was Judith.

A black jacket, full helmet, and opaque visor had made her as anonymous and menacing as any other biker. She reached back to unhook another dark-visored helmet and thrust it at me. "Ram this on!"

I stared at the bike. "What's this thing?"

"A Yama Five Hundred. Hide your face in that pot!"

I got the helmet over my head and tried to unbend my ears. "Can you drive it?"

"No—but I can ride it! Put on those leathers. Fasten your chin strap. Now go split-assed behind me. Feet on the pegs. Clamp on to me. Tight! I don't want to dump you balls-up on the Plaza. Haven't you ever been on a bike?"

"When I was a kid." This was oscillating between nightmare and farce.

"Thank Christ for that!" Judy had adopted a speech-mode to match her rig. "Now—hang on. I may have to take evasive action."

The prospect of being aboard a motorcycle taking evasive action froze me. I clutched Judy's waist as she swerved down the lane, across an open lot, and onto a side road. She was riding with skill if not with caution as she raced through a narrow gap between houses and shot out onto the plaza. A bike can go where a car cannot.

And provided a disguise. Who would expect Doctor Judith Grenfell to be riding a motorcycle? Bikers are the best-disguised creatures on the highway. When the weather is cool one cannot tell the girls from the boys. With visors down we circled the plaza, then drove past the Council Chamber and the waiting limousine. The agents, who were starting to walk toward the Bachelor Cloister, hardly glanced at us.

We roared through the main gates of the Settlement as shouts rose from behind us. I glanced back and saw the agents running for the limousine. I clutched Judy tighter and yelled, "They're after us!"

"I'll drop 'em. Don't worry!" She swerved to avoid a truck coming toward Sherando and I glimpsed the open mouth of the cursing driver. Then the road plunged down the hill and into the trees. We skidded around a curve and skidded again so we were broadside across the road. For a moment I thought Judy had lost control, then I realized it was her way of making a right-angled turn. We shot forward off the hard-top and down a horse trail among the trees.

The limousine roared past, brakes screeched, I heard it backing up at full throttle, and then we were deep in the woods, skidding and slewing in showers of mud and leaves.

"For God's sake—take it easy!" I yelled. "They're way back but they'll catch up if you dump us."

She slowed somewhat but we still had a breathtaking ride until we reached a dirt road running beside the river. "With luck we may make it!" said Judy as she turned in the direction of Waynesboro.

I started to breath easier and Judy started to drive more sensibly when we reached the outskirts of the town. There were more motorcyles weaving through the traffic than I remembered from the past and when we stopped for gas I realized this was one effect of the fuel restrictions. Hydrides for some unknown reason were becoming short and gasoline was back in fashion. And bikes had always used gasoline.

She parked among a bunch of bikes at a shopping center, and we dismounted. Judy in black biking gear and helmet was a different person from the earlier Judiths I had got to know. She was letting her suppressed delight in theatrics have full rein. "I knew they wouldn't let me out of that place. Anslinger's turning it into a Jonesville-in-Virginia! So I got hold of this Yama and loaded the panniers, ready for takeoff."

"Where are you going now?"

"Sutton Cove."

"You plan to go to Maine on that thing? Disguised as a biker?"

"That's how I've always gone. Part-way at least. That's why nobody ever trailed me. But not disguised—I *am* a biker. It's the fastest, most exciting, and least obvious way to travel." She laughed, as though delighted at my expression. "Want to come along?"

"Riding pillion? For a thousand kilometers?"

"I'd rather have a sore ass than a sore back! Let me give you a lift to somewhere safe anyway."

"Nowhere's safe for me now!"

She snapped down her visor, as though irritated by my pessimism. "I know one place where we can merge with the natives. If it's still going. You said you were a biker once?"

"I had a trail bike as a kid."

"Good enough. Climb aboard!"

"Where are we going?" I asked as she took off with a roar, leaving a plume of dust astern.

"Like I said. To merge with some of the native fauna. If it's not been destroyed by the new austerity. Now hang on!"

By the time we reached the thruway I had no breath left to ask anything, and once we were on it Judy began riding too fast for conversation. She headed north and I rode pressed tightly against her for the next hour, enjoying the body contact too much to be concerned about the speed. She slowed as we approached the outskirts of Frederick, and turned off the thruway onto a secondary road where there were more motorcycles than automobiles, then onto a dirt road, joining a stream of bikers, riding singly or paired like ourselves. The road wound through vacant lots, wrecking yards, and dilapidated factories until it finally spewed us out onto a wasteland of disused sandpits; a breeding ground for mosquitoes and bikers.

The bikers were out in force; mating, inspecting machines, and riding in, out, and around the sandpits. Judy wove her way through the mob of men, women, and bikes until she reached the far side where she stopped and said, "Here we are!"

"Which is where?" I dismounted and stared at the biker hordes.

"The Bikers Bi-monthly Bargain Boozeup! The best buys in bikes, booze, and broads. Also grass, spares, customizing—babes or bikes. The last hold-out of unadulterated male chauvinism. Gross in the extreme!" She looked around with evident relish. "It's nice to find some remnants of the old barbarism still exist."

"This isn't the kind of crowd I expected you to—"

"Cram your expectations, Gavin! This gang are totally irresponsible! They don't give a damn about the President's pleas, about prophets of doom, about the probability there'll be no tomorrow. This is the swansong of a civilization. And these are people who have the guts to sing!"

"Judy, that's nonsense. Anyway, why did you come here?"

"Because nobody except a biker would dare to come searching through this mob. And most cops are too tight-assed these days to ride bikes. You can dehelmet now. Nobody recognizes anybody without an invitation. Like Sanctuary—or Saturnalia! I used to come here when I was a med student. Too seldom since then!" She had the satisfied air of an old grad at a homecoming. "Let's go buy you a bike. That Slada's about your speed. Light enough to go cross-country but fast enough if you wind her up to outrun most things on the road."

Of all possible futures, becoming a biker again had never entered my prevision. I eyed a gleaming Slada while Judy haggled with its owner. Presently she asked, "Like to try it out on the track? It's supposed to have only three thousand clicks on the clock. Or maybe you want me to test-ride it before I close with this crook?"

"I'll test it myself if I've got to ride it!" I sat astride and touched the starter.

The Slada started sweetly and went well. Almost too well, for after a few cautious turns around the impromptu test track I opened the throttle as I had in the past and my front wheel climbed into the air. I completed part of the circuit with it still up, steering with desperate body-English in a controlled panic reaction. After that near miss I made several cautious circuits, trying to look as if I was listening for piston-slap but actually gaining time for my pulse to drop back to near normal before I returned to Judy.

The design of motorbikes had plateaued in the last decade of the twentieth century. There was not much left to be done. A good bike had the best power-weight ratio of any roadworthy vehicle. If there had been tires to grip a bike could have raced up a vertical wall. Japanese engineers had produced a near-perfect machine, a superb example of engineering elegance, unmatched efficiency, and with the lethal potential of a ground-to-ground missile.

When my heart and breathing had steadied I coasted the Slada back to where Judy was watching with an expression of mixed approval, surprise, and chagrin. "Gavin—that was an unnecessary bit of showoffery. This is no time for risk-taking!"

I had been about to apologize for letting the bike get away from me, but sank in a surge of adolescent pride. "Just seeing what she'll do!"

A bearded beer-bellied brute who had been adjusting the triple carbs on a machine that looked like several generations of Guzzi-DKW-Harley cross-breeding, joined the conversation. "That was as pretty a wheel-up as I've seen today." He scowled at Judy. "Slap that chick back if she's uppity. It's what she really wants. They like it!" And he returned to adjusting his carburetors with the care of a first-violinist tuning his instrument.

I moved back from the expected explosion and winced when Judy laughed. "See what I mean? Last hold-out of the hogs this side Georgia! But they care about what they're doing and they want to do things right. That's enough to make me love 'em." She pulled on her helmet and went astride her Yama. "Now—let's go!" She roared her motor and was away across the rough ground, standing up on her rests and waving me to follow.

Beer-belly yelled, "Slap her down when you catch her!" I grinned despite myself, got the Slada started, and took off after the bouncing seat of Judy's tight jumpsuit. God knows what role she was playing now or where she was leading me. For the moment I was happy to admire and be led.

When she reached the hardtop she waited for me and waved toward a cluster of bikers warming up before taking off. "We'll join that squadron!" she yelled. "Now we're criminals we might as well get the benefits!" And the whole gang roared away before she had time to explain.

About twenty kilometers outside Frederick I realized the reason for her maneuver. There was a police roadblock and at least a hundred automobiles were lined up with the cops checking the papers of the occupants in each car. The leading bikers simply swooped over onto the shoulder or out into the opposite lane, weaving among cursing drivers and shouting policemen. One bike skidded and the rider went sprawling. The cops rushed to grab him. The rest of the gang swerved past the roadblock and then, without any apparent order, half a dozen, including Judy, circled back to harrass the police while the fallen biker grabbed his machine and got away to yells of triumph.

Criminal behavior, antisocial in the extreme. Why so exhilarating when it represented everything decadent about our society? I had no answer by the time dusk came, the mob split up, and Judy turned off the highway to park behind a barn.

I joined her as she took off her helmet and shook out her glorious hair. "Those cops were after us," she said. "They'll probably have stake-outs on all motels. We're pretty important people apparently. But they'll be looking for two crooks on one bike—though I'll bet they'll assume we're acting our age and have got ourselves an automobile."

She was probably right. Even if I had been hunting us I doubt I would have considered that we might have acquired a second bike and were riding together. Riding to where?

She waved toward the barn. "Want to join me in the hay?"

"It's a warm night," I agreed.

"Then bring in your bike. No lights. I've got some iron rations in my panniers."

We wheeled the bikes into the sweet-smelling warmth of the barn and sat side by side in the darkness chewing hardtack. Presently she put her head on my shoulder. "Gavin."

"Yes?"

"Today should have been the worst of my life. I thought we'd had it half-a-dozen times. I thought you'd gone crazy and about to get yourself killed and me flogged. I discovered that those bastards who control Sherando are making a deal with the devil. I've behaved like the worst kind of hooligan. But I've felt more alive than I have in years."

I put my arm round her. "My crazy spell is gone for good. Sherando can have Futrell, and he can have Sherando. He can have the whole goddamn United States for all I care. He'll go to hell with the rest of us."

"But we're not going to hell," said Judith. "We're going to Sutton Settlement. At least I hope you are." She reached up to touch my cheek. "Gav, I would have married you if only that sanctimonious bastard Anslinger hadn't ordered me to."

"Judy, I wouldn't have married you anyway." I kissed her.

The kiss turned into an embrace. Horses and motorbikes are powerful aphrodisiacs and Judy had felt the effect as much as I had. Presently she whispered, "Gav—remember my promise? Any time, any way?"

"To hell with that! What matters is your time, your way!"

"Is it?" She kissed me. "Then how about now?" And she began to unzip her jumpsuit.

A hay loft on a warm summer night is a magic place to make love. Something that a thousand generations of farmgirls and farmboys have known but which most men and women of my generation have never discovered.

I discovered it that night and later I slept the sweetest sleep I had slept in years. An outlaw, being hunted across a nation going down into chaos, I awoke as refreshed as if I was a young man without a worry to his name. If such a freak exists!

The sunlight was streaming in through the open door and Judy was sitting up naked, pulling bits of hay from her hair. I started to stroke her back, and then, in default of anything better to say, I asked, "What's all this stuff about Impermease?"

"Impermease?" She turned to look at me. "That's not the kind of subject to bring up on the morning after our marriage. But I guess you'd better know."

"Not if it makes you serious!" I objected.

"Gavin—we've got to be serious again. So I'll start by telling you what I've found out about why everything's breaking down."

I lay back in the hay. "Okay! If you must!"

She raised herself on one elbow and started to deliver a lecture on female reproductive physiology. "Every month my ovaries release an egg that was formed and stored in me six months before I was born."

I studied her stomach, trying to decide where her ovaries were. Then I started stroking it.

She pushed my hand away. "I was born with every fertile egg I'll ever have already inside me."

"But you weren't born looking like you do now. So it's only been during the last few years that anybody's wanted to fertilize one of 'em."

She didn't smile. "Ever heard of a drug called thalidomide?"

"Vaguely. It damaged babies, didn't it? Way back in the last century."

"It was the safest sedative known at the time, except for one terrible side effect. If a woman took it during her first three months of pregnancy her baby might be born without arms or legs. Thalidomide checked the development of the limb buds in the fetus."

I sat up, feeling sick. This was not the kind of thing I like to discuss with a naked woman.

She rammed her point home. "What do you think would have happened if thalidomide had checked the development of the Fallopian tubes? The tubes that take the eggs from the ovary to the uterus?"

I didn't want to think about such unpleasant possibilities, but Judith's expression demanded an answer. "I guess it would have the same effect as tying 'em. The girl would grow up sterile."

"Right. But how would anyone know her tubes weren't there? It's easy to recognize there's something wrong when a baby's born without arms. How would you recognize a baby without tubes?"

"Well—you wouldn't. Not until she tried to get pregnant. Twenty years later, maybe!" I started pulling on my clothes, my sex-drive abolished. "Is that what Impermease does? Block off a girl's tubes before she's born?"

"The effect's much the same. The mechanism's not so simple as blocking the tubes. If it was only the tubes, they could be fixed by surgery these days. Impermease hits the eggs. Prevents them from ever dividing. It's a selective inhibitor of cell division."

I extracted the meaning of that statement after a little thought. "Some woman told me that was how Noncon worked. The monthly pill she was taking. As long as she took one a month she couldn't get pregnant. But if she stopped taking it she could. She swore by it. The great liberator she called it. Had three kids too—none of 'em mine," I added quickly.

"If those kids were girls they were born sterile. Noncon's the trade name for Impermease. Impermease when it's been colored, scented, and packaged in heart-shaped containers!"

"Good God!" I stared at her. "I don't get it. I thought the idea was to stop the woman from getting pregnant. Not to sterilize the fetus when she did."

"That was the idea. They didn't know that the traces of Impermease remaining in the woman's body weren't enough to stop her from getting pregnant. But were enough to cross the placental barrier and sterilize the eggs in the fetus. Because of the time lag, about twenty years, they only found out when the birth rate among girls wanting babies started to fall!"

"So all those women who were taking Noncon are going to have sterile daughters!"

"All the women who've been taking Noncon since the late nineties have been having sterile daughters. They're only starting to discover that now. And most sexually active women in North America have been taking their monthly 'liberator' for the last twenty-five years. They're still taking it!" She came to sit beside me. "I haven't. My mother didn't. She was one of the earliest converts to the Teacher. And he forbade the use of any drug or chemical developed after 1990."

"How the hell did he know?"

"The Light warned him. Not against Impermease specifically. Against all post-1990 chemicals."

"Good for the Light!" I spat in sudden anger. "Typical Jehovah! Warn the elect in vague terms. But don't tell 'em why or what. Save the dumb obedient faithful! Let the infidels die."

"I wouldn't push your God's sense of humor too far!"

I returned to the subject at hand. "So the ladies of the Affluence have been having sterile daughters. But the vast majority of women don't belong to the Affluence. They can't afford to buy colored, scented, and prettily packaged contraceptives. Yet you speak as if this thing's worldwide. How come?"

"Impermease stops cell division, but very selectively. It stops rapidly dividing cells. Such as cancer cells. It's sold as a cancer prophylactic under the trade name Bancan. Black tablets in a container with a crushed crab on the cover."

"Christ! I took those once when I thought—" I stopped, suddenly ashamed of an empty fear. For months I'd been afraid to show my wart to the doc.

"You and a hell of a lot of other people. Cancerphobia—fear of cancer—has been endemic in Europe and North America for years. Men as much as women. Bancan won't have harmed you! If only the stuff had made mens' balls drop off it would have saved a lot of women from a lot of misery."

"Christ! So Bancan's Impermease too! And masses of people take it regularly." I looked at the floor. "And the FTA wouldn't have dared to stop the sale of Bancan. Not even if they'd known."

"Well, they know now! And they're trying to stop it being used without facing the public. The Bancan you buy today is a placebo."

Another bit of Administration flim-flam! But one I could excuse. I thought of the howl if they'd tried to ban it openly. "So they've stopped it. But I still don't see how that affects the non-affluent. They can't afford Bancan any more than their women can afford Noncon."

"Impermease is easy and cheap to produce. For over twenty years they've been making it by the megakilo." Judith sighed, then clenched her fists. "Not to sell as expensively packaged tablets of Noncon and Bancan. When I described how it stopped division in rapidly dividing cells I gave the clue to its third use. Probably by far its most important use. It stops cell division in insect pupa. So it's a first-class insecticide. And the insects never have a chance to develop resistance. It's now the pesticide of choice all over the world. Mogro—the farmer's friend. Without it the cost of food would quadruple and most farmers would go bankrupt."

"And millions would starve in the famines. That seems a legitimate use for Impermease. As long as the farmer's daughter keeps her hands out of the insecticides. I suppose—" I looked up at her. "Oh no!"

"Oh yes! It's a persistent insecticide. Most washes off but traces remain. The worst thing about Impermease is that it accumulates in the human body. The way DDT used to do. Only DDT was harmless to everything except birds and insects. In the seventies—just before it was banned—every man, woman and child in the United States had measurable amounts of DDT stored in their body fat. Absorbed with the food they ate and even the air they breathed. The stuff didn't break down, but it didn't do much harm either. Humans slowly got rid of it over the next ten years. Even those people who ate it by the kilo to prove how safe it was."

"It was banned so it must be dangerous. When I was a kid I heard of an aunt who killed herself with DDT."

"It wasn't the DDT that killed her. It was drinking the several liters of kerosine in which it was dissolved." Judith gave an impatient gesture. "I only mentioned DDT to show you how one insecticide got into everyone. Impermease has done the same. Accumulated in every woman who's eaten regularly food from crops treated with Mogro. Now do you see how the stuff's reached almost everybody? Affluent and starving. The starving got it with relief shipments as insecticide contamination. The poor got it as a discreet additive. An additive added by governments trying to control their runaway birth rates. They've reduced the birth rates—with a vengeance! That's why the truth hasn't yet been published. Would you like to be a Minister in some country where every peasant would try to tear you apart if he found you'd sterilized his new-bought bride?"

"Judy—surely they've come up with an answer by now?"

"They've been researching the stuff like hell for years. Under the blanket of the Social Stability Act. Trying to find some way to reverse the Impermease effect." She sighed. "It's hopeless! The eggs were made infertile twenty years ago. It's as hopeless as trying to bring a twenty-year-old corpse back to life!"

That left me with a lot to think about during our thousand click ride north.

XII

The road ended abruptly at the bridge. The spans were intact but the roadway had been taken up; the planks for a makeshift replacement were piled on the far side. I skidded my Slada to a halt and grabbed my CB. "Hold it!"

"Why?" Judith's signal was too strong. She should be way astern.

"There's a bridge down. Stay where you are and let me scout." The wrecked cars we had passed during our journey north had been warnings that bandits were now a hazard on back roads. Since leaving the highway at Standish I had insisted on riding point. For the last few kilometers we had been following a dirt road winding along beside a creek with the deep woods of Maine on each side of us and the tang of the sea ahead.

"The Settlement's only a little way beyond the bridge. I'm coming up!"

It was no good my telling her once again to stay where she was. I searched the creek and the woods as I heard her bike rounding the bend. When she pulled up beside me there was a flicker of movement among the trees. I muttered, "We're being watched."

"Good!" She took off her helmet, shook out her Titian hair, and smiled at the woods and the stream.

"Someone's watching the bridge." I saw the movement again. "Up there—by those beech trees."

"Doctor Grenfell!" A girl's voice came from the far bank. I did not see her until she broke cover, slipping from the bushes less than fifty meters from us. A slim youngster in a dark-blue jersey and jeans who came jumping from stone to stone across the creek, golden hair flying.

"Barbara!" Judith put her bike on its side-stand and ran to

meet her. "Barbara Bernard!" They kissed, then Judith held the girl at arm's length, smiling down at her. "You've grown so! I hardly recognized you."

"You look older too, Doctor." She was returning Judith's smile, humor and affection in her voice. "We thought you were dead."

"You can see I'm not." Judith put her arm around the girl and brought her over to me. "This is Barbara, an old friend of mine. Barbara, meet Mister Gavin—a new friend."

I took her hand with that benign courtesy men of my age and type use as a defense against teenage girls. Her fingers were slim, her grip was firm. Everything about her was firm from the set of her mouth and chin to the way she stood, from the assurance with which she had greeted Judith to the way she studied me. I put her age at a young seventeen, but her gray eyes mirrored confidence and experience. I was both fascinated and warned.

"Barb!" A boy had stepped from behind the beech trees. "Who are they? What shall I call in?" Glancing up I was startled to see he was hefting a rifle. We had been covered as well as watched.

"Say that Doctor Grenfell's here. That she has a man with her." She looked at Judith's Yama. "When Ruth radioed that a woman biker was heading this way I should have known it must be you."

"You've got lookouts up the road?"

"Back to the fork. We like to be warned when visitors are coming. And to know who they are." She called across the creek. "Bring up the bridge squad. And have Hilda tell Chairman Yackle that the Doc's on her way." She turned to Judith. "We'll have the planks on within ten minutes. Then you'll be able to ride in."

"No need for them to haul lumber." Judith pulled on her helmet and studied the creek. "The old ford still passable?"

"For you—yes. For Mister Gavin—I don't know." She regarded me with frank skepticism.

Judith laughed and tightened the chin strap of her helmet. "Gavin, wait to see if I get across. If I dump—don't you try!" And she was astride her bike and away, weaving down the bank, plunging through the creek, and roaring up the far side.

"She makes it look easy," said Barbara, watching Judith's maneuver with detached admiration. "It isn't! You'd better wait till we've got the planks down."

I was not going to play second string under the critical eyes of this teenage brat. I didn't dump but I did stall in mid-creek and finally arrived beside Judith muddy, sweating, and annoyed. My temper was not improved when she greeted me with advice to the effect that I should keep my revs high when my pipes were under water. I called my Slada something I usually reserve for horses. Then the bridge squad arrived and, finding they were not needed, formed an honor guard to escort us into Sutton Cove.

Judith made a triumphant entry, with me trailing astern. At first sight the Settlement was not much to look at; several hundred wooden houses clustered around a small cove at the end of a narrow valley. Men, women, and hordes of children came pouring from the houses to greet the returning doctor; their display of affection for Judith in sharp contrast to the looks they gave me. I parked my bike beside hers outside a building which seemed to serve the duties of Council Chamber, Chapel, and Town Hall and stood ignored while she was being embraced by people of all ages and both sexes.

A plump little man emerged from the building. "Doctor Grenfell—the Light has led you back to us! And at a time when your skills are sorely needed!"

"Chuck Yackle—Chairman Yackle!" Judith threw her arms about him, kissing his bald head. "I thank the Light for guiding me home!"

Amused and depressed, I turned to look down the village street toward the cove. Boats were coming in from the sea: word of her arrival had apparently reached even the fishing fleet. I watched boat after boat shouldering through the rip across the mouth of the harbor. These people looked poor, but—

"Gavin!" Judith's hand was on my arm. "This is Chuck Yackle—Chairman of the Settlement Council."

He beamed as he wrung my hand. "We thank the Light for returning our Physician. And we thank you, Brother Gavin, for aiding her return." He moved to the steps of the Hall, holding up his arms to quiet the crowd. "Let us enter and give thanks to the Light for having shone upon us! Enter, all of you. And tonight we will eat together." Chairman Yackle evidently doubled as the local Minister of Religion.

Judith flashed me a smile before disappearing into the Hall. I watched the others crowding in after her, astonished at the excitement our arrival had caused, at the warmth of Judy's reception. What was so great about a doctor coming back to a village? Although the American Medical Association had striven to keep the physician/population ratio reasonably low to hold the fee scale unreasonably high, there was still a surplus of doctors in most cities.

In most cities! Of course. It would be very different for these people living on the edge of an empty ocean, isolated from the nearest town by thirty kilometers of dirt road and woods still reputed to be filled with unexploded missiles. The old and sick wouldn't have been getting much in the way of physician care during the time Judith had been in jail. Physicians and soldiers have the same public image. I remember the rhyme I had seen on an old tombstone in Gibraltar:

"God and the Soldier, all men adore
In times of troubles, and then no more.
When wars are over and wrongs are righted
God is forgotten, the Soldier is slighted."

I understood better the pleasure on the faces of the men and women coming up the street from the cove. Small-boat fishing is a dangerous trade at best. A lot of these people probably had had fish hooks taken from their hands, lacerations sewn up, bones reset, without benefit of anesthetics or strong analgesics. I remembered how uncomfortable even we Troopers had been if there was no medical corpsman with us when we went on a mission. Of how we would protect the one guy who could look after us, give us relief from pain—or a painless death—if we were hit.

There were many babies here. Most of them would have been born without even a skilled midwife in attendance. I had had to deliver a baby once myself and the memory still tended to leave me nauseated. The mother and child had lived, thank God! But during those terrible hours crouching in a ruined house, trying to help a young mother through her first labor with an ignorant old crone muttering that girl and child were lost because the head was locked or something—during those hours I would have welcomed the arrival of the worst product of any second-rate medical school in America.

Yackle reappeared on the porch. "Join us, Brother Gavin. Come and join us. Come and pray wih us. Praise the Light with us!"

I hesitated. Should I avoid hasslement by pretending to be a Believer? No, by God! I didn't believe in their Light, but I'd be damned if I'd insult It—or Him—or Her—with hypocrisy. "I'm sorry, Mister Yackle. But I'm not one of the chosen."

"Not a Believer?" His smile turned to a flustered frown. "But you came with Doctor Grenfell—I had assumed—then please wait while we have our little service of thanksgiving." He attempted another smile and followed his flock into the Hall.

I stood on the porch, alone with myself, two motorcycles, and an empty street. From inside the Hall came the roar of voices, lustily singing a hymn whose tune roused childhood memories but whose words differed from those I remembered. Their Teacher had borrowed tunes as well as myths to weave into his synthetic religion.

A single boat glided into the cove and moored alongside the pier. A heavyset weatherbeaten man in a windbreaker, cap, and seaboots climbed onto the wharf and started up the village street, moving like a sturdy ship breasting a rip tide. When he reached the steps he held out his hand. "You must be Mister Gavin. The gentleman who's brought the Doc back. Heard about you on the radio. Like to thank you myself. My name's Enoch."

As we were shaking hands Barbara appeared in the doorway and snapped, "Come on, Dad! We've just started."

"Coming, girl!" He smiled at me. "Reckon you've met my little girl already?"

"I have indeed!" I looked from one to the other. This large and friendly man seemed an unlikely father for the slim, detached Barbara, but the shape of his nose confirmed that he was.

She tugged at his sleeve, ignoring me. "Move it, Dad! Everybody else is inside."

"Then I'd better be too!" He winked at me over the top of his daughter's blonde head. "See you later, I hope, Mister Gavin." And he followed her into the Hall. I looked after him. At least one of the natives appeared to be friendly.

The psalm-singing began to get on my nerves. To escape I walked down the village street toward the wharf, and began to revise my initial impression of Sutton Cove as a poor and primitive Settlement. The houses, though clad in unpainted shingles, were solidly built on permacrete foundations. The people crowding into the Hall had been wearing worn but serviceable working clothes and were obviously well fed. And the boats at anchor in the cove made me realize that there was a lot more here than met the superficial eye.

They looked like traditional Cape Islanders. Between twelve and fifteen meters from stem to stern, high bows to shoulder through cresting waves and low counters for the easy hauling of lobster traps and trawl, a hull-form evolved from a hundred years of power-boat fishing on some of the roughest seas in the world. But the traditional Cape Islander had been planked with softwood and had had a working life of little more than a decade. These boats were built of veralloy and had a potential life of centuries. I hunkered down on the edge of the wharf, inspecting the boat moored alongside, Enoch's *Aurora*.

Powered by a miniturbine, she had ample take-offs for traps, lines, and trawl. Inside her wheelhouse I could see the display scopes of radar, echometers, fish-finders, and navsat. I myself was no sailor, but like every Trooper in the Special Strike Force I had been taught to handle minicopters, aircushions, hydrofoils, and light armored fighting vehicles. Even to ride horses. Almost anything that could be used to get a Strike Force section into position to strike. What I saw below me was an example of elegant engineering; a seaworthy hull, an advanced power unit, and the electronic technology of picrochip and minicomp. A boat which a lone helmsman could take through dangerous waters and fog-shrouded seas. A boat fitted to hunt the shoals of fish which were returning to the Bay of Fundy.

The hymn singing in the Hall rose to a crescendo, dropped to silence, and a few minutes later the population of Sutton Cove began to pour down the steps. Enoch was among the first out, and I stood up, not knowing how he might react to my inspecting his boat. But when he saw me he smiled and came toward the wharf, his daughter at his side.

"I hope you don't mind my admiring your boat," I said.

"Mind? It's good to meet an outsider with the eyes to see and the sense to understand!" He stood beside me, looking down at *Aurora* with the pride of a man who owns something that is both beautiful and useful. "She's trim! She's trim! Best seaboat that ever fished these waters. Me and the missus—we've taken seven thousand kilos of cod in three hours. Filled her to the gun'ls, we did!" His face clouded. "That was when Vera was alive and fishing. Vera had a nose for the fish." The cloud passed. "But me and my girl here, we've done almost as well at times." He ruffled Barbara's hair. "That was afore she got her boat. Now I fish *Aurora* by myself. Still do pretty good." He filled his pipe.

I glanced at the slim girl beside him. "Barbara—you have a boat of your own?"

She nodded, half resentful of my surprise but too proud of her status to be offended. "There—*Sea Eagle*—lying at that buoy." She pointed to a boat somewhat smaller than her father's but with more radio antennae. "I got her last spring."

"And you fish alone?"

"Sometimes!" Her father laughed. "But not often. The boys around here, they like to go fishing with Barb. She must have her ma's nose for the fish—or something!"

"Daddy!" For a moment she was a typical daughter embarrassed by a father's idea of humor. Then she looked up the street and frowned. "Here comes Doctor Grenfell—and Baldy's grabbed her already!"

"Hush girl!" Her father gave her an affectionate cuff. "Becos' you've got your boat young's no cause to talk like some bad-mouthing oldster." He smiled and took out his pipe to greet Judith and the Chairman. "It's good to have you back, Doc. Chuck—that was a right good sermon you gave."

"Thank you, Enoch. Thank you. The Light shone through me." He looked at Barbara. "Child, go and light a fire in Mistress Grenfell's cottage. And stack plenty of wood for the Doctor to use."

"Yes sir!" said Barbara, stressing the honorific in a way I would have judged insolent but which seemed to please Yackle. I watched her dart off up the village street, surprised by her instant obedience. Most of the teenagers I had known never obeyed any order instantly until after they'd been through boot camp.

"You're going to let me have my mother's cottage?" Judith looked pleased. "It's still empty?"

"We've left it vacant, hoping her daughter would return to us. Even after they tried to tell us you were dead the Light told us to expect your return. We never believed those lies the outsiders tell!" He remembered I was an outsider and added hastily, "No offense, Mister Gavin."

"No offense taken, Mister Yackle. You're wise not to believe Administration stories."

"Then I'll go wash up and get rested," Judith broke in. "We've been riding all day."

"I sent Prudence and Clara to air the rooms and spread fresh linen," said Yackle quickly. "And Nora's dusting and polishing. While they're making it snug for you, maybe you'll take a look at my eldest. Bernice has had a nasty cough on her for weeks."

"I'll check Bernice now." Judith's face showed her resignation to the cares which descend on a community doctor as soon as he or she reappears. "Gavin, I'll see you later up at the house. It's over there—above the cove." She pointed to a cottage backing against the cliff, its yard bright with fall flowers. The doors and windows were open and several girls were shaking out rugs and mops, preparing a home for their Doctor. Barbara was trudging up the pathway towards it with a load of kindling.

"Mister Gavin—he'll be staying with you?" Yackle's voice faltered under Judith's steady glance.

"Of course! He arrived with me. Enoch, would you show him around and then bring him up to the cottage."

"Be a pleasure, Doc!"

"But—" Yackle started to say something.

"You wanted me to take a look at Bernice?" Judith turned away from the wharf.

"Yes—if you would." Yackle glanced uncertainly at me, then trotted after Judith toward the largest house on the village street.

Enoch was refilling his pipe. "Don't judge Chuck Yackle too hard, Mister Gavin. We need Chuck to remind us of the lighted path. Barb, she's like all young 'uns. Critical of their elders." He lit his pipe. "At times she's right to be critical. At times she's wrong. She'll get no smarter as she grows older, but she'll get more understanding. Leastwise, I hope she does." He drew on his pipe, then added, "Though not too understanding."

"She does as she's told. That's unusual. Most kids these days—too raw to eat and too green to burn."

Enoch laughed. "She does as she's told when what she's told is sensible. All the youngsters here do as they're told, when they're told what's sensible. It's the sea that teaches 'em. In a boat you learn not to argue." He puffed on his pipe and chuckled. "But those kids, they do a lot of things they're not told. And it's a good thing for all of us that they do!" I waited for him to expand on that cryptic remark, but he said, "Before I show you around, maybe you'd like a tot of rum? To refresh you after a long day. I keep a bottle in the boat."

"There's nothing I'd like better," I said and followed him down the ladder and into the cabin of the *Aurora*.

I didn't see much of the Settlement that day, and when Barbara hailed us from the wharf it was almost dark. She was waiting at the top of the ladder and gave a disapproving sniff when we joined her. "The Doc sent me to find out what the two of you were doing. Now I know! She's waiting up at the cottage for Mister Gavin."

"And he's coming right up," said Enoch jovially. We had actually done more talking than drinking, but this was evidently the kind of community where to smell of alcohol was to be judged intoxicated.

Judith had already acquired the community attitude. She was standing in the doorway when we climbed up the path. "Enoch! You haven't changed! But don't start introducing Gavin to your habits."

"Gavin don't need no introducing!" Enoch chuckled and started back toward the cove, his daughter hovering beside him.

"He's not drunk!" I protested, following Judith into the cottage. "Neither am I."

"He used to be a drinking man. And this isn't a drinking Settlement." She inspected me, decided I was reasonably sober, and announced. "I'm going to take a bath. You need one too. I'll leave you some hot water." And she disappeared. I heard the sound of a bath being filled. So the Settlement had both electricity and a piped water supply. I had half-expected to be drawing buckets of icy water from a well and heating it in a wood-fired copper.

I went to warm my hands at the log fire blazing in the large stone fireplace, looking around the living room of Mistress Grenfell's old home. A snug and comfortable room. The girls Yackle had sent to prepare it for Judith had done a good job. The mahogany table gleamed a rich brown. The silver candlesticks on the mantel, the tea service on the sideboard, the brass fire-irons, shone in the firelight. A pendulum clock ticked on the wall. Above the fireplace a portrait of Judith as a girl watched me as I wandered round the room. The portrait of a woman—I assumed she was Judith's dead mother—watched me from another wall. If Judith looked like her when she was fifty she would be as beautiful as she was now and a good deal easier to live with. A trace of her mother's perfume still seemed to linger as did the sense of peace and order she had impressed upon her home.

I sat down and looked into the fire. The cottage, the whole Settlement, was a refuge from the rising chaos of the world outside. After the turmoil of my last few years, after the hectic activity of my whole life, here was a place where I could rest and regain my sanity. I hoped that these Believers would let me stay long enough to do it.

Judith came from the bathroom, pulling an embroidered robe over her long woolen nightdress, brushing out her golden-auburn hair which now hung to her shoulders and glinted in the firelight. I jumped to my feet and stood staring at her. She looked like a woman from an earlier age. She looked completely feminine. And she had never looked more beautiful.

But the essential Judith was still there. "If you're sufficiently sober, Gav—go and get cleaned up!" The disapproval in her voice was an echo of the elderly supervisor in the Pen who had been fond of reminding me to wash my hands before supper.

My panniers had been brought up from the bike and I had returned, shaved and in a clean shirt, when there was a knock on the door. The visitor was Yackle. He seemed embarrassed to find Judith in her night-dress and robe, although I could not imagine more modest sleeping garments. "We're having a communal supper tonight. Down at the Hall. We were hoping you'd join us, Doctor." He glanced at me. "And Mister Gavin too, of course."

"Thanks, Chuck. But not tonight. I'm exhausted. There's food somebody's kindly put in the larder. I'll fix us something to eat here."

"No need for that! Not for you cooking on your first night home." He was obviously relieved that he would not have to explain my presence at the feast. "I'll have the girls bring you up a meal." He gave me a weak smile and disappeared.

Judith was wandering round rearranging things, the way a woman does when she moves into new quarters, starting to make the place her own. She ignored me, so presently I asked, "Didn't Yackle say something about sending up supper?" I was hungry.

She turned, pushed back her hair, and studied me. She had put on perfume, the first time since I had met her when she smelt of anything except herself. She had made up her face; something she hadn't done since distracting the salesman at Hucksters' Haven and impressing the doorman at the Sheraton-Ritz. She had never used cosmetics in the Pen and they were forbidden in Sherando.

"Supper, Gavin? First booze, then food? Is that all you have on your mind?"

"I had two shots of rum with Enoch and I haven't had anything to eat all day!" Why was she so jumpy? We had escaped the Feds. We had survived a dangerous journey, made more dangerous by the way she had ridden her Yama. We had been welcomed—at least she had—by the Settlement. We were in comfortable quarters. Yet when I mentioned I was hungry she reacted as if I had insulted her. That's the trouble with having a female partner on any mission. Single-minded and resolute in the crunch; illogical and unpredictable when out of it.

Before I could annoy her further there was a knock at the door. Barbara and the boy from the woods had arrived with trays of food. "Supper," announced Barbara, stepping into the room. "Compliments of Chairman Yackle. George, put that tray over there!"

George grinned at me, stared open-mouthed at Judith, and put the tray on the sideboard. Barbara started to lay the table with the quick efficiency which seemed to govern all her actions, issuing an occasional command to George. She had just told him to fill the water glasses when Judith took her by the shoulders and turned her toward the door.

"Thanks, Barbara. We can look after ourselves now. There'll be lots of time to talk tomorrow, I promise you. George—take her back to the others. And show her how to enjoy herself! Will there be dancing?"

"If Chairman Yackle approves," said George.

"Tell him I hope he will. After all, I'm the reason for the gala. And I always thought dancing was the best part."

"I'll pass your message ma'am. Come on Barb!"

The girl still lingered. "If there's anything else you want, anything at all, just call me. There's a scrambled com in that cabinet."

"Yes, dear! I remember." She urged the two youngsters out, closed the door, and turned toward me.

"A scrambled com?" I asked.

"Ever the electronics tech!" Judith sighed. "We use a closed CB net here. Better than telephones. You can call anybody within five kilometers of the Cove." She began dishing up the steaming container of clam chowder which Barbara had brought. "I suppose my only hope is to feed you!"

We ate in silence for several minutes, then I said, "That

kid—she's Enoch's daughter all right. But her mother must have been quite something."

"Vera was a fine woman. Her eldest daughter—Barbara's sister—is a lot like her. She's a computer expert somewhere now. But Barbara takes after her grandmother—in looks and character." The expression on Judith's face suggested she had not liked Barbara's grandmother. "She was the first female Captain of an American airliner. So you can guess the kind of woman she was!"

"Like Barbara will be at forty?"

"I hope not!" Judith stopped eating and looked into the fire. "Barb doesn't know it—and you mustn't tell her—but she's an example of what Freyer, the geneticist, calls 'dominant genetic clumping.' A group of sex-linked genes which are transmitted as a group and surface every few generations in a female offspring." She looked up from the flames and at me. "High-survival traits—not all of them pleasant!"

"So if Barbara has any grand-daughters, some of them may look like her?"

"Daughters, granddaughters, great-granddaughters! Those traits may not show up as a group for several generations."

"And you don't approve of them?"

"I don't know!" Judith sighed. "Her grandmother was very competent, very single-minded, very ambitious."

"To make airline skipper in the nineties she'd have had to be!"

"She was also completely ruthless."

She'd have had to be that too. "Barbara's strong-minded all right. But I'd say there's a lot of Enoch in her. And he's the kindest guy—and the most sensible—that I've met for some time. While you and Barbara assumed we were boozing he was actually clueing me in how things are here."

"What sort of things?" Judith glanced sharply at me.

"Enoch says that Chuck Yackle and most of the Council—all oldsters or midders—think that being out in the boondocks is all the protection the Settlement needs. That they're not going to be bothered because outsiders believe the woods are still full of unexploded missiles and the sea lousy with mines. That nobody's going to come and try to loot this place if law and order break down."

"Isn't that true? Isn't that what the Teacher said? When he told us to settle somewhere isolated and become self-sufficient in essentials?"

"I don't know what your Teacher said. But he seems to

have talked more sense than most gurus. And 'self-sufficient' includes being able to defend yourself."

"It won't come to that!" Judy returned to her study of the fire.

"There are weapons here," I persisted. "We saw some this afternoon. What do you think Barbara and her friends were doing in the woods? Playing cowboys and Indians? They had real guns."

"They watch the road. That's good. But they also hunt. That's why they were carrying guns."

"Do you hunt deer with veralloy-clad bullets?"

"How the hell should I know?" Judith made an impatient gesture. "I've never killed anything in my life. You said so yourself!"

"You've never killed people. Or deer. But what about rats?"

"Rats? That's different. That was in the lab."

"So you're ready to kill for knowledge, but not for meat? And you won't kill to defend the Faith?"

"Gavin, quit riding me! I suppose I might. If there was no other way. I'm a doctor, remember? Those kids—"

"Barbara's no kid! She's seventeen, and she has her own boat."

"Her own boat?" Judith looked up, startled.

"She told me she got her ticket last spring. And a boat to go with it. How can a girl of her age get a boat of her own? A fully equipped fishing boat worth God knows how much?"

"It's not hers! It belongs to all of us!" Judith looked back into the fire. "Though once the boat's been allotted it's as good as hers for as long as she fishes it profitably."

"Profitably? Profitable for who? Her or the Settlement?"

"Profitable for both. Sutton Cove isn't a commune, not like Sherando. We're a cooperative. Everybody owns an equal share. Like a common stock company. And everybody gets an equal cut of any profits. The people who fish—and that's all of us at one time or another—earn a share in the catch. Those of us who fish regularly get a boat allotted—if we show we're good enough. In effect the boat's ours so long as we can pay the rental and the operating costs. What's left is our own. The best—the high-liners, men or women, make the most. The others, whether we're carpenters, or doctors, or mechanics, or any other of the trades we have, get paid for what we do. The teachers and so on get a salary, indexed to what the average fisherman earns. A few don't work at anything profitable but live on their share in the Settlement's profits. Basic living with no luxuries. We had a poet like that once. A good poet but a lousy fisherman. He should have stuck to poetry but insisted on fishing. He drowned! He was a sweet guy too!"

That memory had touched some nerve. I returned to Barbara. "How could she have had a boat allotted to her at seventeen?"

"By being good and proving it, I suppose!"

"She seems to be good at everything."

"She's also damned pretty and has every boy in the Settlement after her ass!" Judith could be as crude as any other educated woman when she wanted to be. "I've heard quite enough about that girl for tonight. Don't get ideas! She's out of your age group! More important, what are your plans, now you've deposited me safely here?"

"I'd like to stay awhile. Perhaps do the same job I was doing at Sherando."

"No!" Her green eyes flashed in the firelight. "For God's sake, don't mention Sherando. Or any other violent job you've done. They'll try to throw you out if you do. Yackle and the Council abhor violence. They're peaceable folk here. I haven't told them where we've been or what we've done. And they won't ask." Her voice grew calmer. "As far as the Council is concerned you're an electronics tech. And a good one. They need an electronics tech. You've seen the amount of electronics they have around. And the techs they've got are outdated."

"Do you think they'll let me stop over? Yackle was really spooked when he found I wasn't a Believer."

"Do you want to stay?"

"Only if you do."

She studied me with her clinical stare. Then her eyes became warm and her smile female. "I'll make sure they let you." She put her arms around me, kissed me with a mouth that was no longer hard and firm but passionate and soft. "Let's go to bed! I've been trying to get you there all the evening."

I woke once during the night to lie close against Judith's smooth curves; comforted by her nearness, by the scent of her hair, by her gentle breathing. Breathing as regular as the rhythm of the seas running into the Cove.

The thunder of rollers breaking onto the beach, the rumble

of shingle sucked back by retreating waves. Sea sounds from my boyhood. As I drifted into sleep I drifted back in time. Back to my father's manse on Nantucket, back to my old fantasies. But the face which floated into my first dream was a new face. A girl with golden hair and cool gray eyes. The face of Enoch's daughter—Barbara.

XIII

"He's not a heretic. He's an unbeliever," Judith insisted, facing the Settlement Council. "That's quite different. A heretic believes the wrong thing. An unbeliever doesn't believe anything!"

Chairman Yackle looked nonplused, the other Councilors confused. We had been in Sutton Cove for a week and Yackle had suggested that I, as a heretic, could not be allowed to stay much longer. Judith had countered with a theological argument. But the Council were not interested in theology; they were only interested in avoiding discord. They had created a snug haven for themselves and their children in a world where the storms were rising and the number of children was falling. I was an intruder, a source of disruptive ideas who had arrived with two guns and a murky background.

"If you want to keep me, then you've got to take my husband!" Judith fell back from theological argument to open threat.

I sat up, opened my mouth to protest, then shut it again. For Judith the fact of marriage seemed derived from the act of love; our consummation in the hay had established our married state to her satisfaction, and I was in no position to deny it. Later, perhaps, I could claim annulment.

The Councilors went in a huddle. They didn't want me but they did want her. Enoch took the pipe from his mouth and remarked, "Mister Gavin's a good electronics tech. He fixed my radar."

"We need an electronics man," added Jehu, another elderly fisherman with a taste for rum. "Old Shipley don't see so well now, and young Rustin ain't learned enough yet."

Yackle got the message. "I did not realize that you and

Mister Gavin were married, Doctor. That, of course, alters the situation. We would offend the Light were we to be responsible for putting asunder two people who are joined in matrimony." He looked around the table. "Perhaps we can employ Mister Gavin on a temporary basis. Providing he does not parade his unbelief before our children."

"I've learned never to parade my views on politics or religion."

Yackle rubbed his hands together. "Good! Good! I am confident that you will become Brother Gavin after you have lived among us for a while." The same hope that Anslinger had expressed. "That the Light will illuminate you as it illuminates us."

I could match him pietism for pietism. "The Light is the true Light which lighteth every man who cometh into the world." However doubtful the validity of the first chapter of the Gospel according to Saint John, the King James translation is among the glories of the English language.

The fact that only Yackle, Enoch, and Judith seemed to recognize the source of the quotation told me a good deal about the general education of the Sutton Settlement Believers. After the Council had accepted me as a temporary stranger within their gates and we were outside on the steps of the Hall, Judith snapped, "For an agnostic gunman, you're a fast man with a pious phrase!"

"My father was a Presbyterian minister and force fed me the Bible. I can quote scripture to suit any occasion!"

"Your father a minister—and he let you join the Army?"

"Dad said at seventeen I should make up my own mind. So when he sent me off to college I took Gramps' advice and went to the SSF for my education."

"You jumped from one authority to another."

I swung on her, suddenly furious. "What the hell do you mean?"

She faced me. "You've made a career of being a faithful follower. You're feudal. A samurai always looking for a Lord. Your father—your grandfather—Colonel Jewett—Arnold Grainer. And whoever told you to kill Futrell. In the Pen you were adrift—"

"Until you took over, I suppose!"

She shrugged. "You needed a push. Remember? At Sherando you latched onto Anslinger—"

"Judy, you're no psychologist! So lay off analyzing me."

"I'm only trying to tell you that here you'll have to be your own man."

"A few minutes back I found I'd been married without being asked!"

"Well? Do you want to split?"

I looked into her green eyes. "Do you?"

"No!" She stared back, defiant.

"Then I'm still a masterless man! But I've got a damned pretty mistress!" I grabbed her and kissed her long and hard, despite her initial protests and the embarrassment of Chuck Yackle, who emerged from the Council Chamber just as Judy was starting to respond.

Enoch had told me the story of the Sutton Cove Settlement when we had sat drinking in his boat. It had been founded by a group of Believers some twenty years before after they had heard their Teacher advise them to pick some remote place and start living the simple life. A slightly bemused look had come over Enoch's face, and I had again been astonished at the effect the man had had on so many diverse people. Enoch, for example, was a jovial, good-hearted, and pragmatic person, yet a word from the Teacher had been enough for him and his wife to uproot themselves and move into this deserted fishing village to start a new life.

He had been one of the few fishermen among the original group of Believers; in fact one of the few displaced Fundy fishermen who returned to inshore fishing. But he would have gone to establish a Settlement in the middle of Texas if the Teacher had told him. The group had picked Sutton Cove principally because the land and buildings had cost them almost nothing, and it was as remote as anywhere on the eastern seaboard.

Much of the Maine coast and the whole coastline of the Bay of Fundy had been desolated in 1990 when the *Joseph Kinross* loaded with crude for the refinery at Pocolagon, had collided with the chemical carrier *Jenny Wren*, outward bound from Eastport with a cargo of tritorridine. They had run into each other at the entrance to the Bay of Fundy in a typical radar-assisted collision; the category of maritime disasters which included those in which watch-officers had preferred to watch a radar screen in a warm wheelhouse than look over a dodger on a cold bridge. A collision of two aging monsters manned by incompetents and officered by fools. In 1990, despite high pay and luxurious accommodation, it had already become difficult to persuade sensible seamen to ship out in single-bottomed, single-boilered, single-screwed behemoths, rescued from the scrap yard by anonymous owners and chartered through Caribbean-based agents.

The *Jenny Wren* had been the prototype for a class of chemical carriers, a class which in a few years acquired a reputation which made them almost uninsurable. She had been cut in two and her bows had gone straight to the bottom. Her stern had lingered long enough for the whole crew to get away in the boats; the sea had been as calm as Fundy ever gets and the visibility good.

The *Joseph Kinross*, listing to port, had continued to sail northeast, trailing crude from her ripped tanks. She had been abandoned as quickly as the *Jenny Wren*. The only engineer on watch at the time of the collision had been her dedicated engine-room computer. (Since the late nineteen-sixties human engineers on supertankers had kept office hours.) It had manfully tried to maintain the last-ordered speed despite the list and the gashed hull. When the engine room flooded, the computer had drowned. The more rugged fuel-pumps had continued to fuel the furnaces, even after the boiler feed-pumps had burned out their bearings. So the boiler had blown up, tearing a section out of her bottom.

That had stopped her engines but the momentum of one of the largest man-made masses ever to put to sea had carried her on for another fifteen kilometers. Then the spring tides, roaring up the Bay of Fundy, had taken over and swept her level with Saint John where she had hung for half an hour before sinking.

The *Joseph Kinross* had been over a kilometer from stem to stern and rated at a million metric tons. By the time she sank she had discharged half a billion liters of crude onto the Bay of Fundy, with the result that the waters of the Bay had been less troubled during the subsequent spring gales than ever before in history. During the next few months, as her remaining half billion liters came welling up, the Fundy tides and the Fundy winds had laid a black strip of crude oil between high and low watermarks from Portland to Brier Island.

This was a disaster that marine experts had been predicting for years. The Governments of Canada and the United States reacted as though it were an unexpected Act of God. The disappearance of the anonymous owners and the bankruptcy of the charter parties left a financial hiatus which delayed action, and by the time action was taken there was no effective action to take. Both governments finally announced that, given time, the coast would recover its unsoiled condition. Then the seepage from the *Jenny Wren* began to take effect.

TTD, tritorridine, is an innocuous compound used in the synthesis of neoplastics. Under sufficient pressure, however, it reacts with free chloride ions to produce ritidine chloride, toxic to most organisms. At a depth of three hundred meters the ocean provided both chloride ions and pressure. As TTD seeped out, ritidine was formed, currents and tides distributed it and killed off what marine life had survived the oil. Within a year the Bay of Fundy was a dead sea, and over its whole coast hung the stench of death.

By then the entire population of the littoral had been evacuated. Both the US and the Canadian Governments compensated its dispossessed citizens by buying them out. The Canadians, with rare bureaucratic humor, declared the devastated strip of coast to be a wildlife sanctuary. The US Government, more realistic (or with a more subtle wit) gave theirs to the military. The oil-soaked, death-strewn beaches provided a training area which (apart from the cold) simulated conditions troops were likely to meet going ashore when the Persian Gulf again went critical.

Once the need for amphibious training was past, the deserted coast had become a proving-ground for bombs, shells, and guided missiles, with Jona's Point as a prime target. The peninsula and its hinterland had been bombarded by high-explosive, antipersonnel spreaders, napalmite, smokes, defoliants, and God knows what else. The fuse-failure rate was low, but even at one percent the number of unexploded missiles with various contents scattered through woods, beaches, and inshore shallows accumulated until the Point was among the most heavily mined areas in the world. The ideal site for both the new Federal Penitentiary and the prototype fusion reactor.

By then TTD has ceased to seep from the *Jenny Wren*, the sea had given up its dead, and the lower forms of marine life had started to thrive on the rich organic remains of the original inhabitants. The cod, the pollack, the herring, the hake, and the halibut followed to gorge once more on the biota the Fundy tides swept over the ledges, and lobsters crawled slowly back up the coast to their cold feeding grounds. The only major species made extinct by the combination of oil and TTD was the Fundy Inshore Fisherman.

Inshore fishing is a hard way to earn a living. It requires a mastery of many skills, including an intimate knowledge of where, when, and how. By the time the fish returned the fishermen who knew had gone and nobody was interested in relearning. During the Affluence only the rich went to sea in small boats and bad weather, only the rich enjoyed cold, wet, and exhaustion as they raced sailboats, each of which cost more than the whole fleet which had once fished from Sutton Cove.

The Believers had moved in to fill the ecological niche left vacant by the extinction of the local fishermen. The original founders had been devout, enthusiastic, and educated but all they had known about commercial fishing was what young Enoch and two old fishermen had been able to tell them, and what they had read in books. Their first catches had been pitifully small, but as they learned about the sea and developed their own fishing techniques, the Settlement had grown and prospered.

The Believers were simpleminded in their religion but not in their thinking. The technological constraints of their creed had made them apply "elegant engineering" to small-boat fishing. Offshore the great factory ships steamed over the Grand Banks, their fish-pumps sucking up everything that swam, converting live fish to canned, frozen or powdered forms, untouched by human hands. But they could not invade the rocky inshore grounds where the underwater ledges would smash their pump intakes and rip their hulls. Yet it was along those ledges that the rich feeding grounds lay; waters that could only be harvested by hand-line and trawl.

The original Believers had been a mixed lot and, like my companions in the Pen, had had a variety of skills. After twenty years of learning the waters the fleet out of Sutton Cove was bringing in catches as large as those of the sixteenth century when fishermen from Britain, France, and Portugal first discovered the richest fishing grounds in the world.

At the time of the Settlement's founding the locals had looked upon Believers as I had done at first; a group of religious nuts trying to live a simple life of semiproverty while the rest of America was riding the Affluence. That patronizing but friendly attitude had started to fade as the Settlement had advanced from rural poverty to quiet prosperity. Now many of the locals were starting to talk of the Believers as a bunch of foreigners who had moved in to steal their lobsters, although there was not a local left who knew how to bait a trap.

During the first few years the people of Sutton Settlement had lived on what they had caught and sold what they didn't eat as cattle feed and fertilizer. By 2010 Fundy waters were declared clear and its products approved for export to foreigners. In 2015 its fish and lobsters were found fit for consumption by Americans and the Settlement gained a ready market for all it could catch. Fresh fish was at a premium; in the judgment of epicures, free-ranging lobsters from the cold waters of Maine tasted far better than the tanked product. Sutton Settlement was one of the few sources. The Settlement had brought prosperity and population back to Standish, though nobody except Believers dared live any closer than thirty kilometers to the coast. The lethal reputation of the Fundy shoreline persisted as a legend more powerful that the facts about Impermease.

I settled down well enough into this seafaring society and earned my keep as the resident electronics tech. The Settlement had been suffering from the usual complaint of organizations which purchase sophisticated equipment without ensuring there shall be adequate service backup. I had all the work I could handle overhauling the gear in the boats, the com system in the Cove, and the radio station, which kept the Settlement in touch with other Settlements all over the world.

It was officially a ham radio station, but the transmitter was a good deal simpler than most twenty-first-century ham stations. For one thing it was strictly code in an age when few hams bothered to learn the International Morse Code and even commercial operators couldn't handle code at any speed. The kids who manned the Sutton station passed traffic at over thirty words a minute, and could have matched keys with the expert radio operators of a century before.

The station intrigued me more than the sophisticated microcircuitry in the boats, and I came to enjoy sitting in the radio shack watching some youngster copying signals so faint that I could hardly hear them through the interference and static.

When I asked Kitty, one of the more talkative operators, why they made life difficult for themselves in this way, she explained, "Here in North America we can get almost any kind of electronic gadget we want—at present. But a lot of the Settlements are away to hell and gone. They may have to keep going for years with the gear they've got now. They may be powering their transmitters from somebody peddling a bicycle-generator. That means we've got to get used to CW only—morse code. And we've got to learn to read signals through heavy QRM and QRN—interference and noise." She broke off our conversation to swivel around in her chair and fine-tune her receiver. These kids seemed to be able to carry on a discussion with one ear and monitor a channel with the other. "Some Aussie calling. At this time of day the Aussies come rolling in on fourteen megahertz. Could be a genuine ham." She checked the call sign against a list. "No—it's one of ours." She pressed the phones against her ears, then rattled out an acknowledgment on her key. She listened a moment, touched her key again, and made an entry in the log. "Near Wiluna, Western Australia. Out in a damned great desert. Routine report that all's as well as can be expected."

"You can sure handle traffic fast!"

"Two half-decent code operators can pass traffic with zero error at twice the speed of two oldsters bellowing over mikes and misunderstanding each other. You should listen to some of our boats trying to report where they've found fish!"

"I have!"

"If it wasn't for the scramblers so would the whole of the Eastern seaboard. If the Council want to keep us out of the public ear they'd better lock up the radiophones on half the boats in the fleet." She paused. "I'll bet the Coast Guard have decoders."

"Not any that'll sort out our mix," I said. "Not since I lined 'em up. But how come you don't attract attention? I mean, this whole net you've set up between Settlements?"

"We use minimum power and stay in the ham bands. Fourteen megahertz at twenty watts lets us contact almost anywhere in the world at some time of the day or night. And we always follow ham procedures—although we usually work too fast for any normal ham to copy unless they go to the trouble of taping. And we always answer any ham who calls us in code. There were hardly any before last year. Now a lot more are starting to switch to CW from radiophone. They're starting to learn code again. I guess that means more and more of them are being isolated, running out of power and spares. In some parts of the world—the things I hear! It's pathetic!" She listened a moment. "There're those bastards at Sherando calling. That's a Settlement somewhere in Virginia.

Blasting away at full power as usual. Guess I'll have to answer." And she turned to her task, the headphones around her neck, the morse echoing loud and hard through the room. I went slowly back to my workshop, sentimental enough to enjoy hearing about the revival of an old communication skill, depressed by the reasons for its revival.

Judith and I seemed to be the only people in the Settlement who were depressed, or even much interested, in what was happening in the outside world. All through the winter news bulletins on radio and TV became increasingly cheerful as the news itself worsened. The population decline was accelerating, there were few convincing examples of women under twenty becoming pregnant. News from some parts of the world, especially those where a girl of fourteen was considered to be of marriageable age, was catastrophic. Whole populations were beginning to see disaster ahead and, lacking the Affluence's faith in Science, were turning to older faiths, resurrecting fertility rites which tended to be barbarous and bloody.

Believers, while deploring what was going on, tended to show an element of self-satisfaction as they heard of these disasters. One of the least attractive aspects of a "chosen people" is their indifference to what happens to the non-chosen. There was some excuse for those Settlements which were already suffering from persecution, for persecution seldom develops unselfishness or improves the character of those persecuted. So far the Believers in Sutton Cove, thanks to their isolation and their economic importance to the merchants of Standish, had only had black looks and curses hurled at them. But, after all, they too were Americans and should have been as anguished as I when, in the spring, the news broadcasts started to play the flip side of the American dream.

Yet even Judith, a fine scientist, who might have been adding her brains and skill to the struggle to discover some solution to the Impermease disaster, was more worried about the health of the few hundred children in the Settlement than the sterility of millions of American girls.

I mentioned this to her once. She sighed and said, "I've told you already, Gavin. All their research is hopeless. The eggs in those girls were sterilized years ago. I won't waste my time trying to bring the dead back to life. What I can do is to help the living to grow up healthy and strong, fit to build a better world."

"So America means nothing to you anymore?"

She turned to stare at me. "Oh yes it does! The new America. The America which will rise from the cesspool of the Affluence. That is what we are working for here!"

That was what she was working for. Since my moment of enlightenment when she had saved me from getting killed trying to kill Futrell I had been working chiefly for my own survival—and hers. If any marriage can be called satisfactory, ours was satisfactory. Because of our shared love, or our shared guilt, or because we were both working so hard we had neither the inclination nor the energy to criticize each other. Marriage was less of an entrapment than I had feared. In fact that first winter in Sutton Cove was among the happiest times of my life.

XIV

"Want to take a ride into town?" Barbara was standing in the door of my workshop. "Truck's leaving in half an hour."

"Sorry!" I gestured toward the bench. "I promised to fix Jehu's radar by tonight."

"It was Jehu who sent me to ask. He's the trader. Sam and I are driving. But there's room for a third. Especially if the third has a gun."

"You're expecting—?"

"I'm just passing on Jehu's message. Trailer's loading from the lobster pens. We're taking the Brinks." She gave me a cool stare and turned back toward the wharf.

It was the first time that Barbara and I had exchanged more than a few words since my arrival. As Judith had remarked, Barbara was out of my age group—a hint that had kept me away from her through the winter. But if we live as men we dream as boys, and Barbara's face often floated into my dreams, usually regarding me with disdain. Had I really been her age I would have been chasing her ass with the other youngsters; a prize which few of them seemed to win.

Now she had thrown down a clear challenge. The Settlement owned five large trucks and one second-hand armored car—the Brinks. A beast of a vehicle whose only virtues were its armor and an ability to go cross-country. As rural roads became more dangerous the Settlement had started using it more often to haul lobsters to Standish and bring back the proceeds in gold. I walked to the door and looked toward the cove. The lobster pens were large slatted boxes floating just beneath the surface of the water. Trapped lobsters, their claws pegged to stop them from fighting, were stored in the pens until they could be trucked in one shipment to the Standish dealers and thence air-freighted all over the United States.

An old coaster, the *Ranula*, lay alongside the wharf. The Council had bought her to shop fish down the coast to Clarport, now that the dealers could no longer persuade their drivers to make the risky run to Sutton Cove. But she was too slow for the rapid transit from sea to table demanded by the epicures who paid astronomical prices for our free-ranging lobsters. So Settlement trucks continued to go into Standish. Jehu was asking me to join him on this trip; Barbara was challenging me to come.

Jehu must be expecting trouble; Barbara was probably hoping for it. Damnation! Judith had been insistent that I keep my bloody past to myself. But the news that I was a professional gunman must have leaked out. Jehu's invitation had the force of an appeal. Barbara's delivery had turned it into a challenge. I cursed again, put on my windbreaker and cap, took my Luger from the locked cupboard where I kept it, and went down to watch the large trailer being loaded.

"Glad to have you along, Mister Gavin," said Jehu, looking up from his tally sheet as he counted the crates going aboard.

"Nice day for a ride through the woods!" I remarked. "Are we in for a storm?"

"Maybe! Maybe! Time's about ripe for one."

"Do you think that kid should be driving if it starts?"

"If a blow comes I'd rather have that kid at the wheel than any man in the Cove. That's why I asked her to drive this trip. And why I asked you along. We'll be coming back with more gold than I like to consider. This is settling-up day!" Which meant we'd be returning with payment for the last six loads.

"The last settling-up day, Jehu?"

"The last for me. Chuck can collect the next payment himself." The final sling-load of crated prisoners swung up onto the trailer and Jehu slammed the tailgate closed. He shouted to Sam, "Back her up, lad! Let's get moving."

I watched Sam backing the Brinks onto the wharf, and helped Jehu hitch on the trailer. Not an easy task. The Brinks had been designed to frustrate robbers, not tow trailers.

Jehu opened its rear door. "Mind riding up front, Mister Gavin? Nothing won't happen on the way into town."

I glanced past him into the back and saw Midge, a girl of

small size and immense energy, sitting with headphones around her neck. "What's she doing?"

"Workin' the radio." Jehu climbed aboard.

"But to take another kid on a trip like this—"

"Barbara wants her along." Jehu closed the door.

"Mister Gavin, are you coming?" Barbara called from the cab.

Sam, a lean and loose-jointed youth, was behind the wheel. He grinned at me. "I drive up. Barb drives back. So if I sight a deer—or something—I can use that!" And he pointed to a hunting rifle in the roof rack. We had at least one other decent weapon aboard.

The dirt road had deteriorated since Judith and I had ridden down it ten months before. "Damn the Department of Highways!" said Sam as he steered the Brinks between the ruts and past an overhanging bank. "We've told 'em a dozen times that lot's going to slide and block the road."

"We pay our taxes and they do nothing for us," complained Barbara.

The shutter between the cab and the back of the Brinks slid open and Midge's freckled face appeared. "I've made contact with the State Police. They say the road's clear right into Standish."

"So they say!" muttered Sam. "How the hell do they know when they don't look?" But he began to drive faster, which was not very fast with the heavy trailer lurching along behind.

The forest stretched away unbroken on each side of the road. "Do outsiders ever go into these woods?" I asked.

"Nope. Too many unexploded missiles lying around."

"But you kids hunt in them?"

"We know where the missiles are!" Sam and Barbara both laughed. "The folks in Standish—they hear explosions in the woods at times. When a deer steps on one." Or when some kid sets off a stick of dynamite to scare the townsfolk!

Judith and I had not been impressed by what little we had seen of Standish when we had ridden through it on our bikes. Now that I saw more of it as we drove in from the highway I was even less impressed. A small decaying town on a railroad where few trains ran, off a thruway which now led to nowhere. The inhabitants seemed as unattractive as their town. The expression on the faces of the people we passed as the Brinks jolted down Main Street showed their dislike of us, and loungers on the corner of the town square shouted abuse as we turned into the trucking center where the semitrailer was waiting to take our lobsters to the airport at Augusta.

Jehu climbed stiffly from the rear of the Brinks as the dealer, a short fat man, came bustling up. "Good to see you, Jehu! Good to see you! You've got a full load?"

"A full load, Mister Goodson," said Jehu. "You've got what's due us? I aim to start back for the Cove afore dark."

"Sergeant Carver's escorting the gold over from the bank now. Nuisance you people not taking paper anymore. But I can't say I blame you. Maybe it's best to have your capital in something solid these days—even at the premium. Here comes the Sergeant now."

A police cruiser was turning into the trucking center and I slipped out of the cab. It wasn't likely that I would be recognized by a local cop, but there was no point in taking chances. I was dressed like the out-of-town truckers who were standing and talking together while their trucks were being loaded. I joined them. Nobody took any notice of me. I heard the Sergeant saying to Jehu, "I checked it at the bank. It's all there."

"Thanks, Mike." Jehu accepted the Sergeant's word without question. And he did look like the type of cop I remembered. "Expecting trouble?"

"I'm always expecting trouble these days!" The Sergeant sighed. "And you folks down at the Cove aren't getting more popular. There's a lot of ugly stories going around about what you're doing down there. Grabbing kids, keeping young girls against their will. That sort of thing. All lies—I know!" He glanced round, then added, "Best not come come up with your lobsters for a while. Those dealers will be mad at me for saying so, 'cos your Settlement's just about the only thing that's keeping this town afloat. But I don't like some of the talk I hear."

"Thanks for the tip, Mike."

"I hope it don't come to nothing!" The Sergeant noticed Midge, Barbara, and Sam getting out of the Brinks and started toward a soda fountain across the street. "Hey—you kids! Get back in your truck."

"Why?" asked Sam, swinging around.

The Sergeant nodded to a group of youths who had gathered at the entrance of the trucking center, and were starting to jeer. "Want to mix it with those bums?"

"I wouldn't mind," said Sam.

"Do like the Sergeant says!" ordered Jehu.

Sam cursed, Barbara scowled, and Midge grumbled, "I only came on this trip to get a fudge sundae!" But all three climbed back into the Brinks.

The dealer was tallying the lobsters while Jehu and the Sergeant went to the police cruiser, and returned carrying a small money chest between them. After they had stowed it in the back of the Brinks the Seregant dusted his hands and hitched up his belt. "Think I'll go and break up that gang of young loafers!" He walked toward them and they responded first by shifting their insults from us to him, and then by piling into their autos and roaring away.

The Sergeant came back and got into his cruiser. "Gotta go into Augusta now, Jehu. Don't hang around town, and have a safe trip home. Radio the station if you run into trouble." He raised his hand and drove off.

"Wish there were more like Mike," said Jehu, when I joined him. "He's been a good friend to the Settlement for a long time. We ain't got too many friends left no more. Maybe he's our last friend in this damned town."

"I'd like to pick up some stuff from the hardware," I said. "Mind if I take off for half an hour?"

"Sure! You don't look like no Believer. And we're safe enough here in the loading bay. These truckers are out of town and they'd beat shit outta anybody who tried to jump a truck. Even ours! But don't hang around. I want to get out of this dump."

I promised to be quick and looked into the cab of the Brinks. "Midge, I'll fetch you a pack of sundae."

"Me too!" Barbara and Sam showed their residual youth.

I promised to bring them all sundaes and walked around the warehouse to emerge at the side of the square. Dressed like a trucker nobody took any particular notice of me. I bought the items I wanted in the hardware at the end of Main Street, then walked back toward the loading bays. There was a bar on the corner, and I hesitated. I hadn't tasted bourbon since our arrival in Sutton Cove, and God knows when I'd get another chance.

Although it was early afternoon, the place was full of drinkers; noisy evidence of Standish's commercial stagnation. The drinkers along the bar were complaining about the Government, the drinkers standing grouped at the window were looking at the Brinks on the far side of the square and exchanging absurd and scurrilous stories about what went on at Sutton Cove.

Stories that Believers were polygamous, which was absurd. Descriptions of supposed sexual orgies in obscene and fantastic detail. Rumors that the Settlement was kidnapping children, when there were few children around to kidnap. These were men and women who had started to realize that something terrible was happening and were looking for scapegoats. The Believers at Sutton Cove filled the bill, as far as this part of Maine was concerned.

The stories circulating among the watchers in the bar followed the same hate-raising pattern as the slanders which in the past had been aimed at Jews, Mormons, Catholics, Quakers, Masons, Protestants, and almost every minority which claimed superiority and appeared better off than their neighbors. Rumors listened to with excitement and passed on with eagerness for the same conscious or unconscious reason; to raise a sense of public indignation which might later justify burning the homes and looting the property of the minority concerned. And the hatred behind that desire was fueled by more than common resentment. It was fired by the fact that the Sutton Settlement still contained fertile women.

Even ordinarily decent people were looking for targets on whom to vent their anger at the impending collapse of their civilization. Most of them had realized by this time that the real fault lay with frightened and incompetent governments. But the Federal Government was remote and still too strong and brutal to attack. The Settlement, on the other hand, was nearby and apparently defenseless.

The more I listened to the talk in the bar the angrier and more alarmed I became. By the time I had finished my bourbon I had heard all the lies I could stomach. I myself was no Believer, but I knew they were a moral, hard-working, and decent group of men and women, even if their own view of the future was essentially selfish and they believed they were the elect. More important, they were raising a crop of youngsters with decent manners and some morals. Children who might grow into self-reliant civilized adults, capable of rebuilding the kind of free and strong society which the United States had once been. Or which I hoped it had once been. Anyway, whatever the truth about the past, the kids in Sutton Cove were a notable improvement on the kids I had encountered elsewhere in America, and particularly the examples of arrested social development hanging around the square.

I left the bar, stopped at the supermarket to pick up the sundaes I had promised the three child-adults in the Brinks, and made my way back to where the group of truckers were still smoking and talking. They were talking about neither the Settlements nor the Government, but about how many women they had managed to lay during their last trip. And how much easier it was to lay a woman now that the bitches didn't worry about getting knocked up.

Jehu and the dealer were exchanging receipts. I stooped to examine the axles of the trailer and called Jehu over. "That bearing ain't goin' to last until we get her back to the Cove."

He squatted down beside me. "Mister Gavin—it's always been like that. No call to get clutched up."

"It's not the axle," I growled. "It's those damned townies. I stopped for a drink in that bar across the square and the talk was turning ugly. As they get smashed they'll start pushing each other to start something. We should fade right now. And with this thing trailing astern we won't be able to move fast or back up."

He saw my expression and nodded. "Mister Goodson," he called, "I'm going to leave our trailer here. Ask Joe Clarke to come over tomorrow and fix the axle, will you?"

"Sure, Jehu! Sure!" The dealer was too nervous looking at the louts to look at the axle. The Sergeant had chased them off, but they had seen him driving out of town and were now returning to bait us. "Have a good trip home. Better wait a week or two before you come up again. Maybe I'll be able to persuade one of my drivers to bring your trailer down to you." And he scurried off toward his office.

I helped Jehu unhitch the trailer and swung into the cab as he jumped into the back of the Brinks. Barbara had the motor running and was behind the wheel. Some of the louts had brought their old autos to the square and were waiting outside the entrance of the truck-park. The truckers were still talking about women. Their only interest in law and order was maintaining it inside the trucking center.

"There's trouble!" I muttered to Barbara.

"You call that trouble?" She gunned the motor and spoke over her shoulder to Midge and Jehu. "Close up and strap down. Heavy weather ahead!" Then she sent the Brinks rolling toward the exit.

A rock bounced off the armored windshield and a car swung across the road to block our way out. "You want me to radio the Sergeant?" asked Midge from the back.

"No need to bother the Sergeant." Barbara had the arrogant self-confidence of youth. "We can handle these dead-necks." She headed the Brinks at the car blocking the exit. "Maybe have a little fun ourselves!"

More rocks bounced off the cab. The driver of the car yelled, "Whatcha' going to do now, little girl?"

"Flatten that heap of yours!" muttered the little girl, keeping the Brinks rolling.

The driver suddenly realized that the Brinks was about to ram, and tried to shoot ahead. He stalled the motor and his acned face showed stark terror as the armored car loomed above him. Then he threw open the door and went tumbling out into the roadway, scrambling for safety.

Barbara braked the Brinks with its front bumper resting against the car door. Sam picked up the bullhorn and roared, "Get that crate outta the way or we'll roll it over. You've got thirty seconds!"

The driver clambered back in, started his motor at the second attempt, and skidded away up the street. Barbara accelerated through the exit and sent the Brinks charging along Main.

Sam swung the periscope. "They're following." He didn't seem worried.

I was! Behind us were more than six cars, packed with hoodlums, trailing us along Main, with the leaders attempting to slip past, careless of other traffic. They might—"Hey! You're dead-ending!" I shouted as Barbara swung off Main and down a narrow road which finished in what looked like a junk yard.

"Just having our bit of fun!" she yelled, as the Brinks crashed from pothole to pothole.

"Fun?" Ahead was a wooden fence and an overgrown lot filled with the rusting remains of generations of pre-veralloy autos. I looked astern. A string of cars had turned off Main after us, the leader only a meter from our tail. I eased out my Luger.

"No need for that!" yelled Sam. "Not yet!"

"Hang on, all!" shouted Barbara and hit the brakes.

An instant later the lead car hit us. The Brinks gave a ponderous lurch. From astern came a cadence of tinkling glass and screeching metal. The lead car was concertinaed between us and the car behind it. The lane was clogged with rear-end collisions.

"Got 'em!" shouted Sam.

"How many?" asked Barbara.

"Six—no—eight!"

"Right on!" She headed the Brinks at the wooden fence. It went down as we hit and she took us swerving among the wrecks. The yells and curses behind us faded as she went through another fence on the far side of the junk yard and then out onto a lane. "That'll teach the cabron to leave us alone!"

"You young idiots!" I raged. "The Settlement's unpopular enough already. Are you trying to make things worse?"

"We couldn't," said Barbara as we reached the highway. Then, as she turned onto the dirt road leading to the Cove, she added, "We're already as unpopular as we can get. All we can do now is to show those nerds that it's expensive to tangle with us."

We started winding through the woods. The setting sun was hidden by the trees so that on the road it was already dusk, but the farther we got from Standish the less the tension in the cab. Barbara paid me one of her rare compliments. "It was smart of you to fake the axle of the trailer, Mister Gavin. I couldn't have pulled off that rear-end caper if we'd been dragging it behind."

"You'd have thought of something equally infuriating!" I stared out of the window at the woods jolting past. "The talk I heard in Standish was bad!"

"This is my last trip to town!" said Sam. "At least, it's my last trip looking like I'm from the Settlement." His grin hinted that trips by youngsters to town while not looking like Believers were common.

"If Goodson wants our lobsters he can come and fetch 'em," said Jehu from the rear. "He was talking about renting an amphibian to air-freight 'em direct to Boston. He won't like it. It'll cut into his profits. But from now on the only trading I'll do is on the wharf or aboard *Ranula*."

I twisted round to speak through the hatch. "Goodson! That unctuous little bastard's making an enormous profit. You sell lobsters to him at twenty bucks a kilo. In the Boston market they wholesale for eighty!"

"Eighty and more," said Jehu, nodding.

"So why don't you demand a fair price?"

"If it was up to me, I would. But the Council say we're earning more than we need right now. They let the dealers make a big profit to keep them friendly."

"You're paying protection?"

"That's how Chuck Yackle and most of the Council see it. They call it insurance against the future." He spat on the floor of the Brinks. "Not much of an insurance, not to my mind."

I agreed. *"Once you have paid them the Dane-geld, you never get rid of the Dane."* We rode without talking for some time, conversation was an effort in the Brinks. When the road dipped down into a cutting and we passed the entrance to an old logging trail, I remarked, "I thought the locals never came as far as this to cut lumber?"

"They don't," said Sam. "Why?"

"There's a bulldozer hidden back among those trees."

My words acted like an alarm blast. Barbara hit the brakes without warning. We skidded round a bend and stopped a few meters short of a heavy truck parked slantwise across the road. The next instant she was in reverse. Then she braked again as the bulldozer lumbered out onto the road, lurching toward us.

"Christ! A hijack!" We were in a cutting with the truck ahead, the bulldozer astern, and steep banks on each side. "Close up!" She grabbed a lever, dropping the armored shields over the windows. "Sam—can I shove that bastard astern into the ditch?"

"You can try. No—hold it! He's broadside on and the driver's bolted. Won't help any to roll it over. Nor that truck ahead neither." Sam took his deer rifle from the roof rack, and began loading the magazine.

"Keep that thing out of sight!" snapped Barbara, then called through the hatch. "Midge—get on the blower and call Kitty. Tell her we've been bushwacked at fifteenth click. Then call Sergeant Carver and ask him to come and get these thugs to move out of our way." She switched off the motor.

Jehu said nothing. I checked my Luger, then asked, "What are you proposing to do—whichever of you's in charge around here?"

"Orders are to sit and wait," said Jehu as though he was. He put his face to the hatch. "This truck's got veralloy armor, so nobody can get in. We just stay closed up. The plan is that they'll get tired eventually and go away."

"That's what happened last time," said Sam.

So there had been a last time! Nobody'd mentioned a "last time" when they'd invited me to come this time. I suppressed my fury and spoke in a cold voice, slowly and clearly, making sure my message got through. "I don't know who told you that nobody can cut through veralloy armor. Whoever it was, they're wrong! A fluorine torch will cut through any armor, even sintered veralloy. And this armor isn't sintered. It's plain plate!"

"Bandits don't have fluorine torches," said Jehu, producing a pump-action shotgun. "And if they come too close Chuck Yackle says I can tingle them with this. He thinks I'm loaded with sparrow-hail." From his grin I gathered he was probably loaded with buckshot.

"Maybe I could bounce a round or two off that truck's cab?" suggested Sam hopefully.

"No shooting!" said Jehu in a loud voice. Then, more softly, he added, "Not unless we has to."

I peered through the periscope. A group of shadowy figures were crouching behind the cover of the truck. A bullhorn roared, "Open up and get out! All of you!"

"Don't answer them!" snapped Barbara, as if she were now in charge. She produced a high-velocity .22 from under her seat. This crew had been expecting trouble. That's why they had asked me along. But they hadn't made it clear how much trouble they expected.

"Open up or we'll spray you with gasoline and burn you out!" roared the bullhorn.

"Let 'em try!" murmured Barbara. "This thing's guaranteed safe against a brew-up. With luck they'll set fire to themselves. Midge, anything on the radio?"

"Kitty's sent somebody to fetch Chairman Yackle. I can't raise the cops."

"With the Sergeant off in Augusta those blues won't answer," said Sam.

There was silence outside. I swung the periscope, trying to see what our hijackers were doing.

"Chuck Yackle's on the blower," said Midge, and the next moment the voice of the Chairman came from the loudspeaker.

"Jehu, are you there?"

"That is just where I am, Chuck. Blocked in at the fifteen-kilometer post. Down in the cutting. Truck ahead. Bulldozer astern. Can't move more'n five meters either way."

"And you can't take to the woods?"

"Not unless you ship us a pair of wings!"

"You've called the police?"

"We're still calling. And they're still not answering. The Sergeant's in Augusta, and we ain't got no other friends among the azuls."

Silence, as Yackle digested all this. Then he asked, "What do the people who've stopped you want?"

"Dunno. They've just been yellin' at us to come out."

"Don't do that!" Yackle's rising tone reflected his rising alarm.

"Like you say, Chuck—we won't! You sending a posse to rescue us?"

"Well—I will if have to. But we don't want a confrontation."

"What the hell does he think we've got now?" muttered Barbara.

"The fleet's out so there aren't enough men with guns for a posse," murmured Sam.

"Not enough men with guts!" snapped Barbara, easing the spring on her .22.

"Any suggestions for us, while you're getting a posse together?" asked Jehu.

"Try to come to some arrangement. Offer them half the gold to let you pass."

Jehu choked. "Offer these bastards half our earnings?"

"All of it, if you have to. Better to lose gold than to lose life. Who's with you?"

"Barbara Bernard—she's driving."

"That young hothead! Don't let her do anything rash! Who else?"

"Sam Summers."

"He's as thoughtless as the Bernard girl!"

"And Midge—she's working the radio."

"Jehu—you went up into Standish with only three juniors?"

"Mister Gavin's here. I asked him to come along."

"Gavin? Don't let him start trouble."

"Chuck—the trouble's already started. And we didn't start it. We're sitting here in a cutting, can't move either way, and bandits all around us."

"Stay in the truck. I'm calling a meeting of Council."

"Call the State Troopers too. They might come."

"We don't want to involve the State Police if we can help it, Jehu. You know that. Remember—you're quite safe if you stay in the truck."

"If you say so, Brother Yackle. Is Enoch there?"

"He's fishing off Gull Rock. I don't want to radio him yet. He'll only worry about his daughter. Jehu, just stay calm."

"We're calm. Not so sure about you! Over and out." Jehu put down the microphone and spoke through the hatch. "You heard! We can't expect no help for hours. Not until Enoch gets in anyway."

"We may not have hours," I said.

"How do you mean?"

"Three men just slipped out of the ditch and they're underneath us now. No good trying to run over 'em, Barbara!" I said, as she reached to start the motor. "They'll be well clear of the wheels and you've got no room to swing."

"What are they doing under the Brinks?" asked Sam.

"My guess is that they're about to cut up through the floor with a fluorine torch."

Jehu stiffened and cursed. "Fluorine torch? And they said the bandits didn't have such things! No way we can get at 'em down there. Not from here!" He started for the door, shotgun in hand.

"Hold it, Jehu!" I shouted. "They'll zap you as soon as you poke your head outside!"

He turned to glare at me, saw the truth in my warning, and sat down on the floor. Then he looked at me. "Mister Gavin, you're a fighting man. I knowed you were when I asked you to come along. What should we do?"

"Try offering them the gold," I suggested.

"It's not just the gold they're after," said Barbara in a low voice, and in it I heard a trace of fear. "It's Midge and me they'll want as well!"

The situation was a microcosm of the eternal charade. Civilians get themselves into desperate situations by not listening to the military. Then shuck their responsibilities onto the soldiers and demand the soldiers get them out of it. And the hell of it is that the soldiers are never in a position to refuse the civilians' request.

And, of course, the obverse is true. Soldiers get themselves into the shit, and then shout for civilians to pull them out. We are all members, one of another. Et cetera, et cetera. I attempted to think like neither a soldier nor a civilian, but like an intelligent gunman trying to save his own neck and, hopefully, the necks of those with him.

"They've got a torch going," said Midge quietly. "I can feel a hot spot on the deck."

"Relax, Midge," I said to reassure her, although she seemed the calmest of the lot of us. "Keep calling the cops.

It'll take 'em half an hour to get through." If they knew how to use the fluoride they could be into us in ten minutes. I could only hope they were not experts. "We've got to flush 'em out from under." I studied as much as I could see of our surroundings through the periscope and view-slits. "Sam, do you remember if there's underbrush along the crest of that bank?"

"Thick bushes all the way."

"Then here's what we do. I'll go out the side door and into the ditch. They'll see me and start shooting. I'll move along the ditch, and zap those three underneath us. While they're trying to nail me, you go up that bank. It's almost dark, and they'll be too shaken by a Believer shooting back to notice you. You hunt deer, so you know how to move quietly at night, don't you Sam?"

"Sure do, Mister Gavin!"

"When you reach cover at the top of the bank, hide there. And pick your targets."

"Then I start shooting?"

"God, no! Keep hidden but ready to shoot. I'll be crawling along the ditch, letting go the odd round to hold their interest. When I'm in position to make a dash for that truck I'll call you on the com. Then I'll wait for your shot—you'll be giving me covering fire."

"Got it, Mister Gavin!" He repeated his orders, almost like a trained Trooper. The boy had potential.

I called back through the hatch to Jehu. "Hear that? When I make my run you open up too. That buckshot spreads, so aim at anything except me. Midge—you stay on the radio."

"Gav—don't! You'll get killed!" Barbara's hand was on my arm.

She had never before called me anything but "Mister Gavin." She had never spoken to me with such agonized concern. And never before had I seen her gray eyes glisten.

"I'll be okay, Barb!" I squeezed her hand. "This is my specialty." I suddenly realized how much I cared for these four people. Whatever happened to me I must get them out of this mess alive. Barbara must never be taken by the pack around us. I kissed her. "Start the motor! When I get that truck rolling, you roll right behind. I'll drive for a couple of clicks, then ditch it to let you pass. And you keep going. Don't stop for Sam or me!"

"I'm not going to leave—"

"You'll do as you're damn well told! We can look after ourselves, can't we Sam?"

"Sure can! Barb—do like Mister Gavin says. If those cabron come into the woods, maybe I'll get myself a brace of 'em!" His laugh was too much like mine had once been. But, hell, I hadn't any choice! If they got into the Brinks we'd be dead and they'd have both the gold and the girls.

"I'll wait for you at the twelfth post," said Barbara stubbornly.

There was no time to argue with her. I made sure everybody understood what we were about to try without letting them realize how desperate it was. Then I put my hand on the door-lock. "I can guarantee to make it far enough to zap those bastards with the torch. If I don't get any farther, then sit it out. Sam, don't hang around trying to be a hero. Hot-tail it through the woods and shame the Council into sending up a posse. You try doing the same on the radio, Midge!"

"But Mister Gavin—"

I eased the door open, slipped into the shadows outside, and rolled into the ditch. Somebody shouted. I pulled myself back to the edge of the road, saw a face in the glow of the flourine torch underneath the truck, and fired at it once. The torch dropped, the jet touched somebody who screamed. I fired twice more at writhing shadows and the screaming stopped. I glimpsed a flicker sliding up the bank toward the bushes. These kids knew how to hunt deer. If I lived, I'd teach them how to hunt men.

Jehu's shotgun roared through the slit at the rear of the Brinks. Buckshot bounced off the road and the truck. Somebody yelled from behind it. Then the bandits, or whoever they were, recovered from their shock and began shooting at the place where I had been. I fired from farther along the ditch, dropped a silhouette running across the road, and moved again. Fire and movement! Give Sam time to get into position. I faced a dash across ten meters of open ground to reach the truck. You never hear the shot that zaps you! And when I reached the cab there might be a gun to meet me, or no starter key, or the motor wouldn't fire. I was shivering with fear when I lifted my com to my mouth and said, "Start shooting, Sam!"

He hit his target with his first round. Good hunting, boy! Somebody was writhing on the road. Another shot, and a figure lurched out from behind the truck. An instant later somebody tossed a thermite grenade. These people weren't as good as they thought they were! Never been under fire before, I'll bet. The thermite blazed. Eyes covered I raced for the cab. There was a man in it, but he was still blinded by the thermite. I jerked him from the driver's seat and shot him as he sprawled at the roadside. The motor was running.

I rammed the shift ahead, blew off the face of a man tugging at the far door, felt the cab tilt as one wheel started to slide into the ditch, then leveled as I fought the truck around to head down the road. I switched on the headlights.

More light flooded round me as Barbara switched on hers. There were men in the rear of the truck; illuminated for Sam. He was picking them off, his rounds thudding into the back of the cab but well clear of me. Men were shouting and screaming. In the rear-view mirror I saw others rolling on the road, trying to avoid the pounding wheels of the Brinks. Then we were out of the cutting and among the good clean woods. Pointless bullets whistling past the truck from the goons left behind.

Round the next bend. Fourteenth post. Thirteenth post. I pulled over and waved Barbara past. She didn't pause. Good girl! I watched her tail-lights disappear as the Brinks went hammering away toward safety. Then I slewed the truck across the road, dropped the nose into the ditch, and faded into the darkness under the trees, waiting for my prey.

An automobile came hurtling round the bend, swerved, and skidded to a halt when its headlights picked up the truck. Men were jumping out of the car. Fools! They hadn't the sense to know they were in my sights.

A rifle cracked from the far side of the road. Shouts and confusion. The auto reversed madly away. Sam had cheated me of my kill. I lowered my Luger, wiped my forehead, and tried to quench my anger. I waited for him to cross the road.

He was behind me! I swung around. Automatic reaction, Luger coming up. But he had moved already. "It's only me—Sam!" His hand had touched my arm before I knew he was there. "Follow me, Mister Gavin. I know how we can cut through the woods across this bend."

I went with him through the darkness among the trees and we nearly got shot by Midge who had thought we were bandits. When she recognized us she dropped her gun and started hugging me. I passed her on to Sam and went to Barbara, sitting silent behind the wheel.

I kissed her, and she let me, but other thoughts were already filling her mind. "All aboard—let's get the hell out of here! I'm set to shake the shit out of Council."

Barbara was herself again.

XV

I had not expected that we would be hailed as heroes, but neither had I thought that we would be criticized as hotheads who had endangered the security of the Settlement. Yackle didn't put it in so many words, but that was what I sensed in his expression and comments when we reported what had happened to the Council that evening. Several Councillors seemed to feel that it was our fault we had been bushwacked. They disapproved of the fact that we had left several of our attackers dead while none of us had even been wounded. I began to experience the fury of a woman who reports she's been raped and then finds herself the target of criticism for putting herself into a situation where she could be.

"I told you to offer them the gold, Jehu," said Yackle fretfully. "You should have thrown it out of the truck. Then they'd have let you proceed without any shooting."

"Damnation!" I burst out before Jehu could answer. "Those bastards were after the girls too! If you wanted us to toss out Barbara and Midge, why didn't you say so?"

Yackle opened his mouth, hesitated, then shut it again. Some oldster farther down the table muttered that two young girls should never have been allowed to visit Standish. Not only was that exposing them to temptation, they themselves were a temptation to the outsiders.

"I took Barbara because she handles the Brinks better'n any driver we've got," said Jehu. "And she proved it today!"

"And I wanted Midge because she's our best operator," said Barbara, who had been listening without expression to the debate. "Anyway, this won't happen again. Because none of us are going to take a truck up to Standish again!"

Again Yackle started to speak, then he shrugged. "What's

done is done! Now we're likely to have the State Police coming down here to investigate."

"They didn't come when we called on them for help. So what makes you think they'll come and tell us why they didn't?" asked Midge. The juniors were starting to speak up.

"It's my belief that the cops are in cahoots with that gang who jumped us," remarked Jehu. "Maybe it was the police themselves—"

"None of this talk's giving us a course to steer." Enoch puffed on his pipe and studied his fellow Councillors. "Ain't the time come when we'll have to start changing our attitudes? Haven't we got to decide what to do if trouble comes to us?"

There were murmurs of assent and dissent all along the council table. "What do you mean exactly, Enoch?" asked Yackle, putting his elbows on the table and his fingertips together.

"I mean we've got to make some plan to defend ourselves if them there townies gets it into their heads to come and burn us out. That is, if we want to stay on in the Cove."

"Of course we want to stay!" snapped Amanda from beside Yackle. "This is our home."

"Then we'd better get ready to keep them wolves from our doors."

"You're suggesting we build defenses?"

"Defenses won't do us no good. Not unless we plan to shoot from behind 'em!"

From the silence which followed his remark, Enoch might have voiced some obscene suggestion. Yackle pressed his fingertips so tightly together that they went white. Then he said, "Brother Enoch, the Light led us to this remote haven at a time when the world was full of war. We came here to avoid the killings and other horrors that go with war. For over twenty years we have lived righteous and peaceful lives. They never came to take our young men and women away to fight against other young men and women. Are you suggesting that we now arm ourselves to fight against our nearest neighbors?"

"That's about it, Chuck. Unless we want to see 'em come and take those young women of ours off to divide up among themselves. Like the radio tells us they've been doin' to other Settlements. Settlements right here in America!"

Yackle put his face in his hands. Amanda asked, "What have we got to fight with?"

"We all carry rifles in our boats," said Enoch. "And ever

since that killer whale attacked Martha's most of us have had a few sticks of dynamite along. I know I have." He looked around the table and met either nods of assent or eyes that avoided his.

Yackle took his hands away from his face. "We are all weary from today's events, and the subject is too important to debate while we are tired. We will discuss it at length tomorrow. But before we break up I would like to suggest a vote of thanks to Mister Gavin. For better or worse, he risked his life today to save four of our own from the sword of the despoiler."

There was a general mutter of assent and, to my surprise, even the disapproving oldster joined in. I said, "It's young Sam over there who was the real hero today."

Yackle smiled sadly. "When we first came to Sutton Cove we hoped that the only heroes we would have would be those who face the anger of the sea. Now, alas, it seems as if they may have to face the anger of our enemies." He stood up and began the invocation of the Light which closed the meeting.

When the prayer was over I started toward the door with the rest of the crowd who had been listening to the debate. Yackle called me back. "Mister Gavin, may I have a private word with you?"

"They don't want heroics around here," I muttered to Judith. "Today I pretended to be a hero, so now they're going to blackball me!" I went back to the council table expecting to be told I was being thrown out because I was an unhealthy example for their young.

Yackle waited until the room was empty, then said in a low voice, "Our gratitude was genuine. I know what your opinion of me is, Mister Gavin. I can only say that the path of diplomacy must be followed in the hope that it will avoid the abyss. But once one knows that the abyss lies ahead and there is no detour, then I must persuade others like myself to stand aside and let those more skilled in the arts of—of—" For once Yackle seemed at a loss for the right word.

"The art of killing?" I suggested. "You could learn that art quickly enough, I'm afraid, Chairman Yackle. And you're going to have to learn it. You've been the shepherd of this flock for a long time, and you've been a good one, though too optimistic perhaps. But, like Enoch said, the wolves are howling around and the shepherd must go for his gun."

He looked up at me. "I have been a dove since my boyhood. Now you are suggesting I metamorphose into an eagle?"

"Just trust in the Lord. He will show you how to preserve your people." I could not refrain from capping my advice with a quotation of Gramps: *"Blessed be the Lord my strength, who giveth my hand to war and my fingers to fight."* I left him staring at me and went to join Judith outside on the steps.

As we walked back through the village toward our cottage I said, "Now the truth's out! They know I'm a killer by profession."

Judith had been restraining her curiosity until I spoke. Now she asked, "What did Chuck want? If he sends you away—I'll be coming with you."

"Send me away?" I laughed although I found little humor in the situation. "That's the last thing on his mind. He wants me to tell him how to keep the ungodly out of Sutton Cove. He didn't say so in as many words, but that's what he's after. Chuck's like a lot of decent men. Hates having to ask for help from a killer, but knows he'll have to. I tried to encourage him to do his own dirty work."

"You think that defending ourselves is dirty work?"

"Of course not, Judy. But I wish people wouldn't talk about having to fight as though it was all dirty. Damnation, you're a surgeon! You cut into living flesh. Do people treat you as if you were a butcher?"

We had climbed the path to the door of our cottage and I stopped to look back at the cove below, at the soft yellow lights reflected in the calm waters of the harbor, at the fishing boats moving easily at their buoys. Despite myself, I liked this place and admired the people in it. But defend it? That was impossible!

Judith took my arm and led me inside. "The first thing you need is supper. Sit down at the table, prepared to eat." She disappeared into the kitchen and returned with a bowl of fish stew. Its scent drove depression from my mind, at least for as long as I was still hungry.

She finished her stew quickly, then watched me as I finished mine. She had that surgical look in her green eyes. I was in no mood to be dissected, but I had no escape. "Go ahead! Ask!" I pushed my empty plate away from me.

"You don't think we've much chance of holding Sutton Cove if we're attacked, do you?"

I shrugged. "Believers are non-fighters. Pacifists, almost by definition. The kids seem to see what we're in for. So do some of the oldsters. Enoch, Jehu, Amanda, for instance. Even Yackle. In fact Yackle sees better than anybody else here—including me. But the rest—" I threw up my hands.

"Gavin, why did you become a soldier?"

A question for which I was completely unprepared and answered with a joke. "Like they used to say: Join the army and see the world. Join the air force and see the next!"

She persisted. "I'm serious. Why did you?"

"Because I wanted to. That's the only answer I can give. I used to be ashamed to give it. Like admitting to want kinky sex—though God knows there's not much left that's still considered kinky." I fiddled with my desert spoon. "I used to give myself all sorts of excuses for my unnatural desire—to become a fighting man."

"And you don't give excuses anymore?"

"Not since I realized that I was born that way. And that I wasn't abnormal. Just archaic! And that there was still a market for guys like me."

"Gav—if there were more guys like you this world would be a better place." She was still studying me as if looking for a site to start an incision. "And you're not really a fighting man. Or is that the same as being a soldier?"

I laughed. "Not quite! Soldiering's an old trade. As old as man. For the last hundred years it's been out of fashion—at least in the Affluence. Out of fashion—in an age that's been spending more money on weapons than any age has ever spent. Real money, percentage of GNP, I mean. That's the paradox! Except for a few throwbacks like me, no sane individual, no sane government, wanted to fight. So they built weapon systems that will annihilate everybody if anybody starts! Which was the craziest thinking. Because, sooner or later, somebody would have started. Maybe Impermease is a blessing in disguise. At least people will die off naturally. Fighting's natural too. Bloody but natural—like childbirth."

"It's natural for men to fight like animals?"

"The trouble is that men don't fight like animals. They fight like men. And women too, these days!" I shrugged. "If your Teacher's only half right, there's going to be a lot of natural selection for animal traits in the next few years."

She persisted. "You mean that those humans with the greatest lust for blood will be the ones who'll survive to breed?"

"No!" I stood up. Then I sat down. "Natural selection

doesn't work like that. And you know it! Also, blood-lust, whatever that is, has nothing to do with it. Some men who like fighting are bloody-minded murderers. Some are meek slobs who turn sick at the sight of blood when away from the action. It's not some kind of an addiction—it's not like being hooked on alcohol or drugs or sex. If you can't have it, you can go without it. I never wanted to fight anybody in the Pen. I never missed not having a drink in the Pen. But I enjoy a bourbon when it's available, and so I go to places where it is available when opportunity offers. Because when it's available, then I want it." I stood up again. "Soldiers aren't psychopaths—"

"Sit down, Gav! I know they aren't. And there's apple pie for dessert. I baked it while you were fighting off those bandits. It kept my hands and mind busy while I was wondering if I'd ever see you alive again!" She disappeared into the kitchen and returned with the pie in her hands. She put it on the table and again her eyes began to probe me. "So you think fighting's inborn? Are there enough of us with the talent to defend this place?"

I gave her stare for stare. "There's you—for one!"

"Me?" She bent to help out the pie, then said quietly, "I suppose I would fight if I have to."

"If the Settlement stays in the Cove, then you will have to. And you'll find you won't need blood-lust or anything else so degrading. Just talent. And you've got the talent, if anybody here has. I've seen you in action. You may not have the instinct to kill—but, by God, you've got the drive to fight and the brains to win!"

She looked uncomfortable, as though I were praising her for a skill of which she was ashamed. She handed me my plate and pushed the cream pitcher toward me. "Eat your pie. I was crying while I baked it. That's how tough I am!"

"Homer's heroes and Elizabethan sea captains wept buckets. All over the place and at any excuse. So you can't cop out because you sob as you shoot. Of course, you won't. Not when you're having to aim." I started on the pie. "God, but this is good!"

We finished our dessert in silence and I began to clear the table. She followed me into the kitchen. "Gavin, if there were more of us talented people, could we defend the Settlement?"

"No! Sutton's indefensible against anything more than a mob. But enough to defend the Settlement if it were some place it could be defended." I went and threw a couple of logs on the fire. "Fairhaven for instance."

"I don't think the Council will move."

"If they don't—I will! Judy, you've seen the kind of signals we're getting from other Settlements. Federal Marshals arriving to arrest 'suspects.' 'Rescue teams' coming to rescue children. 'Deprogramming experts' to deprogram Believers. I'm not going to hang around waiting to be picked up and shipped to some 'rehab center'—that's what they're calling the concentration camps. That's where the Administration is mind-wiping Believers and distributing children, especially girls, for adoption by the Administration's friends. As soon as the Feds come—I go!"

"You'd leave me?"

"I don't want to. But if you won't come with me I'll not wait to watch you arrested, mind-wiped, and bound over to the custody of some damned Executive."

"Gavin—I can't leave. I have to stay! These are my people."

"From what I hear they'll need a doctor in those 'rehab centers.' The methods they're using seem pretty rough. If you'll be in any shape to practice medicine after they've rehabilitated you!"

She bit her lip, but remained stubborn. "I have to stay with my fellow Believers."

"Then try and persuade the Council to get out of this trap. A move to Fairhaven might buy them time."

Fairhaven was the remains of a once-prosperous fishing village farther north up the Bay. It was still a safe small-boat anchorage but within a year of the *Joseph Kinross* meeting the *Jenny Wren* it had become a wilderness of collapsing wooden houses and now, some forty years later, the only sign to show that people had once lived there was the remains of a stone wharf. The forest, unchecked, had invaded the village from three sides; a forest still reputed to be filled with unexploded shells. The Navy had used it as a target for off-shore bombardment, and the inshore approach was dangerous. Fairhaven was isolated enough for the most devout Believer.

Enoch took Judith and me to look at the place. Boats from the Cove sometimes used it as a shelter from bad weather when fishing up the Bay, but ashore there was only desolation. The forest had grown right down to the rocky beach. At least there wasn't space to land a gun-ship. It was a refuge, but what a refuge! Both the near and the distant future of the Settlement depressed me. It would be a case of just surviving. They would have to revert to wood and canvas, muscle power and homespun. Living off the fish they caught and the deer they shot—while they still had ammunition for their rifles. And if they were left alone.

Most governments had started cautious campaigns trying to persuade their citizens to cut down on their use of Impermease, but cancerphobia was as endemic as ever, farmers weren't going to give up their cheapest, safest, and most effective insecticide without a very good reason, and women took no more notice of vague warnings about possible side effects from using the "liberator" than they had of Papal warnings of probable punishments in the life to come.

No government had yet had the guts to publish the real reason for caution. That the panaceas they had all been pushing for over twenty years were a sterilizing agent with a twenty-year delay. And even less did they dare to tell their people that the time for caution was past. That the damage was already done. I suspect that Impermease was bringing the governments of the world closer together than had anything else in human history. Even obtuse politicians who had seen the true statistics could see the common disaster ahead. And have the self-preserving reflex of hiding the true statistics as long as possible, while they planned for their personal futures.

Through the summer one could almost sense the percolating down of the dread information through the layers of government by the changing reactions of public servants toward the Settlements. The police, once helpful, had become so hostile that radio reports from other Settlements told us how they were starting to set up their own armed patrols. Both State and Federal Goverments were shrugging off Settlement charges of discrimination, and those Believers still holding positions in various bureaucracies kept warning us to avoid attracting attention to ourselves.

Outsiders were beginning to skulk along the road to Sutton Cove. News from other Settlements spoke of vigilante groups forming in the cities and of bands of goons ranging the countryside. The authorities were accusing Settlements of harboring such bands; another excuse for liquidating them. As yet the declining population of young people was having no real effect on the operation of vital industries and systems. But a whole generation of teachers were losing their jobs as classrooms progressively emptied, and they added to the general atmosphere of resentful anger.

The spreading social disintegration was the result of desperation and despair from people who could now see the darkness ahead. Settlements were only one of the targets for popular anger. Most minority groups everywhere were being assaulted. Racism and sexism were returning in their worst forms. But those Settlements within reach of the cities were special targets. They were definable, localized minorities who had acted like moral elites for years. And they had something the majority of outsiders wanted.

Governments used Settlements to divert popular anger from themselves. And the destruction of vulnerable Settlements made useful examples of what happens to "troublemakers, revolutionary groups, un-American activists, fascists, and plain traitors."

XVI

"There's Jona's Point," said Barbara. "Away on the port bow." She stood at the wheel of *Sea Eagle,* handling her Cape Islander with the skill and confidence of a veteran fisherman. "Anything on the fuzzmeter?"

"Nothing," I said. "Not even the old radiobeacons. All bands silent."

"Is it safe to go any closer?" Judith picked up the binoculars and studied the smudge on the horizon.

"It's safe enough. I've run to within five clicks of the Point and nothing happened. According to those people in Clarport nobody stays there overnight now."

"Captain Rideout didn't say that!" I objected. "He just said that the warehouses at Clarport are filled with containers waiting to go aboard the *John Howard.*"

Barbara shrugged and didn't answer. Judith continued to study Jona's Point through the binoculars. I moved to the rear of the wheelhouse, moodily wondering why I had come on this expedition with these two females. They had decided to take a look at the Pen after the Skipper of *Ranula* had told them that it was being used as a supply dump. I had been less than enthusiastic about seeing our old home, but Judith had insisted I join Barbara and herself in a voyage up the Bay. It was probably part of some wild plan to save the Settlement.

If it was I wasn't privy to it, nor to any of the other schemes the Council was debating. I had given them my opinion; that the Cove was indenfensible against any organized attack. Their only rational course was to evacuate to some remote place like Fairhaven while they could.

But rationality was not the Council's forte when religion was involved, and some members were arguing that this was another of those rigorous tests the Light inflicted on Believers. I had told Judith plainly that, when the time came, we must get out before the Settlement went under. She had insisted she would stay to the end. I hadn't argued further. When I went, she'd go with me, unconscious if necessary. My wife wasn't going to be grabbed by the Feds.

The fuzzmeter beeped and I looked at the radar display. "Something's leaving the Point."

"That'll be the *Howard*. She's finished unloading and is heading back to Clarport." Barbara glanced at the bulkhead clock. "And she's on time."

"You knew she'd be leaving the Pen this afternoon?"

"Sure. Unless there was fog or bad weather. We've all watched her heading north on Tuesdays and south on Thursdays."

"You didn't warn us we might meet the *Howard!*" I protested.

"I'll stand offshore while she passes." Barbara spun the wheel. "Her skipper's used to seeing us fishing around here."

I watched the blip on the radar screen, then studied the supply ship through binoculars. There was no minicopter on her poop now. Her siren gave a short blast and we acknowledged with a blast from our own. The old maritime acts of courtesy still functioned when all other civilized gestures were disappearing.

"She's making thirty knots," remarked Barbara, as we watched her race by. "She'll reach Clarport in six hours. *Ranula* takes over twenty to get there from the Cove. Why didn't those shortsighted oldsters on Council spend more and buy us a decent ship? We've got the capital."

"The *Ranula*'s old, but she's basic. You'll be able to keep her seaworthy for another hundred years—if you have the chance."

Barbara ignored me. Our relationship, which should have been improved by our moments of tenderness and terror in the Brinks, had actually worsened. She altered course again to head directly for Jona's Point.

The Pen rose out of the summer haze. "Barb," said Judith, with a trace of alarm. "The seas around the Point used to be deadly!"

"They're safe enough now. The *Howard* docks there every week. And she doesn't carry any special mine-detection gear."

"How do you know that?" I demanded.

"Midge spent a night with her Skipper. While she was working in the hash house at Clarport."

"Midge—working in Clarport?" I stared at her.

"She took a job as a waitress and slept around among the truck drivers bringing loads to Clarport for shipping to the Pen. The oldsters—most of 'em, not Dad—thought they could ignore what was happening outside." She glanced at me as though I was one of them. "We knew we couldn't! We needed information. And you have to pay for information."

"How the hell could Midge get away from the Cove for a week?"

"Fishing for hake," said Barbara, her eyes on the compass, a slight smile on her lips. "We're always away for up to a week when we're after hake. Every fisherman knows that!"

To be called ignorant of fishing was an insult in the Cove. I wasn't a fisherman, but the gibe stung. "I suppose the 'we' are your gang of arrogant young brats?"

"Cool it! Both of you!" snapped Judith. "You're behaving like spoiled children! Barbara, you shouldn't have told Gavin about Midge! If he tells her father—"

"I'm no stoolie!" I snarled. "Midge's secret is safe with me. And Barbara's too—if she's been making similar purchases!"

Barbara went scarlet, the first time I had ever seen her blush, and I deduced she had.

"Gavin—you can be a real bastard!" said Judith.

"She started it!" I protested. "Oh hell! Did we come all this way just to fight! What are we here for anyway?"

"Keep looking ahead," said Judith wearily.

I seized the binoculars and glared through them at the Pen. It was taking shape as we closed on the Point; the menacing silhouette I had last seen during our escape. I forgot my anger as I began to identify the changes. Through binoculars I could see the effects of weather and lack of care. The Yagis and the parabolic reflectors high on the antenna tower were askew from loose clamps and the winds of two winters. They drooped like weary arms or stared at empty seas. Not a single radio channel among them could be operational.

"Have you ever been to San Francisco?" asked Barbara, in a tone that suggested truce.

"Yes. Ten years ago. Why?"

"I went there once with my grandmother and my sister. There's an island in the harbor with a museum. Used to be a prison. Place called Alcatraz. Heard of it?"

"Sure—closed down back in the sixties."

"It was abandoned. In the seventies a group of Amerinds walked in and took it over. Some political row. The cops had a job getting them out."

"I didn't know that." I paused. "Barbara, have you got some crazy idea about grabbing the Pen?"

"It may be crazy. But not as crazy as staying where we are until we're stomped. I've heard you trying to warn Council that the Cove is a trap if things get tough. You suggested Fairhaven to them." She shrugged. "None of us fancy a future in Fairhaven!"

"It's isolated enough not to attract attention."

"The object of our lives isn't going to be avoiding attention! We—I mean my friends—can read the future as well as you can, Mister Gavin. And we don't plan on waiting around to be grabbed as living loot when outsiders move into the Cove. I hear you don't intend to wait around for that either! Sure, we've thought about the Pen as a possible hideout."

Judith said quietly, "It wouldn't do any harm to scout the place."

I looked at the two. "That's what you both had in mind when you suggested this trip up the Bay, wasn't it? You know what Council would say—"

"Shuck the Council!"

"Okay—if you're willing to risk a row! Ease in slowly so we can see if there's a guard on the place."

"There isn't any guard. The dockers who unload the containers go out with the *Howard* and come back in her."

"So Midge says! I don't trust bedroom information! Stay offshore until dusk. Then we can take a closer look—if you still want to."

"Mister Gavin—this is my boat!"

"Miss Barbara, it surely is. But it's my neck you're risking!"

"You'd rather chance grounding after dark than being seen by people who aren't there?" demanded Barbara, the wrath of a Skipper overridden aboard her own boat adding to her normal resentment of me as a person.

"Barbara, I have complete confidence in your seamanship! We know the channel's clear right up to the dock because the *Howard*'s been going alongside for years. And I know your radar and depthfinders are accurate because I calibrated them myself."

"Then dusk it is, Boss!" She swung the wheel hard over, the *Eagle* heeled sharply, and I went floundering across the wheelhouse. Then she snarled at Judith, "Doc—you take over! I'll fix supper."

"I'll fix the supper!" Judith seized her chance to escape.

We lay offshore while we ate, watching a summer sunset spreading over the forests of Maine. As I mellowed Barbara slowly thawed and began to talk, showing me a new aspect of life in Sutton Settlement. The attitude of the generation who were growing up there.

They were a type almost extinct elsewhere in the Affluence. Born and brought up in a seafaring community where the strict discipline of nature outweighed the prejudices of parents and the whims of pedagogues. Educated by an ocean on which they either learned to do the right thing the right way or they drowned, Barbara and her fellows had come from the same mold as had those earlier Americans who had spread out to conquer a continent.

Superficially the generation gap seemed narrower in Sutton Cove than in any place I'd known. But I was discovering that many things in the Settlement were not as they seemed. What the youngsters did share with the midders and oldsters was an ability to avoid confrontations while still achieving their ends—a convoluted approach to decision making. The final outcome of a discussion was often the one to which most people had seemed initially opposed.

Their parents, the founders of the Settlement, were neither unintelligent nor uneducated, but they lived in a world governed by their faith and worked too hard to worry about problems which were neither practical nor spiritual. They had rejected the Affluent Society twenty years before, and most of them were still uninterested in what was happening in it.

The youngsters were educated in the basics, in the peculiar theology of the Teacher, and in practical skills. The Settlement had a large library of teaching tapes covering most areas of higher education, for those who wanted it. The way of life was neither restrictive nor oppressive; the rules were fair and obviously for the general good. Most of the founders had been pacifist liberals who had never made any particular issue of sex, so one major cause of conflict between parents and children was reduced.

Anyone could leave the Settlement at any time, but those who did usually came back. Children who had grown up in a close society with the vastness of the Atlantic always before them, did not take kindly to anonymous crowds, vertical boxes, and scented deodorizers. Most Affluent occupations tasted insipid to youngsters who had fished Fundy, where their success had depended on the correctness of their decisions and the exercise of their skills.

Neither did the professions attract them. Judith had not really been a Settlement child and Barbara's mysterious elder sister was an exception, but most Sutton youngsters could not endure the prolonged adolescence a professional education demanded. In the Settlement a junior was treated as responsible from the time he or she was judged fit to handle a boat. They did not slip back into semi-literacy because the high technology of boats and gear required theoretical as well as practical knowledge. Most important, for youngsters with the idealism of youth, was knowing the real value of their work. That in a good day's fishing a boat could produce sufficient carbohydrates, fats, and proteins to feed fifty families for a week. In a world where millions were starving that was a reward few members of the Affluence enjoyed.

They tended to be prigs like their parents; something I could accept. Without a leavening of prigs people behave like herds of swine. But until that evening I had not realized their awareness of reality. If the Settlement survived long enough for juniors like Barbara to become leaders, then it could survive for centuries. Although, like most survivor communities, it might not be the easiest place in which to live.

At dusk we crept into the loom of the land. The Pen hung black above us. "No lights—so there's nobody there!" said Barbara with the smug satisfaction of a junior who has been proved right.

"There are no lights because there are no windows or doors in the outer walls," I snapped. "Inside it could be lit up like Times Square. See if you can coast up alongside the pier. It's the last of the ebb, so if there is a watchman the boat'll be hidden." The tides around the Point averaged five meters.

She put us alongside so gently that I hardly knew we had arrived. "Make fast!" I whispered, and went scrambling up the ladder to go flat on the wharf with my gun ready.

I lay listening. Only silence. A few meters away was a cluster of rectangular silhouettes, containers which had been offloaded but not yet moved into storage. The rest of the pier was dark and deserted. I went back to the ladder and hissed down, "Wharf's clear. Judy, come on up!"

Judith arrived, and then Barbara. I caught the girl's shoulder. "Not you! You stay and watch the boat."

She said nothing, but I sensed her anger. Slowly she started to lower herself back down the ladder.

I relented. "All right—come on. But keep quiet and don't use your flash!"

We slipped between the containers, heading for the main entrance. I had assumed that it would be closed and our exploration would be confined to the wharf, but Judith whispered, "I think the tunnel's open. There are containers lined up the whole length of the ramp."

Her night vision was better than mine and she was right. Dodging from container to container we found ourselves moving through the outer walls and under the inner courtyards. Then we rounded a bend and froze. There was a light ahead.

"See that! I warned you!" I hissed at Barbara.

"It's the inspection station," murmured Judith. "Stay here. I'll go take a look."

Before I could stop her she had disappeared into the shadows of the tunnel. I reached out to locate Barbara and felt a rifle. The kid had come armed! Foolishness or good sense? I didn't know, but crouching in the dark I was glad I was not the only one of us with a gun.

Judith came slipping back. "Nobody there. But there was somebody earlier on. Somebody who left gum wrappers. There may be watchmen around."

"Then we'd better get back to the boat."

"And lose this chance of seeing what's inside? We may never get another as good!"

"We can reach the boat faster than anybody who spots us," urged Barbara.

Some African tyrant had once remarked that nobody can outrun a bullet. I didn't quote him, but whispered, "No shooting! For God's sake—no shooting!"

"Then keep moving!" hissed Judith.

There is an Inuit saying to the effect that the woman walks behind the man so she can give him a push when he stops. I was being shoved by two women seized by the exploratory drive. "Okay—but one at a time. Go from cover to cover. Barbara, you guard the rear. I'll go point." And I inched forward toward the inspection station.

There was a light burning above the container platform but the glass-fronted inspection booth was dark and empty. I sent a brief flash back to signal Judith it was safe for her to move while I went on up the tunnel, passing one open gate after another, going deeper and deeper into the Pen.

An occasional light was burning—they had either brought in an auxiliary generator or the fusion reactor was still operating. Moving cautiously, I reached the main distribution hall. A single flood hung high above the vast room, now filled with containers. A place of shapes and shadows, but it seemed deserted. I signaled the women to join me and we crouched together between two containers, staring around us.

"They've been shipping stuff in here so fast they haven't had time to stow," muttered Barbara. "Chock-a-block's the term!" She studied the doors around the hall. "Where to now?"

"Gavin—do you know your way from here to the Surveillance Center?"

"I think so. Why?"

"If we can reach it, and if the gear's still operating, we can check out the whole place."

"Christ—we'd have to get into the guard ring. All the doors are coded. And we don't know the code."

"Maybe the one I used to get us out might get us back. There's no harm in trying."

No harm unless by trying we'd set off every alarm in the place. "Judy, haven't we seen enough?"

"Is this really the guy who made the break with you, Doc?" whispered Barbara.

I choked; stung by her derision and startled by the knowledge it implied.

"Quiet, brat!" snapped Judith. "Gavin, which of those doors leads to the ring?"

"That one in the corner—I think. I wasn't allowed to wander free around here, you know!"

"Let's try it!" Judith was away into the shadows, as silent as a shade.

"Relax, Mister Gavin!" Barbara squeezed my arm.

Being told to relax by a kid who had just questioned my courage made me reckless. I snapped, "Stay here!" and went after Judith. She was trying various half-remembered combinations on the lock and I was about to haul her off before she tripped an alarm when the door swung open onto a stairwell.

The next instant Barbara arrived. I held her back and stepped through the doorway. Dust lay heavy on the stairs.

Nobody had used them for a long time. "Landing by landing," I whispered. "And one by one! Yes, I can see that nobody's been here lately, but somebody might come here tonight."

The surviving lights had probably been burning ever since the Pen had been abandoned as a prison. I began to get the impression that this surveillance circle, lying between the outer quarters where the guards had lived and the central prison complex, was either unknown or of no interest to whoever was using the place now. The dust was thick everywhere, many of the lights had burned out and never been replaced, and the whole section had a musty disused smell. But there was some positive pressure ventilation so the fusion generator must still be running; no auxiliary could supply sufficient power to maintain the load of an installation this size.

We reached the top level and started down a corridor along which I had often gone under surveillance during my days as the Pen's captive tech. By now my hopes that the whole place was unoccupied were rising. The door to the Surveillance Center opened to the same code as the doors behind us, and then we were standing in front of the array of screens and controls I had serviced more than two years before.

Dusty and deserted like everywhere else. The screens were blank. The speakers were silent. Barbara stared around her. "So this is where they watched what you were up to. Quite a rig!"

"Wonder if it's still working?" Judith stepped forward and, before I could check her, had snapped on the main switch and brought a dozen screens alive.

I stopped in mid-grab. Most of the screens showed empty cells, rooms, and corridors. But five showed living people. On one screen two men and two women were sitting round a table playing cards. On another, one man and one woman were lying on a bed making love. On a third a man and a woman in combat kit were standing in an alcove on the roof, glancing intermittently into the darkness of the Bay but spending most of their time looking at each other. All, except the pair making love, were in the uniform of Federal Marshals.

"Christ!" I breathed. "The place is guarded by Feds!"

"Some guards!" said Barbara, studying the pair on the bed.

I jumped forward to bring up the wharf cameras. Only the dark shapes of the containers were visible, even when I went to infrared. Our boat was hidden by the wharf.

"She'll float up into view when the tide rises," said Barbara. "But that'll be hours yet."

"We'd better get to hell out of here!" The sight of so many Feds was making me nervous. The whole atmosphere of the Pen was making me nervous.

"No rush. The tide won't be full for another five hours." Barbara was prowling round the Surveillance Center, inspecting the gadgetry. "What are those?" She pointed to the banks of controls on the wall.

"For God's sake—don't touch! Or you'll lock every door in the place. And then we'll really be screwed." I breathed easier as she moved back to the display console. "There are trick interlocks all over!"

"That pair can't imagine they're being watched!" Judith nodded toward the couple on the bed who had started to add imagination to passion.

I switched off the monitor. After all, one of us was a young girl. "I think we've seen as much of the setup as we need to see. Let's talk about it when we're safely out on the Bay."

But when we were offshore they would not talk. Most women are talkative; even Barbara had chattered away earlier in the evening. But back on the Bay neither would talk about the Pen.

It was Barbara who finally gave a sort of explanation. "It's not that we don't trust you. It's because you're outside our group. We need your help. But please don't say anything about this until we ask you to speak up."

"Then why the hell did you drag me along?"

Judith smiled and touched my hand. "Barbara said that, besides her father, you were the only man over thirty who had both guts and brains."

"Barb!" I looked at her. "Did you really say that?"

In the moonlight I could not be sure but I had the impression she blushed again. And I was certain of her quick nod.

XVII

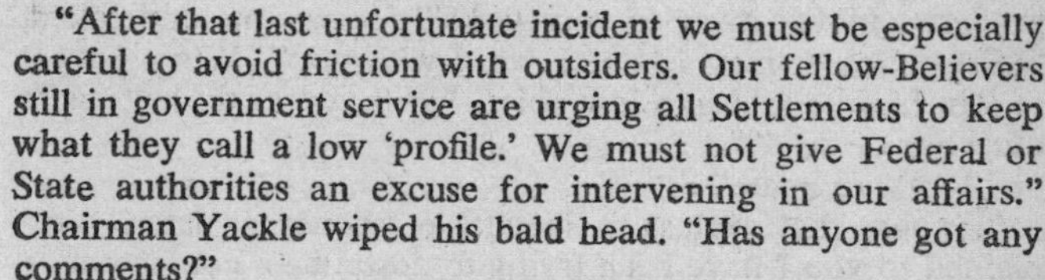

"After that last unfortunate incident we must be especially careful to avoid friction with outsiders. Our fellow-Believers still in government service are urging all Settlements to keep what they call a low 'profile.' We must not give Federal or State authorities an excuse for intervening in our affairs." Chairman Yackle wiped his bald head. "Has anyone got any comments?"

"A low profile didn't save Cellerton!" objected Martha, a large and resolute woman. Cellerton, a Settlement in Ohio, had been overrun by a mob, looted, and its people dispersed, arrested, or abducted. We had heard its last despairing signals on the radio network. Its fate had gone unmentioned in the media.

"Cellerton was sited too near Akron." Yackle was continuing to urge upon us our need for a "low profile" (military metaphors were creeping into even the Chairman's exhortations) when Kitty burst into the room. "What is it, child?"

"Joe just called from twelfth click. There's a stream of autos taking the fork toward us!"

"Who are they?" Yackle was on his feet.

"Joe says they look like a mob on wheels. Some seem drunk. They're shooting at road signs!"

"Sheriff Zimpfer—call the State Police. And have the planks removed from the bridge across the creek!" Yackle sat down. "That should delay them if they come this far. And if they're looking for trouble."

"They're probably looking for girls!" said Martha.

"We can't assume that. But in case there are rowdies among them we had better remove temptation." He stood up again. "Susan, take all the schoolchildren down to the boats. Kitty, signal the boats out fishing to return to the cove as fast as they can. Martha, have all the women with babies and preschool children put aboard *Ranula* and tell Captain Rideout to stand offshore." He looked around. "All other young women will gather on the wharf, ready to embark if these people invade the village."

"You mean—clear out and let them smash up our homes?" demanded Lucy, twenty-two and pregnant.

"Of course not! All of us with essential tasks must remain in the village. If these outsiders do come as far as the Cove we will treat them with courtesy. Use restraint. Don't tempt them into violence!"

"And if they don't need tempting?" asked Jehu.

"Then we must use the least force necessary to protect our property. Now—away to your tasks!" He saw me and called, "Mister Gavin, may I have a word with you?" When I went to join him he said in a low voice, "Will you again help us in our hour of need?"

"Any way I can."

"I know that a clash is inevitable, sooner or later. I explained to you I have been trying to postpone a confrontation between ourselves and outsiders for as long as possible. But if this mob crosses the creek and starts to break into our houses, if violence follows insults, then those of us still here must resist. Please go and offer your services to Sheriff Zimpfer. Tell him I want you made a deputy. Then you will have a legal right to help maintain law and order."

There was a hardness in Yackle's voice and expression. If he was cornered he would fight; most of the Believers would fight if cornered. But the most important aspect of any fight is to avoid being driven into a corner before it starts. I went to find Sheriff Zimpfer.

Zimpfer, a fat pleasant man, had served in the Army—as an office-equipment technician. The Council had made him Sheriff because he was the only Believer with any kind of military experience. His five Deputies were the five largest men in the Settlement and, like most large men, they were five of the most inoffensive. Three of them were out fishing, the two in the Sheriff's office when I arrived looked as though they wished they were.

Zimpfer had been trying to raise the State Police on the radio. When I came in he gave up, took off his hat, wiped his forehead, and shook my hand. "Glad to have you, Mister Gavin. From what I hear you know more about this policing business than I do!" He pinned a star on my windbreaker and gave me an ancient revolver in an open holster. "I hope you don't have to use this."

"So do I!" I glanced at my colleagues and prayed they wouldn't try to use theirs. My Luger was already strapped on under my windbreaker. "I'll take my bike up to the bridge, if that's all right with you?"

He nodded. "Mister Gavin, the kids are watching the bridge and the road. You talk to 'em. They'll listen to you. Don't let 'em start shooting. Leastwise, not unless they're directly attacked."

"I'll hold 'em back if I can," I promised and rode out of the village. I parked my bike round the bend and went scrambling up the hillside to what was, in effect, Barbara's command post.

She and Sam seemed pleased at my arrival. "Thank the Light that Yackle's had the sense to make you legal!"

"No shooting, Barbara! Not unless I say."

"We won't. And I doubt we'll be attacked." She pointed to the woods and undergrowth fringing the bank above the road and on the far side of the creek. "We're all along that ridge. And on this side too."

"Glenda's just called," said Midge, appearing out of nowhere. "Those goons are at fifth. Almost a hundred cars. Every jerk in Standish must have come hunting. And Kitty says the cops aren't answering."

"They won't. Not even Sergeant Carver'll come and face that kind of a mob."

"The bridge isn't going to stop 'em!" Only guns or gas would stop the drunken crowd coming toward us. And we hadn't got any gas. I began to assemble my Luger. If I kept the creek crossing covered, if I could pick off the leaders, if the mob lacked guts—then there was a chance—

Barbara touched my arm. "Put your hardware together if you want to, Mister Gavin. But I don't think you'll be needing it. We knew that something like this was going to happen, sooner or later. And we know what to do."

Alarmed by the cold anticipation in her voice, I asked, "What's that?"

Before she could answer there was a rumble of motors from farther up the road and the first automobile appeared round the bend. It skidded to a halt when the driver saw there was no roadway on the bridge.

The five occupants, all with rifles, tumbled out, stared at the banks and woods, saw nothing and walked to examine the bridge. Then they walked back to discuss the problem with the second group to arrive. None of them seemed worried about what might be in the woods.

"They can't have heard about our shoot-out with the Brinks," whispered Sam. "Which means that that hijack, and the killings, have been kept quiet. Guess who by?"

I was in no mood for guessing games and didn't care who'd been behind the attempt to jump us. Our present troubles were enough for now. But it was apparent from the behavior of the men and women arriving in the cars that they had no hint of any Believer reacting to violence with violence.

"They've come to loot us, and they don't expect the loot to shoot!" There was an undertone of pleasure in Barbara's voice. More and more cars were arriving. She spoke on her com. "Let 'em all come. The more the better! Hold it until they're all here!"

"For Christ's sake!" I saw her expression and had a sudden vision of the men and women crowding the creekside below us going down under a volley from the kids above them. It would be a massacre! "If you start shooting you'll kill half that mob and bring the National Guard down on us!"

She glanced at me. "And you don't want that?"

"God no! The Settlement would be wiped out."

"Perhaps." She laughed without humor. "Don't worry, Mister Gavin. We're not planning to kill anybody—not yet!"

"Then what the hell are you planning to do?"

"Discourage 'em." She again called on her com. "Is that the lot?"

"Road's clear back to the fork. Except for five autos in the ditch. Drunks!" came Joe's voice from the com.

"Any sign of the cops?"

"Not a cruiser or chopper in sight."

Below us cars and pickups were parking on the shoulders of the road. Men and a few women were getting out, most armed with rifles or shotguns, most of them still drinking. A typical old-fashioned lynch mob. I tried to identify the leaders, but if there were any they were not making themselves conspicuous.

A group detached itself from the crowd and began to ford the creek. "This is it!" hissed Barbara on her com. "Let go!"

"Let go what?" I demanded. Then I saw. Some twenty Molotov cocktails arced from the trees and bushes above the road to smash among the cars below and burst into flames.

"You little idiot!" I turned on her furiously. "You'll roast some of them with those things!"

"I doubt it." Barbara was watching the confusion below with relish. "There's only enough gasoline in each bottle to fire the parapitch. Lots of smoke. Not much flame." She licked her lips. "But those clods down there don't realize that yet!"

They obviously didn't. The sudden arrival of flaming missiles had sent the mob into a turmoil. Some were bolting for cover. Some were running back to their cars. A few were clambering up the bank to where the Molotov throwers were hiding. Acrid smoke swirled around the cars and across the creek.

The lead car tried to turn and crashed into the car behind it, which had been attempting to do the same. There were more crashes and curses from drivers trying to extricate themselves from what they assumed was a general conflagration. Cars and pickups were backing into each other, drivers were shouting at each other, several fist fights had started. Women were screaming. Men were yelling. And some were too busy coughing the smoke from the parapitch out of their lungs to do anything.

The men who had climbed the bank after the Molotov throwers were searching through the underbrush and finding nobody. In their frustration they started to shoot at shadows under the trees. Somebody fired back, and the searchers went tumbling and sliding down the bank, to add to the general confusion.

The last cars to arrive were the first to leave, backing away or trying to turn. A pickup, reversing too fast, went out of control, dropped a wheel into the ditch, and spun around, blocking the road. The next vehicle rammed it. A gang of cursing drivers from the trapped cars combined to push both vehicles down the bank and into the creek. The group who had reached the far side came splashing back, running to their cars.

"That's cooled 'em off!" said Barbara. "They won't try that again!"

"Not that they won't!" I snarled. "Next time it won't be a drunken mob looking for a good time. The next gang will come sober, armed, and shooting!"

Sheriff Zimpfer and his Deputies arrived in the Brinks as the road was starting to clear of smoke, mob, and cars. He walked to the edge of the creek with his bullhorn and roared an order to disperse in an orderly fashion. The goons still trying to recover their cars yelled threats and curses back.

Somebody from among the trees fired a burst over their heads. The goons stopped shouting, abandoned their ditched cars, and scrambled aboard those still mobile. Joe called on the com to report that the whole mob were streaming back toward Standish, some still firing wildly into the woods. "Most of their autos look battered!"

Nobody seemed to have been killed or seriously hurt. Barbara and I slid down to join Sheriff Zimpfer just as Judith arrived with Yackle on the pillion of her Yama. Both were armed with revolvers. So the Settlement did have some weapons stashed away, and Yackle was starting to issue them. They joined us to study the six wrecked and two burning automobiles on the road beyond the bridge.

"Reckon you can tell everybody to go home now, Chairman Yackle," said the Sheriff. "This lot won't be back!"

"Not today," said Judith. "But another day perhaps." She hitched up her gunbelt and stared up the road. Things were changing with Judith. Things were changing in Sutton Cove. I could only hope they were not changing too late to matter.

"A bloodless victory!" Yackle was nodding with satisfaction. "Well done, Barbara!" He gave the girl an approving pat on the shoulder. "Better than I dared hope."

So Yackle had known about Barbara's plan all the time. Perhaps it wasn't her plan at all but Chairman Yackle's. Barbara, however, seemed quite happy to take the credit for it. And from the way Judith avoided my eye I suspected she had been in on it too! Suddenly and illogically I was angry not to have been included in their planning sessions. I was supposed to be the professional around here. Me—not a bunch of kids, a pacifist Chairman, and a female surgeon!

Yackle moved to stand beside me. "Mister Gavin, you and I will have to discuss how we can best meet future threats."

"You met that one pretty well without my advice!"

"Without your advice?" He stared at me in simulated astonishment. "But the strategy was yours! We simply devised the tactics. It was the same strategy you advised Sherando to follow. When you told them to fire the cars of any mob which drove out to attack the Settlement. You said that the outsiders would rush to rescue their vehicles and forget about burning the Settlement."

"Sherando? You knew that I'd been at Sherando?"

"Recently, Mister Gavin. I only learned it recently. When Judith realized an attack upon us was inevitable and came to tell me we had one defense expert among us. Please do not be concerned about having stayed in Sherando. We know you are not a heretic!" And he walked away to start arranging the return of the women and children to their homes.

Being judged a heretic was the least of my concerns. I rode my bike back to the village, furious with Judith, with Yackle, with the whole damned lot of them.

The first hint of an official threat came from the State Police the next day when two cruisers arrived in Sutton Cove for the first time in a year. It was not a belated answer to our call for help; it was to investigate a report that we had ambushed and set fire to the cars of some harmless citizens who had approached the Settlement. The officers inspected the damaged cars, listened to Sheriff Zempfer's account of the incident, and threatened to arrest several adults for the unlawful discharge of firearms within a hundred meters of a public highway plus a number of kids as juvenile delinquents. They finally went away without arresting anybody but they left us with the impression that we would be hearing more about our offenses against law and order.

A week later Sergeant Carver arrived, alone and unofficially. The Settlement Council was about to be charged with civil disobedience under the Social Stability Act, a Federal offense which put us in the clutches of the Federal authorities. We could expect a squad of Federal Marshals to arrive and arrest the Council for trial and take off our children for "deprogramming." We could also expect that others of us, particularly the girls and young women, would be taken into "protective custody" as "material witnesses."

The Sergeant's advice was for us to get to hell out of Sutton Cove while the going was good. "Find some place where you can lie low until they've forgotten about you. It's my belief that things are going to get so bad in the next few months that the Feds will have more to do than hound peaceful folks, like yourselves." He sighed, hitched up his belt, touched his hat, and departed, after saying he'd appreciate our not mentioning his visit.

"This kid isn't going to be taken off and deprogrammed," remarked Barbara, after the sergeant had gone. But she refused to tell me how she planned to prevent it. When I asked Yackle, he shrugged. "I expect they'll take to the woods. Or go up the coast in their boats for a while. They'll come back after the Federal Marshals have left."

"The Feds may not leave until they've grabbed every girl they can get. Every young woman, for that matter. And what about you and the rest of Council?"

He smiled sadly. "I suppose we'll have to surrender to superior force if they insist on arresting us. But I cannot believe that the Federal Authorities really want to saddle themselves with a group of oldsters. I pray they will let us be when they find the children and young women are no longer here."

"Chuck—for God's sake, listen to me! You don't know the present breed of Fed like I do. Like Judith does. Ask her if you don't believe me. They're quite capable of forcing you to tell them where the women and children have gone. This is 2030, not 2010!"

"They won't be able to force us to tell them. Because we won't know."

"Christ—that's even worse! It's bad enough being interrogated when you know what they're trying to get out of you. It's pure hell when you're a loser—when you don't know but they think you do! They'll work you over in ways that went out with the Inquisition—updated for greater effect!"

"If that is the Light's wish—then so be it."

Another martyr in the making! I walked away, cursing his foolishness and wondering how many martyrs had changed their minds after they discovered what martyrdom was really like. Changed their minds too late! I went to Judith, who might have a martyr complex but also had a strong survival drive. All she would tell me was that she planned to leave with the women and children. She wouldn't tell me where. Even Judith, my wife, did not trust me. And she was right not to.

The Feds arrived on a Sunday morning when the whole adult population of the Settlement was worshipping together. Everybody except the single unbeliever—me. I had watched the kids, the women and children, disappearing into the woods the moment the radar aboard the *Ranula* had picked up the approaching choppers. A well-planned exodus that would result in tragedy for everybody still in the village. If I had had any sense I would have gone with Judith, but some obscure bond held me in the Settlement so long as Yackle waited there to be picked up. But I stayed well hidden.

The Feds came in three gunships and one large transport. The moment the squads jumped from their ships and ran to take up positions around the Council Hall I knew that was no collection of Federal Marshals; these were men from the Special Strike Force in the uniforms of Federal Marshals. They were commanded by a tall Captain, who must have been well briefed about Believer customs, for he put a cordon around the hall and sent patrols to search the empty houses and the *Ranula,* now lying deserted alongside the wharf.

When a patrol had checked my workshop I came out of hiding and slipped between the buildings until I was as close to the Captain as I dared. He evidently knew that one strict rule of life in a Settlement was that all Believers not too sick to get out of bed must attend the Sunday service. He was sure that the whole population was inside the Hall. When Chairman Yackle led his flock out of the main entrance he stepped forward and said, politely enough, "Mister Yackle? Then you are under arrest for offenses against the Social Stability Act. As are all your colleagues on Council."

"Captain! I must protest! This is both illegal and immoral. We are peaceful citizens of the United States who have never caused any trouble to our neighbors or threatened social stability in any way."

"Sorry, sir. That's not my concern. You will be given a fair trial. I also have orders to take into protective custody a number of minors and material witnesses." He looked at the crowd. "Is everybody here?"

"Everybody who is in the Settlement at present, Captain."

"Where are all the children? And the—the others?" He could not bring himself to say "girls." He didn't like this job, but he was doing it.

"Perhaps I can help you." Barbara wormed her way from the crowd, she had been hiding God knows where, and now emerged to stand facing the officer. I cursed her for showing herself, then stiffened as I heard her voice on the com. If I could hear, so could her squad. Nobody in the crowd could for she was speaking softly and Yackle had moved away to comfort his congregation.

"Where are the other youngsters?" The Captain was looking down at Barbara and now, faced with the fact that he was about to seize a number like her, take them away for a fate he was keeping out of his mind, his expression showed that he was disliking his job more and more. But he continued to perform it.

"Before I tell you, Captain, will you promise not to hit me? Not to shout at me or anything?"

"Hit you? Of course I won't hit you. You don't want the others to hear what you're going to tell me? Is that it?"

"Please sir!"

The Captain nodded and bent so she could whisper in his ear. He heard. I heard. Barbara's squad heard. Her words were clear. "You had better tell your men to stand fast. And you had better stand fast yourself."

"And why should I do that, Miss?"

"Because if you look very slowly up the hillside, toward that pile of rocks halfway up the cliff behind me, you will see a young man with a rifle. He is well camouflaged so he is not easy to pick out except by a well-trained soldier's eye—such as yours!" She moved backwards, beyond reach of the Captain's grasp, as he casually scanned the apparently bare cliff, then stiffened when he saw the hidden rifleman. "What—?"

"Still!" hissed Barbara. "Telescopic sights. Veralloy-coated bullets! They'll puncture your armor, Captain. And he won't miss." She was watching his frozen face. "The charge is high-velocity." She was still speaking so softly that nobody except myself and the Captain appreciated the threat she was making. Or her skill in holding his attention long enough to deliver the whole of it. "There are forty other marksmen hidden on both sides of the Cove. All with telescopic sights, veralloy-coated rounds, and high-velocity charges. By now each of them has identified a target. Forty marksmen with their sights on thirty Federal Marshals. All knowing the range to a meter and all behind good cover."

The Captain made an instinctive movement toward her.

She stepped back, then stood firm. "If you grab me. Or if I signal. You—and every one of your men—will be dead in the first volley."

"You wouldn't dare! You're bluffing!" But he kept his voice low, and that showed he feared she wasn't.

"I'm not bluffing. Though I'd rather like you to believe I am." Her gray eyes were fixed on his face. "Because the quickest solution to our problem would be to kill the lot of you with one salvo."

Watching the Captain's face, I could almost read his mind.

This child might have some boy fool enough to shoot at him. But to have forty marksmen hidden—that was so far outside his image of young girls—of pacifist Believers—that he was about to lunge forward, call her bluff, and start a massacre. I stepped from behind the building where I had been hiding and called, "Hold it, Captain! She's right!"

He checked his move and stared at me. I walked over to stand where I was within his hearing but outside the reach of both him and Barbara. My Luger was now strapped openly at my hip and the sight of it convinced the Captain that here was the person he really had to face. "Who are you?"

"Once a Trooper. Third Section. Under Colonel Jewett. Before your time, Captain."

"Colonel Jewett!" The name still echoed through the Force.

"The same." I moved closer and spoke as softly as had Barbara. "Every word this brat has said is true. Those oldsters are pacifists. These kids are killers. They've hunted deer through those woods all their lives. Now they're aching for a chance to hunt men. They're first-class shots and they don't plan on being taken off for reprogramming. Though most of 'em sure need it!"

Slowly he surveyed the cliffs on both sides of the Cove. Then he looked back at me. "My orders are to arrest the ringleaders of this Settlement. And to rescue the children."

"I was with the Third when General Grainer was ordered to capture Eastern Moonbase. Grainer had the guts to obey his reason rather than his orders. That's why I—and you—are still alive. Take the time to satisfy youself that each of your men is on the wrong end of a rifle. Then get them out of here alive. Let the politicos do their own dirty work. Let them do the dying for a change."

He still hesitated. He had not believed he had walked into a trap set by children. He was having trouble accepting a trap set by even a Trooper of the Third. I said to Barbara, "Tell them to hold their fire. I have something I must show the Captain." I put my hand slowly in my hip pocket, as terrified as I have ever been in my life. The rifles were up on that hillside all right, and they were aimed at us by excellent marksmen. But they were rifles in the hands of kids, and I was asking them to act like veterans.

I eased my Secret Service badge from my pocket and held it for both of them to see. "Captain," I said. "Some bastard has fooled you into dressing up in the wrong uniform. Sent you on the wrong mission at the wrong time. I'm in charge here. I don't want to have thirty Troopers shot. But I will if you don't get your men out—pronto!"

He stared at my badge, then at me. "What the hell are you people up to now?"

"That's my business. I work for the President—not for the Attorney General!"

He understood enough of that implication to think that he was caught in the middle of some political bloodbath. He stared at Barbara. "Girl—if you're helping the SS take over—you'll end by wishing it had been us."

"Captain—get your ass out of here!"

"Quiet, brat!" I snapped. "Captain, call over your Second. Let him see my badge too. So he'll know why you're aborting the mission."

He met my eyes. I was giving him an out and he took it. He gestured his Lieutenant over to stare at my badge, then shouted, "Stand down all! Mission's terminated. Sergeant—get everybody back aboard!"

The Lieutenant looked livid, the squad baffled. But, being what they were, they obeyed without question. I watched them boarding the gunships, keeping the Captain at my side. Then I walked with him to his ship. Barbara followed.

He muttered to her, "I hope you know what you're getting into!"

"We know," she said, and laughed. "You go! And I advise you to keep going before they con you into doing something that obliterates what's left of your honor! Special Strike Force dressed up as Feds!" She laughed again, with more contempt than I had heard in the laugh of any woman.

It stung the Captain into swinging around, staring at this terrible girl-child. She stared back, her gray eyes as hard as agate. "And if you're thinking of shooting us up after you're airborne—don't try it! The first ship to fire a burst will get hit by five Strelas."

"Strelas! You've got Strelas? How the hell—"

"Old models. But still fully operational. So flake off, and keep going!"

He still hesitated, then asked quietly, "How old are you?"

"A little younger than Alexander when he'd conquered half of Asia. Older than Cleopatra when she'd captured all Egypt. And older than Von Helm when he'd shot down his fiftieth enemy. Does that answer your question?"

"Hell on earth!" He turned and climbed into his ship. The

hatch slammed and the choppers took off. They circled above us, as though deciding what to do, then shot away inland.

I swung on Barbara. "You've got Strelas? Why didn't you tell me?"

"Strelas? Of course we haven't got Strelas! But if that poor bastard of a Captain reports we have—that might keep their gunships away!"

Now we had no option; we had to evacuate the Cove. We had used up our real source of strength; the belief by outsiders that we were weak and helpless. We had been able to ambush our attackers only because they had thought they were about to overrun or arrest a bunch of unarmed pacifists. Now they would over-react—especially if the Captain reported how we had jumped him and threatened him with Strelas. Personally I doubted that he would. From his expression when he left I suspected he would take Barbara's parting advice and keep going. Probably he and his squad would convert to bandits. Anything to avoid explaining to his Colonel how he had let himself be ambushed by children and bluffed by one fake SS agent.

We had to move, and we prepared to move, but the prospect of Fairhaven as our future home was so depressing that we hung on in the Cove, hoping that in the growing confusion, we would be ignored. That the Feds would leave us alone. As they did. When our next threat came it was not from the Federal Government but from the Government of Maine, which had taken upon itself to start acting like an independent state. As its Governor had taken on the role of a local Dictator, with the National Guard as his private army, "keeping the peace" throughout Maine. And for all Settlements the term keeping the peace carried overtones of "getting the girls."

Soon they would come and try to get ours and we prepared to evacuate when they did. Evidently they had heard rumors of Strelas for their aircraft kept well away from the Cove, but our scouts, watching the road into Standish, reported that truckloads of troops and tanks on transporters were moving into the town, ostensibly to restore law and order after outbreaks of rioting. But Guardsmen were filling the local bars with stories about the number of fertile women they had liberated from the other three Settlements in the State, and how they would soon be rescuing the ones we were supposed to be holding captive.

Legally we were now in revolt. Outlawed. "Wearing the wolf's head." Fair game for anyone. We knew we had a way out, but we didn't want to take it until we had to. And when we had to we found that way suddenly blocked.

XVIII

Our escape route was blocked by the arrival offshore of a Coast Guard cutter. Our relationship with the US Coast Guard had always been good; they were fellow sailors and our boats seldom got into trouble. But on that foggy September morning the sight of the white ship with her blue and red stripe lying off the Cove was an omen of trouble to come.

Enoch went out to find why the cutter was there and returned with bad news. "Lieutenant Jenson's the Skipper. All he'll say is that his orders are to stop any boats from leaving Sutton Cove."

"His orders? Whose orders?" demanded Yackle. "The Federal Government has no right to interfere with our fishing. We have an agreement with Washington—"

"He doesn't take orders from the Federal Government no more. Told me Coast Guard's reverted to local control. The States are regaining their rights—they are!" He sucked moodily on his empty pipe. "Jenson's taking his orders from the Governor of Maine. When I asked him why, he said he had to take orders from somebody!"

So Lieutenant Jenson was stamped by the same die as had marked the Captain of the Strike Force. In a collapsing civilization they were disciplined men cut adrift, looking for some authority to tell them what to do. Judith had accused me of being feudal, of seeking someone to serve. To serve perhaps—not to obey blindly!

"One cutter can't blockade us," said Jehu. "We've more'n fifty boats, most of 'em faster than that one out there. He can't stop us all—even if he tries to sink us. And I doubt he'd do nothing like that. Not Craig Jenson!"

"Craig Jenson'll do as he's told," snapped Yackle. "It's the

Ranula he'll want to stop. And board. Captain Rideout, do you think you could get past him?"

The Captain of *Ranula* tugged on his moustache and shook his head mournfully. "No way I can think of. He could come alongside as he liked, and I couldn't stop him. Not without a lot of shooting. And against his guns there wouldn't be much point to that now, would there? Not with the children aboard."

"What about at night? Could you slip past him in the dark?"

"With his radar—night's as clear as day."

"Not quite," I interrupted. "I've got a radar spoiler in the shop. I've been rigging it in *Sea Eagle*." They turned to listen and I explained, "It's a gadget that masks a radar echo by making it look like a rain storm. Useful for creeping inshore on a raid." I fidgeted, uncomfortable at having to confess I knew about such things. "Of course, it doesn't work if there's good ECM defense—"

"Good what?" asked Yackle.

"Electronic Counter Measures. Sophisticated radar. But that cutter of the Coast Guard will only have a standard rig, and the spoiler might fool it."

"It'd have to be at night, then?" said Captain Rideout. He sighed. "I guess it's worth trying." He looked out of the window. "There's a fog closin' in."

"That cutter's come here today," said Enoch. "So to my mind it looks as if those tanks of theirs are likely to be coming down the road right soon. What do you think, Chuck?"

"I think you're probably right." Yackle rested his face in his hands, then looked up. "In fact I'm sure you're right. Cutter or no cutter, we'll have to move today. Gavin, can you finish rigging that spoiler thing by this afternoon. That may be all the time we've got."

I promised to try, and went to my workshop, cursing the indecision which was endemic in the Settlement. As usual, everything had been left too late. I lugged the spoiler unit down to *Sea Eagle*, which was lying alongside, and found her with engines running, Barbara at the wheel, and Midge about to cast off.

"Where the hell are you going?" I shouted down.

"Out to try to persuade Craig Jenson to let us past."

"Some hope!" I grumbled, climbing down the ladder, clutching the spoiler. "Anyway, you'll have to belay that. Chuck told me to finish rigging this."

"You can finish it as we go out," said Barbara. Before I could argue Midge had cast off and jumped aboard.

Perhaps the girls would be able to persuade Lieutenant Jenson to disobey his orders, but I doubted it. I set to work rigging the radar spoiler while Barbara picked her way among the moored boats crowding the Cove. The fog was thickening, but the Coast Guard cutter was still clearly visible lying offshore, her white topsides glinting in the misty sunshine.

I hadn't much hope that we would ever have a chance to use the spoiler, but I worked at it because it was the only thing I could do. In Standish the armored column would be starting to form up. Astern of us the children were starting to go aboard *Ranula.* Ahead of us lay the cutter, making it certain that they wouldn't get out of the cove. How the hell did Barbara think she was going to persude this Lieutenant Jenson to let us go? Her methods of persuasion were unorthodox and inclined to be dangerous. She might have some crazy idea—

I threw down my side-cutters and went up to the wheelhouse. "Barbara, if you are going to try to ram that cutter—"

"Do you think I'm mad?" she said over her shoulder, without turning her eyes from the swell ahead.

"We're only going to talk to them," said Midge. "We're not going to do anything dangerous. But I know one of the Petty Officers—from the time I spent in Clarport—and he might do something to help."

"Pity you didn't choose to sleep with Lieutenant Jenson rather than a Petty Officer," I remarked, studying the cutter ahead.

"Mister Gavin, please get the hell out of my wheelhouse," remarked Barbara.

"It might be better if you did keep out of sight," murmured Midge. "Give us girls a chance to see if we can charm those guys."

"Do that, Mister Gavin," snapped Barbara. "Get below! Two girls in a boat is one thing. A professional gunman is another!"

I cursed and went back to rigging the spoiler while *Sea Eagle* eased her way through the slight swell. When a voice from a bullhorn aboard the cutter hailed us and told us to go back into the cove, Barbara cut the motor and let our way carry us to within a few meters of her.

"Why can't we go fishing?" she demanded. "You know us. You've never hindered us before!"

My curiosity overcame my caution. I went to the scuttle and peered through a gap in the curtains. We were almost alongside and a Lieutenant was leaning from the wing of his bridge. "Sorry, young lady. Orders."

"Whose orders? I'm Barbara Bernard. And this is Midge. We just want to fish. We're not going to break any laws."

"Sorry, Barbara." Jenson's voice showed that he was not enjoying his job any more than the Strike Force Captain had enjoyed his. But, like the Captain, he persisted in doing it. "No boats to be allowed to leave Sutton Cove today."

"Why not?" piped up Midge. "Who are those men you've got with you? What are you going to do to us?"

A group of men in combat gear were coming out onto the after deck of the cutter. Marines! A Marine landing party! In its death spasm the Affluence was befouling everything it touched.

A Sergeant stepped to the rail, leaning down, trying to reassure the young girl below him who seemed about to burst into tears. "We're not here to hurt you, Miss. We want to help you."

"You've come to take us away from our homes!" wailed Midge, starting to weep in earnest.

"No—it's not that!" The Sergeant looked around helplessly, then fished a handkerchief from his pocket. He tossed it down to Midge. "Dry your eyes and go home. There's a good kid!"

Barbara had come from the wheelhouse to stand beside Midge, and now started to weep with her. A weeping Barbara was a phenomenon which I had never seen before and could hardly have imagined. This must be a part of some elaborate scam the girls were attempting. Midge had promised they weren't going to try anything dangerous but—

"Barbara, get back to the wheel!" came a bellow from the bridge. "You men, back from the rail!" All the Marines and half the crew were ranged along the cutter's port rail, trying to reassure the sobbing girls. "Damn you! Mind my paint! Cox'n, move those men back and get fenders overside!" There was a thud as *Sea Eagle* nestled up alongside the cutter. Her skipper was a man who could worry about his paintwork while following orders which were helping to destroy a harmless community. "Barbara, you know how to handle a boat! And for God's sake, stop blubbering. Nobody's going to hurt you!"

By this time I was convinced that if anybody was going to get hurt it would be the Coast Guard. "Sorry, Skipper," sniffed Barbara, from the wheelhouse, shifting to slow astern, backing away from the cutter. Then she put the wheel hard over, swinging our bows toward Sutton Cove, but with sternway on we began to bounce along the cutter's topsides. Sailors ran to fend us off, Jenson started cursing, Marines continued trying to comfort Midge.

"Ahead! Go ahead—you silly little bitch!" Jenson yelled as we drifted, stern first, under the cutter's counter.

"Sorry!" shouted Barbara, shifting to slow ahead. And then I saw Midge stoop and pull the lever which shot out the trawl.

A thousand meters of chronon trawl line went snaking out from the ejection port low in *Sea Eagle*'s stern. So thin as to be almost invisible; strong enough to tow the cutter, it went spewing into the propwash as *Sea Eagle* moved ahead. Neither Jenson leaning from his bridge nor the sailors leaning from the rail seemed to notice it or realize that Barbara had maneuvered to drag the line across the cutter's twin screws.

There was a plop as the buoyed tail of the trawl let go, but instead of inflating and floating, the buoy sank as soon as it hit the water. Barbara went to half-ahead and waved to Jenson who, thankful that she was returning to the Cove, waved back. Midge was waving to the Sergeant who blew her a kiss. Nobody aboard the cutter had yet realized that there was a kilometer of chronon line hanging across both propellers, waiting to be wound in when the cutter's engines were next turned over.

By the time we reached the Cove the fog had thickened and the cutter was only just visible, still on station, still hove-to. "They won't do much intercepting!" said Barbara as we went alongside the wharf. "Have you got that gadget of yours fixed, Mister Gavin!"

"I have, Miss Bernard." I locked the final clamp. "One of these days I'm going to risk my life and paddle your ass!"

But before she could pick up the brawl Yackle appeared above us on the dockside. "How did it go?"

"Perfect! That cutter's out of action." Barbara did not elaborate. So Yackle had known what these two kids had planned!

"Thank the Light!" He glanced at *Ranula,* ready to cast

off, children and young mothers crowding her decks. "That armored column has left Standish. Mister Gavin—is your spoiler working?"

"Far as I can tell it is." I climbed up to join him.

"We won't need it now!" said Barbara, putting me down.

"We may! We may! Mister Gavin—leave it operating. Barbara—you will escort *Ranula* out into the Bay and wait with her offshore."

"But with tanks coming along the road—"

"Get movin', young lady!" said Enoch, looming out of the fog. "We're looking after the road. You're needed at sea."

She scowled and went hard astern, backing away from the dock. I followed Enoch up the now almost deserted village street. "Where is everybody?"

"Aboard the boats or going aboard. We was going to chance it, even if Barb's idea hadn't worked. Only chance we got. We may be able to hinder them tanks. There's no way we can stop 'em."

"Where's Judy?"

"Took her bike and went off up the road."

"What?" I grabbed him by the arm. "You let her go off? They'll grab her! Or kill her!"

"She said you was to wait above the bridge with Kitty. The Doc knows what she's doing, even if we don't."

"Christ—nobody knows what anybody's doing in this place!"

"We know we've got the kids safe aboard the boats. And we know we can put to sea." Enoch gently took my hand from his arm and started to fill his pipe. "Why don't you do like the Doc says. Go and wait above the bridge. This time there will be shooting."

I was on my bike and away while he was still speaking. I couldn't imagine what crazy reason had sent Judith to meet an advancing armored column on a motorbike, but the only thing I could think of was to go after her. I skidded around the bend short of the bridge and found the Brinks parked across the road. Jehu waved me to a halt.

"Where's my wife?" I yelled at him.

"Comin' back! Listen!" He held up his hand and I heard the whine of her Yama in the distance, getting closer. "Best go up to the bridge with that gun of yours. So you can knock down anyone who's chasing her."

I went scrambling up to the command post overlooking the bridge. Only Kitty was there. Her eyes intent up the road she hardly glanced at me. "They've passed the fork," she said. "The lead tank's at the fourth click. And Judith's well ahead."

I flopped down beside her. "What the hell's going on?"

"The tanks are coming. And here they come!"

The Yama came first. Judith, without her helmet, her hair streaming, was racing for the bridge. I suddenly realized that the planking was still in place, but it was too late to do anything about it. At least she would be able to ride across.

Instead she skidded to a halt and let her bike heel over, looking as though she had dumped. The commander of the first tank around the bend evidently thought she had and, seeing her as potential loot, went roaring forward, one of the crew emerging from a hatch, ready to grab her.

Before he could she had wrestled her bike upright, jumped astride, and taken off, splattering crewmen and tank with mud flying from her rear wheel. The tank started after her. The planks rattled as she crossed the creek, glancing back, her hair flying. At the last moment the tank driver doubted that the bridge would carry his weight and locked his treads. The tank skidded onto the bridge and then slowly nosed down into the creek as the planks gave way. Judith waved and disappeared around the bend.

"That's blocked it for the cabron!" said Kitty, picking up her com and calling. "Block in place this end!" As the driver's hatch started to open she added, "You can start shooting now, Mister Gavin."

I had been wanting to shoot at something all day; I bounced a round off the driver's hatch and it snapped shut. The crewman who had been outside the turret waiting to grab Judith had been thrown into the creek. He was scrambling up when I fired and dived back into the mud. An armored personnel carrier came round the bend, its hatches opening. Rifles cracked from along the ridge above the creek, ricochets went screaming away into the woods, hatches crashed closed. More tanks arrived, their turrets traversing, their cannon searching for something to shoot at. But they couldn't elevate sufficiently to sweep the ridge and the holiday warriors who manned them stayed in them.

From farther up the road came a series of dull explosions and the ground shivered beneath us. "There goes the overhang!" said Kitty. "Now they're blocked both ends." She began to call on her com, "Pull out everyone. Back to the boats!" She listened for a moment, then said to me, "They've still got a few things to get aboard. Do you mind staying here for a short time, Mister Gavin? Keeping those tanks closed down until everybody's ready to sail?"

"Glad to be of help!" I growled, bouncing another round off an opening hatch. At last here was something I was able to do.

Kitty disappeared down the slope. I caught glimpses of shadows moving back through the trees toward the village. Presently Sam came out of the woods and dropped down beside me. "I'm the last, Mister Gavin. Everybody's back. And safe too!" He laughed. "Should write a letter of thanks to the Department of Highways for not fixin' our road!"

"Find out how much longer they want us to stay here." The fog was thickening and soon even these troops would be venturing out of the carriers.

Sam called on his com, then said, "Evacuation complete, and the boats are out of the Cove. Them tanks won't catch nobody now. Enoch's waiting alongside for you and me. Let's go!"

"Coming!" I used my last magazine to spray the blocked column, then slid after Sam down to the road.

"Will you give me a lift to the wharf on the back of your bike, Mister Gavin? I've never been on a motorcycle."

"You haven't had enough excitement for one day? Then climb on!" We rode back to the village, down the empty street, past the deserted houses. Our own cottage above the cove was already hidden by the fog, and I wasn't sorry. I'd been happier there than any place I'd ever been.

Enoch was waiting on the wharf. "Coast Guard's drifting with her screws all tangled. The boats are hove-to offshore. That spoiler of yours is working fine. They look like a patch of rainstorm on my radar."

"Where's Judy?"

"Aboard *Ranula* with the kids. Jehu took her out. You ready to leave too?"

I turned to look up the village street. The lights had been left burning in most of the houses, so the Settlement glowed in the mist as though it was still alive. But it was dead, and its people were out on the Bay. Driven out to become refugees in their own country. I shouted curses into the fog, curses at the tanks coming to destroy the remnants of a civilization. A world ending not with a bang but a snarl.

Enoch touched my arm. "Reckon we'd best be moving.

Those soldier-boys will be crossing the creek soon. And they'll come ashooting."

"One last thing!" I wheeled my Slada to the end of the jetty, headed it toward the sea, started the motor, kicked it into gear, and let it go. Its roar died with the splash. None of those bastards up the road were going to ride my bike.

Later on I heard that Judith had done the same to her Yama.

The Council were sitting at the table and some fifty other people were crammed standing in *Ranula*'s saloon. Among them were Barbara and Midge. Even the juniors were being brought into the act. I looked for Judith and saw her in a corner with Jehu. She waved at me to join her but it was impossible to squeeze between bulky windbreakers and I stood with Enoch by the door. I was only there because Yackle had radioed for me to come; I couldn't give much advice now we were at sea. Every fisherman around me knew more about boats and the bay than I did.

They were discussing where to go; arguing out a last-minute decision which should have been firm months earlier. That seemed to be the usual way Believers reached decisions; despite my training I was beginning to see some sense in it. They prepared for a number of possibilities so they had a plan ready for whatever turned up. Something like dynamnic programming in computers. But unnerving to me, who had been taught to plan ahead, check the logic, and act crisply.

They were all agreed that the only place *Ranula* could go safely, at least for the night, was Fairhaven. The argument was now centering on whether everybody should go there with her, or whether some of the boats should set out at once along the coast in search of a more attractive home. We lay, lifting and falling in the slight swell, the fog thick around us, while Chuck Yackle used *Roberts' Rules of Order* to chair a debate which was mostly wistful thinking. I wanted to escape to *Aurora* and consume some of Enoch's rum, but when I tried to slip away he caught my arm and muttered, "We'll be needing you in a moment, Mister Gavin."

"What for? I can't add anything to this."

"Maybe. Maybe not." He took advantage of a halt in the debate to call, "Chairman Yackle—my little girl has an idea that's not half bad."

"Barbara? Where is she?" Yackle peered round the crowded saloon. "Oh, there you are. Well, young lady, what idea do you have? Don't be shy—we need all the ideas we can get."

Telling Barbara not to be shy was rather like telling a Trooper not to be modest. Yackle knew that as well as I did; I sensed another of those prearranged proposals which seemed the Chairman's usual method of obtaining what he wanted from his colleagues.

She pushed her way through the crowd to stand at the end of the saloon table; shyness was the least appropriate term to describe her stance and expression. Like most of the other men and women there she had belted on a revolver and she stood with her feet apart against *Ranula*'s gentle roll, her hand on the butt of her pistol. I remembered a line from Chesterton: "*Barbara of the gunners, with her hand upon the gun.*" Saint Barbara, the patron saint of artillery and those in danger of sudden death. The girl facing us was no saint in any sense. But she might one day figure in the legends of her religion.

"These are our alternatives. We can go to Fairhaven, pray to be left alone, and rot if we are. We can go along the coast, try to slip in some place, and be captured all together. Or we can split up, every boat for herself. Most boats will be captured or sunk when this fog clears and the choppers come after us. Some might escape. But separated—we're nothing!" She made a gesture of disgust.

"So what's your idea, girl?" asked an oldster who had obviously disapproved of Yackle's calling on a junior to speak.

"To try for the only place within range where we'll have a chance to stand off those cabron until their whole rotten system falls apart." Her words made me realize that Barbara and Anslinger had something in common. "Jona's Point."

"Jona's Point? Where the Pen is?"

"Where the Pen was. It's a Federal supply dump now."

Everybody started to talk at once, with the oldster piping up that the child was crazy. Yackle gaveled the meeting to silence. "The Federal Penitentiary is guarded by sophisticated radar and those deadly particle beams. We've been warned often enough not to let any boat stray within ten kilometers of it."

"We haven't been warned lately, because it isn't any more. A boat can go right up to the wharf. The *Howard* does it twice a week."

"But the *John Howard*'s a specially equipped ship. She's—"

"She's got nothing the *Sea Eagle* hasn't got. And I've been alongside that wharf." She glanced across the saloon. "Judith and Mister Gavin were with me. Isn't that right, Mister Gavin?"

Everybody was suddenly looking at me. "We slipped in one night to take a look-see," I admitted.

"And what did you see?" asked Yackle.

Barbara answered before I could. "Ten half-assed guards. All sleeping, fooling around, or screwing. In this fog we could run right in and be on them before they know what's hit. Like the other Feds tried to hit us."

"But their beams! Their radar!"

"Barbara's right. There aren't any defenses operational," I said. "And the main entrance was open when we visited. They had crates all over the wharf and up the tunnel." I paused. "Of course, that was months ago. Things may have changed since then."

"Things may have changed," said Gertrude, "but one thing hasn't. Jona's Point is Federal property—whether they're using it as a prison or a warehouse. And if we invade Federal property we'll bring down a Strike Force on us. That's the last thing we need. We are trying to escape notice, not push ourselves out into the limelight." She paused. "I agree, the Pen would make an ideal base. But why not settle in Fairhaven for the time being, see if Jona's Point is as easy to approach as Barbara thinks it is, and then take it over later on."

Barbara swung on her. "If we wait—somebody else will get there first. And we're not likely to have another night when the fog's thick and the Coast Guard's tied up!"

A babble of voices. Judith's cut through them. "We are being tested! Tested by the Light! If we fail—we will be found unworthy." Pragmatic Judith off on her mystical kick. It brought silence to the saloon and they made way for her when she moved to the table. "Think!" she commanded us. "A calm sea, a thick fog, a moonless night. Gavin's radar spoiler. Barbara's trawl around the cutter's screws. The lead tank in the creek. The overhang across the road. The children safe aboard this ship. All of us gathered here in this saloon. Do you think all these are coincidences?" She dismissed such an absurdity with a shake of her head, her hair glinting auburn and gold. "The Light has given us the means. We must find the way."

Logically and theologically that was absurd. Persuasively, it was effective. Even I was trapped. Yackle broke the silence. "I take it, Doctor, that you favor an attempt to capture Jona's Point now?"

"That is our challenge!" She looked round as if to see if any of us rejected it. For the moment she was not my wife; she was a prophetess, a priestess, a Wise Woman. Or a Valkyrie, choosing those who were to be slain. I shifted uneasily, and was startled when she dropped into her normal voice. "With ten boats and fifty rifles we'd have a chance of capturing the Pen, wouldn't we, Gavin?"

I licked my lips. "If the guard hasn't been beefed up." Her eyes started to flash, and I added, "Even if it has—we have a chance."

Enoch, beside me, spoke up. "That girl of mine, she's young and her manners ain't so good, but her thinking's not bad. Except she hasn't thought things through as she'll learn when she's a mite older! I reckon there's fifty of us willing to take a chance, but there's no call to risk the rest. I propose that we make up what Mister Gavin here would say was a 'hit team' and try for the Pen. The rest go with this ship and the young kids to Fairhaven and wait there. If we make it we can signal 'em to come across. If we don't—" He shrugged. "They'll be no worse off. Neither, in the end, will we. The Light expects us to try. It knows we're not always going to win." He put his empty pipe back into his mouth.

Some of this had been orchestrated; some of it had not. From the way that Yackle put his fingertips together I sensed that Enoch had brought the meeting back to the prearranged program. There was a general chorus of approval in the saloon, with Gertrude loudly insisting that if the attack on the Pen failed, the raiding party must dissociate itself completely from the Settlement to avoid bringing Federal retribution down on the Believers waiting in Fairhaven.

XIX

The fog shrouded us, wet and thick. In the wheelhouse of *Aurora* I could see no farther than the for'rd hatch. Enoch was concentrating on the radar screen and the cluster of bright blips which marked the positions of the other four boats.

The sun was setting somewhere in the west but only the lighter obscurity to port showed that a sun existed. I had been warned about these Fundy fogs, and soon after my arrival in Sutton Cove I had learned their reality. Sculling a dory from the wharf to a boat anchored only a hundred meters across the cove I had not bothered to take a compass. I had lost sight of the wharf after three strokes with the scull, and only regained it an hour later when I ran into the end of the jetty. I had never found the boat whose radar I was supposed to be fixing. That day I had cursed the Fundy fog and my own foolishness in equal measure. Watching the fogbank roll over us as we headed north I thanked the Light—or whoever was responsible—for sending it.

We were moving at ten knots toward Jona's Point, now clear at the top of the radar screen. The echosounder ticked off confirmation of our position as it read the depth of the water and the profile of the seabed beneath us. Astern the radar showed *Ranula* and the rest of the fleet heading toward Fairhaven. To port the Coast Guard cutter was drifting helplessly while her divers were struggling to free a thousand meters of chronon line from her screws. At the rate the tide and current were taking her northeast she was likely to ground before her props were free. We had listened to Lieutenant Jenson's radio calls for aid; calls that had gone unanswered. There was no other Coast Guard cutter within two hundred kilometers; there were probably none still operational north of Boston. Nobody was moving to help the unfortunate Lieutenant or to intercept us. If indeed anybody knew where we had gone.

My spoiler was aboard Barbara's boat just ahead, and working well. Any standard radar more than a few kilometers away would show us as a localized rainstorm. Unless the operator was familiar with Fundy weather, he or she was unlikely to wonder how a localized rainstorm could be moving north on an evening when the sea was calm and the fog thick.

I watched Jona's Point creeping down the screen. The whiteness around us faded through gray to black as the day waned. Ahead was the Pen; the place I must capture with five boats and forty rifles. When the Council had accepted Enoch's suggestion of a "hit team," a term more appropriate to gangsters than Believers, it had also accepted Yackle's proposal that I lead it. My protests had been brushed aside. I wasn't a sailor or a Believer, but the Council knew that I had once been a member of the Special Strike Force; an organization of which it disapproved but for whose efficiency it had an exaggerated respect. I had been a Trooper; therefore I knew how to conduct a seaborne raid. Nobody else did, so I must be the leader sent by the Light for that specific purpose.

During the next hour I discovered that Enoch and his friends had prepared more than a proposal; they had a plan already in operation. The raiding flotilla, five boats which included Enoch's *Aurora* and Barbara's *Sea Eagle,* were lying alongside *Ranula*. The volunteer rifles, ten women and thirty men, were going aboard. Barbara, as the only helmsman who had actually taken a boat into the Point, would lead the flotilla. I would be with Enoch in the command vessel. Everything was planned up to the time when the boats put us ashore. Thereafter I would direct the action. Barbara had told them I knew the inside of the Pen; nobody had asked where and how I had gained that knowledge.

I had had command thrust upon me and, unable to avoid it, I was beginning to feel easier in it. What we were attempting might be crazy, but I knew what I was doing and how to do it—if it could be done at all. It was the kind of thing I had done too often in the past. But this time, for the first time, I knew it was worth doing.

"Should be hearing the foghorn at Jona's soon," I said to Enoch.

He shook his head, his eyes still on the radar screen. "She

don't blow no more, Mister Gavin. Broke down last winter and they never fixed her."

Old Groaner had been allowed to die. For some reason I found that the most ominous of portents. The foghorn at Jona's Point had been warning mariners of danger for over two centuries. Its silence prophesied the chaos to come more clearly than any statistic.

The blip marking the Point crept closer and when we were about twelve kilometers south of where the wharf should be I called the other four boats. "This is a last check. At ten clicks we'll be within com range of the Pen. Anybody ahead who's listening will know we're here, even if they don't understand what we're saying. So after you've reported only use the com in an emergency."

Martha, Jehu, Adam, and Barbara reported in turn that they understood. Then I made my own modification to their plan. "I'm shifting to *Sea Eagle,* so I'll be first on the wharf. After Barbara's put me ashore all boats hang off until I call you in, boat by boat."

"Mister Gavin—" Barbara started to protest.

"I'll be coming over Enoch's bows." I cut my com and looked at him. "Can you nose up to *Sea Eagle*'s stern?"

"If you say so!" He looked up from the radar and smiled at me. "Go for'rd and call back when I'm touching."

I gripped his shoulder, eased past the men and women crowding the wheelhouse, and groped my way along the foredeck toward the bows. For minutes I was alone in palpable darkness—the fog pressing in like a wet wrapping. Then, suddenly, the stern light of the *Sea Eagle* was directly beneath me and I called back for Enoch to ease off. He and his daughter must have been in telepathic communication for *Aurora*'s stem only nudged her boat. I jumped down onto the afterdeck as Enoch dropped back into the fog. Somebody grabbed me. "Welcome aboard!" It was Judith.

"What the hell are you doing? You're supposed to be with the kids in *Ranula.*"

"I'm more use here. I know the Pen too!" She led me for'rd. "If you get hit I'll be able to take over guidance." She stopped at the wheelhouse door. "Please—give me your Jeta. In case I have to shoot somebody!"

Judith was like all the rest. Act first—ask afterwards. I gave her the dart-gun and went into the wheelhouse to join Midge, Sam, and Barbara. Midge welcomed me, Barbara ignored me, and Sam grinned.

I moved beside Barbara at the wheel. "Got a fix?"

She nodded. "We're five clicks southwest of the Point. I'm about to change course and run up to the channel marker."

We stood silent, the night and the fog heavy around us. The only sounds were the low rumble of the turbine and the slap of the waves on our forefoot. The radar showed the other boats taking up line astern. I stared into the murk. Presently Midge said, "The Pen's over there."

I could see nothing until I used the night-sights of my Luger and picked out the silhouette of our target. Barbara called softly, "We're at the channel buoy. Shall I go on in?"

"Can you see where to go?"

"Sonic rangefinder's bouncing well. There's the wharf!" She pointed to the tube and though I couldn't tell what the ultracoustic beeps were bouncing from, she seemed confident it was the metal pilings of the pier.

"Ease in then. Put me off on a ladder. Tide's about half, so I'll have three meters to climb. Then stand away until I signal all clear. Got that?"

She nodded, reluctantly. Either she or Judith had planned to be the first over the top. I was discovering that once women start down the glory road they follow it as blindly as men. But if I was leading this expedition I was damned well going to lead; if somebody was to be shot at first, it was going to be me.

"Better get ready to jump, Mister Gavin," whispered Midge. These girls seemed able to see in the dark. I was reaching out and actually touched the dockside with my hand before I knew we had arrived.

"Ladder's back here!" hissed Judith, catching my arm and urging me aft. I grabbed seaweed, then wet metal rungs. "Good luck!"

I went up the ladder in three bounds; over the top and flat on the wharf in the best assault manner. I hugged the permacrete, trying not to breathe. Silence and darkness; the fog both muffled and hid. I heard nothing from *Sea Eagle* which should be easing away from the wharf. I estimated the direction of the tunnel and started to crawl toward it. After about two meters I rammed my raised face into the side of a container.

I rubbed my skinned forehead and hoped that my nose wasn't bleeding, felt for the edge of the container, crawled round it, and ran into another. The whole wharf was covered with the damned things. By a process of trial and error, the strategy of a dumb automaton, I found a gap between them and at least saw a dim light. The tunnel was still lit. I crawled to the entrance and found both gates blocked open. They'd been offloading containers onto the wharf and just shoving them up the tunnel.

There was no sound or sign of life from the inspection station or beyond. I felt my way back to the wharf, saved myself from falling over the edge, and gave a quick call on my com. "Wharf all clear. First boat, come in!"

The first person to appear out of the darkness was Judith, the second was Barbara. "We're the ones who know our way around!" whispered Judith.

"Midge is moving *Sea Eagle* astern," added Barbara. "Dad's alongside now. Shall I scout the tunnel?"

"You stay here and call the other boats in. I'll scout the tunnel."

"I'll follow as link-up. As I did last time," said Judith. When we reached the dim light of the inspection station she stared at me. "What have you done to your nose?"

I felt my face and found my hand covered with blood. A nosebleed is not a leader's wound. "Rammed a container. Stay here. I'll scout ahead."

The hall was the same dimly lit cavern we had visited months before, now crammed even more tightly with containers. I sidled between them to the door which would let us reach the Surveillance Center. I couldn't open it. Judith knew the code; I didn't. I went back to fetch her and found Enoch and his squad already assembled in the inspection station with Martha's being guided up the tunnel by Barbara.

Colonel Jewett would have approved of the silent and organized manner in which forty rifles were moving themselves from boats to wharf to inspection station, though he would have court-martialed somebody later for exceeding orders. As it was I could only watch the operation complete itself. These inshore fishermen could not only see in the dark, they must communicate by smell. All of them arrived without anybody dropping anything, treading on anyone, or cursing above a whisper.

When they were all hidden in the shadows I hissed, "This time—wait here! Judy, come and help me open that door."

This time they did wait while Judith was attempting to open the door to the stairs. She succeeded in hitting the right combination on her fifth try, by which time I was about to send back for dynamite and risk blowing it in. We couldn't go undetected much longer. "Thank Christ!" I muttered when it swung back to disclose the same deserted and dirty stairwell as before; the only foot marks in the dust were ours. "Now go and guide the rest here. Bring them in small groups."

"You're laying a neat trail with that nose of yours!" she whispered, and disappeared.

They arrived in twos and threes while I reconnoitered ahead. My chief fear now was that the guard had been beefed up or replaced by effectives. My goal was to reach the Surveillance Center and identify who and where they were. The occasional light still burned on the stairs and along the passageways, but there was no sign that anybody had used them since our visit. I reached the Surveillance Center and was again faced with a locked door. Again I went back to fetch Judith, threatening to strangle her if she didn't remember the combination sooner this time.

She opened the door on the third attempt and I burst into the room. Empty! All screens off. I moved quickly down the rows of switches, bringing up the cameras. I was still searching the matrix of images for signs of life when I realized that the whole team were crowding into the room and watching me with fascination. I swung around to curse them, remembered I hadn't told them to wait, and turned back to the screens.

"It doesn't look as though there's anybody here!" said Barbara, in a tone that suggested she had maintained from the start that the Pen was now deserted.

"Can't be sure of that yet!" I continued to study the banked images of rooms, cells, corridors, and stairs. "We'll have to search the whole of the guards quarters. They may be using rooms that aren't monitored." I explained the general layout of the Pen, using the plan on the wall of the Surveillance Center, and then sent out groups to move cautiously through each area. And not to start anything if they did find anybody. While these Believers were giving thanks to the Light for having let them get into the Pen so easily, I could also sense a vague disappointment that our entry had lacked the promised drama. I myself was starting to feel a fool. We could have waited for daylight and simply walked ashore.

By dawn I was fairly certain the place was deserted. It was packed with stores of various kinds, most of them still containerized, as though the rush had been to get as much as possible into the place before some deadline. There were also signs that the guard had only left during the past few days;

half a carton of milk in one of the mess rooms had hardly had time to turn sour. And at daylight, when I went up onto the roof, I found a small chopper pad had been installed near the lucaplex dome. A pad which had recently been used. The area was no longer verboten to aircraft. If anyone came after us, they would probably come by air.

Enoch joined me on the roof. "There're ten boats with another eighty rifles coming from Fairhaven. Should arrive around noon." He looked at the fog swirling across the Point. "It'll be clear by then. Breeze picking up. Blow this lot away." He filled his pipe. "Looks like you've done it. We've got a safe place to stay awhile."

"It won't be safe until we can close the gates. Put all hands to work moving those containers out of the tunnel."

Enoch nodded and left. I stayed on the roof, trying to think like a commander planning consolidation, while feeling more like an escaped con who has been caught and brought back to prison. And the place was a mess! The lucaplex dome was intact but, looking down through it, I could see only a jungle of tangled greenery. Climatic control had been allowed to run wild, and so had the plants we had tended so carefully. I felt the anger of a man who returns to his summer cottage and finds it has been used by hunters who have left the toilets blocked, the kitchen filthy, and the yard full of trash.

But the fusion generator was still pouring out power. We had heat and light. The hydride converter could probably be made operational and would give us fuel for the boats. I stood on the roof, looking around as the sun started to break through. A fresh breeze was sweeping the fog away. Soon it would be as Enoch had forecast: one of those sparkling days when Fundy shows a wild beauty.

It had already cleared sufficiently for me to see the rocks and scrub around the Pen. At the tip of the Point, about nine hundred meters away, the outline of a large chopper pad began to appear with a road running from it to the wharf; they'd been bringing stuff in by air as well as by sea. I began to pick out sites from which launchers and automatics could cover the pad, the road, and the wharf. There might be such weapons packed away in some of the unopened containers. I hoped we'd have time to find them before somebody found us. It would have made defense of the Pen easier if the Charged Particle Beam projectors had still been in position, but even in our need I could not wish they were.

"Gavin!" Judith was climbing up through the hatch onto the roof. Her expression said that her news was bad. "Captain Rideout's calling—"

"He hasn't left Fairhaven, has he?"

"No." She caught her breath. "He says that his radar has just picked up six choppers. Four large and two small. A hundred clicks down the coast. And they're heading our way!"

XX

They came low out of the south, two gunships and four transports. They came closed up and without evasive action, circling the Point as if supremely confident or else unsuspicious. Either they didn't know we were here or they knew we were armed with nothing better than rifles. And that we had not been able to clear the tunnel of containers in the forty minutes which was all the time we had had to get ready for their arrival.

I had done what I could. There were eight of us on the roof, Judith in the Surveillance Center, and the rest under Enoch covering the main hall and the entrance tunnel. We might gain an initial instant of surprise if they thought the Pen was deserted. After they got over that it would be fighting container to container, corridor to corridor, stairway to stairway. If there were green troops in those choppers then we stood a small chance of driving them off. If they were experienced fighters we stood no chance at all. The only tactics I had been able to tell the team was to stay behind cover and shoot straight when the shooting started.

Banks of fog were still driving across the Point but it had cleared enough for me to be able to see the landing pad at its tip. The four transports were going down to land, one by one. The two gunships were circling above them. I picked up my binoculars and watched the first transport down. I watched the hatches snap open and the lead section jump out. And my guts cramped. This was the end. Those were Troopers!

But they didn't act like Troopers making an assault landing. The first men out moved almost casually to the edge of the pad, hardly glancing toward the Pen as they stood waiting for the rest of the squad to deplane. There was a flash of color in the open door. Sam, beside me, gripped my arm. "Women!" he hissed. "Women—by the Light!"

And not ladies being helped down from the hatch. Women being pushed through it, to be rounded up by the waiting Troopers and herded off the pad and into the scrub. Captive women! Three more Troopers followed the last woman pushed out, then the turbines of the transport picked up speed and it lifted off, women and Troopers crouching together against the blast from its rotors.

In quick succession the other three transports landed, discharged their prisoners, and took off as soon as they were empty. Each in turn went lifting into the overcast, heading east, as if each was trying to get away as quickly as possible from something of which it was ashamed. Fifteen minutes after the aircraft had arrived there were only the two gunships circling overhead and some sixty women being herded along the road toward the Pen by twenty Troopers.

"What's going on?" asked Sam from beside me.

"Evil in action!" came Judith's voice in our earplugs. She must have slewed a wharf camera round and watched the landing. Her voice was thick with fury. "Those are women taken from looted Settlements. Brought here—"

I cut her off. "Cool it! There are only twenty guards. We can take twenty easily if we keep our heads." I wasn't at all certain we could, not twenty Troopers. The Force might have lost its honor; it still had its lethal skills.

"There'll soon be more!" muttered Sam. The two gunships were now landing and their occupants disembarking. I looked through my binoculars. "Civilians!" I said, then I caught the flash of insignia on braided uniforms. "Civilians and brass!"

So that's why the Pen had been filled with stores, why the guard had been withdrawn! That's what the Administration had been planning when it decommissioned the Federal Penitentiary! This was to be one of the refuges, the "safe houses," which it had been preparing for itself and its friends. The same kind of place that Sherando had become. Only here they had had to bring their own girls. Or rather, somebody else's girls.

There were more people disembarking, among them women who were being helped out, not pushed out. Those would be wives, daughters, and female politicians who had played along with Futrell. That bastard—

"Easy, Mister Gavin," said Sam, touching my arm. "Cool it, you said!"

I drove from my mind the face of the man I hated and stared at the evil spread out below me. As the captives were driven nearer the Pen I could see that they were young, some little more than children. Staring at the wildness around them, at the wilderness of rocks, sea, and scrub. At the Pen looming ahead. The Troopers were too occupied with turning back girls trying to escape or urge forward others hanging back to look toward us. This was the ultimate shame. American women being herded like captured cattle. Or like the captives from some defeated Greek city: women being driven toward enslavement by the soldiers of democratic Athens.

The civilians and the brass were still grouped near the gunships, talking together as if trying to dissociate themselves from the infamous scene taking place in front of them. Some were glancing at the sky as if expecting the arrival of more transports or gunships. If we were to take them we must take them soon. But we could not fire into that mixture of guards and captives. Sam, the best marksman in the settlement, was cursing his frustration. "Couldn't knock off any of them soldiers yet. Not without a chance of hitting a girl."

The girls were putting up the kind of fight you don't usually get from prisoners. Groups of them kept breaking away to run back toward the civilians on the pad or into the underbrush. Troopers were chasing them, dragging the ones they caught back to the main herd. Hitting them to keep them moving, but not hard enough to damage them. Usually any group of prisoners can be subdued by killing the first who disobeys orders. But these were prisoners who must not be killed or seriously injured, and now the frustrated guards were trying to persuade rather than force their captives to keep moving. They too were starting to glance at the sky.

A couple of fast-running girls got back among the civilians, dodging between them with two Troopers on their heels. The brass and civilians scattered, some of them obviously protesting to the Troopers. Men and women who perhaps only now had realized what was going on. A couple of civilians were knocked down, a General lost his hat, the girls dodged round the choppers, were grabbed by the crew, and dragged fighting back along the road. The officer in charge of the guards halted his squad just short of the wharf to let the two be brought in and other escapers be rounded up. His curses, threats, and entreaties floated up to us watching from the roof.

My com pinged and I heard Midge's voice. "Mister Gavin—I'm offshore. I've just picked up another chopper. Twenty clicks southeast and coming fast."

Only one ship; so there was still hope.

"Also, Mister Gavin, those boats from Fairhaven. They know what's happening and they're coming full speed. Should be here by eleven."

"Midge—you stay offshore. And if we've gone under by then, tell those boats to high tail it back to Fairhaven. You go back there too!"

I didn't get any answer and was still repeating my order when out of the west came a command ship, flying at full speed. It swept over us, banked, and then hung above the wharf. The officer in charge of the guards was looking up toward it, obviously receiving orders. "Their boss is in that chopper," I muttered. "If only there was some way to nail him."

I was studying the machine through binoculars when Sam's rifle cracked. I swung on him in fury, there was no way to down a command ship with a rifle. I choked back my curses and spoke on my com. "They know we're here! Fire at will!" Then I looked back at the chopper.

The chances of hitting an aircraft with rifle fire are remote. A miracle however appeared to have happened. The command ship was in difficulty; Sam's shot had hit something vital. From his smile something he had aimed at. We watched it pass across the point, its rotors stabilizing wildly. Then it disappeared into the mist off the Point, fluttering out to sea and still losing height. "Reckon that's taken their boss out of things!" said Sam.

It had also thrown the Troopers into the action mode. All of them were out of sight, leaving their charges huddled together at the edge of the wharf. Abandoning a task they disliked for one they knew and enjoyed. The crack of Sam's rifle had been like the call of a bugle; they had faded into the underbrush as one man.

"What the hell are they doing?" asked Sam, perplexed at the loss of his targets. He looked over the edge of the roof.

A burst of fire whistled past his head and he dropped flat, his face suddenly white, looking at me.

"They're good, Sam," I said, in mixed pride and sadness. "Keep your head down!" A grenade arced up from the scrub to burst just short of the roof. "Now they know we're up here. We've got to get out—fast." I sent him and the rest of the group scrambling back through the hatch and down the ladder. I moved along the roof, waited until I saw the flash of another grenade being launched, and fired at the spot. A man half rose, then dropped at the same moment that his missile exploded farther along the roof. I crouched as the fragments sprayed over me, then ran for the hatch as half-a-dozen grenades came arcing up. I dropped through it as they began to go off, sweeping the roof with shrapnel. Well, that one shot had been worthwhile. They'd know they were up against real riflemen and they wouldn't rush things.

In the Surveillance Center Judith was bent over the displays. She had slewed every external camera she could bring to bear toward the wharf and the Point. "Good shooting, Gavin!" she said as I arrived, panting, from the roof. "That one you hit looks as though he's dead. And the rest are moving with great caution!" She laughed, with a cold pleasure that made my skin crawl. I glimpsed how faith can convert the kindest of men and women into killers. These Believers, these peaceful people, had been driven into a corner and were now intent on fighting their way out. For them this was just another of the fitness tests their Light used to try them out while on Earth, so It could decide whether they would be useful in Heaven. Good is no match for Evil unless it is ready to defend itself.

I moved beside her to study the screens. The fog had been swept away and in the bright sunshine the viewing was excellent. I could see nothing of the Troopers, only an occasional flash as they exchanged fire with our group covering the approach of the wharf. The girls were crouching together showing both strong nerves and good sense. The civilians were clustered around the ships, trying to persuade the crews to lift them out. I couldn't see any brass among them, so the Troopers had probably been reenforced by three Generals and one Admiral.

"The girls are the threat," I muttered.

"How do you mean?"

"As soon as the guards get formed up they'll drive those girls toward the entrance. Use them as mobile cover."

"That's too horrible! How could they?"

"It's standard practice." I was too concerned with the situation to worry about whitewashing. "I wish to hell I could get a message to them."

"What message?" Barbara had appeared at my elbow.

"I'd like to tell 'em to either scatter into the bush and accept a few casualties. Or to move back to the pad in one body and mingle with that gang of civilians. So they'll be clear of grabs by the guard and out of our line of fire."

"I'll tell 'em to move back to the pad." And Barbara was gone before I could stop her.

"Oh God!" said Judith. "She'll get herself killed trying to impress you."

"Impress me—hell! She's glory-hunting." And I ran after her.

I lost her in the main distribution hall, and only sighted her again after she had stripped down to her panties and was out on the wharf dodging between containers. I started after her and Enoch hauled me back. "You go out there you'll get shot, Mister Gavin."

"But Barbara—your daughter—!" She was breaking from cover, sprinting toward the prisoners.

"She's banking on them not shooting at a girl." The strength of his grip on my arm suggested he was not as confident as his daughter. Then it relaxed. "And they ain't. They think she's a runaway running back now there's shooting."

Barbara had arrived among the captives and presently the whole group began to move in an amoebalike fashion toward the chopper pad. A Trooper came out of the brush, tried to stop them, got nicked, and dived back to cover. The girls went flat as the subsequent volleys whistled over their heads, then started to crawl. When they were about half-way to the pad they rose together and ran. They were among the civilians before the chopper crews realized they were arriving.

I had only wanted the girls out of the way. Barbara had offensive ideas. Within seconds they were swarming into the cockpits of both ships. By the time they were ejected, both tail-rotors were fouled and neither was in shape for an immediate takeoff. The girls then started fighting the civilians and the chopper crews retreated into their ships, drawing their pistols and threatening anyone who approached.

I got back to the Surveillance Center to hear Midge calling on her com. At extreme range her voice was weak but readable. "I've picked up a survivor from that chopper which went into the sea. A bit battered. He's safely roped. Won't say who he is, but I think he's one of their honchos."

I looked at Judith. "Maybe we've got a hostage—if we can bring him here."

"How can we get him across the wharf from the boat?"

"Easy! We just have to drive those Troopers farther into

the scrub so they can't shoot up the wharf." I went to the door. "Tell Midge to stand by offshore and come in when it's safe."

"And when will that be?"

"When we've driven those Troopers back. I'll call when we have." I ran down the stairs and across the hall to the tunnel where men and women were still struggling to shift containers so the gates could be closed.

I found Enoch and explained what was happening. "I need some volunteers to help me keep the wharf free of fire while Midge drops off her prisoner."

"Volunteers? You need the best. I'll go get 'em." He disappeared among the containers and presently returned with a squad headed by Martha. "Here're your volunteers. They know what you want and they're willing to go out with you."

Willing perhaps, but no more eager than I was. In this kind of action everybody knows that somebody is going to die. We might not like it but we had to risk it. We had a chance of grabbing the enemy Number One. We had to drive the Troopers back so Midge could come alongside.

"Drive them back if you can. Give me covering fire if you can't. Those bastards will have used up their grenades by now. So it's rifle against rifle."

Martha nodded, taking automatic command, and began to despatch each of her squad to take cover behind a different container. Before she disappeared herself she said, "Shout when you want us to start shooting."

I went to hide behind the container projecting the farthest onto the wharf, trying to think of some way to save myself from having to run twenty meters while being shot at from a range of one hundred. Smoke? The wind would blow it away across the neck. Just as well or they'd have used it against us by now. Shove this container out to the edge of the wharf as a shield? The damned thing was off the rollers and immovable. Some other place for Midge to off-load her captive? There wasn't one.

I was convincing myself that the risk to me wasn't worth grabbing some unknown politico as reward, when Midge came on the com and her voice was loud and clear. "I'm tucked in under the end of the wharf. . . . A few dents and the wheelhouse glass. . . . Tell Mister Gavin to come and collect this honcho."

She had brought her boat in among the rocks, reached the cover of the pier, and cancelled my options. I shouted to

Martha, "Give me all you've got!" swallowed twice, and launched myself before my resolution evaporated.

The Troopers weren't expecting a target to pop out from between containers like a clay pigeon from a trap. They were slow in shifting their attention to me and the first burst whined over my head as I vaulted down into the well of *Sea Eagle*. The tide was not yet full and the dockside gave the boat cover. I picked myself up and swung round. Midge was crouching amid shattered glass in the wheelhouse, one hand on the wheel.

"Where is he?"

"On the bunk in the cabin. Wrists tied behind him. I think he can walk." She paused. "Pilot's down there too. Dead. I had to shoot him."

I plunged into the cabin, stepped across a body, rolled over the damp form on the bank. And found myself facing Gerald Futrell. Gaunt and gray-haired, etched by pain and fatigue, it was still the face of the man I hated.

I drew my Luger, aimed at his right eye. He recognized me, flinched, but did not speak. With an effort I reholstered my gun. I pulled him to his feet, pushed him up to the wheelhouse. "I'm going to get you into the Pen—alive or dead!"

"Be careful with him, Mister Gavin," called Midge. "Remember—he's my prisoner. Not yours!"

"I'll keep him alive as long as I can—if his pals let me!" I lifted him bodily and shoved him over the edge of the wharf. Then I followed, calling back to Midge, "Now get to hell out of here! Lie offshore until you're called in."

Beside me Futrell murmured, "Knox—Gavin Knox! Fucking things up again!"

For the moment the shooting had stopped. I pulled my handkerchief out of my pocket, tied it to the muzzle of my Luger, and waved it in the air above us. "That's the best I can do for you," I growled. "Now—stand up! Let your boys see you!"

"Stand up?" He got to his knees, mouth set in a feral snarl. "I can't. Not unless you help me."

I hesitated, seized him around the waist and pulled him to his feet, supporting him, waiting for a burst to kill us both.

No burst came. For the Troopers out in the scrub a white flag was a signal that we wanted to talk. And by now they were probably ready to talk. Time was passing and their ammunition would be running low. Then their officer must have recognized Futrell, for I heard him shout, "Hold your fire!"

Still waving my handerchief like a pennant I urged Futrell across the wharf to the cover of the nearest container. Enoch was waiting and caught him as he fell.

"Is this the one?"

"That's him. The devil himself! Get him up to the Surveillance Center."

They dragged Futrell away. I waited until I was sure there would be no rescue attempt. Then I followed.

Futrell was slumped in a chair with Judith standing over him. She turned when I came in. "He's got his com with him. He's going to call the troops. Arrange for a cease-fire. So we can get the girls into the Pen."

"He'd better!" I went over, caught his hair, jerked his head back to face me. "Listen well! There's a gallows in this place. The designers put one in—just in case the Government decided to start hanging murderers again. It's never been used. You'll be its first customer—if you're lucky and do as you're told. If you don't—you'll die slowly over the next two days. I know all the tricks of the trade. I've never had to use 'em. But I'd be delighted to start on you!"

He stared back at me, fear mixed with defiance.

Judith tried to pull me away. "He's Midge's prisoner. Like she told you. She just called on the com. You're not to hurt him, do you hear?"

I swung around. "If he does as I tell him, I won't hurt him. I'll hang him painlessly like I promised. But if he doesn't—then I'll hurt him all right!"

Futrell's eyes were on Judith. Without meaning to we had moved into the "bad cop" versus "good cop" routine. His eyes went wide. I turned and saw Judith was raising the Jeta. "Not that—you silly bitch! We want him conscious."

Then I realized she was pointing it at my chest. I jumped toward her, the dart hit, and I found myself collapsing at her feet.

XXI

Consciousness came back slowly. I rose through a phase of disorientation as I realized that I had been knocked out by a Jeta and tried to remember where and by whom. I still hadn't solved that problem when I discovered I couldn't move. I opened my eyes, stared at the lights above me, and decided I was in an operating room. Then that I was strapped to an operating table.

It was going to be forced mind-wipe! I'd been caught and brought back to the Pen. Or I'd never escaped! Or—

"He's awake." That was Judith's voice. Her face swam over me. Then Barbara's. And memory flooded back.

"What the hell are you doing? Where's Futrell?"

"Safe in a cell." Judith bent to pull up my left eyelid and stare at my pupil. "Relax, Gavin. Everything's under control."

"Futrell!" I tried to sit up. "He'll be the first murderer to swing from the Pen's gallows!"

"No he won't," said Judith, filling a syringe. "I gave him my word that if he persuaded the soldiers to let those women come into the Pen we'd turn him loose unharmed."

"You had no right to do that!"

"I did. You went crazy and I had to take over." She came toward me, syringe in hand. "If we'd had to fight it out, a lot more poeple would have been killed." She put a tourniquet around my arm and began to swab the skin. "He accepted my word."

"Well—he hasn't got mine." I wrenched at the straps holding me. "Let me up, will you!"

"Not till after you've been debugged."

"What the hell do you mean?"

"Gavin, I told you after you went berserk in Sherando that

someone's planted a directive in you. You thought you'd licked it. You haven't. The sight of Futrell still triggers it. You'll still try to kill him when you see him. You can only control yourself long enough to delay—as you did when you fetched him from the boat. I've got to help you find out who planted that directive, and why."

"Balls! Keep that needle away from me! Post-hypnotic suggestion doesn't work."

"It does on rigid-minded duty-bound individuals—if it's something they really want to do. And you want to kill Futrell all right! The compulsion's forcing you to try to kill him, regardless of everything else. Futrell's face can still switch you to automatic."

I found the straps would not loosen and lay panting. "What are you doing?" She was slapping the skin of my bound arm and the veins were starting to stand out as the tourniquet cut off the return blood flow.

"Trying to pick a good vein." She was bending, intent, over my arm. Running her little finger across the skin to feel the bulging vessels. "This stuff damages tissue if it leaks outside the vein."

"What stuff?"

"Neoscopolamine. It'll send you to sleep and let you abreact."

"Leave me alone! Abreact—hell! I want to kill Futrell because he's a traitor to the United States!"

"That he may be. Or he may only be trying to salvage something from the wreck. Either way, you can hunt him later. When he's left Jona's Point. And when you don't go crazy at the sight of his face." She sank the needle into a vein, drew back the plunger so that blood mixed with the liquid in the syringe, pulled off the tourniquet, and looked at me. "Gavin, you'll go to sleep when I inject this. You'll dream about being conditioned. That memory's been suppressed. I want you to remember. Remembering may break the compulsion. I hope so—for all our sakes."

"Judy! This is nonsense." I heard the rattle of an automatic from somewhere outside. "There's still fighting. You can't drug me while there's still fighting!"

"Not fighting. Just mopping up. You're not needed for that. Now lie quiet while I'm injecting!" Her voice had acquired the ring of authority that went with her white coat. She looked down at me, helpless on the table, and her words came hard and clear. The words of the Wise Woman. "Go back and re-live being ordered to kill Gerald Futrell."

I passed out with her command reverberating in my skull.

I woke slowly into a dream. But a dream of unique completeness. A dream which included every perception, every sensation. After the first few moments I forgot it was a dream. I only remembered that it was a fine April afternoon on the Chesapeake, that Grainer and I had taken Gloria and Helga sailing. I was lying half-asleep on the port locker, the boat moving gently under me, the sun warm on my bare chest. When I opened my eyes I could see white sails curving above me and blue sky beyond.

"You awake, Gavin?"

That was Arnold Grainer's voice. I raised my head and looked around. We were coasting along under a light breeze a few kilometers off the Eastern Shore. And he was at the wheel. Helga had my hand on her lap. Gloria was kissing my ear. Two beautiful women. Like everybody in Grainer's employ they were superb performers. Like most people in his personal service they were his devoted admirers. And because he treated me as an intimate on these pleasure expeditions both girls were gladly intimate with me.

He looked at me and laughed. "Gav—maybe we should anchor and let me relax too!"

"Fine!" I disengaged myself from the girls and went forward to furl the jib and drop the anchor as Grainer brought the sloop into the wind. The Coast Guard cutter discreetly escorting us hove-to a couple of kilometers astern. The watching chopper drifted down to land on the beach. Ashore the primary campaigns were in full swing. Grainer had lost Maine and only held Massachusetts by the barest margin. The politicos expected New York to finish him and were preparing to celebrate his rejection; here on the Chesapeake the President and I prepared to enjoy ourselves.

I snugged down the boat, then went back to the cockpit. Grainer had already taken Gloria into the cabin. Helga had slipped out of her bikini and was waiting for me on the starboard cushions.

Afterwards I dozed off and only woke when Grainer came up the companionway, a bourbon in each hand. He gave me one and said, "Helga, go and help Gloria fix supper."

She kissed me and disappeared below. Grainer sat down. I sipped my bourbon and waited. One of my jobs was to act as a wall against which the President could bounce ideas. After a moment he asked, "How do you think the Convention will go?"

"You'll take it. Not by much. But you'll get the delegates." He knew that already, so there was something else he wanted to bounce off me. I pulled on my slacks, then my sweater. It was growing cooler as the afternoon waned.

"I will! I must! I've got to finish the job. The most important job any President ever tackled." He sat, nursing his bourbon, watching me drink mine. "The girls have been bugging me about Futrell. They're scared of him."

"Futrell's ruthless. A real bastard. They're afraid that if—"

"If anything happens to me he'll silence everybody close to me? Is that it?"

"More or less." I shrugged. "Futrell likes to play it safe. And the only safe way to silence anybody is to silence them permanently."

"Like I silenced Shantz?"

I looked into my glass. "I didn't hear that! Anyway, Shantz deserved what he got. The girls don't. They're afraid that Futrell will assume that they've picked up more than they have and he'll—well—take precautions. They'd be happier if he wasn't AG." I took another mouthful of bourbon. "So would I! He's turned the Secret Service into a Secret Police."

"I know! I know! The goddamn thing is that's what I may need! And that's why I need Futrell." He swirled his whiskey. "I'll tell him to leave the girls alone—whatever happens."

"Whatever happens? What might happen?" The sun, the love-making, the bourbon, were all combining to make me sleepy. Even had I been interested in the machinations of politicians I was too drowsy to care. "What do you expect to happen?"

Grainer leaned forward across the cockpit. Our knees were almost touching, his face was directly opposite mine. I felt the aura of his power more intensely than I had ever felt it before. "Gav—there are people who'll try to kill me if they think I'm likely to win in November."

"After New York they'll know you will! Arnold—what—" Under his stare I could only ask weakly, "What do you want me to do?"

"Protect me if you can. Protect Futrell if you can't."

That didn't make sense, but I was too sleepy and confused to question the logic. Grainer was saying something about

Futrell's ruthless dedication when Gloria called him down to the cabin and I fell asleep.

I was partly awakened by Helga shaking me, clamping her hand over my mouth, hissing in my ear. "If anything happens to Arnold—kill Futrell! Kill him before he kills us!"

That made more sense. I mumbled, "If Arnold's killed, I kill Futrell. Yes! I hate that bastard."

Helga was gone; Grainer was back in the cockpit, cursing because he'd given me too much of something. I managed to sit up. He was gripping my arm. "Do you understand, Gavin? Do you understand what you've been told to do?"

"Sure." I struggled to order my thoughts, but everything was confused and hazy. In the middle of the haze Grainer's eyes burned like twin fires and from out of it Helga's voice echoed in my ear. "Yes, Arnold. I know what to do."

"And you will forget about this conversation?"

"I will forget about this conversation." I'd forget gladly.

He let me fall back onto the cushions, and said something about Gavin having had too much bourbon and to let him sleep it off.

I returned from my dream to my reality. The straps were hurting my wrists. The light was blinding my eyes. My mind was aching from the blow.

"Gavin—are you all right?" Judith's voice, anxious and insistent.

I saw her face. Gray and drawn. "Yes. I'm okay. Safe to untie!" I sat up as the straps were freed. Barbara was staring at me as though I were a ghost rising from a grave.

"You remembered?"

"I remembered!" I put my face in my hands. Rubbed my aching eyes. I remembered Helga and Gloria. Both murdered by Futrell's men. As he had meant to murder me. The Pen had saved me. "Every detail!" I staggered as I got down from the table.

Barbara caught me, steadied me. "You'd better sit down." There was compassion in her gray eyes, the first I had ever seen in them. "You look like hell!"

"Feel like I've been there." I recovered control of my legs. "I'll be all right. The fighting? What's happened?"

"Fighting finished hours ago. Chuck Yackle arrived with reinforcements. Landed on the far side of the Point and came charging across it like the US Cavalry."

"Oh Christ!" I had seen religious fanatics charging Troopers. "How many killed?"

"None! A lot of bruises and a few cracked ribs from falling on the rocks. That's all. By the time Yackle got here Futrell had almost persuaded the soldiers that the best thing they could do was to fix those two gunships and take off. Yackle's arrival with ten boats and eighty rifles convinced 'em. So they did—leaving most of the civilians behind. I've got 'em locked up in separate cells. Maybe they'll tell us what all this is about." If Judith wore her present expression when she asked them they'd tell her without further persuasion.

"Where's Futrell?"

"By himself in your old cell. I've patched him up."

"Can I see him?"

"Are you sure?" She studied me with the uncertainty of a teacher eyeing an untrustworthy pupil. "Can you control yourself now?"

"I think so. If I can't—you've still got the Jeta!"

Futrell was lying on the bed; washed and bandaged he looked more like his TV image than the drowned rat I had dragged from the cabin of *Sea Eagle*. He sat up when I came in, and the hatred in his eyes matched mine. "Hello Knox! Still obeying your master's orders?"

Judith followed me into the cell, then stood with her back to the door, her Jeta at the ready. "No violence!" she warned.

I sat down facing him and for a few moments we stared at each other. Then I said, "Grainer ordered me to protect you."

"Protect me?" His surprise changed to a sneer. "Protect me when you couldn't protect him! Why the hell would Grainer tell you that?"

"Then—I couldn't imagine. Now—I know! Because you were the biggest bastard in his team. Because he could count on you not to crack in the crunch. Grainer saw the crunch coming. He must have known about Impermease. Did you?"

My question caught him off guard. He hesitated, then said, "Only after the damage was done. When all we could do was to reduce its effects."

"By keeping people in line? By forcing industry to fill up these dumps?"

"Of course! And we're one of the few governments who managed to plan for survival."

"Like you planned for your own? And for your pals?"

"For all America!" He clasped his hands around one knee. "Do you think I had Grainer killed?"

"You had him murdered. Like you had Helga and Gloria murdered."

"Helga and Gloria? Who were they?"

"Two of Grainer's friends."

"There were a lot of people keen to kill Grainer's friends—once Grainer was gone." He smiled his ugly smile. "I wish to hell they'd killed you! But I didn't arrange Grainer's assassination. I just let it happen."

"You just let it happen? What the hell do you mean? If you didn't arrange it, who did?"

"Grainer himself!" He laughed at my expression.

I heard the hiss of Judith's breath and felt her hand holding me back as I started to rise. I shook her off, sat down, and spat, "That's a lousy lie! Arnold wouldn't have faked an assassination—"

"Not faked—real. That bullet killed him instantly. As he had expected. As he had hoped!"

Futrell must be lying. "Why the hell should Grainer let himself be murdered? Murdered on the eve of an election he must win to block the big shutdown?"

"An election he was likely to lose."

"Balls! Back in April, after New York, Grainer had enough delegates to get the nomination. You bastards may have thought he hadn't—"

"Us bastards thought he had. When he carried the Convention we were all sure he'd win in November. In October he learned he wouldn't. That even if he won the Presidency he'd lose the game!"

"Bullshit! Randolph ran on Arnold's record. And took every State except Ohio. Roat wouldn't have held even Ohio if he'd been up against Grainer."

"Roat had hard evidence tying Grainer to the veralloy scam."

"A dead issue!"

"Involving a dead man."

"That old lie!" I hesitated. "You mean Shantz? He deserved what he got."

"I agree. But he got it from Grainer in person. And Roat had enough evidence to nail the killing on Grainer—even if Grainer hadn't done it." He studied me. "Why the hell did Grainer kill Shantz himself? When he had guys like you who'd have been glad to do it for him."

"Arnold was that kind of man. He did his own dirty work." I hesitated, and stared at Futrell. "Where did Roat get his evidence? He was the dumbest Senator in Congress."

"And the smartest ward heeler in the United States. That's how he clawed his way into the Senate. His intelligence was minimal but his instincts were unerring. Verbal assassination was his metier. And he'd built up a case against Grainer too convincing to ignore—if made public."

"I never heard a whisper of it. And I heard about most things."

"Neither had the rest of us—not until October. Roat and his pals held back until the Party—until all of us, including Randolph—were completely committed to Grainer. Then he followed his ward-heeler instincts and offered Grainer a deal. He showed Grainer the evidence and said, 'Quit now and I'll keep quiet.' He thought he had Grainer cornered."

"Christ—he was lucky to leave Camp David alive!" I remembered the night of Roat's secret visit. The stink of his sweat when I escorted him from his chopper; the smirk on his face after his meeting with the President. The smirk of a pol who has made a deal. At the time I'd assumed he'd parlayed a lost election into an Embassy.

"We were on the verge of rapprochement with Moscow and Beijing. Both suspected that Impermease was one of our biological weapons which had backfired, but Lobachevsky and Chung trusted Grainer when he showed them the American statistics and proved that we were being hit even harder than them. He convinced them that the danger was universal and acute. He also persuaded them to trust Randolph. If Roat had become President, or if Grainer had been discredited, there'd have been a superpower confrontation and we'd have lost what little stockpiling time we had."

"Arnold should have told me to get Roat!" I breathed.

"Still the simpleminded hit man, eh Knox?" Futrell laughed. "There were a dozen Pubs to inherit Roat's role—and evidence. If Grainer'd won he'd have been the first US President indicted for murder while in office. Whether he quit or ran, the result would have been disaster. Grainer did all he could to postpone it. Pushed the Tripartite Pact through Congress and then let himself be assassinated before Roat could pull the plug. He'd already got planning for Impermease off the ground; he bailed out and left us to cope with the crash!" Futrell gave another of his ugly smiles. "Grainer didn't give a damn about what happened to his friends. Or his enemies. Or his bodyguard. All he cared about was his own niche in history."

"You're claiming he arranged his own death! That's suicide!"

"Suicide dressed up as martyrdom! Grainer made sure he died a hero. That his mantle would cover Randolph and make him the next President. Even Roat and his gang had the sense not to slander a hero who'd been dead less than a month. And once Randolph was safely in, I was able to take care of Roat."

"That auto smash?"

Futrell nodded.

"And Grainer hired the gunman who killed him?"

"No need! The gang who got him knew nothing about Shantz. They were fanatics who believed they were executing a Dictator. Grainer had great confidence in his enemies. And they didn't let him down."

"Were you one of them?"

"Of course not! I only did what Grainer asked me to do."

"Which was?"

"Remove faithful fools like you from his immediate bodyguard. Appoint zealots like Sherry and terrorists like Sline. You almost fucked things up by charging back into the act. You got rid of Sherry. I disposed of Sline later."

"Then Sherry *was* a traitor!"

Futrell shrugged. "In a way we were all traitors."

"It doesn't make sense. He could have done a dozen things to keep Roat quiet without getting himself killed."

"No!" Judith burst out.

We had forgotten about Judith, and we both swung round to stare at her, towering above us, her eyes blazing.

"No!" she repeated. "It's all starting to make sense!"

"What the hell do you mean?" I demanded.

She advanced into the cell, standing between us. "Grainer was a Caesar on the surface, but he was a pagan at heart. He saw himself as the Leader sacrificing himself for the people. The King must die! The Royal victim! One of the oldest and most universal of human myths."

"And the biggist pile of bullshit I've ever heard!"

"Bullshit perhaps." Futrell was smiling up at her. "But bullshit of a superior quality."

"Grainer was either a megalomaniac—or else he was inspired! He saw himself as the Chosen One. That might have been blasphemous—but it wasn't crazy. Not for the man who had held the fate of the world in his hands. Twice. Once on Moonbase. Again when he arranged rapprochement. Especially when the second was a result of the first. Lobachevsky trusted him because he had saved Lobachevsky's life."

She was making a terrible kind of sense. But a sense too silly to consider. "He must have gone mad!"

"He wanted to go out as a hero. To be remembered by history—if there is any history after this mess—as the President who saved civilization long enough for the Affluence to get its act together. Not as the President who went down with the chaos." Futrell looked at his hands, cracked his knuckles. "He left me to do the rough stuff."

"He picked the right man for that!" I was still groping for Grainer's logic. His planning had always been so exact, his ideas so definite. Old questions were reviving in my mind. Why had so many people let themselves be involved in the assassination? Why had he exposed himself so openly at the end of that red carpet? Why had Sherry turned traitor? Had she known that Grainer was seeking his own death? If she had, then my killing of her had been true murder, even if she had hated him as she had claimed. But perhaps that had only been another of her stratagems. The image of her slumped on that sofa, the blood running down between her breasts, swamped my vision. I put my head in my hands. I would never know! I would never know!

Judith's fingers were stroking my hair. "Forget it all, Gavin! Arnold Grainer's death was his personal sacrifice—whatever his reason. Randolph was the only man who could persuade people there was hope for some kind of a future, who could persuade them to work for it. He gave meaning to many lives which otherwise would have become meaningless. And Futrell here was the kind of man needed to drive them on after hope was running thin." She turned to him. "Where is President Randolph?"

"Dead!" Futrell gave another of his ugly smiles. "I strengthened Sherando to serve as his refuge. After two days there he shot himself! Not as any sacrifice. From despair!"

I lunged toward him. I wanted to smash his smiling face. Judith held me back. "Let him be, Gavin. He carried on with Grainer's plan." Then she swung on him. "Was persecuting the Settlements part of that plan?"

Futrell shook his head.

"Then why have you been attacking us?"

"Not my doing! The Government's response to popular request. Five years ago most Americans regarded Believers as a bunch of religious nuts, heretics, or quasicommunists. During the draft your Settlements were bolt-holes for draft-dodgers hiding behind a fake religion. Or cowards who'd taken to the hills during some nuclear scare. Americans who had dropped out of mainstream America while claiming the rights and privileges of American citizens."

"We paid our taxes! We never caused any trouble."

"But you had your private radio network with Settlements in foreign countries. An international conspiracy, but too unimportant to become an issue when the Affluence was in full flood. Just a bunch of misguided fools trying to live the simple life. The woods were full of survivalists preparing for some giant shitstorm." He looked up at Judith. "You know what changed that, as well as I do."

"We escaped Impermease."

"Most people had never heard of Impermease. All they could see were Settlements still full of kids while maternity wards were closing down for lack of business. So they made a natural assumption—you Believers were somehow responsible for their daughters' sterility. That if you were left alone you'd inherit the Earth within a couple of generations. And that you'd planned it that way."

"Lies—and you knew it!"

"Sure—but why should we worry about a gang of bolters who'd already opted out?" Futrell gave another ugly smile. "Anyway, by then our credibility was nil. A statement by us that you weren't involved would only have convinced people you were."

"So you sent in your thugs to rape our women!"

"We sent in disciplined troops to rescue your women. To free your brainwashed girls and give them a chance of living decent lives. Married to men. Not mated to doves!"

"Doves that drove off your Troopers and put you in this cell!"

Futrell scowled. "That was bad luck."

"And good shooting!" Someone was tapping at the door. "Judy, who the hell's that?"

It was Chuck Yackle. He stepped into the cell, breathing heavily, his bald head gleaming. "Ahh—there you are, Mister Gavin. *Ranula*'s due to arrive in an hour. Where are you going to put the mothers with young babies?"

Where was *I* going to put them? I stopped myself from telling Yackle where he could. "Have 'em stay aboard until

Enoch's got the tunnel clear. Tell the crew, and any other freedom fighters you can round up, to lend Enoch a hand. This place won't be secure until we've got those gates closed."

"Yes—of course!" Yackle mopped his forehead, hitched up his gunbelt, and noticed Futrell. "I'm Chairman Yackle. Er—who are you?"

"Meet Gerald Futrell," said Judith. "Attorney General of the United States."

"The Attorney General! I hope they're looking after you properly, Mister Futrell."

"I'm just deciding whether or not to hang him," I said.

"Hang him? I trust you won't. There have been too many killed already today." He sighed. "Remember Mister Gavin, revenge debases just anger." And he departed on that platitude.

Futrell looked after him. "Who's that wimp?"

"Our spiritual leader. One of the doves who grounded your vultures!" I turned to Judith. "How long before this bastard's fit to travel?"

"About a week."

"Then tell Midge he's all hers. Tell her to take him away as soon as he's strong enough to survive. Turn him loose, as you promised, unharmed. And unarmed! Dump him at Fairhaven. Let him take a walk through the woods."

"He'll go to Sherando."

"If he makes it—he deserves it. And Anslinger deserves him!" I looked around my old cell, then I went to ease off the ventilator grill and reach up the duct. My manuscript was still hidden round the elbow and I pulled it out. Filthy with dust, it was still legible. I flung it on the bed. "Here's something to read while you're waiting." I stood in front of him, staring down at him. "And here's something to remember. Grainer told you to protect Helga and Gloria. And you can't even remember who they were! Well—they were two beautiful women who were murdered. For that you'll pay. Here or in Hell!"

Judith tugged my sleeve. "Come on! Leave him! There's still lots to be done."

There was still too much. I needed time to think, and time was the last thing I was allowed. Because I was credited with capturing the Pen people were asking me how to consolidate our victory and what to do with our prisoners. Because I was the combat commander I must count our dead, comfort our wounded, and console our bereaved.

Statistically our losses had been light; in human terms, tragic. The only thing worse than a battle won is a battle lost. I returned to the Surveillance Center exhausted and depressed. Judith was monitoring activities throughout the Pen and issuing instructions with her usual competence. "Barbara wants to see you," she said, without looking up from the displays.

"Everybody wants to see me!" I snarled.

"Barbara deserves to. She's waiting for you to praise her heroics."

"Heroics—hell! She did one of the bravest things I've ever seen."

"Then go and tell her so! She's brooding somewhere in that wilderness of an orchard. Go and give her a pat on the back!"

"I'll go and give her a pat on the ass!"

Barbara too was suffering from post-combat depression, and she greeted me with a scowl when she saw me coming through the underbrush. "Well, we've won! So what now?"

"We've grabbed the Pen. I don't know how long we'll hold it!" I subsided onto the bench where Judith and I had once pretended love and plotted escape.

"Not long if you sit here drooping while the other oldsters argue whether to praise the Light or mount the launchers!"

"Things are under control at last! Chuck's singing some kind of Te Deum on the roof. Enoch's got the tunnel clear and the gates locked, Martha's searching containers for weapons, and Judy's issuing orders." I turned to face her. "Barb—today you showed more guts than I've ever seen."

Her scowl changed to a suspicious stare. Her stare blossomed into the smile that converts a girl to a goddess. Then she flung her arms around me.

I replied with an avuncular hug. "You saved the Pen when you saved those women."

"I did it for you!" Her hand was stroking the back of my neck. She tipped up her face, eyes closed, mouth half open, lips moist.

I kissed her gently.

She responded by pushing her tongue into my mouth.

I tried to ease back; she pulled me forward. I had not planned on carrying congratulations this far; she wanted them to go all the way. She nibbled my ear. "Gav—I've waited so long for you to say something nice to me."

"You've what?" I tried to sit up.

She pulled me down. "I've loved you from the first moment I saw you! I told Judy so. She said you were a sweet guy. But you weren't sweet to me. Gav—why were you so hostile?"

"Hostile? Me? Barb—I've always admired you."

"Then why didn't you show it? Why were you so fond of putting me down?"

"Me putting you down?" But this was no time to argue. "I guess I was afraid." Afraid of what Judith might say or Enoch might do. She was a broadminded woman; he was a broadminded man. But breadth of mind and acute jealousy coexist in the best of women. And few fathers are broadminded about their daughters. "Better your dog than your daughter!" as Gramps used to say. I fell back on my old defense line. "I couldn't trust myself!"

"You were afraid of being carried away?"

I nodded and kissed her.

She raised her head and studied my face. "Gav, why am I so worked up all of a sudden? I don't usually get horny this easily. And why are *you*?"

"Post-combat heat!" I muttered, trying to cool my own. "Fear—rage—guilt—desire. Classical sequence. Kill the men and rape the women. Now women are joining the action—"

"So that's it!" She slid her hand inside my shirt. "Never felt this hot before!" She might never have felt the heat herself but she certainly knew how to raise mine.

Her hands were below my belt and mine were on her breasts when my com pinged. I cursed but continued to explore. Her fingers froze. "Gav—you'd better answer. You're still in command of this show, and that may be important."

Reluctantly I took my right hand from her left breast and eased the com from my belt. It was Midge. "Mister Gavin—Jehu and Margaret and some of the others are going to that Coast Guard cutter. They're ashore on the Needles and with the swell rising she's starting to pound. She'll have broken up by morning. We'd like to rescue the sailors and marines, if that's okay by you?"

"It's okay if you're armed and they're not when you take them aboard. And keep them standing out on the foredeck after you've pulled them from the drink." I shivered as Barbara's fingers started moving again.

"I can't find Barb. So me and Sam are going to take *Sea Eagle*."

Her hands left me abruptly.

"Stand by, Midge!" I looked at Barbara. "What's up?"

"Tell her you'll find me. And tell her to wait!' She was on her feet, tugging up her slacks. "*Eagle*'s my boat. I'll take her out!"

I nodded, frustration tempered with relief. "Midge—hold it! I'll get a message to Barbara. You'd better wait for her!"

"Okay. But tell her to move it! We've got to reach that cutter before dark."

"She'll get the signal!" She had already got it. And so had I. Her infatuation with her boat was a love exceeding the love of men.

She tucked in her blouse and kissed me. "We'll have our victory orgy later!" Then she was away, jumping over the low bushes and the trailing vines, disappearing into the wilderness of the orchard.

I composed myself and my clothes and went slowly back to the Surveillance Center, distributing encouragement and advice to those Believers I met. Judith was still busy watching her displays.

"I congratulated Barbara," I said.

"So I saw!"

"Christ! Is that camera still working? Listen Judy—"

"I listened too!" She swung round to face me. She was laughing. "Saved by the ping!" She moved toward me. "What's this line of yours about post-combat lust? I knew I felt something; I wasn't sure what."

"Judy, I didn't mean—"

She caught my arm. "Let's use my old cell. I left it empty especially for us!"

XXII

Epilogue

Within two years the Settlement had moved back to Sutton Cove, leaving a rotating squad with launchers to protect the riches of the Pen and taking with us sufficient weaponry to hold off an armored brigade. By then the nearest thing to any kind of army in the northeast was a few companies of the National Guard, behaving more like bandits than soldiers. They left us alone, following Gramps' old dictum that it is safer to shear sheep than spear wolves.

Barbara and I never enjoyed our victory orgy. For the first few days we were too busy sorting out prisoners, settling in the rescued women, and preparing to defend the Pen against an attack which never came. Once all that was done we found that our mutual fascination had faded with our post-combat heat, and Barbara had developed other interests.

As soon as the Pen was secure, Chairman Yackle broadcast the news of its capture on the inter-Settlement radio network, and thereafter our boats spent more time picking up refugees from overrun Settlements and escapees from "reeducation centers" than they did in fishing. Among the reasons for our eventual return to Sutton Cove was the population explosion which resulted as more and more Believers managed to reach us.

A month after Yackle spread the news that we held the Pen, Barbara's mysterious sister appeared literally out of the blue, flying a chopper, and whisked the kid off to some unknown but exciting future. After an evening talking with her sister, Barbara transferred her infatuation from boats to choppers, leaving *Sea Eagle* to Sam, much as she left me to Judith. Enoch looked sad for a while but had already resigned himself to losing his daughter, sooner or later. "She's got too much of her grandma in her to ever settle down to a quiet life like the rest of us."

Midge left with Futrell and the Marines she rescued from the Coast Guard cutter. She dumped Futrell at Fairhaven, watched him limping away into the forest, and then radioed that she was staying with the Marines. Their Sergeant had heard some story about a gang of mercenaries who had set themselves up as a protection organization somewhere. Sam, who brought the *Eagle* back from Clarport, assured us that she was going of her own free will—she was in love with the Sergeant. Midge was another not cut out for the quiet life of a Settlement.

Neither was I, but that was what I had to endure. Judith was still hoping for children. I tried to share her enthusiasm and fulfill her need, but in truth I had lost what little urge I might have had to reproduce. I was disgusted with myself and the human race; the past had been wasted and the future mortgaged. The beginning of the Chaos was the time when Benevolent Presentism was abandoned for Factual Futurism. When civilized men used sophisticated weapons to grab women too uncivilized to have been made sterile by Impermease.

The first excitement to enter our placid lives in the three years after we had captured the Pen was a signal from the Teacher himself. He had returned from wherever he had been meditating during the onset of the Chaos to set up shop in an area called the Enclave, a patch of territory controlled by Believers somewhere in Syria. His signal was an invitation for Doctor Judith Grenfell to come and join his entourage.

Of course she accepted. With tears in her eyes she swore that only the Teacher could take her from me. She must go. The amphibian which had started to operate a kind of Inter Settlement Airline would arrive in the Cove some time during August to pick her up.

After all my attempts to dissuade her had failed, I went to see Chuck Yackle. "You're the local representative of the Light. When we first came here you called the break-up of a marriage a sin against the Light. Remember? So why isn't this seduction of my wife by your Teacher a sin?"

He fiddled with his stylus and rubbed his bald head. "We had hoped that this wouldn't break up your marriage. We had hoped you would go with Judith."

"Me? Go to the Enclave? What the hell could I do there? Anyway, they'd never take me. I'm an unbeliever."

Yackle shrugged. "They'll accept you. In fact—" He hesitated. "In fact it's you the Teacher wants."

"Me? Your Teacher doesn't even know I exist."

"Apparently he does. I had a signal some time back asking if I thought you'd go. I answered that I thought you wouldn't."

"You never asked me!"

"I knew your answer, Gavin." He sighed. "I was right, wasn't I?"

I admitted he was, but it would have been nice to have been asked.

He sighed again. "We didn't want to lose you."

"But you're prepared to lose Judith. I know there are two other Docs in the Cove now. But they're quacks compared to her!"

"True! But if the Teacher calls—we must answer."

"You claimed he was calling me!" Then what he had just said sank in, and it took all my willpower not to reach across the table, grab Chairman Yackle by the throat, and ram his head against the wall.

He eased back his chair, moving out of my reach. "Judith is answering the call. We hope you will follow."

"What a lousy trick! Wait until I tell Judy!" I started for the door.

"And lacerate her pride? Would you do that to her?"

I stopped and turned. I could see her face collapsed if I claimed that her beloved Teacher was using her as a bait to entice me. Entice me for what? Once again I was being manipulated. Once again I was being maneuvered into the service of some authority I didn't understand. Proving the truth of what Judy had once called me—a feudal retainer always looking for a Lord to serve.

"Tell her you're going with her!" urged Yackle. "Follow her the way you followed her when you both came here. Be honest, Gavin! You're bored with our peaceful life. In the Enclave there'll be excitement. Probably more than you want!"

"To hell with the Enclave!" But I still stood facing him.

"Aren't you curious to find out why the Teacher should want you?"

Of course I was.

And I did.